BALLASWIN
Aluminium Works
OEY MACHAN
CULDEE FELL
(2046 feet)
PEEL GODRED
SHANE DOOINEY
SKARLOEY
RHENEAS
CHIBBYR ULF
ULFSTED
SHEN
VEN
WARDFELL
GLENNOCK
CROS-NY
-CRUIN
Public School
CRONK
KILLDANE
KELLSTHORPE
SUDDERY
ROLF'S
CASTLE
BALLADWAIL
Girls' School
BRENDAM
KIRKRONAN
CROVANS
GATE
BALLAHOO
NORMANBY
VICARSTOWN
MILLOM
ULVERSTON
BARROW
Scale
0 5 10 15 20 25
Miles

THOMAS the TANK ENGINE

THE COMPLETE COLLECTION

The illustrations in this book have been re-originated using the latest digital technology, and reproduced from newly restored artwork wherever possible. On the few occasions where it proved impossible to scan directly from the artwork, great care was taken to match the originals, but some variation in colour and quality may be noticeable.

THOMAS the TANK ENGINE

THE COMPLETE COLLECTION

THE REV. W. AWDRY

A complete edition of all 26 books from the famous Railway Series by the Rev. W. Awdry

RANDOM HOUSE VALUE PUBLISHING
NEW YORK

First published in Great Britain 1996
by Heinemann Young Books
an imprint of Egmont Children's Books Limited
239 Kensington High Street, London W8 6SA

The Three Railway Engines first published in Great Britain 1945
Thomas the Tank Engine first published in Great Britain 1946
James the Red Engine first published in Great Britain 1948
Tank Engine Thomas Again first published in Great Britain 1949
Troublesome Engines first published in Great Britain 1950
Henry the Green Engine first published in Great Britain 1951
Toby the Tram Engine first published in Great Britain 1952
Gordon the Big Engine first published in Great Britain 1953
Edward the Blue Engine first published in Great Britain 1954
Four Little Engines first published in Great Britain 1955
Percy the Small Engine first published in Great Britain 1956
The Eight Famous Engines first published in Great Britain 1957
Duck and the Diesel Engine first published in Great Britain 1958
The Little Old Engine first published in Great Britain 1959
The Twin Engines first published in Great Britain 1960
Branch Line Engines first published in Great Britain 1961
Gallant Old Engine first published in Great Britain 1962
Stepney the "Bluebell" Engine first published in Great Britain 1963
Mountain Engines first published in Great Britain 1964
Very Old Engines first published in Great Britain 1965
Main Line Engines first published in Great Britain 1966
Small Railway Engines first published in Great Britain 1967
Enterprising Engines first published in Great Britain 1968
Oliver the Western Engine first published in Great Britain 1969
Duke the Lost Engine first published in Great Britain 1970
Tramway Engines first published in Great Britain 1972

This 1999 edition is published by Random House Value
Publishing, Inc. 280 Park Avenue, New York, N.Y. 10017

ISBN 0-517-18786-8

Random House
New York • Toronto • London • Sydney • Auckland
http://www.randomhouse.com/

Printed and bound in Spain

Contents

Foreword

Dear Friends,

In my introduction to *Thomas the Tank Engine – The Complete Collection* I have been asked to tell you about how the 'Thomas' books came to be written. This is how it happened.

When I was 3 or 4 years old my father used to take me for walks around his parish in Hampshire. Our favourite was the one to Baddesley Bridge where we would scramble up the embankment and walk along the line. No one ever turned us away. The plate-layers all knew my father, and were happy to talk to him about their work, in which they took a great pride. As far as I can remember there was no question I ever asked my father about railways which he either could not answer, or did not know where to find the answer.

He retired in 1916. We left Hampshire and settled at Box in Wiltshire. Our house was near the Great Western main line which here climbs for 2 miles at 1 in 100. A tank engine was kept at Box station, part of whose duties was to help goods trains up the incline. Lying in bed at night I would hear both engines snorting up the grade, and imagine in their puffings and pantings the conversation they were having with each other. I had no doubt at all that steam engines had personalities.

Many years later in 1943, when I was curate at King's Norton, Birmingham, my three-year-old son caught measles and had to be amused. I told him stories about engines which had to be made up on the spur of the moment, and drew on my childhood memories to do it. 'Edward's Day Out', 'The Sad Story of Henry', and 'Edward and Gordon' were told over and over again. The wordage became fixed, and my son allowed no deviation! I wrote the stories down in pencil on scraps of paper for family use. I had no thought of getting them published.

Mrs Awdry thought otherwise. She kept telling me to do something about it, but could not say what! She told my mother about them. My mother had an idea. She wrote back saying that she was expecting a visit from a distant cousin whom she thought was connected with a firm of literary agents. He was coming in a day or two so 'send the stories at once'. With no time to write a fair copy I sent the pencilled scraps of paper. Our cousin must have had imagination to see a future in those scraps! He hawked them around for several months before he found a publisher who had imagination too. This was Mr Edmund Ward of Leicester who said that he would accept the three stories on condition that I wrote a fourth getting Henry out of his tunnel and providing a happy ending. The book came out in 1945 and sold well. *Thomas the Tank Engine* came next; I was asked to write another and another! There are now 26 books in the series.

Granted the fiction that steam engines have personality and can express it, everything else in the stories must be authentic. Each story is based on some odd incident which has happened to some engine, somewhere, some time. Most are things which readers have written to tell me about, or which I have read in railway books and magazines.

In my study at home I have a thick heavy file which I prize highly. It is full of letters. They are from children, mothers, fathers, grandfathers, grandmothers, aunts and uncles who have written to me over the years to say how much they and their children enjoy the books. I prize these highly of course; but there are some I value even more. They are letters from fathers and grandfathers who are or have been professional railwaymen, saying that they too like the books. To quote one of them: '. . . your background knowledge of railways is so good that yours are the only books about railways which I can read to my children without squirming inside! I myself know of many odd incidents which have happened just as you describe them in your stories . . .' That is praise indeed!

I am happy to commend Thomas' omnibus edition to you, and hope you will enjoy it!

THE AUTHOR

THE RAILWAY SERIES NO. 1

The Three Railway Engines

THE REV. W. AWDRY

with illustrations by

C. REGINALD DALBY

Edward's Day Out

ONCE upon a time there was a little engine called Edward. He lived in a shed with five other engines. They were all bigger than Edward and boasted about it. "The Driver won't choose you again," they said. "He wants big, strong engines like us." Edward had not been out for a long time; he began to feel sad.

Just then the Driver and Fireman came along to start work.

The Driver looked at Edward. "Why are you sad?" he asked. "Would you like to come out today?"

"Yes, please," said Edward. So the Fireman lit the fire and made a nice lot of steam.

Then the Driver pulled the lever, and Edward puffed away.

"Peep, peep," he whistled. "Look at me now."

The others were very cross at being left behind.

Away went Edward to get some coaches.

"Be careful, Edward," said the coaches, "don't bump and bang us like the other engines do."

So Edward came up to the coaches, very, very gently, and the shunter fastened the coupling.

"Thank you, Edward," said the coaches. "That was kind, we are glad you are taking us today."

Then they went to the station where the people were waiting.

"Peep, peep," whistled Edward – "get in quickly, please."

So the people got in quickly and Edward waited happily for the Guard to blow his whistle, and wave his green flag.

He waited and waited – there was no whistle, no green flag. "Peep, peep, peep, peep – where is that Guard?" Edward was getting anxious.

The Driver and Fireman asked the Stationmaster, "Have you seen the Guard?" "No," he said. They asked the porter, "Have you seen the Guard?" "Yes – last night," said the porter.

Edward began to get cross. "Are we ever going to start?" he said.

Just then a little boy shouted, "Here he comes!" and there the Guard was, running

down the hill with his flags in one hand and a sandwich in the other.

He ran on to the platform, blew his whistle, and jumped into his van.

Edward puffed off. He did have a happy day. All the children ran to wave as he went past and he met old friends at all the stations. He worked so hard that the Driver promised to take him out again next day.

"I'm going out again tomorrow," he told the other engines that night in the shed. "What do you think of that?"

But he didn't hear what they thought, for he was so tired and happy that he fell asleep at once.

Edward and Gordon

ONE of the engines in Edward's shed was called Gordon. He was very big and very proud.

"You watch me this afternoon, little Edward," he boasted, "as I rush through with the express; that will be a splendid sight for you."

Just then his Driver pulled the lever. "Goodbye, little Edward," said Gordon, as he puffed away, "look out for me this afternoon!"

Edward went off, too, to do some shunting.

Edward liked shunting. It was fun playing with trucks. He would come up quietly and give them a pull.

"Oh! Oh! Oh! Oh! Oh!" screamed the trucks. "Whatever is happening?"

Then he would stop and the silly trucks would go bump into each other. "Oh! Oh! Oh! Oh!" they cried again.

Edward pushed them until they were running nicely, and when they weren't expecting it he would stop; one of them would be sure to run on to another line. Edward played till there were no more trucks; then he stopped to rest.

Presently he heard a whistle. Gordon came puffing along, very slowly, and very crossly. Instead of nice shining coaches, he was pulling a lot of very dirty coal trucks.

"A goods train! A goods train! A goods train!" he grumbled. "The shame of it, the shame of it, the shame of it."

He went slowly through, with the trucks clattering and banging behind him.

Edward laughed, and went to find some more trucks.

Soon afterwards a porter came and spoke to his Driver. "Gordon can't get up the hill. Will you take Edward and push him, please?"

They found Gordon halfway up the hill and very cross. His Driver and Fireman were talking to him severely. "You are not trying!" they told him.

"I can't do it," said Gordon. "The noisy trucks hold an engine back so. If they were coaches now – clean sensible things that come quietly – that would be different."

Edward's Driver came up. "We've come to push," he said.
"No use at all," said Gordon.
"You wait and see," said Edward's Driver.

They brought the train back to the bottom of the hill. Edward came up behind the brake van ready to push.

"Peep, peep, I'm ready," said Edward.

"Poop, poop, no good," grumbled Gordon.

The Guard blew his whistle and they pulled and pushed as hard as they could.

"I can't do it, I can't do it, I can't do it," puffed Gordon.

"I will do it, I will do it, I will do it," puffed Edward.

"I can't do it, I will do it, I can't do it, I will do it, I can't do it, I will do it," they puffed together.

Edward pushed and puffed and puffed and pushed, as hard as ever he could, and almost before he realized it, Gordon found himself at the top of the hill.

"I've done it! I've done it! I've done it!" he said proudly, and forgot all about Edward pushing behind. He didn't wait to say "Thank you", but ran on so fast that he passed two stations before his Driver could make him stop.

Edward had pushed so hard that when he got to the top he was out of breath.

Gordon ran on so fast that Edward was left behind.

The Guard waved and waved, but Edward couldn't catch up.

He ran on to the next station, and there the Driver and Fireman said they were very pleased with him. The Fireman gave him a nice long drink of water, and the Driver said, "I'll get out my paint tomorrow, and give you a beautiful new coat of blue with red stripes, then you'll be the smartest engine in the shed."

The Sad Story of Henry

ONCE, an engine attached
to a train
Was afraid of a few drops
of rain –
– It went into a tunnel,
And squeaked through
its funnel
And never came out again.

The engine's name was Henry. His Driver and Fireman argued with him, but he would not move. "The rain will spoil my lovely green paint and red stripes," he said.

The Guard blew his whistle till he had no more breath, and waved his flags till his arms ached; but Henry still stayed in the tunnel, and blew steam at him.

"I am not going to spoil my lovely green paint and red stripes for you," he said rudely.

The passengers came and argued too, but Henry would not move.

A Fat Director who was on the train told the Guard to get a rope. "We will pull you out," he said. But Henry only blew steam at him and made him wet.

They hooked the rope on and all pulled – except the Fat Director. "My doctor has forbidden me to pull," he said.

They pulled and pulled and pulled, but still Henry stayed in the tunnel.

Then they tried pushing from the other end. The Fat Director said, "One, two, three, push": but did not help. "My doctor has forbidden me to push," he said.

They pushed and pushed and pushed; but still Henry stayed in the tunnel.

At last another train came. The Guard waved his red flag and stopped it. The two engine Drivers, the two Firemen, and the two Guards went and argued with Henry. "Look, it has stopped raining," they said. "Yes, but it will begin again soon," said Henry. "And what would become of my green paint with red stripes then?"

So they brought the other engine up, and it pushed and puffed, and puffed and pushed as hard as ever it could. But still Henry stayed in the tunnel.

So they gave it up. They told Henry, "We shall leave you there for always and always and always."

They took up the old rails, built a wall in front of him, and cut a new tunnel.

Now Henry can't get out, and he watches the trains rushing through the new tunnel. He is very sad because no one will ever see his lovely green paint with red stripes again.

But I think he deserved it, don't you?

Edward, Gordon and Henry

Edward and Gordon often went through the tunnel where Henry was shut up.

Edward would say, "Peep, peep – hullo!" and Gordon would say, "Poop, poop, poop! Serves you right!"

Poor Henry had no steam to answer, his fire had gone out; soot and dirt from the tunnel roof had spoilt his lovely green paint and red stripes. He was cold and unhappy, and wanted to come out and pull trains too.

Gordon always pulled the Express. He was proud of being the only engine strong enough to do it.

There were many heavy coaches, full of important people like the Fat Director who had punished Henry.

Gordon was seeing how fast he could go. "Hurry! Hurry! Hurry!" he panted.

"Trickety-trock, trickety-trock, trickety-trock," said the coaches.

Gordon could see Henry's tunnel in front.

"In a minute," he thought, "I'll poop, poop, poop at Henry, and rush through and out into the open again."

Closer and closer he came – he was almost there, when crack: "Wheee ———— eeshshsh," he was in a cloud of steam, and going slower and slower.

His Driver stopped the train.

"What has happened to me?" asked Gordon, "I feel so weak." "You've burst your safety valve," said the Driver. "You can't pull the train any more." "Oh, dear," said Gordon. "We were going so nicely, too. . . . Look at Henry laughing at me." Gordon made a face at Henry, and blew smoke at him.

Everybody got out, and came to see Gordon. "Humph!" said the Fat Director. "I never liked these big engines – always going wrong; send for another engine at once."

While the Guard went to find one, they uncoupled Gordon, and ran him on a siding out of the way.

The only engine left in the Shed was Edward.

"I'll come and try," he said.

Gordon saw him coming. "That's no use," he said, "Edward can't pull the train."

Edward puffed and pulled, and pulled and puffed, but he couldn't move the heavy coaches.

"I told you so," said Gordon rudely. "Why not let Henry try?"

"Yes," said the Fat Director, "I will."

"Will you help pull this train, Henry?" he asked. "Yes," said Henry at once.

So Gordon's Driver and Fireman lit his fire; some platelayers broke down the wall and put back the rails; and when he had steam up Henry puffed out.

He was dirty, his boiler was black, and he was covered with cobwebs. "Ooh! I'm so stiff! Ooh! I'm so stiff!" he groaned.

"You'd better have a run to ease your joints, and find a turntable," said the Fat Director kindly.

Henry came back feeling better, and they put him in front.

"Peep, peep," said Edward, "I'm ready."

"Peep, peep, peep," said Henry, "so am I."

"Pull hard; pull hard; pull hard," puffed Edward.

"We'll do it; we'll do it; we'll do it," puffed Henry.

"Pull hard we'll do it. Pull hard we'll do it. Pull hard we'll do it," they puffed together. The heavy coaches jerked and began to move, slowly at first, then faster and faster.

"We've done it together! We've done it together! We've done it together!" said Edward and Henry.

"You've done it, hurray! You've done it, hurray! You've done it, hurray!" sang the coaches.

All the passengers were excited. The Fat Director leaned out of the window to

wave to Edward and Henry; but the train was going so fast that his hat blew off into a field where a goat ate it for his tea.

They never stopped till they came to the big station at the end of the line.

The passengers all got out and said, "Thank you," and the Fat Director promised Henry a new coat of paint.

"Would you like blue and red?"

"Yes, please," said Henry, "then I'll be like Edward."

Edward and Henry went home quietly, and on their way they helped Gordon back to the shed.

All three engines are now great friends.

Wasn't Henry pleased when he had his new coat. He is very proud of it, as all good engines are – but he doesn't mind the rain now, because he knows that the best way to keep his paint nice is not to run into tunnels, but to ask his Driver to rub him down when the day's work is over.

THE RAILWAY SERIES NO. 2

Thomas the Tank Engine

THE REV. W. AWDRY

DEAR CHRISTOPHER,

Here is your friend Thomas the Tank Engine. He wanted to come out of his station yard and see the world. These stories tell you how he did it.

I hope you will like them because you helped me to make them.

YOUR LOVING DADDY

Thomas and Gordon

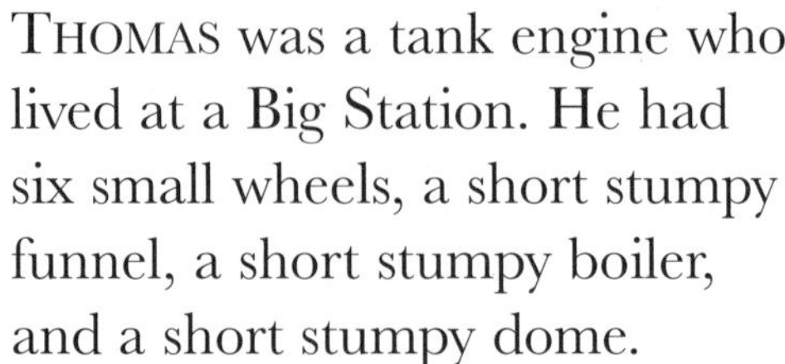

THOMAS was a tank engine who lived at a Big Station. He had six small wheels, a short stumpy funnel, a short stumpy boiler, and a short stumpy dome.

He was a fussy little engine, always pulling coaches about. He pulled them to the station ready for the big engines to take out on long journeys; and when trains came in, and the people had got out, he would pull the empty coaches away, so that the big engines could go and rest.

He was a cheeky little engine, too. He thought no engine worked as hard as he did. So he used to play tricks on them. He liked best of all to come quietly beside a big engine dozing on a siding and make him jump.

"Peep, peep, peep, pip, peep! Wake up, lazybones!" he would whistle, "why don't you work hard like me?"

Then he would laugh rudely and run away to find some more coaches.

One day Gordon was resting on a siding. He was very tired. The big Express he always pulled had been late, and he had had to run as fast as he could to make up for lost time.

He was just going to sleep when Thomas came up in his cheeky way.

"Wake up, lazybones," he whistled, "do some hard work for a change – you can't catch me!" and he ran off laughing.

Instead of going to sleep again, Gordon thought how he could pay Thomas out.

One morning Thomas wouldn't wake up. His Driver and Fireman couldn't make him start. His fire went out and there was not enough steam.

It was nearly time for the Express. The people were waiting, but the coaches weren't ready.

At last Thomas started. "Oh, dear! Oh, dear!" he yawned.

"Come on," said the coaches. "Hurry up." Thomas gave them a rude bump, and started for the station.

"Don't stop dawdling, don't stop dawdling," he grumbled.

"Where have you been? Where have you been?" asked the coaches crossly.

Thomas fussed into the station where Gordon was waiting.

"Poop, poop, poop. Hurry up, you," said Gordon crossly.

"Peep, pip, peep. Hurry yourself," said cheeky Thomas.

"Yes," said Gordon, "I will," and almost before the coaches had stopped moving Gordon came out of his siding and was coupled to the train.

"Poop, poop," he whistled. "Get in quickly, please." So the people got in quickly, the signal went down, the clock struck the

hour, the guard waved his green flag, and Gordon was ready to start.

Thomas usually pushed behind the big trains to help them start. But he was always uncoupled first, so that when the train was running nicely he could stop and go back.

This time he was late, and Gordon started so quickly that they forgot to uncouple Thomas.

"Poop, poop," said Gordon.

"Peep, peep, peep," whistled Thomas.

"Come on! Come on!" puffed Gordon to the coaches.

"Pull harder! Pull harder!" puffed Thomas to Gordon.

The heavy train slowly began to move out of the station.

The train went faster and faster; too fast for Thomas. He wanted to stop but he couldn't.

"Peep! Peep! Stop! Stop!" he whistled.

"Hurry, hurry, hurry," laughed Gordon in front.

"You can't get away. You can't get away," laughed the coaches.

Poor Thomas was going faster than he had ever gone before. He was out of breath and his wheels hurt him, but he had to go on.

"I shall never be the same again," he thought sadly, "My wheels will be quite worn out."

At last they stopped at a station. Everyone laughed to see Thomas puffing and panting behind.

They uncoupled him, put him on to a turntable and then he ran on a siding out of the way.

"Well, little Thomas," chuckled Gordon as he passed, "now you know what hard work means, don't you?"

Poor Thomas couldn't answer, he had no breath. He just puffed slowly away to rest, and had a long, long drink.

He went home very slowly and was careful afterwards never to be cheeky to Gordon again.

Thomas' Train

THOMAS often grumbled because he was not allowed to pull passenger trains.

The other engines laughed. "You're too impatient," they said. "You'd be sure to leave something behind!"

"Rubbish," said Thomas, crossly. "You just wait, I'll show you."

One night he and Henry were alone. Henry was ill. The men worked hard, but he didn't get better.

Now Henry usually pulled the first train in the morning, and Thomas had to get his coaches ready.

"If Henry is ill," he thought, "perhaps I shall pull his train."

Thomas ran to find the coaches.

"Come *along*. Come *along*," he fussed.

"There's plenty of time, there's plenty of time," grumbled the coaches.

He took them to the platform, 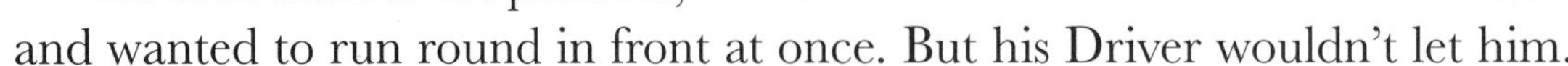 and wanted to run round in front at once. But his Driver wouldn't let him.

"Don't be impatient, Thomas," he said.

So Thomas waited and waited. The people got in, the Guard and Stationmaster walked up and down, the porters banged the doors, and still Henry didn't come.

Thomas got more and more excited every minute.

The Fat Director came out of his office to see what was the matter, and the Guard and the Stationmaster told him about Henry.

"Find another engine," he ordered.

"There's only Thomas," they said.

"You'll have to do it then, Thomas. Be quick now!"

So Thomas ran round to the front and backed down on the coaches ready to start.

"Don't be impatient," said his Driver. "Wait till everything is ready."

But Thomas was too excited to listen to a word he said.

What happened then no one knows. Perhaps they forgot to couple Thomas to the train; perhaps Thomas was too impatient to wait till they were ready; or perhaps his Driver pulled the lever by mistake.

Anyhow, Thomas started. People shouted and waved at him but he didn't stop.

"They're waving because I'm such a splendid engine," he thought importantly. "Henry says it's hard to pull trains, but *I* think it's easy."

"Hurry! Hurry! Hurry!" he puffed, pretending to be like Gordon.

As he passed the first signal box, he saw the men leaning out waving and shouting.

"They're pleased to see me," he thought. "They've never seen *me* pulling a train before – it's nice of them to wave," and he whistled, "Peep, peep, thank you," and hurried on.

But he came to a signal at "Danger".

"Bother!" he thought. "I must stop, and I was going so nicely, too. What a

nuisance signals are!" And he blew an angry "Peep, peep" on his whistle.

One of the Signalmen ran up. "Hullo, Thomas!" he said. "What are you doing here?"

"I'm pulling a train," said Thomas proudly. "Can't you *see*?"

"Where are your coaches, then?"

Thomas looked back. "Why bless me," he said, "if we haven't left them behind!"

"Yes," said the Signalman, "you'd better go back quickly and fetch them."

Poor Thomas was so sad he nearly cried.

"Cheer up!" said his Driver. "Let's go back quickly, and try again."

At the station all the passengers were talking at once.

They were telling the Fat Director, the Stationmaster and the Guard what a bad railway it was.

But when Thomas came back and they saw how sad he was, they couldn't be cross. So they coupled him to the train, and this time he *really* pulled it.

But for a long time afterwards the other engines laughed at Thomas, and said:

"Look, there's Thomas, who wanted to pull a train, but forgot about the coaches!"

Thomas and the Trucks

THOMAS used to grumble in the Shed at night.

"I'm tired of pushing coaches, I want to see the world."

The others didn't take much notice, for Thomas was a little engine with a long tongue.

But one night, Edward came to the shed. He was a kind little engine, and felt sorry for Thomas.

"I've got some trucks to take home tomorrow," he told him. "If you take them instead, I'll push coaches in the Yard."

"Thank you," said Thomas, "that will be nice."

So they asked their Drivers next morning, and when they said "Yes," Thomas ran happily to find the trucks.

Now trucks are silly and noisy. They talk a lot and don't attend to what they are doing. They don't listen to their engine, and when he stops they bump into each other screaming.

"Oh! Oh! Oh! Oh! Whatever is happening?"

And, I'm sorry to say, they play tricks on an engine who is not used to them.

Edward knew all about trucks. He warned Thomas to be careful, but Thomas was too excited to listen.

The shunter fastened the coupling, and, when the signal dropped, Thomas was ready.

The Guard blew his whistle. "Peep! Peep!" answered Thomas and started off.

But the trucks weren't ready.

"Oh! Oh! Oh! Oh!" they screamed as their couplings tightened. "Wait, Thomas, wait." But Thomas wouldn't wait.

"Come — on; come — on," he puffed, and the trucks grumbled slowly out of the siding on to the main line.

Thomas was happy. "Come along. Come along," he puffed.

"All — right! — don't — fuss — all — right! — don't fuss," grumbled the trucks. They clattered through stations, and rumbled over bridges.

Thomas whistled "Peep! Peep!" and they rushed through the tunnel in which Henry had been shut up.

Then they came to the top of the hill where Gordon had stuck.

"Steady now, steady," warned the driver, and he shut off steam, and began to put on the brakes.

"We're stopping, we're stopping," called Thomas.

"No! No! No! No!" answered the trucks, and

bumped into each other. "Go — on! — go — on!" and before his driver could stop them, they had pushed Thomas down the hill, and were rattling and laughing behind him.

Poor Thomas tried hard to stop them from making him go too fast.

"Stop pushing, stop pushing," he hissed, but the trucks would not stop.

"Go — on! — go — on!" they giggled in their silly way.

He was glad when they got to the bottom. Then he saw in front the place where they had to stop.

"Oh, dear! What shall I do?"

They rattled through the station, and luckily the line was clear as they swerved into the goods yard.

"Oo ————— ooh e ————— r," groaned Thomas, as his brakes held fast and he skidded along the rails.

"I must stop," and he shut his eyes tight.

When he opened them he saw he had stopped just in front of the buffers, and there watching him was ———

The Fat Director!

"What are *you* doing here, Thomas?" he asked sternly.

"I've brought Edward's trucks," Thomas answered.

"Why did you come so fast?"

"I didn't mean to, I was *pushed*," said Thomas sadly.

"Haven't you pulled trucks before?"

"No."

"Then you've a lot to learn about trucks, little Thomas.

They are silly things and must be kept in their place. After pushing them about here for a few weeks you'll know almost as much about them as Edward. Then you'll be a Really Useful Engine."

Thomas and the Breakdown Train

EVERY day the Fat Director came to the station to catch his train, and he always said "Hullo" to Thomas.

There were lots of trucks in the Yard – different ones came in every day – and Thomas had to push and pull them into their right places.

He worked hard – he knew now that he wasn't so clever as he had thought. Besides, the Fat Director had been kind to him and he wanted to learn all about trucks so as to be a Really Useful Engine.

But on a siding by themselves were some trucks that Thomas was told he "mustn't touch".

There was a small coach, some flat trucks, and two queer things his Driver called cranes.

"That's the breakdown train," he said. "When there's an accident, the workmen get into the coach, and the engine takes them quickly to help the hurt people, and to clear and mend the line. The cranes are for lifting heavy things like engines, and coaches, and trucks."

One day, Thomas was in the Yard, when he heard an engine whistling "Help! Help!" and a goods train came rushing through much too fast.

The engine (a new one called James) was frightened. His brake blocks were on fire, and smoke and sparks streamed out on each side.

"They're *pushing* me! They're *pushing* me!" he panted.

"On! On! On! On!" laughed the trucks; and still whistling "Help! Help!"

poor James disappeared under a bridge.

"I'd like to teach those trucks a lesson," said Thomas the Tank Engine.

Presently a bell rang in the signal box, and a man came running, "James is off the line – the breakdown train – quickly," he shouted.

So Thomas was coupled on, the workmen jumped into their coach, and off they went.

Thomas worked his hardest. "Hurry! Hurry! Hurry!" he puffed, and this time he wasn't pretending to be like Gordon, he really meant it.

"Bother those trucks and their tricks," he thought, "I hope poor James isn't hurt."

They found James and the trucks at a bend in the line. The brake van and the last few trucks were on the rails, but the front ones were piled in a heap; James was in a field with a cow looking at him, and his Driver and Fireman were feeling him all over to see if he was hurt.

"Never mind, James," they said. "It wasn't your fault, it was those wooden brakes they gave you. We always said they were

no good."

Thomas pushed the breakdown train alongside. Then he pulled the unhurt trucks out of the way.

"Oh —— dear! — oh — dear!" they groaned.

"Serves you right. Serves you right," puffed Thomas crossly.

When the men put other trucks on the line he pulled them away, too. He was hard at work puffing backwards and forwards all the afternoon.

"This'll teach you a lesson, this'll teach you a lesson," he told the trucks, and they answered "Yes — it — will — yes — it — will," in a sad, groany, creaky, sort of voice.

They left the broken trucks and mended the line. Then with two cranes they put James back on the rails. He tried to move but he couldn't, so Thomas helped him back to the Shed.

The Fat Director was waiting anxiously for them.

"Well, Thomas," he said kindly, "I've heard all about it, and I'm very pleased with you. You're a Really Useful Engine.

"James shall have some proper brakes and a new coat of paint, and you ———— shall have a Branch Line all to yourself."

"Oh, Sir!" said Thomas, happily.

Now Thomas is as happy as can be. He has a branch line all to himself, and puffs proudly backwards and forwards with two coaches all day.

He is never lonely, because there is always some engine to talk to at the junction.

Edward and Henry stop quite often, and tell him the news. Gordon is always in a hurry and does not stop; but he never forgets to say "Poop, poop" to little Thomas, and Thomas always whistles "Peep, peep" in return.

THE RAILWAY SERIES NO. 3

James the Red Engine

THE REV. W. AWDRY

with illustrations by

C. REGINALD DALBY

DEAR FRIENDS OF EDWARD, GORDON, HENRY AND THOMAS,

Thank you for your kind letters; here is the new book for which you asked.

James, who crashed into the story of *Thomas the Tank Engine*, settles down and becomes a useful engine.

We are nationalised now, but the same engines still work the Region. I am glad, too, to tell you that the Fat Director, who understands our friends' ways, is still in charge, but is now the Fat Controller.

I hope you will enjoy this book too.

THE AUTHOR

James and the Top-Hat

JAMES was a new engine who lived at a station at the other end of the line. He had two small wheels in front and six driving wheels behind. They weren't as big as Gordon's, and they weren't as small as Thomas'.

"You're a special Mixed-Traffic engine," the Fat Controller told him. "You'll be able to pull coaches or trucks quite easily."

But trucks are not easy things to manage and on his first day they had pushed him down a hill into a field.

He had been ill after the accident, but now he had new brakes and a shining coat of red paint.

"The red paint will cheer you up after your accident," said the Fat Controller kindly. "You are to pull coaches today, and Edward shall help you."

They went together to find the coaches.

"Be careful with the coaches, James," said Edward, "they don't like being bumped. Trucks are silly and noisy; they need to be bumped and taught to behave, but coaches get cross and will pay you out."

They took the coaches to the platform and were both coupled on in front. The Fat Controller, the Stationmaster, and some little boys all came to admire James' shining rods and red paint.

James was pleased. "I am a really splendid engine," he thought, and suddenly let off steam. "Whee — ee — ee — ee — eesh!"

The Fat Controller, the Stationmaster and the Guard all jumped, and a shower of water fell on the Fat Controller's nice new top-hat.

Just then the whistle blew and James thought they had better go – so they went!

"Go on, go on," he puffed to Edward.

"Don't push, don't push," puffed Edward, for he did not like starting quickly.

"Don't go so fast, don't go so fast," grumbled the coaches; but James did not listen. He wanted to run away before the Fat Controller could call him back.

He didn't even want to stop at the first station. Edward tried hard to stop, but the two coaches in front were beyond the platform before they stopped, and they had to go back to let the passengers get out.

Lots of people came to look at James, and, as no one seemed to know about the Fat Controller's top-hat, James felt happier.

Presently they came to the junction where Thomas was waiting with his two coaches.

"Hullo, James!" said Thomas kindly, "feeling better? That's right. Ah! That's my Guard's whistle. I must go. Sorry I can't stop. I don't know what the Fat Controller would do without me to run this branch line," and he puffed off importantly with his two coaches into a tunnel.

Leaving the junction, they passed the field where James had had his accident. The fence was mended and the cows were back again. James whistled, but they paid no attention.

They clattered through Edward's station yard and started to climb the hill beyond.

"It's ever so steep, it's ever so steep," puffed James.

"I've done it before, I've done it before," puffed Edward.

"It's steep, but we'll do it – it's steep, but we'll do it," the two engines puffed together as they pulled the train up the long hill.

They both rested at the next station; Edward told James how Gordon had stuck on the hill, and he had had to push him up!

James laughed so much that he got hiccoughs and surprised an old lady in a black bonnet.

She dropped all her parcels, and three porters, the Stationmaster and the Guard had to run after her picking them up!

James was quiet in the Shed that night. He had enjoyed his day, but he was a little afraid of what the Fat Controller would say about the top-hat!

James and the Bootlace

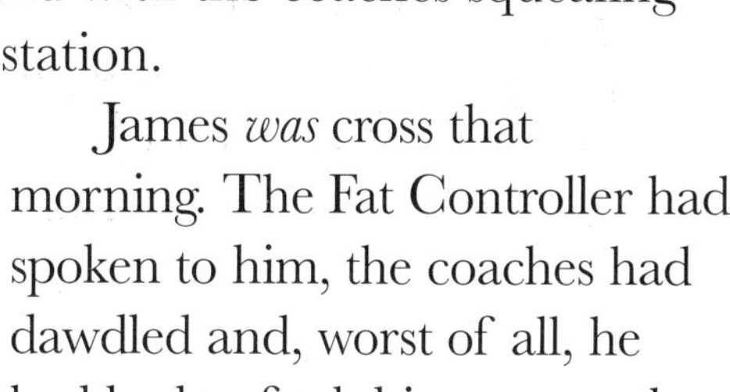

NEXT morning the Fat Controller spoke severely to James: "If you can't behave, I shall take away your red coat and have you painted blue."

James did not like that at all and he was very rough with the coaches as he brought them to the platform.

"Come along, come along," he called rudely.

"All in good time, all in good time," the coaches grumbled.

"Don't talk, come on!" answered James, and with the coaches squealing and grumbling after him, he snorted into the station.

James *was* cross that morning. The Fat Controller had spoken to him, the coaches had dawdled and, worst of all, he had had to fetch his own coaches.

"Gordon never does," thought James, "and he is only painted blue. A splendid Red Engine like me should never have to fetch his own coaches." And he puffed and snorted round to the front of the train, and backed on to it with a rude bump.

"O — ooooh!" groaned the coaches, "that was too bad!"

To make James even more cross, he then had to take the coaches to a different platform, where no one came near him as he stood there. The Fat Controller was in his office, the Stationmaster was at the other end of the train with the Guard, and even the little boys stood a long way off.

James felt lonely. "I'll show them!" he said to himself. "They think

Gordon is the only engine who can pull coaches."

And as soon as the Guard's whistle blew, he started off with a tremendous jerk.

"Come on! — come on! — come on!" he puffed, and the coaches, squeaking and groaning in protest, clattered over the points on to the open line.

"Hurry! — hurry! — hurry!" puffed James.

"You're going too fast, you're going too fast," said the coaches, and indeed they were going so fast that they swayed from side to side.

James laughed and tried to go faster, but the coaches wouldn't let him.

"We're going to stop — we're going to stop — we're — going — to — stop," they said

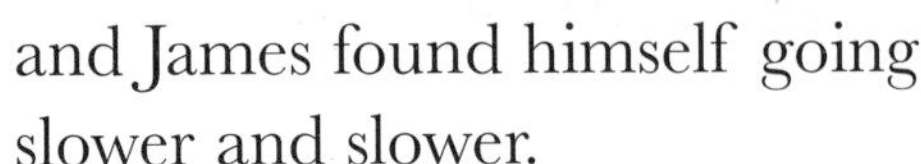

and James found himself going slower and slower.

"What's the matter?" James asked his Driver.

"The brakes are hard on – leak in the pipe most likely. You've banged the coaches enough to make a leak in anything."

The Guard and the Driver got down and looked at the

brake pipes all along the train.

At last they found a hole where rough treatment had made a joint work loose.

"How shall we mend it?" said the Guard.

James' Driver thought for a moment.

"We'll do it with newspapers and a leather bootlace."

"Well, where is the bootlace coming from?" asked the Guard. "We haven't one."

"Ask the passengers," said the Driver.

So the Guard made everyone get out.

"Has anybody got a leather bootlace?" he asked.

They all said "No" except one man in a bowler hat (whose name was Jeremiah Jobling) who tried to hide his feet.

"You have a leather bootlace there I see, sir," said the Guard. "Please give it to me."

"I won't," said Jeremiah Jobling.

"Then," said the Guard sternly, "I'm afraid this train will just stop where it is."

Then the passengers all told the Guard, the Driver and the Fireman what a Bad Railway it was. But the Guard climbed into his van, and the Driver and Fireman made James let off steam. So they all told Jeremiah Jobling he was a Bad Man instead.

At last he gave them his laces, the Driver tied a pad of newspapers tightly round the hole, and James was able to pull the train.

But he was a sadder and a wiser James and took care never to bump coaches again.

Troublesome Trucks

JAMES did not see the Fat Controller for several days. They left James alone in the shed, and did not even allow him to go out and push coaches and trucks in the Yard.

"Oh, dear!" he thought sadly, "I'll never be allowed out any more; I shall have to stay in this shed for always, and no one will ever see my red coat again. Oh, dear! Oh, dear!" James began to cry.

Just then the Fat Controller came along.

"I see you are sorry, James," he said. "I hope, now, that you will be a better Engine. You have given me a lot of trouble. People are laughing at my Railway, and I do not like that at all."

"I am very sorry, Sir," said James. "I will try hard to behave."

"That's a good engine," said the Fat Controller kindly. "I want you to pull some trucks for me. Run along and find them."

So James puffed happily away.

"Here are your trucks, James," said a little tank engine. "Have you got some bootlaces ready?" And he ran off laughing rudely.

"Oh! Oh! Oh!" said the trucks, as James backed down on them. "We want a proper engine, not a Red Monster."

James took no notice and started as soon as the Guard was ready.

"Come along, come along," he puffed.

"We won't! We won't!" screamed the trucks.

But James didn't care, and he pulled the screeching trucks sternly out of the yard.

The trucks tried hard to make him give up, but he still kept on.

Sometimes their brakes would slip "on", and sometimes their axles would "run hot".

Each time they would have to stop and put the trouble right and each time James would start again, determined not to let the trucks beat him.

"Give up! Give up! You can't pull us! You can't! You can't!" called the trucks.

"I can and I will! I can and I will!" puffed James.

And slowly but surely he pulled them along the line.

At last they saw Gordon's Hill ahead.

"Look out for trouble, James," warned his Driver. "We'll go fast and get them up before they know it. Don't let them stop you."

So James went faster, and they were soon halfway up the hill.

"I'm doing it! I'm doing it!" he panted.

But it was hard work.

"Will the top never come?" he thought, when with a sudden jerk it all came easier.

"I've done it! I've done it!" he puffed triumphantly.

"Hurrah!" he thought, "it's easy now." But his Driver shut off steam.

"They've done it again," he said. "We've left our tail behind!"

The last ten trucks were running backwards down the hill. The coupling had snapped!

But the Guard was brave. Very carefully and cleverly he made them stop. Then he got out and walked down the line with his red flag.

"That's why it was easy," said James as he backed the other trucks carefully down. "What silly things trucks are! There might have been an accident."

Meanwhile the Guard had stopped Edward who was pulling three coaches.

"Shall I help you, James?" called Edward.

"No, thank you," answered James, "I'll pull them myself."

"Good, don't let them beat you."

So James got ready. Then with a "peep, peep" he was off.

"I *can* do it, I *can* do it," he puffed. He pulled and puffed as hard as he could.

"Peep pip peep peep! You're doing well!" whistled Edward, as James slowly struggled up the hill, with clouds of smoke and steam pouring from his funnel.

"I've done it, I've done it," he panted and disappeared over the top.

They reached their station safely. James was resting in the yard, when Edward puffed by with a cheerful "peep peep".

Then, walking towards him across the rails, James saw . . . the Fat Controller!

"Oh dear! What will he say?" he asked himself sadly.

But the Fat Controller was smiling. "I was in Edward's train, and saw everything," he said. "You've made the most troublesome trucks on the line behave. After that, you deserve to keep your red coat."

James and the Express

SOMETIMES Gordon and Henry slept in James' shed, and they would talk of nothing but bootlaces! James would talk about engines who got shut up in tunnels and stuck on hills, but they wouldn't listen, and went on talking and laughing.

"You talk too much, little James," Gordon would say. "A fine strong engine like me has something to talk about. I'm the only engine who can pull the Express. When I'm not there, they need two engines. Think of that!

"I've pulled expresses for years, and have never once lost my way. I seem to know the right line by instinct," said Gordon proudly. Every wise engine knows, of course, that the Signalman works the points to make engines run on the right lines, but Gordon was so proud that he had forgotten.

"Wake up, James," he said next morning, "it's nearly time for the Express. What are you doing? – Odd jobs? Ah well! We all have to begin somewhere, don't we? Run along now and get my coaches – don't be late now."

James went to get Gordon's coaches. They were now all shining with lovely new paint. He was careful not to bump them, and they followed him smoothly into the station singing happily. "We're going away, we're going away."

"I wish I was going with you," said James. "I should love to pull the Express and go flying along the line."

He left them in the station and went back to the yard, just as Gordon with much noise and blowing of steam backed on to the train.

The Fat Controller was on the train with other Important People, and, as soon as they heard the Guard's whistle, Gordon started.

"Look at me now! Look at me now!" he puffed, and the coaches glided after him out of the station.

"Poop poop poo poo poop! — Good-bye little James! See you tomorrow."

James watched the train disappear round a curve, and then went back to work. He pushed some trucks into their proper sidings and went to fetch the coaches for another train.

He brought the coaches to the platform and was just being uncoupled when he heard a mournful, quiet "Shush shush shush shush!" and there was Gordon trying to sidle into the station without being noticed.

"Hullo, Gordon! Is it tomorrow?" asked James. Gordon didn't answer; he just let off steam feebly.

"Did you lose your way, Gordon?"

"No, it was lost for me," he answered crossly, "I was switched off the main line on to the loop; I had to go all round and back again."

"Perhaps it was instinct," said James brightly.

Meanwhile all the passengers hurried to the booking office. "We want our money back," they shouted.

Everyone was making a noise, but the Fat Controller climbed on a trolley and blew the Guard's whistle so loudly that they all stopped to look at him.

Then he promised them a new train at once.

"Gordon can't do it," he said. "Will you pull it for us, James?"

"Yes, sir, I'll try."

So James was coupled on and everyone got in again.

"Do your best, James," said the Fat Controller kindly. Just then the whistle blew and he had to run to get in.

"Come along, come along," puffed James.

"You're pulling us well! You're pulling us well," sang the coaches.

"Hurry, hurry, hurry," puffed James.

Stations and bridges flashed by, the passengers leaned out of the windows and cheered, and they soon reached the terminus.

Everyone said "Thank you" to James. "Well done," said the Fat Controller. "Would you like to pull the Express sometimes?"

"Yes, please," answered James happily.

Next day when James came by, Gordon was pushing trucks in the Yard.

"I like some quiet work for a change," he said. "I'm teaching these trucks manners. You did well with those coaches I hear . . . good, we'll show them!" and he gave his trucks a bump, making them cry, "Oh! Oh! Oh! Oh!"

James and Gordon are now good friends. James sometimes takes the Express to give Gordon a rest. Gordon never talks about bootlaces, and they are both quite agreed on the subject of trucks!

THE RAILWAY SERIES NO. 4

Tank Engine Thomas Again

THE REV. W. AWDRY

with illustrations by

C. REGINALD DALBY

DEAR FRIENDS,

Here is news from Thomas' branch line. It is clearly no ordinary line, and life on it is far from dull.

Thomas asks me to say that, if you are ever in the Region, you must be sure to visit him and travel on his line. "They will have never seen anything like it," he says proudly.

I know I haven't!

THE AUTHOR

Thomas and the Guard

THOMAS the Tank Engine is very proud of his branch line. He thinks it is the most important part of the whole railway.

He has two coaches. They are old, and need new paint, but he loves them very much. He calls them Annie and Clarabel. Annie can only take passengers, but Clarabel can take passengers, luggage and the Guard.

As they run backwards and forwards along the line, Thomas sings them little songs, and Annie and Clarabel sing too.

When Thomas starts from a station he sings, "Oh, come along! We're rather late. Oh, come along! We're rather late." And the coaches sing, "We're coming along, we're coming along."

They don't mind what Thomas says to them because they know he is trying to please the Fat Controller; and they know, too, that if Thomas is cross, he is not cross with them.

He is cross with the engines on the Main Line who have made him late.

One day they had to wait for Henry's train. It was late. Thomas was getting crosser and crosser. "How can I run my line properly if Henry is always late? He doesn't realize that the Fat Controller depends on ME," and he whistled impatiently.

At last Henry came.

"Where have you been, lazybones?" asked Thomas crossly.

"Oh dear, my system is out of order; no one understands my case. You don't know what I suffer," moaned Henry.

"Rubbish!" said Thomas, "you're too fat; you need exercise!"

Lots of people with piles of luggage got out of Henry's train, and they all climbed into Annie and Clarabel. Thomas had to wait till they were ready. At last the Guard blew his whistle, and Thomas started at once.

The Guard turned round to jump into his van, tripped over an old lady's umbrella, and fell flat on his face.

By the time he had picked himself up, Thomas and Annie and Clarabel were steaming out of the station.

"Come along! Come along!" puffed Thomas, but Clarabel didn't want to come. "I've lost my nice Guard, I've lost my nice Guard," she sobbed. Annie tried to tell Thomas "We haven't a Guard, we haven't a Guard," but he was hurrying, and wouldn't listen.

"Oh, come along! Oh, come along!" he puffed impatiently.

Annie and Clarabel tried to put on their brakes, but they couldn't without the Guard.

"Where is our Guard? Where is our Guard?" they cried. Thomas didn't stop till they came to a signal.

"Bother that signal!" said Thomas. "What's the matter?"

"I don't know," said his Driver. "The Guard will tell us in a minute." They waited and waited, but the Guard didn't come.

"Peep peep peep peep! Where is the Guard?" whistled Thomas.

"We've left him behind," sobbed Annie and Clarabel together. The Driver, the Fireman and the passengers looked, and there was the Guard running as fast as he could along the line, with his flags in one hand and his whistle in the other.

Everybody cheered him. He was very hot, so he sat down and had a drink and told them all about it.

"I'm very sorry, Mr Guard," said Thomas.

"It wasn't your fault, Thomas; it was the old lady's umbrella. Look, the signal is down; let's make up for lost time."

Annie and Clarabel were so pleased to have their Guard again, that they sang, "As fast as you like, as fast as you like!" to Thomas, all the way, and they reached the end of the line quicker than ever before.

Thomas goes Fishing

THOMAS' branch line had a station by a river. As he rumbled over the bridge, he would see people fishing. Sometimes they stood quietly by their lines; sometimes they were actually jerking fish out of the water.

Thomas often wanted to stay and watch, but his Driver said, "No! what would the Fat Controller say if we were late?"

Thomas thought it would be lovely to stop by the river. "I should like to go fishing," he said to himself longingly.

Every time he met another engine he would say "I want to fish." They all answered "Engines don't go fishing."

"Silly stick-in-the-muds!" he would snort impatiently.

Thomas generally had to take in water at the station by the river. One day he stopped as usual, and his Fireman put the pipe from the water tower in his tank. Then he turned the tap, but it was out of order and no water came.

"Bother!" said Thomas, "I am thirsty." "Never mind," said his Driver, "we'll get some water from the river."

They found a bucket and some rope, and went to the bridge, then the Driver let the bucket down to the water.

The bucket was old, and had five holes, so they had to fill it, pull it up, and empty it into Thomas' tank as quickly as they could.

"There's a hole in my bucket, dear Liza, dear Liza," sang the Fireman.

"Never mind about Liza," said the Driver, "you empty that bucket, before you spill the water over me!"

They finished at last. "That's good! That's good!" puffed Thomas as he started, and Annie and Clarabel ran happily behind.

They puffed along the valley, and were in the tunnel when Thomas began to feel a pain in his boiler, while steam hissed from his safety valve in an alarming way.

"There's too much steam," said his Driver, and his Fireman opened the tap in the feed pipe, to let more water into the boiler, but none came.

"Oh, dear," groaned Thomas, "I'm going to burst! I'm going to burst!"

They damped down his fire, and struggled on.

"I've got such a pain, I've got such a pain," Thomas hissed.

Just outside the last station they stopped, uncoupled Annie and Clarabel and ran Thomas, who was still hissing fit to burst, on a siding right out of the way.

Then while the Guard telephoned for an Engine Inspector, and the Fireman was putting out the fire, the Driver wrote notices in large letters which he hung on Thomas in front and behind, "DANGER! KEEP AWAY."

Soon the Inspector and the Fat Controller arrived. "Cheer up, Thomas!" they said. "We'll soon put you right."

The Driver told them what had happened. "So the feed pipe is blocked," said the Inspector. "I'll just look in the tanks."

He climbed up and peered in, then he came down. "Excuse me, Sir," he said to the Fat Controller, "please look in the tank and tell me what you see."

"Certainly, Inspector." He clambered up, looked in and nearly fell off in surprise.

"Inspector," he whispered, "can *you* see *fish*?"

"Gracious goodness me!" said the Fat Controller, "how did the fish get there, Driver?"

Thomas' Driver scratched his head, "We must have fished them from the river," and he told them about the bucket.

The Fat Controller laughed, "Well, Thomas, so you and your Driver have been fishing, but fish don't suit you, and we must get them out."

So the Driver and the Fireman fetched rods and nets, and they all took turns at fishing in Thomas' tank, while the Fat Controller told them how to do it.

When they had caught all the fish, the Stationmaster gave them some potatoes, the Driver borrowed a frying-pan, while the Fireman made a fire beside the line and did the cooking.

Then they all had a lovely picnic supper of fish and chips.

"That was good," said the Fat Controller as he finished his share, "but fish don't suit you, Thomas, so you mustn't do it again."

"No, Sir, I won't," said Thomas sadly, "engines don't go fishing, it's too uncomfortable."

Thomas, Terence and the Snow

AUTUMN was changing the leaves from green to brown. The fields were changing too, from yellow stubble to brown earth.

As Thomas puffed along, he heard the "chug chug chug" of a tractor at work.

One day, stopping for a signal, he saw the tractor close by.

"Hullo!" said the tractor, "I'm Terence; I'm ploughing."

"I'm Thomas; I'm pulling a train. What ugly wheels you've got."

"They're not ugly, they're caterpillars," said Terence. "I can go anywhere; *I* don't need rails."

"I don't want to go anywhere," said Thomas huffily, "I like my rails, thank you!"

Thomas often saw Terence working, but though he whistled, Terence never answered.

Winter came, and with it dark heavy clouds full of snow.

"I don't like it," said Thomas' Driver. "A heavy fall is coming. I hope it doesn't stop us."

"Pooh!" said Thomas, seeing the snow melt on the rails, "soft stuff, nothing to it!" And he puffed on feeling cold, but confident.

They finished their journey safely; but the country was covered, and the rails were two dark lines standing out in the white snow.

"You'll need your Snow Plough for the next journey, Thomas," said his Driver.

"Pooh! Snow is silly soft stuff – it won't stop me."

"Listen to me," his Driver replied, "we are going to fix your Snow Plough on, and I want no nonsense, please."

The Snow Plough was heavy and uncomfortable and made Thomas cross. He shook it, and he banged it and when they got back it was so damaged that the Driver had to take it off.

"You're a very naughty engine," said his Driver, as he shut the shed door that night.

Next morning, both Driver and Fireman came early and worked hard to mend the Snow Plough; but they couldn't make it fit properly.

It was time for the first train. Thomas was pleased, "I shan't have to wear it, I shan't have to wear it," he puffed to Annie and Clarabel.

"I hope it's all right, I hope it's all right," they whispered anxiously to each other.

The Driver was anxious, too. "It's not bad here," he said to the Fireman, "but it's sure to be deep in the valley."

It was snowing again when Thomas started, but the rails were not covered.

"Silly soft stuff! Silly soft stuff!" he puffed. "I didn't need that stupid old thing yesterday; I shan't today. Snow can't stop me," and he rushed into the tunnel, thinking how clever he was.

At the other end he saw a heap of snow fallen from the sides of the cutting.

"Silly old snow," said Thomas, and charged it.

"Cinders and ashes!" said Thomas, "I'm stuck!" – and he was!

"Back! Thomas, back!" said his Driver. Thomas tried, but his wheels spun, and he couldn't move.

More snow fell and piled up round him.

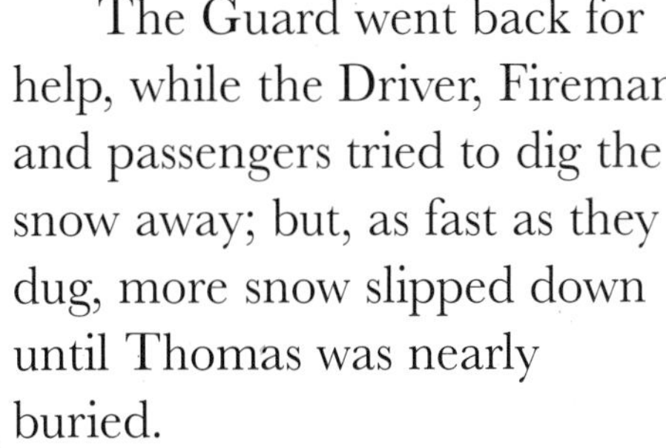

The Guard went back for help, while the Driver, Fireman and passengers tried to dig the snow away; but, as fast as they dug, more snow slipped down until Thomas was nearly buried.

"Oh, my wheels and coupling rods!" said Thomas sadly, "I shall have to stop here till I'm frozen. What a silly engine I am," and Thomas began to cry.

At last, a tooting in the distance told them a bus had come for the passengers.

Then Terence chugged through the tunnel.

He pulled the empty coaches away, and came back for Thomas. Thomas' wheels were clear, but still spun helplessly when he tried to move.

Terence tugged and slipped,

and slipped and tugged, and at last dragged Thomas into the tunnel.

"Thank you, Terence, your caterpillars are splendid," said Thomas gratefully.

"I hope you'll be sensible now, Thomas," said his Driver severely.

"I'll try," said Thomas, as he puffed home.

Thomas and Bertie

ONE day Thomas was waiting at the junction, when a bus came into the Yard.

"Hullo!" said Thomas, "who are you?"

"I'm Bertie, who are you?"

"I'm Thomas; I run this line."

"So you're Thomas. Ah – I remember now, you stuck in the snow, I took your passengers and Terence pulled you out. I've come to help you with your passengers today."

"Help me!" said Thomas crossly, going bluer than ever and letting off steam. "I can go faster than you."

"You can't."

"I can."

"I'll race you," said Bertie.

Their Drivers agreed. The Stationmaster said, "Are you ready? – Go!" and they were off.

Thomas never could go fast at first, and Bertie drew in front. Thomas was running well but he did not hurry.

"Why don't you go fast? Why don't you go fast?" called Annie and Clarabel anxiously.

"Wait and see, wait and see," hissed Thomas.

"He's a long way ahead, a long way ahead," they wailed, but Thomas didn't mind. He remembered the level crossing.

There was Bertie fuming at the gates while they sailed gaily through.

"Goodbye, Bertie," called Thomas.

The road left the railway and went through a village, so they couldn't see Bertie.

They stopped at the station. "Peep pip peep! Quickly, please!" called Thomas. Everybody got out quickly, the Guard whistled and off they went.

"Come along! Come along!" sang Thomas.

"We're coming along! We're coming along!" sang Annie and Clarabel.

"Hurry! Hurry! Hurry!" panted Thomas, looking straight ahead.

Then he whistled shrilly in horror, for Bertie was crossing the bridge over the railway, tooting triumphantly on his horn!

"Oh, deary me! Oh, deary me!" groaned Thomas.

"He's a long way in front, a long way in front," wailed Annie and Clarabel.

"Steady, Thomas," said his Driver, "we'll beat Bertie yet."

"We'll beat Bertie yet; we'll beat Bertie yet," echoed Annie and Clarabel.

"We'll do it; we'll do it," panted Thomas bravely. "Oh, bother, there's a station."

As he stopped, he heard a toot.

"Goodbye, Thomas, you must be tired. Sorry I can't stop, we buses have to work you know. Goodbye!"

The next station was by the river. They got there quickly, but the signal was up.

"Oh, dear," thought Thomas, "we've lost!"

But he felt better after a drink. Then James rattled through with a goods train, and the signal dropped, showing the line was clear.

"Hurrah, we're off! Hurrah, we're off!" puffed Thomas gaily.

As they rumbled over the bridge they heard an impatient "Toot, Toot," and there was Bertie waiting at the red light, while cars and lorries crossed the narrow bridge in the opposite direction.

Road and railway ran up the valley side by side, a stream tumbling between.

Thomas had not crossed the bridge when Bertie started with a roar, and soon shot ahead. Excited passengers in train and bus cheered and shouted across the valley. Now Thomas reached his full speed and foot by foot, yard by yard he gained, till they were running level. Bertie tried hard, but Thomas was too fast; slowly but surely he drew ahead, till whistling triumphantly he plunged into the tunnel, leaving Bertie toiling far behind.

"I've done it! I've done it," panted Thomas in the tunnel.

"We've done it, hooray! We've done it, hooray!" chanted

Annie and Clarabel; and whistling proudly, they whooooshed out of the tunnel into the last station.

The passengers gave Thomas "three cheers" and told the Stationmaster and the porters all about the race. When Bertie came in they gave him "three cheers" too.

"Well done, Thomas," said Bertie. "That was fun, but to beat you over that hill I should have to grow wings and be an aeroplane."

Thomas and Bertie now keep each other very busy. Bertie finds people in the villages who want to go by train, and takes them to Thomas; while Thomas brings people to the station for Bertie to take home.

They often talk about their race. But Bertie's passengers don't like being bounced like peas in a frying-pan! And the Fat Controller has warned Thomas about what happens to engines who race at dangerous speeds.

So although (between you and me) they would like to have another race, I don't think they ever will.

THE RAILWAY SERIES NO. 5

Troublesome Engines

THE REV. W. AWDRY

with illustrations by

C. REGINALD DALBY

DEAR FRIENDS,

News from the Line has not been good. The Fat Controller has been having trouble. A short while ago he gave Henry a coat of green paint; but as soon as he got his old colour back again, Henry became conceited. Gordon and James, too, have been Getting Above Themselves.

I am glad to say, however, that the Fat Controller has, quite kindly but very firmly, put them In Their Place; and the trains are running as usual.

I hope you will like meeting Percy; we shall be hearing more of him later.

THE AUTHOR

Henry and the Elephant

HENRY and Gordon were lonely when Thomas left the Yard to run his branch line. They missed him very much.

They had more work to do. They couldn't wait in the Shed till it was time, and find their coaches at the platform; they had to fetch them. They didn't like that.

Edward sometimes did odd jobs, and so did James, but James soon started grumbling too. The Fat Controller kindly gave Henry and Gordon new coats of paint (Henry chose green), but they still grumbled dreadfully.

"We get no rest, we get no rest," they complained as they clanked about the Yard; but the coaches only laughed.

"You're lazy and slack, you're lazy and slack," they answered in their quiet, rude way.

But when a Circus came to town, the engines forgot they were tired. They all wanted to shunt the special trucks and coaches.

They were dreadfully jealous of James when the Fat Controller told him to pull the train when the Circus went away.

However, they soon forgot about the animals as they had plenty of work to do.

One morning Henry was told to take some workmen to a tunnel which was blocked.

He grumbled away to find two trucks to carry the workmen and their tools.

"Pushing trucks! Pushing trucks!" he muttered in a sulky sort of way.

They stopped outside the tunnel, and tried to look through it, but it was quite dark; no daylight shone from the other end.

The workmen took their tools and went inside.

Suddenly with a shout they all ran out looking frightened.

"We went to the block and started to dig, but it grunted and moved," they said.

"Rubbish," said the foreman.

"It's not rubbish, it's big and alive; we're not going in there again."

"Right," said the foreman, "I'll ride in a truck and Henry shall push it out."

"Wheeeesh," said Henry unhappily. He hated tunnels (he had been shut up in one once), but this was worse; something big and alive was inside.

"Peep peep peep pip pip pee — eep!" he whistled, "I don't want to go in!"

"Neither do I," said his Driver, "but we must clear the line."

"Oh dear! Oh dear!" puffed Henry as they slowly advanced into the darkness.

BUMP————————!!!!

Henry's Driver shut off steam at once.

"Help! Help! We're going back," wailed Henry, and slowly moving out into the daylight came first Henry, then the trucks, and last of all, pushing hard and rather cross, came a large elephant.

"Well I never did!" said the foreman. "It's an elephant from the Circus."

Henry's Driver put on his brakes, and a man ran to telephone for the keeper.

The elephant stopped pushing and came towards them. They gave him some sandwiches and cake, so he forgot he was cross and remembered he was hungry. He drank three buckets of water without stopping, and was just going to drink another when Henry let off steam.

The elephant jumped, and "hoo —— oosh", he squirted the water over Henry by mistake.

Poor Henry!

When the keeper came, the workmen rode home happily in the trucks, laughing at their adventure, but Henry was very cross.

"An elephant pushed me! an elephant hooshed me!" he hissed.

He was sulky all day, and his coaches had an uncomfortable time.

In the Shed he told Gordon and James about the elephant, and I am sorry to say that instead of laughing and telling him not to be silly, they looked sad and said:

"You poor engine, you have been badly treated."

Tenders and Turntables

THE Big Stations at both ends of the line each have a turntable. The Fat Controller had them made so that Edward, Henry, Gordon and James can be turned round. It is dangerous for Tender Engines to go fast backwards. Tank Engines like Thomas don't need turntables; they can go just as well backwards as forwards.

But if you had heard Gordon talking a short while ago, you would have thought that the Fat Controller had given him a tender just to show how important he was.

"You don't understand, little Thomas," said Gordon, "we Tender Engines have a position to keep up. You haven't a Tender and that makes a difference. It doesn't matter where *you* go, but We are Important, and for the Fat Controller to make us shunt trucks, fetch coaches, and go on some of those dirty sidings it's —— it's —— well it's not the Proper Thing."

And Gordon puffed away in a dignified manner.

Thomas chuckled and went off with Annie and Clarabel.

Arrived at the Terminus, Gordon waited till all the passengers had got out; then, groaning and grumbling, he shunted the coaches to another platform.

"Disgraceful! Disgraceful!" he hissed as he ran backwards to the turntable.

The turntable was in a windy place close to the sea. It was only just big enough for Gordon, and if he was not on it just right, he put it out of

balance, and made it difficult to turn.

Today, Gordon was in a bad temper, and the wind was blowing fiercely.

His Driver tried to make him stop in the right place; backwards and forwards they went, but Gordon wasn't trying.

At last Gordon's Driver gave it up. The Fireman tried to turn the handle, but Gordon's weight and the strong wind prevented him. The Driver, some platelayers, and the Fireman all tried together.

"It's no good," they said at last, mopping their faces, "your tender upsets the balance. If you were a nice Tank Engine, you'd be all right. Now you'll have to pull the next train backwards."

Gordon came to the platform. Some little boys shouted, "Come on quick, here's a new Tank Engine."

"What a swiz!" they said, when they came near, "it's only Gordon, back to front."

Gordon hissed emotionally.

He puffed to the junction. "Hullo!" called Thomas, "playing Tank Engines? Sensible engine! Take my advice, scrap your tender and have a nice bunker instead."

Gordon snorted, but didn't answer. Even James laughed when he saw him. "Take care," hissed Gordon, "you might stick too."

"No fear," chuckled James, "I'm not so fat as you."

"I mustn't stick," thought James anxiously, as he ran to the turntable later. He stopped on just the right place to balance the table. It could now swing easily. His Fireman turned the handle . . . James turned . . . much too easily! The wind puffed him round like a top. He couldn't stop! . . .

At last the wind died down, and James stopped turning, but not before Gordon, who had been turned on the loop line, had seen him.

"Well! Well!" he said, "are you playing roundabouts?"

Poor James, feeling quite giddy, rolled off to the Shed without a word.

That night the three engines had an "indignation meeting".

"It's shameful to treat Tender Engines like this! Henry gets 'hooshed' by elephants; Gordon has to go backwards and people think he's a Tank Engine. James spins round like a top, and everyone laughs at us. And added to that, the Fat Controller makes us shunt in dirty sidings. Ugh ——— ! !" said all three engines together.

"Listen," said Gordon. . . . He whispered something to the others: "We'll do it tomorrow. The Fat Controller *will* look silly!"

Trouble in the Shed

THE Fat Controller sat in his office and listened. The Fat Controller frowned and said, "What a nuisance passengers are! How can I work with all this noise?"

The Stationmaster knocked and came in, looking worried.

"There's trouble in the Shed, Sir. Henry is sulking; there is no train, and the passengers are saying this is a Bad Railway."

"Indeed!" said the Fat Controller. "We cannot allow that. Will you quieten the passengers, please; I will go and speak to Henry."

He found Henry, Gordon and James looking sulky.

"Come along, Henry," he said, "it is time your train was ready."

"Henry's not going," said Gordon rudely.

"We *won't* shunt like Common Tank Engines. We are Important Tender Engines. You fetch our coaches and we will pull them. Tender Engines don't shunt," and all three engines let off steam in a cheeky way.

"Oh indeed," said the Fat Controller severely. "We'll see about that; engines on My Railway do as they are told."

He hurried away, climbed into his car and drove to find Edward.

"The Yard has never been the same since Thomas left," he thought sadly.

Edward was shunting.

"Leave those trucks please, Edward; I want you to push coaches for me in the Yard."

"Thank you, Sir, that will be a nice change."

"That's a good engine," said the Fat Controller kindly, "off you go then."

So Edward found coaches for the three engines, and that day the trains ran as usual.

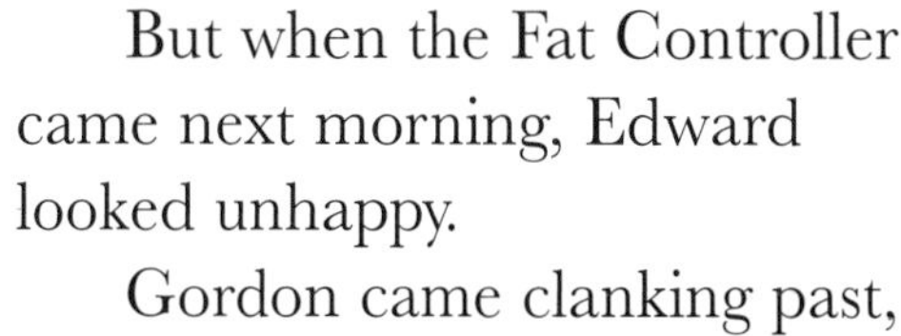

But when the Fat Controller came next morning, Edward looked unhappy.

Gordon came clanking past, hissing rudely. "Bless me!" said the Fat Controller. "What a noise!"

"They all hiss me, Sir," answered Edward sadly. "They say 'Tender Engines don't shunt', and last night they said I had black wheels. I haven't, have I, Sir?"

"No, Edward, you have nice blue ones, and I'm proud of you. Tender Engines do shunt, but all the same you'd be happier in your own Yard. We need a Tank Engine here."

He went to an Engine Workshop, and they showed him all sorts of Tank Engines. There were big ones, and little ones; some looked happy, and some sad, and some looked at him anxiously, hoping he would choose them.

At last he saw a smart little green engine with four wheels.

"That's the one," he thought.

"If I choose you, will you work hard?"

"Oh Sir! Yes Sir!"

"That's a good engine; I'll call you Percy."

"Yes Sir! Thank you Sir!" said Percy happily.

So he bought Percy and drove him back to the Yard.

"Edward," he called, "here's Percy; will you show him everything?"

Percy soon learned what he had to do, and they had a happy afternoon.

Once Henry came by hissing as usual.

"Whee ——— eesh!" said Percy suddenly; Henry jumped and ran back to the Shed.

"How beautifully you wheeshed him," laughed Edward. "I can't wheesh like that."

"Oh!" said Percy modestly, "that's nothing; you should hear them in the workshop. You have to wheesh loudly to make yourself heard."

Next morning Thomas arrived. "The Fat Controller sent for me; I expect he wants help," he said importantly to Edward.

"Sh! Sh! Here he comes."

"Well done Thomas; you've been quick. Listen, Henry, Gordon and James are sulking; they say they won't shunt like Common Tank Engines. So I have shut them up, and I want you both to run the line."

"Common Tank Engines indeed!" snorted Thomas. "We'll show them."

"And Percy here will help too," said the Fat Controller.

"Oh Sir! Yes Sir! Please Sir!" answered Percy excitedly.

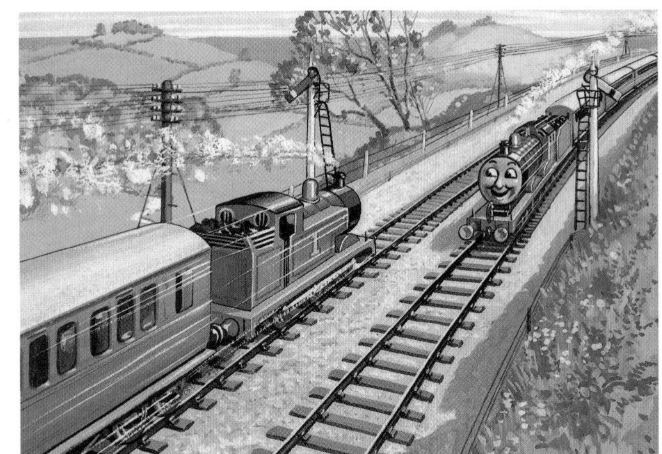

Edward and Thomas worked the line. Starting at opposite ends, they pulled the trains, whistling cheerfully to each other as they passed.

Percy sometimes puffed along the branch line. Thomas was anxious, but both Driver and Guard promised to take care of Annie and Clarabel.

There were fewer trains, but the passengers didn't mind; they knew the three other engines were having a Lesson.

Henry, Gordon and James stayed shut in the Shed, and were cold, lonely and miserable. They wished now they hadn't been so silly.

Percy Runs Away

HENRY, Gordon and James were shut up for several days. At last the Fat Controller opened the Shed.

"I hope you are sorry," he said sternly, "and understand you are not so important after all. Thomas, Edward and Percy have worked the Line very nicely. They need a change, and I will let you out if you promise to be good."

"Yes Sir!" said the three engines, "we will."

"That's right, but please remember that this 'no shunting' nonsense must stop."

He told Edward, Thomas and Percy that they could go and play on the Branch Line for a few days.

They ran off happily and found Annie and Clarabel at the junction. The two coaches were so pleased to see Thomas again, and he took them for a run at once. Edward and Percy played with trucks.

"Stop! Stop! Stop!" screamed the trucks as they were pushed into their proper sidings, but the two engines laughed and went on shunting till the trucks were tidily arranged.

Next, Edward took some empty trucks to the Quarry, and Percy was left alone.

Percy didn't mind that a bit; he liked watching trains and being cheeky to the engines.

"Hurry! Hurry! Hurry!" he would call to them. Gordon, Henry and James got very cross!

After a while he took some trucks over the Main Line to another siding. When they were tidy, he ran on to the Main Line again, and waited for the Signalman to set the points so that he could cross back to the Yard.

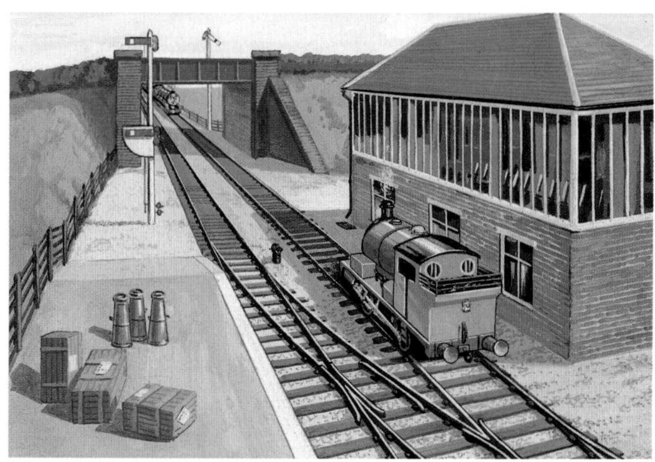

Edward had warned Percy: "Be careful on the Main Line; whistle to tell the Signalman you are there." But Percy didn't remember to whistle, and the Signalman was so busy, and forgot Percy.

Bells rang in the signal box; the man answered, saying the line was clear, and set the signals for the next train.

Percy waited and waited; the points were still against him. He looked along the Main Line . . . "Peep! Peep!" he whistled in horror for, rushing straight towards him, was Gordon with the Express.

"Poop poop poo-poo-poop!" whistled Gordon. His Driver shut off steam and applied the brakes.

Percy's Driver turned on full steam. "Back Percy! Back!" he urged; but Percy's wheels wouldn't turn quickly. Gordon was coming so fast that it seemed he couldn't stop. With shut eyes Percy waited for the crash. His Driver and Fireman jumped out.

"Oo —— ooh e —— er!" groaned Gordon. "Get out of my way."

Percy opened his eyes; Gordon had stopped with Percy's buffers a few inches from his own.

But Percy had begun to move. "I — won't — stay — here — I'll — run — a — way," he puffed. He was soon clear of the station and running as fast as he could. He went through Edward's station whistling loudly, and was so frightened that he ran right up Gordon's Hill without stopping.

He was tired then, and wanted to stop, but he couldn't . . . he had no Driver to shut off steam and to apply the brakes.

"I shall have to run till my wheels wear out," he thought sadly. "Oh dear! Oh dear!"

"I — want — to — stop, I — want — to — stop," he puffed in a tired sort of way.

He passed another signal box. "I know just what you want, little Percy," called the man kindly. He set the points, and Percy puffed wearily on to a nice empty siding ending in a big bank of earth.

Percy was too tired now to care where he went. "I — want — to — stop, I — want — to — stop ——— I — *have* — stopped!" he puffed thankfully, as his bunker buried itself in the bank.

"Never mind, Percy," said the workmen as they dug him out, "you shall have a drink and some coal, and then you'll feel better."

Presently Gordon arrived.

"Well done Percy, you started so quickly that you stopped a nasty accident."

"I'm sorry I was cheeky," said Percy, "you were clever to stop."

Percy now works in the Yard and finds coaches for the trains. He is still cheeky because he is that sort of engine, but he is always *most* careful when he goes on the Main Line.

THE RAILWAY SERIES NO. 6

Henry the Green Engine

THE REV. W. AWDRY

with illustrations by

C. REGINALD DALBY

DEAR FRIENDS,

Here is more news from the Region. All the engines now have numbers as well as names; you will see them in the pictures. They are as follows: THOMAS 1, EDWARD 2, HENRY 3, GORDON 4, JAMES 5, PERCY 6.

Then I expect you were sorry for Henry who was often ill and unable to work. He gave Sir Topham Hatt (who is, of course, our Fat Controller) a lot of worry. Now Henry has a new shape and is ready for anything. These stories tell you all about it.

THE AUTHOR

Coal

"I SUFFER dreadfully, and no one cares."

"Rubbish, Henry," snorted James, "you don't work hard enough."

Henry was bigger than James, but smaller than Gordon. Sometimes he could pull trains; sometimes he had no strength at all.

The Fat Controller spoke to him too. "You are too expensive, Henry. You have had lots of new parts and new paint too, but they've done you no good. If we can't make you better, we must get another engine instead of you."

This made Henry, his Driver, and his Fireman very sad.

The Fat Controller was waiting when Henry came to the platform. He had taken off his hat and coat, and put on overalls.

He climbed to the footplate and Henry started.

"Henry is a 'bad steamer'," said the Fireman. "I build up his fire, but it doesn't give enough heat."

Henry tried very hard, but it was no good. He had not enough steam, and they stopped outside Edward's station.

"Oh dear!" thought Henry sadly, "I shall have to go away."

Edward took charge of the train. Henry stopped behind.

"What do you think is wrong, Fireman?" asked the Fat Controller.

The Fireman mopped his face. "Excuse me, Sir," he answered, "but the coal is wrong. We've had a poor lot lately, and today it's worse. The other engines can manage; they have big fireboxes. Henry's is small and can't make the heat. With Welsh coal he'd be a different engine."

"It's expensive," said the Fat Controller thoughtfully, "but Henry must have a fair chance. James shall go and fetch some."

When the Welsh coal came, Henry's Driver and Fireman were excited.

"Now we'll show them, Henry old fellow!" They carefully oiled all his joints and polished his brass till it shone like gold.

His fire had already been lit, so the Fireman "made it" carefully.

He put large lumps of coal like a wall round the outside. Then he covered the glowing middle part with smaller lumps.

"You're spoiling my fire," complained Henry.

"Wait and see," said the Fireman. "We'll have a roaring fire just when we want it."

He was right. When Henry reached the platform, the water was boiling nicely, and he had to let off steam, to show how happy he was. He made such a noise that the Fat Controller came out to see him.

"How are you, Henry?"

"Pip peep peep!" whistled Henry, "I feel fine!"

"Have you a good fire, Driver?"

"Never better Sir, *and* plenty of steam."

"No record breaking," warned the Fat Controller, smiling. "Don't push him too hard."

"Henry won't need pushing, Sir; I'll have to hold him back."

Henry had a lovely day. He had never felt so well in his life. He wanted to go fast, but his Driver wouldn't let him. "Steady old fellow," he would say, "there's plenty of time."

They arrived early at the junction.

"Where have you been, lazybones?" asked Henry, when Thomas puffed in, "I can't wait for dawdling tank engines like you! Goodbye!"

"Whoooosh!" said Thomas to Annie and Clarabel as Henry disappeared, "have you ever seen anything like it?"

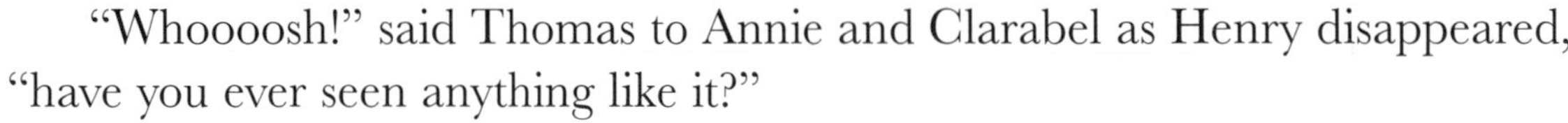

Both Annie and Clarabel agreed that they never had.

The Flying Kipper

LOTS of ships use the harbour at the Big Station by the sea. The passenger ships have spotless paint and shining brass. Other ships, though smaller and dirtier, are important too. They take coal, machinery and other things abroad, and bring back meat, timber and things we need.

Fishing boats also come there. They unload their fish on the quay. Some of it is sent to shops in the town, and some goes in a special train to other places far away.

The railwaymen call this train "The Flying Kipper".

One winter evening Henry's Driver said: "We'll be out early tomorrow. We've got to take 'The Flying Kipper'."

"Don't tell Gordon," he whispered, "but I think if we pull the 'Kipper' nicely, the Fat Controller will let us pull the Express."

"Hurrah!" cried Henry, excited. "That will be lovely."

He was ready at 5 o'clock. There was snow and frost. Men hustled and shouted, loading the vans with crates of fish. The last door banged, the Guard showed his green lamp, and they were off.

"Come on! Come on! dontbesilly! — dontbesilly!" puffed Henry to the vans, as his wheels slipped on the icy rails.

The vans shuddered and groaned. "Trock, Trick, Trock, Trick; all right, all right," they answered grudgingly.

"That is better, that is better," puffed Henry more happily, as the train began to gather speed.

Thick clouds of smoke and steam poured from his funnel into the cold air; and when his Fireman put on more coal, the fire's light shone brightly on the snow around.

"Hurry, hurry, hurry," panted Henry.

They hooshed under bridges, and clattered through stations, green signal-lights showing as they passed.

They were going well, the light grew better and a yellow signal appeared ahead.

"Distant signal – up," thought Henry, "caution." His Driver, shutting off steam, prepared to stop, but the home signal was down. "All clear, Henry; away we go."

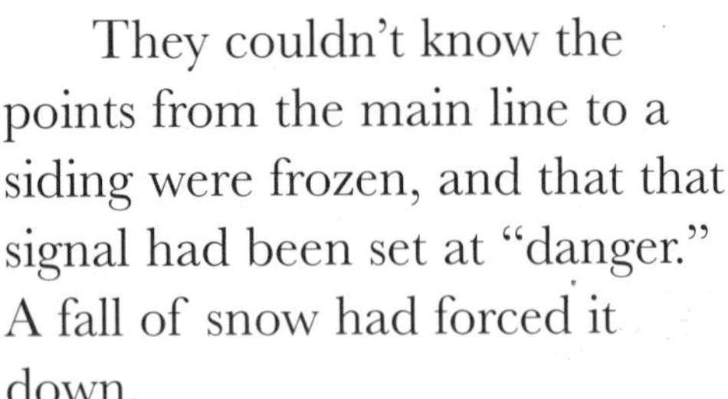

They couldn't know the points from the main line to a siding were frozen, and that that signal had been set at "danger." A fall of snow had forced it down.

A goods train waited in the siding to let "The Flying Kipper" pass. The Driver and Fireman were drinking cocoa in the brake van.

The Guard pulled out his watch. "The 'Kipper' is due," he said.

"Who cares?" said the Fireman. "This is good cocoa."

The Driver got up, "Come on Fireman, back to our engine."

"Hey!" the Fireman grumbled, "I haven't finished my cocoa yet."

A sudden crash – the brake van broke – the three men shot in the air like Jacks-in-the-box, and landed in the snow outside.

Henry's Driver and the Fireman jumped clear before the crash. The Fireman fell head first into a heap of snow. He kicked so hard that the Driver couldn't pull him out.

Henry sprawled on his side. He looked surprised. The goods train Fireman waved his empty mug.

"You clumsy great engine! The best cup of cocoa I've ever had, and you bump into me and spill it all!"

"Never mind your cocoa, Fireman," laughed his Driver, "run and telephone the breakdown gang."

The gang soon cleared the line, but they had hard work lifting Henry to the rails.

The Fat Controller came to see him.

"The signal was down, Sir," said Henry nervously.

"Cheer up, Henry! It wasn't your fault. Ice and snow caused the accident. I'm sending you to Crewe, a fine place for sick engines. They'll give you a new shape and a larger firebox. Then you'll feel a different engine, and won't need special coal any more. Won't that be nice?"

"Yes, Sir," said Henry doubtfully.

Henry liked being at Crewe, but was glad to come home.

A crowd of people waited to see him arrive in his new shape. He looked so splendid and strong that they gave him three cheers.

"Peep peep pippippeep! Thank you very much," he whistled happily.

I am sorry to say that a lot of little boys are often late for school because they wait to see Henry go by!

They often see him pulling the Express; and he does it so well that Gordon is jealous. But that is another story.

Gordon's Whistle

GORDON was cross.

"Why should Henry have a new shape?" he grumbled. "A shape good enough for ME is good enough for him. He goes gallivanting off to Crewe, leaving us to do his work. It's disgraceful!"

"And there's another thing. Henry whistles too much. No *respectable* engine ever whistles loudly at stations."

"It isn't wrong," said Gordon, "but we just don't do it."

Poor Henry didn't feel happy any more.

"Never mind," whispered Percy, "I'm glad you are home again; I like your whistling."

"Goodbye, Henry," called Gordon next morning as he left the Shed. "We are glad to have you with us again, but be sure and remember what I said about whistling."

Later on Henry took a slow train, and presently stopped at Edward's station.

"Hullo Henry," said Edward, "you look splendid; I was pleased to hear your happy whistle yesterday."

"Thank you, Edward," smiled Henry . . . "Sh Sh! Can you hear something?"

Edward listened – far away, but getting louder and louder, was the sound of an engine's whistle.

"It sounds like Gordon," said Edward, "and it ought to be Gordon, but Gordon never whistles like that."

It *was* Gordon.

He came rushing down the hill at a tremendous rate. He didn't look at Henry, and he didn't look at Edward; he was purple in the boiler, and whistling fit to burst.

He screamed through the station and disappeared.

"Well!!!" said Edward, looking at Henry.

"It isn't wrong," chuckled Henry, "but we just don't do it," and he told Edward what Gordon had said.

Meanwhile Gordon screeched along the line. People came out of their houses, air-raid sirens started, five fire brigades got ready to go out, horses upset their carts, and old ladies dropped their parcels.

At a Big Station the noise was awful. Porters and passengers held their ears. The Fat Controller held his ears too; he gave a lot of orders, but no one could hear them, and Gordon went on whistling. At last he clambered into Gordon's cab.

"Take him away," he bellowed, "**AND STOP THAT NOISE!**"

Still whistling, Gordon puffed sadly away.

He whistled as he crossed the points; he whistled on the siding; he was still whistling as the last deafened passenger left the station.

Then two fitters climbed up and knocked his whistle valve into place ——

—— and there was SILENCE.

Gordon slunk into the Shed. He was glad it was empty.

The others came in later. "It isn't wrong," murmured Henry to no one in particular, "but we just don't do it."

No one mentioned whistles!

Percy and the Trousers

ON cold mornings Percy often saw workmen wearing scarves.

"My funnel's cold, my funnel's cold!" he would puff; "I want a scarf, I want a scarf."

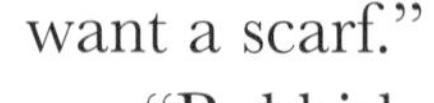

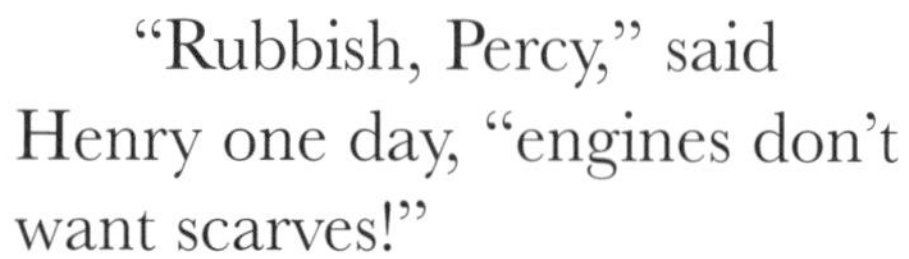

"Rubbish, Percy," said Henry one day, "engines don't want scarves!"

"Engines with proper funnels do," said Percy in his cheeky way. "You've only got a small one!"

Henry snorted; he was proud of his short, neat funnel.

Just then a train came in and Percy, still puffing "I want a scarf, I want a scarf," went to take the coaches to their siding.

His Driver always shut off steam just outside the station, and Percy would try to surprise the coaches by coming in as quietly as he could.

Two porters were taking some luggage across the line. They had a big load and were walking backwards, to see that none fell off the trolley.

Percy arrived so quietly that the porters didn't hear him till the trolley was on the line. The porters jumped clear. The trolley disappeared with a crunch.

Boxes and bags burst in all directions.

"Oo —— ooh e —— r!" groaned Percy and stopped. Sticky streams of red and yellow jam trickled down his face. A top hat hung on his lamp-iron. Clothes, hats, boots, shoes, skirts and blouses stuck to his front. A pair of striped trousers coiled lovingly round his funnel. They were grey no longer!

This story is adapted from one told by Mr. C. Hamilton Ellis in *The Trains We Loved*.
We gratefully acknowledge his permission to use it.

Angry passengers looked at their broken trunks. The Fat Controller seized the top hat.

"Mine!" he said crossly.

"Percy," he shouted, "look at this."

"Yes Sir, I am Sir," a muffled voice replied.

"My best trousers too!"

"Yes Sir, please Sir," said Percy nervously.

"I am very cross," said the Fat Controller. "We must pay the passengers for their spoilt clothes. My hat is dented, and my trousers are ruined, all because you *will* come into the station as if you were playing 'Grandmother's Steps' with the coaches."

The Driver unwound the trousers.

The Fat Controller waved them away.

"Percy wanted a scarf; he shall have my trousers for a scarf; they will keep him warm."

Percy wore them back to the Yard.

He doesn't like scarves now!

Henry's Sneeze

ONE lovely Saturday morning, Henry was puffing along. The sun shone, the fields were green, the birds sang; Henry had plenty of steam in his boiler, and he was feeling happy.

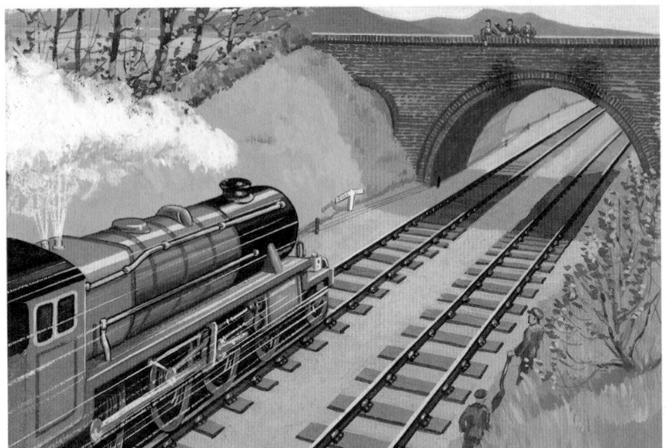

"I feel so well, I feel so well," he sang.

"Trickety trock, Trickety trock," hummed his coaches.

Henry saw some boys on a bridge.

"Peep! Peep! Hullo!" he whistled cheerfully.

"Peep! Peep! Peeeep!" he called the next moment. "Oh! Oh! Oooh!" For the boys didn't wave and take his number; they dropped stones on him instead.

They were silly, stupid boys who thought it would be fun to drop stones down his funnel. Some of the stones hit Henry's boiler and spoilt his paint; one hit the Fireman on the head as he was shovelling coal, and others broke the carriage windows.

"It's a shame, it's a shame," hissed Henry.

"They've broken our glass, they've broken our glass," sobbed the coaches.

The Driver opened the first-aid box, bandaged the Fireman's head, and planned what he was going to do.

They stopped the train and the Guard asked if any passengers were hurt. No one was hurt, but everyone was cross. They saw the Fireman's bumped head, and told him what to do for it, and they looked at Henry's paint.

"Call the Police," they shouted angrily.

"No!" said the Driver, "leave it to Henry and me. We'll teach those lads a lesson."

"What will you do?" they asked.

"Can you keep a secret?"

"Yes, yes," they all said.

"Well then," said the Driver, "Henry is going to sneeze at them."

"What!" cried all the passengers.

The Driver laughed.

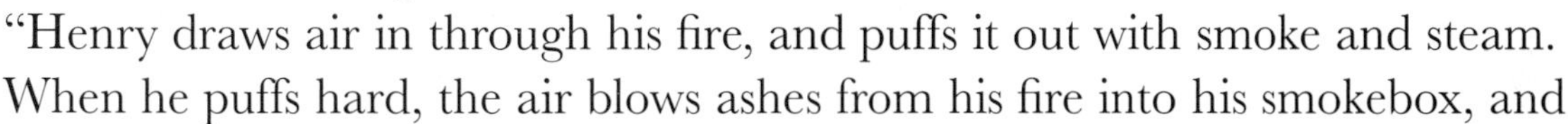

"Henry draws air in through his fire, and puffs it out with smoke and steam. When he puffs hard, the air blows ashes from his fire into his smokebox, and these ashes sometimes prevent him puffing properly.

"When your nose is blocked, you sometimes sneeze. If Henry's smoke box is blocked, I can make air and steam blow the ashes out through his funnel.

"We will do it at the bridge and startle those boys."

Henry puffed on to the terminus, where he had a rest. Then he took the train back. Lots of people were waiting at the station just before the bridge. They wanted to see what would happen.

"Henry has plenty of ashes," said the Driver. "Please keep all windows shut till we have passed the bridge. Henry is as excited as we are, aren't you old fellow?" and he patted Henry's boiler.

Henry didn't answer; he was feeling "stuffed up", but he winked at his Driver, like this.

The Guard's flag waved, his whistle blew, and they were off. Soon in the distance they saw the bridge. There were the boys, and they all had stones.

"Are you ready, Henry?" said his Driver. "Sneeze hard when I tell you."

"NOW!" he said, and turned the handle.

"Atisha Atisha Atishoooooh!"

Smoke and steam and ashes spouted from his funnel. They went all over the bridge, and all over the boys who ran away as black as soot.

"Well done, Henry," laughed his Driver, "they won't drop stones on engines again."

"Your coat is all black, but we'll rub you down and paint your scratches and you'll be as good as new tomorrow."

Henry has never again sneezed under a bridge. The Fat Controller doesn't like it. His smoke box is always cleaned in the Yard while he is resting.

He has now gone under more bridges than he can count; but from that day to this there have been no more boys with stones.

THE RAILWAY SERIES NO. 7

Toby the Tram Engine

THE REV. W. AWDRY

with illustrations by

C. REGINALD DALBY

DEAR FRIENDS,

Poor Thomas has been in trouble. So the Fat Controller asked Toby to come and help run the Branch Line. Thomas and Toby are very good friends.

Toby is a funny little engine with a queer shape. He works very hard and we are fond of him. We hope you will like him too.

THE AUTHOR

Toby and the Stout Gentleman

TOBY is a Tram Engine. He is short and sturdy. He has cow-catchers and side-plates, and doesn't look like a steam engine at all. He takes trucks from farms and factories to the Main Line, and the big engines take them to London and elsewhere. His tramline runs along roads and through fields and villages. Toby rings his bell cheerfully to everyone he meets.

He has a coach called Henrietta, who has seen better days. She complains because she has few passengers. Toby is attached to Henrietta and always takes her with him.

"She might be useful one day," he says.

"It's not fair at all!" grumbles Henrietta as the buses roar past full of passengers. She remembers that she used to be full, and nine trucks would rattle behind her.

Now there are only three or four, for the farms and factories send their goods mostly by lorry.

Toby is always careful on the road. The cars, buses and lorries often have accidents. Toby hasn't had an accident for years, but the buses are crowded, and Henrietta is empty.

"I can't understand it," says Toby the tram engine.

People come to see Toby, but they come by bus. They stare at him. "Isn't he quaint!" they say, and laugh.

They make him so cross.

One day a car stopped close by, and a little boy jumped out. "Come on Bridget," he called to his sister, and together they ran across to Toby. Two ladies and a stout gentleman followed. The gentleman looked important, but nice.

The children ran back. "Come on grandfather, do look at this engine," and seizing his hands they almost dragged him along.

"That's a tram engine, Stephen," said the stout gentleman.

"Is it electric?" asked Bridget.

"Whoosh!" hissed Toby crossly.

"Sh Sh!" said her brother, "you've offended him."

"But trams *are* electric, aren't they?"

"They are mostly," the stout gentleman answered, "but this is a steam tram."

"May we go in it grandfather? Please!"

The Guard had begun to blow his whistle.

"Stop," said the stout gentleman, and raised his hand. The Guard, surprised, opened his mouth, and the whistle fell out.

While he was picking it up, they all scrambled into Henrietta.

"Hip Hip Hurray!" chanted Henrietta, and she rattled happily behind.

Toby did not sing. "Electric indeed! Electric indeed," he snorted. He was very hurt.

The stout gentleman and his family got out at the junction, but waited for Toby to take them back to their car.

"What is your name?" asked the stout gentleman.

"Toby, Sir."

"Thank you, Toby, for a very nice ride."

"Thank *you*, Sir," said Toby politely. He felt better now. "This gentleman," he thought, "is a gentleman who knows how to speak to engines."

The children came every day for a fortnight. Sometimes they rode with the Guard, sometimes in empty trucks, and on the last day of all the Driver invited them into his cab.

All were sorry when they had to go away.

Stephen and Bridget said "Thank you" to Toby, his Driver, his Fireman, and the Guard.

The stout gentleman gave them all a present.

"Peep pip pip peep," whistled Toby. "Come again soon."

"We will, we will," called the children, and they waved till Toby was out of sight.

The months passed. Toby had few trucks, and fewer passengers.

"Our last day, Toby," said his Driver sadly one morning. "The Manager says we must close tomorrow."

That day Henrietta had more passengers than she could manage. They rode in the trucks and crowded in the brake van, and the Guard hadn't enough tickets to go round.

The passengers joked and sang, but Toby and his Driver wished they wouldn't.

"Goodbye, Toby," said the passengers afterwards, "we are sorry your line is closing down."

"So am I," said Toby sadly.

The last passenger left the station, and Toby puffed slowly to his shed.

"Nobody wants me," he thought, and went unhappily to sleep.

Next morning the shed was flung open, and he woke with a start to see his Fireman dancing a jig outside. His Driver, excited, waved a piece of paper.

"Wake up, Toby," they shouted, "and listen to this; it's a letter from the stout gentleman."

Toby listened and . . .

But I mustn't tell you any more, or I should spoil the next story.

Thomas in Trouble

THERE is a line to a quarry at the end of Thomas' Branch; it goes for some distance along the road.

Thomas was always very careful here in case anyone was coming.

"Peep pip peep!" he whistled; then the people got out of the way, and he puffed slowly along with his trucks rumbling behind him.

Early one morning there was no one on the road, but a large policeman was sitting on the grass close to the line. He was shaking a stone from his boot.

Thomas liked policemen. He had been a great friend of the Constable who used to live in the village; but he had just retired.

Thomas expected that the new Constable would be friendly too.

"Peep peep," he whistled, "good morning."

The policeman jumped and dropped his boot. He scrambled up, and hopped round on one leg till he was facing Thomas.

Thomas was sorry to see that he didn't look friendly at all. He was red in the face and very cross.

The policeman wobbled about, trying to keep his balance.

"Disgraceful!" he spluttered. "I didn't sleep a wink last night, it was so quiet, and now engines come whistling suddenly behind me! My first day in the country too!"

He picked up his boot and hopped over to Thomas.

"I'm sorry, Sir," said Thomas, "I only said 'good morning'."

The policeman grunted, and, leaning against Thomas' buffer, he put his boot on.

He drew himself up and pointed to Thomas.

"Where's your cow-catcher?" he asked accusingly.

"But I don't catch cows, Sir!"

"Don't be funny!" snapped the policeman. He looked at Thomas' wheels. "No side plates either," and he wrote in his notebook.

"Engines going on Public Roads must have their wheels covered, and a cow-catcher in front. You haven't, so you are Dangerous to the Public."

"Rubbish!" said his Driver, "we've been along here hundreds of times and never had an accident."

"That makes it worse," the policeman answered. He wrote "regular lawbreaker" in his book.

Thomas puffed sadly away.

The Fat Controller was having breakfast. He was eating

toast and marmalade. He had the newspaper open in front of him, and his wife had just given him some more coffee.

The butler knocked and came in.

"Excuse me, Sir, you are wanted on the telephone."

"Bother that telephone!" said the Fat Controller.

"I'm sorry, my dear," he said a few minutes later, "Thomas is in trouble with the police, and I must go at once."

He gulped down his coffee and hurried from the room.

At the junction, Thomas' Driver told the Fat Controller what had happened.

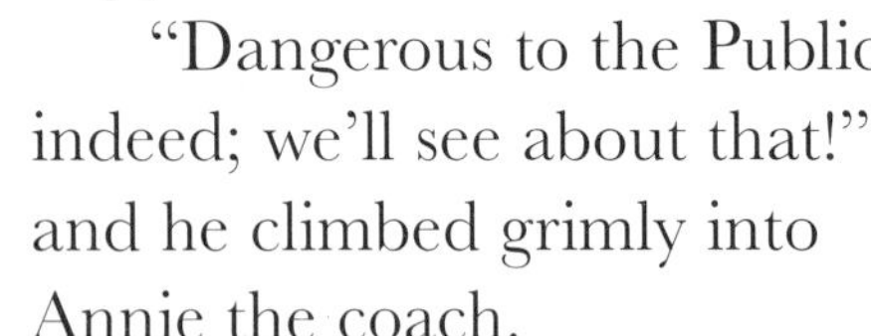

"Dangerous to the Public indeed; we'll see about that!" and he climbed grimly into Annie the coach.

The policeman was on the platform at the other end. The Fat Controller spoke to him at once, and a crowd collected to listen.

Other policemen came to see what was happening and the Fat Controller argued with them too; but it was no good.

"The Law is the Law," they said, "and we can't change it."

The Fat Controller felt exhausted.

He mopped his face.

"I'm sorry Driver," he said, "it's no use arguing with policemen. We will have to make those cow-catcher things for Thomas, I suppose."

"Everyone will laugh, Sir," said Thomas sadly, "they'll say I look like a tram."

The Fat Controller stared, then he laughed.

"Well done, Thomas! Why didn't I think of it before? We want a tram engine! When I was on my holiday, I met a nice little engine called Toby. He hasn't enough work to do, and needs a change. I'll write to his Controller at once."

A few days later Toby arrived.

"That's a good engine," said the Fat Controller, "I see you've brought Henrietta."

"You don't mind, do you, Sir?" asked Toby anxiously. "The Stationmaster wanted to use her as a hen house, and that would never do."

"No, indeed," said the Fat Controller gravely, "we couldn't allow that."

Toby made the trucks behave even better than Thomas did.

At first Thomas was jealous, but he was so pleased when Toby rang his bell and made the policeman jump that they have been firm friends ever since.

Dirty Objects

TOBY and Henrietta take the workmen to the Quarry every morning. At the junction they often meet James.

Toby and Henrietta were shabby when they first came, and needed new paint. James was very rude. "Ugh! What *dirty* objects!" he would say.

At last Toby lost patience.

"James," he asked, "why are you red?"

"I am a splendid engine," answered James loftily, "ready for anything. You never see *my* paint dirty."

"Oh!" said Toby innocently, "that's why you once needed bootlaces; to be ready, I suppose."

James went redder than ever, and snorted off.

At the end of the line James left his coaches and got ready for his next train. It was a "slow goods", stopping at every station to pick up and set down trucks. James hated slow goods trains.

"Dirty trucks from dirty sidings! Ugh!" he grumbled.

Starting with only a few, he picked up more and more trucks at each station, till he had a long train. At first the trucks behaved well, but James bumped them so crossly that they determined to pay him out.

Presently, rumbling over the viaduct, they approached the top of Gordon's Hill. Heavy goods trains halt here to "pin down" their brakes. James

had had an accident with trucks before, and should have remembered this.

"Wait, James, wait," said his Driver, but James wouldn't wait. He was too busy thinking what he would say to Toby when they next met.

Too late he saw where he was, and tried to stop.

"Hurrah! Hurrah!" laughed the trucks, and banging their buffers they pushed him down the hill.

The Guard tightened his brakes until they screamed.

"On! On! On!" yelled the trucks.

"I've *got* to stop, I've *got* to stop," groaned James, and setting his brakes he managed to check the trucks' mad rush, but they were still going much too fast to stop in time.

Through the station they thundered, and lurched into the Yard.

James shut his eyes ——

There was a bursting crash, and something sticky splashed all over him. He had run into two tar wagons, and was black from smokebox to cab.

James was more dirty than hurt, but the tar wagons and some of the trucks were all to pieces. The breakdown train was in the Yard, and they soon tidied up the mess.

Toby and Percy were sent to help, and came as quickly as they could.

"Look here, Percy!" exclaimed Toby, "whatever is that dirty object?"

"That's James; didn't you know?"

"It's James' shape," said Toby thoughtfully, "but James is a splendid red

engine, and you never see *his* paint dirty."

James shut his eyes, and pretended he hadn't heard.

They cleared away the unhurt trucks, and helped James home.

The Fat Controller met them.

"Well done, Percy and Toby," he said.

He turned to James. "Fancy letting your trucks run away. I *am* surprised. You're not fit to be seen; you must be cleaned at once."

"Toby shall have a coat of paint – chocolate and blue I think."

"Please, Sir, can Henrietta have one too?"

"Certainly Toby," he smiled, "she shall have brown like Annie and Clarabel."

"Oh thank you, Sir! She will be pleased."

Toby ran home happily to tell her the news.

Mrs Kyndley's Christmas

IT was nearly Christmas. Annie and Clarabel were packed full of people and parcels.

Thomas was having very hard work.

"Come on! Come on!" he puffed.

"We're feeling *so* full!" grumbled the coaches.

Thomas looked at the hill ahead. "Can I do it? Can I do it?" he puffed anxiously.

Suddenly he saw a handkerchief waving from a cottage window. He felt better at once.

"Yes I can, yes I can," he puffed bravely. He pulled his hardest, and was soon through the tunnel and resting in the station.

"That was Mrs Kyndley who waved to you, Thomas," his Driver told him. "She has to stay in bed all day."

"Poor lady," said Thomas, "I am sorry for her."

Engines have heavy loads at Christmas time, but Thomas and Toby didn't mind the hard work when they saw Mrs Kyndley waving.

But then it began to rain. It rained for days and days.

Thomas didn't like it, nor did his Driver.

"Off we go Thomas!" he would say. "Pull hard and get home quickly; Mrs Kyndley won't wave today."

But whether she waved or not, they always whistled when they passed the little lonely cottage. Its white walls stood out against the dark background of the hills.

"Hello!" exclaimed Thomas' Fireman one day. "Look at that!"

The Driver came across the cab. "Something's wrong there," he said.

Hanging flapping and bedraggled from a window of the cottage was something that looked like a large red flag.

"Mrs Kyndley needs help I expect," said the Driver, and put on the brakes. Thomas gently stopped.

The Guard came squelching through the rain up to Thomas's cab, and the Driver pointed to the flag.

"See if a Doctor's on the train and ask him to go to the cottage; then walk back to the station and tell them we've stopped."

The Fireman went to see if the line was clear in front.

Two passengers left the train and climbed to the cottage. Then the Fireman returned.

"We'll back down to the station," said the Driver, "so that Thomas can get a good start."

"We shan't get up the hill," the Fireman answered. "Come and see what's happened!"

They walked along the line round the bend.

"Jiminy Christmas!" exclaimed the Driver, "go back to the train; I'm going to the cottage."

He found the Doctor with Mrs Kyndley.

"Silly of me to faint," she said.

"You saw the red dressing-gown? You're all safe?" asked Mrs Kyndley.

"Yes," smiled the Driver, "I've come to thank you. There was a landslide in the cutting, Doctor, and Mrs Kyndley saw it from her window and stopped us. She's saved our lives!"

"God bless you, ma'am," said the Driver, and tiptoed from the room.

They cleared the line by Christmas Day, and the sun shone as a special train puffed up from the junction.

First came Toby, then Thomas with Annie and Clarabel, and last of all, but very pleased at being allowed to come, was Henrietta.

The Fat Controller was there, and lots of other people who wanted to say "Thank you" to Mrs Kyndley.

"Peepeep, Peepeep! Happy Christmas!" whistled the engines as they reached the place.

The people got out and climbed to the cottage. Thomas and Toby wished they could go too.

Mrs Kyndley's husband met them at the door.

The Fat Controller, Thomas' Driver, Fireman, and Guard went upstairs, while the others stood in the sunshine below the window.

The Driver gave her a new dressing-gown to replace the one spoilt by the rain. The Guard brought her some grapes, and the Fireman gave her some woolly slippers, and promised to bring some coal as a present from Thomas,

next time they passed.

Mrs Kyndley was very pleased with her presents.

"You are very good to me," she said.

"The passengers and I," said the Fat Controller, "hope you will accept these tickets for the South Coast, Mrs Kyndley, and get really well in the sunshine. We cannot thank you enough for preventing that accident. I hope we have not tired you. Goodbye and a happy Christmas."

Then going quietly downstairs, they joined the group outside the window, and sang some carols before returning to the train.

Mrs Kyndley is now at Bournemouth, getting better every day, and Thomas and Toby are looking forward to the time when they can welcome her home.

THE RAILWAY SERIES NO. 8

Gordon the Big Engine

THE REV. W. AWDRY

with illustrations by

C. REGINALD DALBY

DEAR IAN,

You asked for a book about Gordon. Here it is. Gordon has been naughty, and the Fat Controller was stern with him.

Gordon has now learnt his lesson and is a Really Useful Engine again.

THE AUTHOR

Off the Rails

GORDON was resting in a siding.

"Peep peep! Peep peep! Hullo, Fatface!" whistled Henry.

"What cheek!" spluttered Gordon. "That Henry is too big for his wheels; fancy speaking to me like that! Me e e e e!" he went on, letting off steam, "Me e e e who has never had an accident!"

"Aren't jammed whistles and burst safety valves accidents?" asked Percy innocently.

"No indeed!" said Gordon huffily, "high spirits – might happen to any engine; but to come off the rails, well I ask you! Is it right? Is it decent?"

A few days later it was Henry's turn to take the Express. Gordon watched him getting ready.

"Be careful, Henry," he said, "You're not pulling the 'Flying Kipper' now; mind you keep on the rails today."

Henry snorted away, Gordon yawned and went to sleep.

But he didn't sleep long. "Wake up, Gordon," said his Driver, "a Special train's coming and we're to pull it."

Gordon opened his eyes. "Is it Coaches or Trucks?"

"Trucks," said his Driver.

"Trucks!" said Gordon crossly. "Pah!"

They lit Gordon's fire and oiled him ready for the run. The fire was sulky and wouldn't burn; but they couldn't wait, so Edward pushed him to the turntable to get him facing the right way.

"I *won't* go, I *won't* go," grumbled Gordon.

"Don't be silly, don't be silly," puffed Edward.

Gordon tried hard, but he couldn't stop himself being moved.

At last he was on the turntable, Edward was uncoupled and backed away, and Gordon's Driver and Fireman jumped down to turn him round.

The movement had shaken Gordon's fire; it was now burning nicely and making steam.

Gordon was cross, and didn't care what he did.

He waited till the table was half-way round. "I'll show them! I'll show them!" he hissed, and moved slowly forward.

He only meant to go a little way, just far enough to "jam" the table, and stop it turning, as he had done once before. But he couldn't stop himself, and, slithering down the embankment, he settled in a ditch.

"Oooosh!" he hissed as his wheels churned the mud. "Get me out! Get me out!"

"Not a hope," said his Driver and Fireman, "you're stuck, you silly great engine, don't you understand that?"

They telephoned the Fat Controller.

"So Gordon didn't want to take the Special and ran into a ditch," he answered from his office. "What's that you say? The Special's waiting – tell Edward to take it please – and Gordon? Oh leave him where he is; we haven't time to bother with him now."

A family of toads croaked crossly at Gordon as he lay in the mud. On the other side of the ditch some little boys were chattering.

"Coo! Doesn't he look silly!"

"They'll never get him out."

They began to sing:

Silly old Gordon fell in a ditch,
fell in a ditch,
fell in a ditch,
Silly old Gordon fell in a ditch,
All on a Monday morning.

The School bell rang and, still singing, they chased down the road.

"Pshaw!" said Gordon, and blew away three tadpoles and an inquisitive newt.

Gordon lay in the ditch all day.

"Oh dear!" he thought, "I shall never get out."

But that evening they brought floodlights; then with powerful jacks they lifted Gordon and made a road of sleepers under his wheels to keep him from the mud.

Strong wire ropes were fastened to his back end, and James and Henry, pulling hard, at last managed to bring him to the rails.

Late that night Gordon crawled home a sadder and a wiser engine!

Leaves

TWO men were cleaning Gordon.

"Mind my eye," Gordon grumbled.

"Shut it, silly! Did ever you see such mud, Bert?"

"No I never, Alf! You ought to be ashamed, Gordon, giving us extra work."

The hosing and scrubbing stopped. Gordon opened one eye, but shut it quickly.

"Wake up, Gordon," said the Fat Controller sternly, "and listen to me. You will pull no more coaches till you are a Really Useful Engine."

So Gordon had to spend his time pulling trucks.

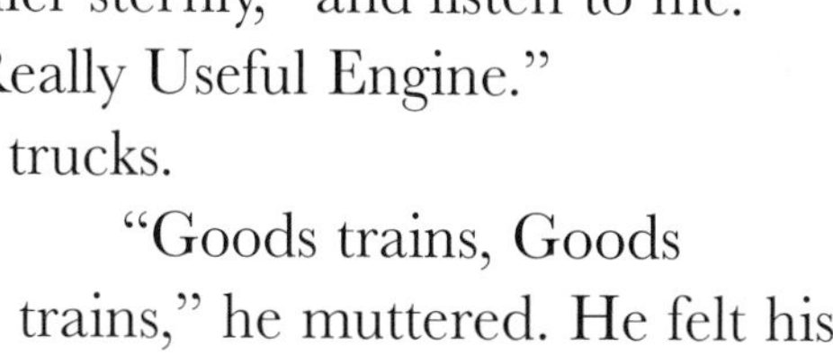

"Goods trains, Goods trains," he muttered. He felt his position deeply.

"That's for you! – and *you*! – *and* you!" Gordon said crossly.

"Oh! Oh! Oh! Oh!" screamed the trucks as he shunted them about the Yard.

"Trucks will be trucks," said James, watching him.

"They won't with *me*!" snorted Gordon. "I'll teach them. Go on!" and another truck scurried away.

"They tried to push me down the hill this morning," Gordon explained. "It's slippery there. You'll probably need some help."

"*I* don't need help on hills," said James huffily.

Gordon laughed, and got ready for his next train.

James went away to take the Express.

"Slippery hills indeed," he snorted. "*I* don't need help."

"Come on! Come on!" he puffed.

"All in good time, all in good time," grumbled the coaches.

The train was soon running nicely, but a "Distant" signal checked them close to Gordon's Hill.

Gordon's Hill used to be bleak and bare. Strong winds from the sea made it hard to climb. Trees were planted to give shelter, and in summer the trains run through a leafy avenue.

Now autumn had come, and dead leaves fell. The wind usually puffed them away, but today rain made them heavy, and they did not move.

The "Home" signal showed "clear", and James began to go faster.

He started to climb the hill.

"I'll do it! I'll do it!" he puffed confidently.

Half-way up he was not so sure! "I *must* do it, I *must* do it," he panted desperately, but try as he would, his wheels slipped on the leaves, and he couldn't pull the train at all.

"Whatsthematter? Whatsthematter?" he gasped.

"Steady old boy, steady," soothed his Driver.

His Fireman put sand on the rails to help him grip; but James' wheels spun so fast that they only ground the sand and leaves to slippery mud, making things worse than before.

The train slowly stopped. Then –

"Help! Help! Help!" whistled James; for though his wheels were turning

forwards, the heavy coaches pulled him backwards, and the whole train started slipping down the hill.

His Driver shut off steam, carefully put on the brakes, and skillfully stopped the train.

"Whew!" he sat down and mopped his face. "I've never known *that* happen before."

"I have," said the Fireman, "in Bincombe tunnel – Southern Region."

The Guard poked his head in the cab. "Now what?" he asked.

"Back to the station," said the Fireman, taking charge, "and send for a 'Banker'."

So the Guard warned the Signalman, and they brought the train safely down.

But Gordon, who had followed with a goods train, saw what had happened.

Gordon left his trucks, and crossed over to James.

"I thought you could climb hills," he chuckled.

James didn't answer; he had no steam!

"Ah well! We live and learn," said Gordon, "we live and learn. Never mind, little James," he went on kindly, "I'm going to push behind. Whistle when you're ready."

James waited till he had plenty of steam, then "Peep! Peep!" he called.

"Poop! Poop! Poop!"

"Pull hard," puffed Gordon.

"We'll do it!" puffed James.

"Pull hard! We'll do it," the engines puffed together.

Clouds of smoke and steam towered from the snorting engines as they struggled up the hill.

"We *can* do it!" puffed James.

"We *will* do it!" puffed Gordon.

The greasy rails sometimes made Gordon's wheels slip, but he never gave up, and presently they reached the top.

"We've done it! We've done it!" they puffed.

Gordon stopped. "Poop! Poop! He whistled. "Goodbye."

"Peep! Peep! Peep! Peep! Thank you! Goodbye," answered James. Gordon watched the coaches wistfully till they were out of sight; then slowly he trundled back to his waiting trucks.

Down the Mine

ONE day Thomas was at the junction, when Gordon shuffled in with some trucks.

"Poof!" remarked Thomas, "what a funny smell!"

"Can you smell a smell?"

"I can't smell a smell," said Annie and Clarabel.

"A funny, musty sort of smell," said Thomas.

"No one noticed it till you did," grunted Gordon. "It must be yours."

"Annie! Clarabel! Do you know what I think it is?" whispered Thomas loudly. "It's ditchwater!"

Gordon snorted, but before he could answer, Thomas puffed quickly away.

Annie and Clarabel could hardly believe their ears!

"He's *dreadfully* rude; I feel quite ashamed." "I feel *quite* ashamed, he's dreadfully rude," they twittered to each other.

"You mustn't be rude, you make us ashamed," they kept telling Thomas.

But Thomas didn't care a bit.

"That was funny, that was funny," he chuckled. He felt very pleased with himself.

Annie and Clarabel were deeply shocked. They had a great respect for Gordon the Big Engine.

Thomas left the coaches at a station and went to a mine for some trucks.

Long ago, miners, digging for lead, had made tunnels under the ground.

Though strong enough to hold up trucks, their roofs could not bear the weight of engines.

A large notice said: "DANGER, ENGINES MUST NOT PASS THIS BOARD."

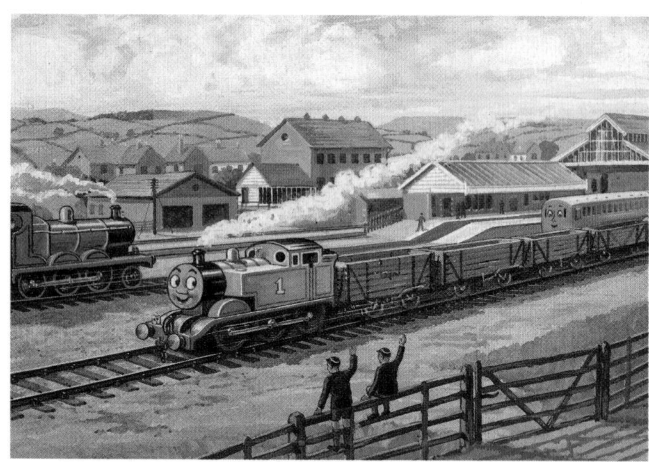

Thomas had often been warned, but he didn't care.

"Silly old board," he thought. He had often tried to pass it, but had never succeeded.

This morning he laughed as he puffed along. He had made a plan.

He had to push empty trucks into one siding, and pull out full ones from another.

His Driver stopped him, and the Fireman went to turn the points.

"Come on," waved the Fireman, and they started.

The Driver leaned out of the cab to see where they were going.

"Now!" said Thomas to himself, and, bumping the trucks fiercely, he jerked his Driver off the footplate.

"Hurrah!" laughed Thomas, and he followed the trucks into the siding.

"Stupid old board!" said Thomas as he passed it. "There's no danger; there's no danger."

His Driver, unhurt, jumped up. "Look out!" he shouted.

The Fireman clambered into the cab. Thomas squealed crossly as his brakes were applied.

"It's quite safe," he hissed.

"Come back," yelled the Driver, but before they could move, there was rumbling and the rails quivered.

The Fireman jumped clear. As he did so the ballast slipped away and the rails sagged and broke.

"Fire and Smoke!" said Thomas, "I'm sunk!" – and he was!

Thomas could just see out of the hole, but he couldn't move.

"Oh dear!" he said, "I am a silly engine."

"And a very naughty one too," said a voice behind him, "I saw you."

"Please get me out; I won't be naughty again."

"I'm not so sure," replied the Fat Controller. "We can't lift you out with a crane, the ground's not firm enough. Hm . . . Let me see . . . I wonder if Gordon could pull you out."

"Yes Sir," said Thomas nervously. He didn't want to meet Gordon just yet!

"Down a mine is he? Ho! Ho! Ho!" laughed Gordon.

"What a joke! What a joke!" he chortled, puffing to the rescue.

"Poop! Poop! Little Thomas," he whistled, "we'll have you out in a couple of puffs."

Strong cables were fastened between the two engines.

"Poop! Poop! Poop!"

"Are you ready? HEAVE," called the Fat Controller.

But they didn't pull Thomas out in two puffs; Gordon was panting hard and nearly purple before he had dragged Thomas out of the hold, and safely past the board.

"I'm sorry I was cheeky," said Thomas.

"That's all right, Thomas. You made me laugh. I like that. I'm in disgrace," Gordon went on pathetically, "I feel very low."

"I'm in disgrace too," said Thomas.

"Why! so you are Thomas; we're both in disgrace. Shall we form an Alliance?"

"An Ally – what – was – it?"

"An Alliance, Thomas, 'United we stand, together we fall'," said Gordon grandly.

"You help me, and I help you. How about it?"

"Right you are," said Thomas.

"Good! That's settled," rumbled Gordon.

And buffer to buffer the Allies puffed home.

Paint Pots and Queens

THE stations on the line were being painted.

The engines were surprised.

"The Queen is coming," said the painters. The engines in their Shed were excited and wondered who would pull the Royal Train.

"I'm too old to pull important trains," said Edward sadly.

"I'm in disgrace," Gordon said gloomily. "The Fat Controller would never choose me."

"He'll choose me, of course," boasted James the Red Engine.

"You!" Henry snorted, "*You* can't climb hills. He will ask *me* to pull it, *and* I'll have a new coat of paint. You wait and see."

The days passed. Henry puffed about proudly, quite sure that he would be the Royal Engine.

One day when it rained, his Driver and Fireman stretched a tarpaulin from the cab to the tender, to keep themselves dry.

Henry puffed into the Big Station. A painter was climbing a ladder above the line. Henry's smoke puffed upwards; it was thick and black. The painter choked and couldn't see. He missed his footing on the ladder, dropped his paint pot, and fell plop on to Henry's tarpaulin.

The paint poured over Henry's boiler, and trickled down each side. The paint pot perched on his dome.

The painter clambered down and shook his brush at Henry.

"You spoil my clean paint with your dirty smoke," he said, "and then you take the whole lot, and make me go and fetch some more." He stumped crossly away.

The Fat Controller pushed through the crowd.

"You look like an iced cake, Henry," he said. "*That* won't do for the Royal Train. I must make other arrangements."

He walked over to the Yard.

Gordon and Thomas saw him coming, and both began to speak.

"Please Sir ——"

"One at a time," smiled the Fat Controller. "Yes Gordon?"

"May Thomas have his Branch Line again?"

"Hm," said the Fat Controller, "well Thomas?"

"Please, Sir, can Gordon pull coaches now?"

The Fat Controller pondered.

"Hm —— you've both been quite good lately, and you deserve a treat —— When the Queen comes, Edward will go in front and clear the line, Thomas will look after the coaches, and Gordon —— will pull the train."

"Ooooh Sir!" said the engines happily.

The great day came. Percy, Toby, Henry and James worked hard bringing people to the town.

Thomas sorted all their coaches in the Yard.

"Peep! Peep! Peep! They're coming!" Edward steamed in, looking smart

with flags and bright paint.

Two minutes passed – five – seven – ten. "Poop! Poop!" Everyone knew that whistle, and a mighty cheer went up as the Queen's train glided into the station.

Gordon was spotless, and his brass shone. Like Edward, he was decorated with flags, but on his buffer beam he proudly carried the Royal Arms.

The Queen was met by the Fat Controller, and before doing anything else, she thanked him for their splendid run.

"Not at all, Your Majesty," he said, "thank *you*."

"We have read," said the Queen to the Fat Controller, "a great deal about your engines. May we see them please?"

So he led the way to where all the engines were waiting.

"Peep! Peep!" whistled Toby and Percy, "they're coming!"

"Sh Sh! Sh Sh!" hissed Henry and James.

But Toby and Percy were too excited to care.

The Fat Controller told the Queen their names, and she talked to each engine. Then she turned to go.

Percy bubbled over, "Three cheers for the Queen!" he called.

"Peeeep! Peeeep! Peeeep!" whistled all the engines.

The Fat Controller held his ears, but the Queen, smiling, waved to the engines till she passed the gate.

Next day the Queen spoke specially to Thomas, who fetched her coaches,

and to Edward and Gordon who took her away; and no engines ever felt prouder than Thomas, and Edward, and Gordon the Big Engine.

THE RAILWAY SERIES NO. 9

Edward the Blue Engine

THE REV. W. AWDRY

with illustrations by

C. REGINALD DALBY

DEAR FRIENDS,

I think most of you are fond of Edward. His Driver and Fireman, Charlie Sand and Sidney Hever, are fond of him too. They were very pleased when they knew I was giving Edward a book all to himself.

Edward is old, and some of the other engines were rude about the clanking noise he made as he did his work.

They aren't rude now! These stories tell you why.

THE AUTHOR

Cows!

EDWARD the Blue Engine was getting old. His bearings were worn, and he clanked as he puffed along. He was taking twenty empty cattle trucks to a market-town.

The sun shone, the birds sang, and some cows grazed in a field by the line.

"Come on! Come on! Come on!" puffed Edward.

"Oh! Oh! Oh! Oh!" screamed the trucks.

Edward puffed and clanked; the trucks rattled and screamed. The cows were not used to trains; the noise and smoke disturbed them.

They twitched up their tails and ran.

They galloped across the field, broke through the fence, and charged the train between the thirteenth and fourteenth trucks. The coupling broke, and the last seven trucks left the rails. They were not damaged, and stayed upright. They ran for a short way along the sleepers before stopping.

Edward felt a jerk but didn't take much notice.

He was used to trucks.

"Bother those trucks!" he thought. "Why can't they come quietly?" He ran on to the next station before either he or his Driver realised what had happened.

When Gordon and Henry heard about the accident, they laughed and laughed. "Fancy allowing cows to break his train! They wouldn't dare do that to US. WE'd show them!" they boasted.

Edward pretended not to mind, but Toby was cross.

"You couldn't help it, Edward," he said. "They've never met cows. I have, and I know the trouble they are."

Some days later Gordon rushed through Edward's station.

"Poop poop!" he whistled, "mind the cows!"

"Haha, haha, haha!" he chortled, panting up the hill.

"Hurry, hurry, hurry!" puffed Gordon.

"Don't make such a fuss! Don't make such a fuss!" grumbled his coaches. They rumbled over the viaduct and roared through the next station.

A long straight stretch of line lay ahead. In the distance was a bridge. It had high parapets each side.

It seemed to Gordon that there was something on the bridge. His Driver thought so too. "Whoa, Gordon!" he said, and shut off steam.

"Pooh!" said Gordon, "it's only a cow!

"SHOOH! SHOOH!" he hissed, moving slowly on to the bridge.

But the cow wouldn't "Shooh"! She had lost her calf, and felt lonely. "Mooooh!" she said sadly, walking towards him.

Gordon stopped!

His Driver, Fireman and

some passengers tried to send her away, but she wouldn't go, so they gave it up.

Presently Henry arrived with a train from the other direction.

"What's this?" he said grandly. "A cow? I'll soon settle *her*. Be off! Be off!" he hissed; but the cow turned and "moohed" at him. Henry backed away. "I don't want to hurt her," he said.

Drivers, Firemen and passengers again tried to move the cow, but failed. Henry's Guard went back and put detonators on the line to protect his train. At the nearest station he told them about the cow.

"That must be Bluebell," said a porter thoughtfully, "her calf is here, ready to go to market. We'll take it along."

So they unloaded the calf and took it to the bridge.

"Mooh! Mooh!" wailed the calf. "MOOH MOOH!" bellowed Bluebell.

She nuzzled her calf happily, and the porter led them away.

The two trains started.

"Not a word."

"Keep it dark," whispered Gordon and Henry as they passed; but the story soon spread.

"Well, well, well!" chuckled Edward, "two big engines afraid of one cow!"

"Afraid —— Rubbish," said Gordon huffily. "We didn't want the poor thing to hurt herself by running against us. We stopped so as not to excite her. You see what I mean, my dear Edward."

"Yes, Gordon," said Edward gravely.

Gordon felt somehow that Edward "saw" only too well.

Bertie's Chase

"PEEP! Peep! We're late," fussed Edward. "Peep! Peeppipeep! Where is Thomas? He doesn't usually make us wait."

"Oh dear, what can the matter be? . . ." sang the Fireman, "Johnnie's so long at . . ."

"Never you mind about Johnnie," laughed the Driver, "just you climb on the cab, and look for Thomas."

"Can you see him?"

"No."

The Guard looked at his watch. "Ten minutes late!" he said to the Driver, "we can't wait here all day."

"Look again, Sid," said the Driver, "just in case."

The Fireman got to his feet.

"Can you see him?"

"No," he answered, "there's Bertie bus in a tearing hurry. No need to bother with him though; likely he's on a Coach Tour or something." He clambered down.

"Right away, Charlie," said the Guard, and Edward puffed off.

"Tooooot! TOOOOT! Stop! STOP!" wailed Bertie roaring into the Yard, but it was no good. Edward's last coach had disappeared into the tunnel.

"Bother!" said Bertie. "Bother Thomas' Fireman not coming to work today. Oh why did I promise to help the Passengers catch the train?"

"That will do, Bertie," said his Driver, "a promise is a promise and we must keep it."

"I'll catch Edward or bust," said Bertie grimly, as he raced along the road.

"Oh my gears and axles!" he groaned, toiling up the hill. "I'll never be the same bus again!"

"Tootootoo Tootoot! I see him. Hurray! Hurray!" he cheered as he reached the top of the hill.

"He's reached the station," Bertie groaned the next minute.

"No . . . he's stopped by a signal. Hurray! Hurray!" and he tore down the hill, his brakes squealing at the corners.

His passengers bounced like balls in a bucket. "Well done, Bertie," they shouted. "Go it! Go it!"

Hens and dogs scattered in all directions as he raced through the village.

"Wait! Wait!" he tooted, skidding into the Yard.

He was just in time to see the signal drop, the Guard wave his flag, and Edward puff out of the station.

His passengers rushed to the platform, but it was no good, and they came bustling back.

"I'm sorry," said Bertie unhappily.

"Never mind, Bertie," they said. "After him quickly. Third time lucky you know!"

"Do you think we'll catch him at the next station, Driver?"

"There's a good chance," he answered. "Our road keeps close to the line, and we can climb hills better than Edward."

He thought for a minute. "I'll just make sure." He then spoke to the Stationmaster, while the passengers waited impatiently in the bus.

"This hill is too steep! This hill is too steep!" grumbled the coaches as Edward snorted in front.

They reached the top at last and ran smoothly into the station.

"Peepeep!" whistled Edward, "get in quickly please."

The porters and people hurried and Edward impatiently waited to start.

"Peeeep!" whistled the Guard, and Edward's Driver looked back; but the flag didn't wave. There was a distant "Tooootoooot!" and the Stationmaster, running across, snatched the green flag out of the Guard's hand.

Then everything seemed to happen at once.

"Too too TOOOOOOT!" bellowed Bertie; his passengers poured on to the platform and scrambled into the train. The Stationmaster told the Guard and Driver what had happened, and Edward listened.

"I'm sorry about the chase, Bertie," he said.

"My fault," panted Bertie, "late at junction. . . . You didn't know . . . about Thomas' passengers."

"Peepeep! Goodbye, Bertie, we're off!" whistled Edward.

"Three cheers for Bertie!" called the passengers. They cheered and waved till they were out of sight.

Saved from Scrap

THERE is a scrap yard near Edward's station. It is full of rusty old cars and machinery. They are brought there to be broken up. The pieces are loaded into trucks, and Edward pulls them to the Steelworks, where they are melted down and used again.

One day Edward saw a Traction-engine in the Yard.

"Hullo!" he said, "you're not broken and rusty. What are you doing there?"

"I'm Trevor," said the Traction-engine sadly, "they are going to break me up next week."

"What a shame!" said Edward.

"My Driver says I only need some paint, Brasso, and oil, to be as good as new," Trevor went on sadly, "but it's no good, my Master doesn't want me. I suppose it's because I'm old-fashioned."

Edward snorted indignantly, "People say *I'm* old-fashioned, but I don't care. The Fat Controller says I'm a Useful Engine."

"My Driver says I'm useful too," replied Trevor. "I sometimes feel ill, but I don't give up like these tractors; I struggle on and finish the job. I've never broken down in my life," he ended proudly.

"What work did you do?" asked Edward kindly.

"My Master would send us from farm to farm. We threshed the corn,

hauled logs, sawed timber, and did lots of other work. We made friends at all the farms, and saw them every year. The children loved to see us come. They followed us in crowds, and watched us all day long. My Driver would sometimes give them rides."

Trevor shut his eyes —— remembering ——

"I like children," he said simply. "Oh yes, I like children."

"Broken up, what a shame! Broken up, what a shame!" clanked Edward as he went back to work. "I *must* help Trevor, I *must*!"

He thought of the people he knew, who liked engines. Edward had lots of friends, but strangely none of them had room for a Traction-engine at home!

"It's a shame! It's a shame!" he hissed as he brought his coaches to the station.

Then ——

"Peep! Peep!" he whistled, "why didn't I think of him before?"

Waiting there on the platform was the very person.

"'Morning Charlie, 'Morning Sid. Hullo Edward,

you look upset!"

"What's the matter, Charlie?" he asked the Driver.

"There's a Traction-engine in the scrap yard, Vicar; he'll be broken up next week, and it's a shame. Jem Cole says he never drove a better engine."

"Do save him, Sir! You've got room, Sir!"

"Yes, Edward, I've got room," laughed the Vicar, "but I don't need a Traction-engine!"

"He'll saw wood, and give children rides. Do buy him, Sir, please!"

"We'll see," said the Vicar, and climbed into the train.

Jem Cole came on Saturday afternoon. "The Reverend's coming to see you, Trevor; maybe he'll buy you."

"Do you think he will?" asked Trevor hopefully.

"He will when I've lit your fire, and cleaned you up," said Jem.

When the Vicar and his two boys arrived in the evening, Trevor was blowing off steam. He hadn't felt so happy for months.

"Watch this, Reverence," called Jem, and Trevor chuffered happily about the Yard.

"Oh Daddy, DO buy him," pleaded the boys, jumping up and down in their excitement.

"Now *I'll* try," and the Vicar climbed up beside Jem.

"Show your paces, Trevor," he said, and drove him about the Yard.

Then he went into the office, and came out smiling. "I've got him cheap, Jem, cheap."

"D'ye hear that, Trevor?" cried Jem. "The Reverend's saved you, and you'll live at the Vicarage now."

"Peep! Peep!" whistled Trevor happily.

"Will you drive him home for me, Jem, and take these scallywags with you? They won't want to come in the car when there's a Traction-engine to ride on!"

Trevor's home in the Vicarage Orchard is close to the railway, and he sees Edward every day. His paint is spotless and his brass shines like gold.

He saws firewood in winter, and Jem sometimes borrows him when a tractor fails. Trevor likes doing his old jobs, but his happiest day is the Church Fête. Then, with a long wooden seat bolted to his bunker, he chuffers round the Orchard giving rides to children.

Long afterwards you will see him shut his eyes —— remembering ——

"I like children," he whispers happily.

Old Iron

ONE day James had to wait at Edward's station till Edward and his train came in. This made him cross. "Late again!" he shouted.

Edward only laughed, and James fumed away.

"Edward is impossible," he grumbled to the others, "he clanks about like a lot of old iron, and he is so slow he makes us wait."

Thomas and Percy were indignant. "Old iron!" they snorted. "SLOW! Why! Edward could beat you in a race any day!"

"Really!" said James huffily, "I should like to see him do it."

One day James' Driver did not feel well when he came to work. "I'll manage," he said, but when they reached the top of Gordon's Hill, he could hardly stand.

The Fireman drove the train to the next station. He spoke to the Signalman, put the trucks in a siding, and uncoupled James ready for shunting.

Then he helped the Driver over to the station, and asked them to look after him, and find a "Relief".

Suddenly the Signalman shouted, and the Fireman turned round and saw James puffing away.

He ran hard but he couldn't catch James, and soon came back to the signal box. The Signalman was busy. "All traffic halted," he announced at last. "Up and down main lines are clear for thirty miles, and the Inspector's coming."

The Fireman mopped his face. "What happened?" he asked.

"Two boys were on the footplate; they tumbled off when James started. I shouted at them and they ran like rabbits."

"Just let me catch them," said the Fireman grimly, "I'll teach them to meddle with my engine."

Both men jumped as the telephone rang; "Yes," answered the Signalman, "he's here . . . Right, I'll tell him.

"The Inspector's coming at once in Edward. He wants a shunter's pole, and a coil of wire rope."

"What for?" wondered the Fireman.

"Search me! But you'd better get them quickly."

The Fireman was ready and waiting when Edward arrived. The Inspector saw the pole and rope. "Good man," he said, "jump in."

"We'll catch him, we'll catch him," puffed Edward, crossing to the up line in pursuit.

James was laughing as he left the Yard. "What a lark! What a lark!" he chuckled to himself.

Presently he missed his Driver's hand on the regulator . . . and then he realised there was no one in his cab . . .

"What shall I do?" he wailed, "I can't stop. Help! Help!"

"We're coming, we're coming."

Edward was panting up behind with every ounce of steam he had. With a

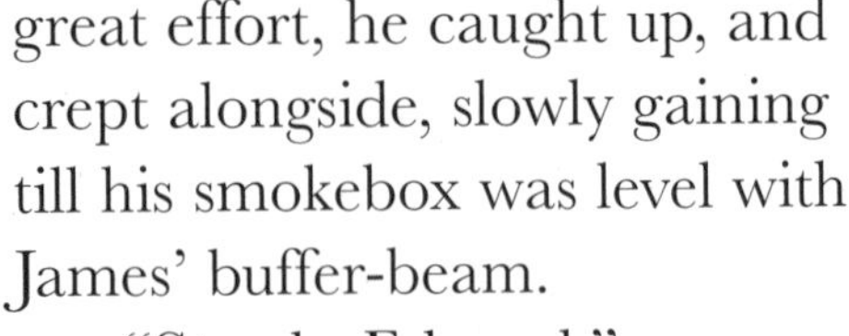

great effort, he caught up, and crept alongside, slowly gaining till his smokebox was level with James' buffer-beam.

"Steady, Edward."

The Inspector stood on Edward's front, holding a noose of rope in the crook of the shunter's pole. He was trying to slip it over James' buffer. The engines swayed and lurched.

He tried again and again; more than once he nearly fell, but just saved himself.

At last – "Got him!" he shouted. He pulled the noose tight and came back to the cab safely.

Gently braking, so as not to snap the rope, Edward's Driver checked the engines' speed, and James' Fireman scrambled across and took control.

The engines puffed back side by side. "So the 'old iron' caught you after all!" chuckled Edward.

"I'm sorry," whispered James, "thank you for saving me."

"That's all right."

"You were splendid, Edward."

The Fat Controller was

waiting, and thanking the men warmly. "A fine piece of work," he said. "James, you can rest, and then take your train. I'm proud of you, Edward; you shall go to the Works, and have your worn parts mended."

"Oh! Thank you, Sir!" said Edward happily. "It'll be *lovely* not to clank."

The two naughty boys were soon caught by the police, and their fathers walloped them soundly.

They were also forbidden to watch trains till they could be trusted.

James' Driver soon got well in hospital, and is now back at work. James missed him very much, but he missed Edward more, and you will be glad to know that, when Edward came home the other day, James and all the other engines gave him a tremendous welcome.

The Fat Controller thinks he will be deaf for weeks!

THE RAILWAY SERIES NO. 10

Four Little Engines

THE REV. W. AWDRY

with illustrations by

C. REGINALD DALBY

DEAR FRIENDS,

Sir Handel Brown is the owner of a little Railway which goes to Skarloey and Rheneas. Skarloey means "Lake in the Woods", and Rheneas means "Divided Waterfall". They are beautiful places, and lots of people visit them.

The Owner is very busy, so Mr Peter Sam, the Thin Controller, manages the railway.

The two Engines, who are called Skarloey and Rheneas, grew old and tired; so the Owner bought two others.

The stories tell you what happened.

THE AUTHOR

Skarloey Remembers

THE Fat Controller had sent Edward to the Works to be mended. Near the Works Station, Edward noticed a narrow-gauge engine standing in an open-sided shed.

"That's Skarloey," he thought, "what's he doing there?" He remembered Skarloey and his brother Rheneas, because in the old days he had often brought passengers who wanted to travel up to the Lake in their little train.

As the men at the Works could not mend him at once, Edward asked them to put him on a siding close to Skarloey.

Skarloey was pleased to see Edward.

"The Owner has just bought two more engines," he said.

"He told me I was a Very Old Engine, and deserved a good rest. He gave me this shed so that I could see everything and not be lonely. But I am lonely all the same," he continued sadly, "I miss Rheneas very much. Yesterday one of the new engines pushed him on a truck, and now he's gone to be mended.

"I wish I could be mended too, and pull coaches again."

"Have your coaches got names?" asked Edward.

"Oh, yes, there's Agnes, Ruth, Jemima, Lucy and Beatrice. Agnes is proud.

She has cushions for first-class passengers. She pities Ruth, Jemima and Lucy, who are third-class with bare boards; but they all four sniff at Beatrice. Beatrice often smells of fish and cheese, but she is *most* important," said Skarloey earnestly, "she has a little window through which the Guard sells tickets. I sometimes leave the others behind, but I always take Beatrice. You *must* have tickets and a Guard you know."

"Of course," said Edward gravely.

"Rheneas and I," continued Skarloey, "used to take turns at pulling the trains. We know everybody, and everybody knows us. We whistle to the people in the fields, at level crossings, and in lonely cottages and farms, and the people always wave to us.

"We love passing the school playgrounds at break-time, for then the children will always run over to the fence to watch us go by. The passengers always wave, because they think the children are waving to them; but we engines know better, of course," said Skarloey importantly.

"Yes, we do indeed," agreed Edward.

"We take your tourists to the Lake and then get ready to pull the train back.

"We enjoy the morning journey home, because then our friends from the villages come down to do their shopping.

"We whistle before every station, 'Peep! Peeeep! Look out!' and the people are there ready.

" 'Where's Mrs Last?' asks the Guard.

" 'She's coming.'

" 'Peep peeeeeep!' we whistle, and Mrs Last comes running on to the platform. 'We'll leave you behind one of these days, Missis,' laughs our Driver, but we know he never will.

"We stop elsewhere too, at farm crossings and stiles, where paths lead to lonely houses. Rheneas and I know all the places very well indeed, and our Driver used to say that we would stop even if he didn't put on the brakes!

"Sometimes, on Market Day, Ruth, Jemima, and Lucy were so full of people that the Guard would allow third-class passengers to travel in Agnes. She didn't like that at all, and would rumble. 'First —— class —— coach —— third —— class —— people.'

"That made me cross. 'Shut up,' I'd say, 'or I'll bump you!' That soon stopped her rudeness to my friends."

Just then some workmen came. "We're going to mend you now, Edward," they said. "Come along."

"Goodbye, Skarloey. Thank you for telling me about your Railway. It's a lovely little line."

"It is! It is! Thank you for talking to me, Edward. You've cheered me up. Goodbye!"

Skarloey watched Edward being taken back to the Works; then, shutting his eyes, he dozed in the warm afternoon sun. He smiled as he dozed, for he was dreaming, as old engines will, of happy days in the past.

Sir Handel

THE new engines looked very smart. One was called Sir Handel, and the other Peter Sam.

"What a small shed!" grumbled Sir Handel. "This won't do at all!"

"I think it's nice," said Peter Sam.

"Huh!" grunted Sir Handel. "What's that rubbish?"

"Sh sh!" said Peter Sam, "that's Skarloey, the famous old engine.

"I'm sorry, Skarloey," he whispered, "Sir Handel's upset now, but he's quite nice really."

Skarloey felt sorry for Peter Sam.

"Now Sir Handel," said the Fireman next morning, "we'll get you ready."

"I'm tired," he yawned, "let Peter Sam go, he'd love it."

"No," said the Fireman, "Owner's orders, you're first."

"Oh well!" said Sir Handel sulkily, "I suppose I must."

When his Driver arrived, Sir Handel puffed away to fetch the coaches.

"Whatever next?" he snorted. "Those aren't coaches; they're cattle trucks!"

"Oooooh!" screamed Agnes, Ruth, Lucy, Jemima, and Beatrice, "what a horrid engine!"

"It's not what I'm used to," clanked Sir Handel rebelliously, making for the station.

He rolled to the platform just as Gordon arrived.

"Hullo!" he said. "Who are you?"

"I'm Gordon. Who are you?"

"I'm Sir Handel. Yes, I've heard of you; you're an Express engine I believe. So am I, but I'm used to bogie coaches, not these cattle trucks. Do you have bogie coaches? Oh yes, I see you do. We must have a chat sometime. Sorry I can't stop; must keep time, you know."

And he puffed off, leaving Gordon at a loss for words!

"Come along! COME ALONG!" he puffed.

"Cattle trucks! CATTLE TRUCKS!" grumbled the coaches. "We'll pay him out! WE'LL PAY HIM OUT!"

Presently they stopped at a station. The line curved here and began to climb. It was not very steep, but the day was misty, and the rails were slippery.

"Hold back!" whispered Agnes to Ruth. "Hold back!" whispered Ruth to Jemima. "Hold back!" whispered Jemima to Lucy. "Hold back!" whispered Lucy to Beatrice, and they giggled as Sir Handel started and their couplings tightened.

"Come on! COME ON!" he puffed as his wheels slipped on the greasy rails, "Comeon comeon COMEON COMEON!"

His wheels were spinning, but the coaches pulled him back, and the train stopped on the hill beyond the station.

"I can't do it, I can't do it," he grumbled, "I'm used to sensible bogie coaches, not these bumpy cattle trucks."

The Guard came up. "I think the coaches are up to something," he told the Driver. So they decided to bring the train down again to a level piece of line, to give Sir Handel a good start.

The Guard helped the Fireman put sand on the rails, and Sir Handel made a tremendous effort. The coaches tried hard to drag him back; but he puffed and pulled so hard that they were soon over the top and away on their journey.

The Thin Controller was severe with Sir Handel that night.

"You are a Troublesome Engine," he said. "You are rude, conceited, and much too big for your wheels. Next time I shall punish you severely."

Sir Handel was impressed, and behaved well for several days!

Then one morning he took the train to the top station. He was cross; it was Peter Sam's turn, but the Thin Controller had made him go instead.

"We'll leave the coaches," said his Driver, "and fetch some trucks from the Quarry."

"Trucks!" snorted Sir Handel, "TRUCKS!"

"Yes," his Driver repeated, "Trucks."

Sir Handel jerked forward; "I won't!" he muttered, "so there!" He lurched, bumped, and stopped. His Driver and Fireman got out.

"Told you!" said Sir Handel triumphantly.

He had pushed the rails apart, and settled down between them.

They telephoned the Thin Controller. He came up at once with Peter Sam, and brought some workmen in a truck. Then he and the Fireman took Peter Sam home with the coaches, while the Driver and the workmen put Sir Handel back on the rails.

Sir Handel did not feel so pleased with himself when he crawled home, and found the Thin Controller waiting for him. "You are a very naughty engine," he said sternly. "You will stay in the Shed till I can trust you to behave."

Peter Sam and the Refreshment Lady

As Sir Handel was shut up, Peter Sam had to run the line. He was excited, and the Fireman found it hard to get him ready.

"Sober up, can't you!" he growled.

"Anybody would think," said Sir Handel rudely, "that he *wanted* to work."

"All *respectable* engines do," said Skarloey firmly. "I wish I could work myself. Keep calm, Peter Sam, don't get excited, and you'll do very well."

But Peter Sam was in such a state that he couldn't listen.

When his Driver came, Peter Sam ran along to fetch the coaches. "Peep pip pip peep! Come along, girls!" he whistled, and although he was so excited, he remembered to be careful. "That's the way, my dears, gently does it."

"What did he say?" asked Jemima who was deaf.

"He said 'Come along, girls,' and he . . . he called us his dears," simpered the other coaches. "Really one does not know *what* to think . . . such a handsome young engine too . . . *so* nice and well mannered." And they tittered happily together as they followed Peter Sam.

Peter Sam fussed into the station to find Henry already there.

"This won't do, youngster," said Henry. "*I* can't be kept waiting. If you are late tonight, I'll go off and leave your passengers behind."

"Pooh!" said Peter Sam; but secretly he was a little worried.

But he couldn't feel worried for long.

"What fun it all is," he thought as he ran round his train.

He let off steam happily while he waited for the Guard to blow his whistle and wave his green flag.

Peter Sam puffed happily away, singing a little song. "I'm Peter Sam! I'm running this line! I'm Peter Sam! I'm running this line!"

The people waved as he passed the farms and cottages, and he gave a loud whistle at the school. The children all ran to see him puffing by.

Agnes, Ruth, Jemima, Lucy, and Beatrice enjoyed themselves too. "He's cocky . . . trock trock . . . but he's nice . . . trock, trock; he's cocky . . . trock trock . . . but he's nice . . . trock, trock," they sang as they trundled along. They were growing very fond of Peter Sam.

Every afternoon they had to wait an hour at the station by the Lake.

The Driver, Fireman, and the Guard usually bought something from the Refreshment

Lady, and went and sat in Beatrice. The Refreshment Lady always came home on this train.

Time passed slowly today for Peter Sam.

At last his Driver and Fireman came. "Peep peeeeeep! Hurry up, please!" he whistled to the passengers, and they came strolling back to the station.

Peter Sam was sizzling with impatience. "How awful," he thought, "if we miss Henry's train."

The last passengers arrived. The Guard was ready with his flag and whistle. The Refreshment Lady walked across the platform.

Then it happened! . . .

The Guard says that Peter Sam was too impatient; Peter Sam says he was sure he heard a whistle . . . Anyway, he started.

"Come quickly, come quickly!" he puffed.

"Stop! . . . Stop! . . . STOP!" wailed the coaches. "You've . . . left . . . her . . . behind . . . ! YOU'VE . . . LEFT . . . HER . . . BEHIND . . . !"

The Guard whistled and waved his red flag. The Driver, looking back, saw the Refreshment Lady shouting and running after the train.

"Bother!" groaned Peter Sam as he stopped. "We'll miss Henry now." The Refreshment Lady climbed into Beatrice, and they started again. "We're sure to be late! We're sure to be late!" panted Peter Sam frantically. His Driver had to keep checking him. "Steady, old boy, steady."

"Peep peep!" Peter Sam whistled at the stations. "Hurry! Please hurry!" and they reached the big station just as Henry steamed in.

"Hurrah!" said Peter Sam, "we've caught him after all," and he let off steam with relief. "Whoooosh!"

"Not bad, youngster," said Henry loftily.

The Refreshment Lady shook her fist at Peter Sam. "What do you mean by leaving me behind?" she demanded.

"I'm sorry, Refreshment Lady, but I was worried about our passengers," and he told her what Henry had said.

The Refreshment Lady laughed. "You silly engine!" she said, "Henry wouldn't dare go; he's *got* to wait. It's a *guaranteed connection*!"

"Well!" said Peter Sam, "Well! Where's that Henry?"

But Peter Sam was too late that time, for Henry had chortled away!

Old Faithful

SIR HANDEL stayed shut up for several days. But one market day, Peter Sam could not work; he needed repairs.

Sir Handel was glad to come out. He tried to be kind, but the coaches didn't trust him. They were awkward and rude. He even sang them little songs; but it was no use.

It was most unfortunate, too, that Sir Handel had to check suddenly to avoid running over a sheep.

"He's bumped us!" screamed the coaches. "Let's pay him out!"

The coaches knew that all engines must go carefully at a place near the Big Station. But they were so cross with Sir Handel that they didn't care what they did. They surged into Sir Handel, making him lurch off the line. Luckily no one was hurt.

Sir Handel limped to the Shed. The Thin Controller inspected the damage. "No more work for you today," he said. "Bother those coaches! We must take the village people home, and fetch the tourists, all without an engine."

"What about me, Sir?" said a voice.

"Skarloey!" he exclaimed, "can you do it?"

"I'll try," answered the old engine.

The coaches stood at the platform. Skarloey advanced on them hissing crossly. "I'm ashamed of you," he scolded, "such behaviour; you might have hurt your passengers. On Market Day too!"

"We're sorry, Skarloey, we didn't think; it's that Sir Handel, he's . . ."

"No tales," said Skarloey firmly, "I won't have it, and don't you dare try tricks on me."

"No Skarloey, of course not Skarloey," quavered the coaches meekly.

Skarloey might be old, and have dirty paint, but he was certainly an engine who would stand no nonsense.

His friends crowded round, and the Guard had to "shoo" them away before they could start. Skarloey felt happy; he remembered all the gates and stiles where he had to stop, and whistled to his friends. The sun shone, the rails were dry. "This is lovely," he thought.

But presently they began to climb, and he felt short of steam.

"Bother my tubes!" he panted.

"Take your time, old boy," soothed his Driver.

"I'll manage, I'll manage," he wheezed; and, pausing for "breath" at the stations, he gallantly struggled along.

After a rest at the Top Station, Skarloey was ready to start.

"It'll be better downhill," he thought.

The coaches ran nicely, but he soon began to feel tired again. His springs were weak, and the rail-joints jarred his wheels.

Then with a crack, a front spring broke, and he stopped.

"I feel all crooked," he complained.

"That's torn it," said his Driver, "we'll need a bus now for our passengers."

"No!" pleaded Skarloey, "I'd be ashamed to have a bus take my passengers. I'll get home or bust," he promised bravely.

The Thin Controller looked at his watch, and paced the platform. James and his train waited impatiently too.

They heard a hoarse "Peep Peep", then groaning, clanging, and clanking, Skarloey crept into sight. He was tilted to one side, and making fearful noises, but he plodded bravely on.

"I'll *do* it, I'll *do* it," he gasped between the clanks and groans, "I'll. . . I've done it!" and he sighed thankfully as the train stopped where James was waiting.

James said nothing. He waited for his passengers, and then respectfully puffed away.

"You were right, Sir," said Skarloey to the Owner that evening, "old engines can't pull trains like young ones."

The Owner smiled. "They can if they're mended, Old Faithful," he said, "and that's what will happen to you, you deserve it."

"Oh, Sir!" said Skarloey happily.

Sir Handel is longing for Skarloey to come back. He thinks Skarloey is the best engine in the world. He does his fair share of the work now, and the coaches never play tricks on him because he always manages them in "Skarloey's way".

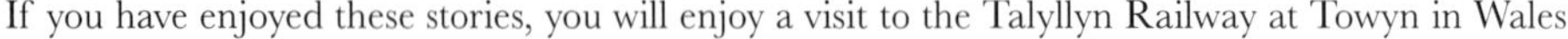

If you have enjoyed these stories, you will enjoy a visit to the Talyllyn Railway at Towyn in Wales.

THE RAILWAY SERIES NO. 11

Percy the Small Engine

THE REV. W. AWDRY

with illustrations by

C. REGINALD DALBY

DEAR CHRISTOPHER, AND GILES, AND PETER, AND CLIVE,

Thank you for writing to ask for a book about Percy. He is still cheeky, and we were afraid (the Fat Controller and I) that if he had a book to himself, it might make him cheekier than ever, and that would never do!

But Percy has been such a Really Useful Engine that we both think he deserves a book. Here it is.

THE AUTHOR

Percy and the Signal

PERCY is a little green tank engine who works in the Yard at the Big Station. He is a funny little engine, and loves playing jokes. These jokes sometimes get him into trouble.

"Peep peep!" he whistled one morning. "Hurry up, Gordon! The train's ready."

Gordon thought he was late and came puffing out.

"Ha ha!" laughed Percy, and showed him a train of dirty coal trucks.

Gordon didn't go back to the Shed.

He stayed on a siding thinking how to pay Percy out.

"Stay in the Shed today," squeaked Percy to James. "The Fat Controller will come and see you."

James was a conceited engine. "Ah!" he thought, "the Fat Controller knows I'm a fine engine, ready for anything. He wants me to pull a Special train."

So James stayed where he was, and nothing his Driver and Fireman could do would make him move.

But the Fat Controller never came, and the other engines grumbled dreadfully.

They had to do James' work as well as their own.

At last an Inspector came. "Show a wheel, James," he said crossly. "You can't stay here all day."

"The Fat Controller told me to stay here," answered James sulkily. "He sent a message this morning."

"He did not," retorted the Inspector. "How could he? He's away for a week."

"Oh!" said James. "Oh!" and he came quickly out of the Shed. "Where's Percy?" Percy had wisely disappeared!

When the Fat Controller came back, he *did* see James, and Percy too. Both engines wished he hadn't!

James and Gordon wanted to pay Percy out; but Percy kept out of their way. One morning, however, he was so excited that he forgot to be careful.

"I say, you engines," he bubbled, "I'm to take some trucks to Thomas' Junction. The Fat Controller chose me specially. He must know I'm a Really Useful Engine."

"More likely he wants you out of the way," grunted James.

But Gordon gave James a wink. . . . Like this.

"Ah yes," said James, "just so. . . . You were saying, Gordon . . . ?"

"James and I were just speaking about signals at the junction. We can't be too careful about signals. But then, I needn't say that to a Really Useful Engine like you, Percy."

Percy felt flattered.

"Of course not," he said.

"We had spoken of 'backing signals'," put in James. "They need extra special care, you know. Would you like me to explain?"

"No thank you, James," said Percy airily. "I know all about signals," and he bustled off importantly.

James and Gordon solemnly exchanged winks!

Percy was a little worried as he set out.

"I wonder what 'backing signals' are?" he thought.

"Never mind, I'll manage. I know all about signals." He puffed crossly to his trucks, and felt better.

He saw a signal just outside the station. "Bother!" he said. "It's at 'danger'."

"Oh! Oh! Oh!" screamed the trucks as they bumped into each other.

Presently the signal moved to show "line clear". Its arm moved up instead of down. Percy had never seen that sort of signal before. He was surprised.

" 'Down' means 'go'," he thought, "and 'up' means 'stop', so 'upper still' must mean 'go back'. I know! It's one of those 'backing signals'. How clever of me to find that out."

"Come on, Percy," said his Driver, "off we go."

But Percy wouldn't go forward, and his Driver had to let him "back" in order to start at all.

"I am clever," thought Percy, "even my Driver doesn't know about 'backing signals'," and he started so suddenly that the trucks screamed again.

"Whoah! Percy," called his Driver. "Stop! You're going the wrong way."

"But it's a 'backing signal'," Percy protested, and told him about Gordon and James. The Driver laughed, and explained about signals that point up.

"Oh dear!" said Percy, "let's start quickly before they come and see us."

But he was too late. Gordon swept by with the Express, and saw everything.

The big engines talked about signals that night. They thought the subject was funny. They laughed a lot. Percy thought they were being very silly!

Duck Takes Charge

"DO you know what?" asked Percy.

"What?" grunted Gordon.

"Do you know what?"

"Silly," said Gordon crossly, "of course I don't know what, if you don't tell me what what is."

"The Fat Controller says that the work in the Yard is too heavy for me. He's getting a bigger engine to help me."

"Rubbish!" put in James. "Any engine could do it," he went on grandly. "If you worked more and chattered less, this Yard would be a sweeter, a better, and a happier place."

Percy went off to fetch some coaches.

"That stupid old signal," he thought, "no one listens to me now. They think I'm a silly little engine, and order me about.

"I'll show them! I'll show them!" he puffed as he ran about the Yard. But he didn't know how.

Things went wrong, the coaches and trucks behaved badly and by the end of the afternoon he felt tired and unhappy.

He brought some coaches to the station, and stood panting at the end of the platform.

"Hullo Percy!" said the Fat Controller, "you look tired."

"Yes, Sir, I am, Sir; I don't know if I'm standing on my dome or my wheels."

"You look the right way up to me," laughed the Fat Controller. "Cheer up!

The new engine is bigger than you, and can probably do the work alone. Would you like to help build my new harbour at Thomas' Junction? Thomas and Toby will help; but I need an engine there all the time."

"Oh yes, Sir, thank you, Sir!" said Percy happily.

The new engine arrived next morning.

"What is your name?" asked the Fat Controller kindly.

"Montague, Sir; but I'm usually called 'Duck'. They say I waddle; I don't really, Sir, but I like 'Duck' better than Montague."

"Good!" said the Fat Controller. " 'Duck' it shall be. Here Percy, come and show 'Duck' round."

The two engines went off together. At first the trucks played tricks, but soon found that playing tricks on Duck was a mistake! The coaches behaved well, though James, Gordon and Henry did not.

They watched Duck quietly doing his work. "He seems a simple sort of engine," they whispered, "we'll have some fun.

"Quaa-aa-aak! Quaa-aa-aak!" they wheezed as they passed him.

Percy was cross; but Duck took no notice. "They'll get tired of it soon," he said.

Presently the three engines began to order Duck about.

Duck stopped. "Do they tell you to do things, Percy?" he asked.

"Yes they do," answered Percy sadly.

"Right," said Duck, "we'll soon stop *that* nonsense." He whispered something . . . "We'll do it tonight."

The Fat Controller had had a good day. There had been no grumbling passengers, all the trains had run to time, and Duck had worked well in the Yard.

The Fat Controller was looking forward to hot buttered toast for tea at home.

He had just left the office when he heard an extraordinary noise. "Bother!" he said, and hurried to the Yard.

Henry, Gordon and James were Wheeeeeshing and snorting furiously; while Duck and Percy calmly sat on the points outside the Shed, refusing to let the engines in.

"STOP THAT NOISE," he bellowed.

"Now Gordon."

"They won't let us in," hissed the big engine crossly.

"Duck, explain this behaviour."

"Beg pardon, Sir, but I'm a Great Western Engine. We Great Western Engines do our work without Fuss; but we are *not* ordered about by other engines. You, Sir, are our

Controller. We will of course move if you order us; but, begging your pardon, Sir, Percy and I would be glad if you would inform these – er – engines that we only take orders from you."

The three big engines hissed angrily.

"SILENCE!" snapped the Fat Controller. "Percy and Duck, I am pleased with your work today; but *not* with your behaviour tonight. You have caused a Disturbance."

Gordon, Henry and James sniggered. They stopped suddenly when the Fat Controller turned on them. "As for you," he thundered, "you've been worse. You made the Disturbance. Duck is quite right. This is My Railway, and I give the orders."

When Percy went away, Duck was left to manage alone.

He did so . . . easily!

Percy and Harold

PERCY worked hard at the harbour. Toby helped, but sometimes the loads of stone were too heavy, and Percy had to fetch them for himself. Then he would push the trucks along the quay to where the workmen needed the stone for their building.

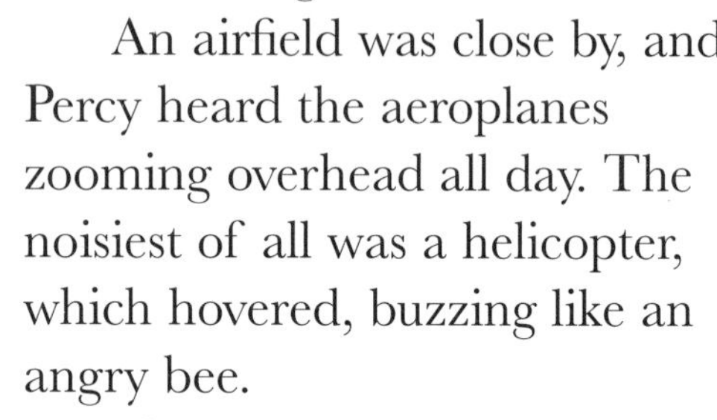

An airfield was close by, and Percy heard the aeroplanes zooming overhead all day. The noisiest of all was a helicopter, which hovered, buzzing like an angry bee.

"Stupid thing!" said Percy, "why can't it go and buzz somewhere else?"

One day Percy stopped near the airfield. The helicopter was standing quite close.

"Hullo!" said Percy, "who are you?"

"I'm Harold, who are you?"

"I'm Percy. What whirly great arms you've got."

"They're nice arms," said Harold, offended. "I can hover like a bird. Don't you wish *you* could hover?"

"Certainly not; I like my rails, thank you."

"I think railways are slow," said Harold in a bored voice. "They're not much use, and quite out of date." He whirled his arms and buzzed away.

Percy found Toby at the Top Station arranging trucks.

"I say, Toby," he burst out, "that Harold, that stuck-up whirlibird thing, says I'm slow and out of date. Just let him wait, I'll show him!"

He collected his trucks and started off, still fuming.

Soon above the clatter of the trucks they heard a familiar buzzing.

"Percy," whispered his Driver, "there's Harold. He's not far ahead. Let's race him."

"Yes, let's," said Percy excitedly, and quickly gathering speed, he shot off down the line.

The Guard's wife had given him a flask of tea for "elevenses". He had just poured out a cup when the van lurched and he spilt it down his uniform. He wiped up the mess with his handkerchief, and staggered to the front platform.

Percy was pounding along, the trucks screamed and swayed, while the van rolled and pitched like a ship at sea.

"Well, I'll be ding-dong-danged!" said the Guard.

Then he saw Harold buzzing alongside, and understood.

"Go it, Percy!" he yelled. "You're gaining."

Percy had never been allowed to run fast before; he was having the time of his life!

"Hurry! Hurry! Hurry!" he panted to the trucks.

"We-don't-want-to; we-don't-want-to," they grumbled; but it was no use, Percy was bucketing along with flying wheels, and Harold was high and alongside.

The Fireman shovelled for dear life, while the Driver was so excited he could hardly keep still.

"Well done, Percy," he shouted, "we're gaining! We're going ahead! Oh good boy, good boy!"

Far ahead, a "distant" signal warned them that the wharf was near. Shut off steam, whistle, "Peep, peep, peep, brakes, Guard, please." Using Percy's brakes too, the Driver carefully checked the train's headlong speed. They rolled under the Main Line, and halted smoothly on the wharf.

"Oh dear!" groaned Percy, "I'm sure we've lost."

The Fireman scrambled to the cab roof. "We've won! We've won!" he shouted and nearly fell off in his excitement.

"Harold's still hovering. He's looking for a place to land!"

"Listen boys!" the Fireman called. "Here's a song for Percy."

Said Harold helicopter to our Percy, "You are slow!
Your Railway is out of date and not much use, you know."
But Percy, with his stone-trucks, did the trip in record time;
And we beat that helicopter on Our Old Branch Line.

The Driver and Guard soon caught the tune, and so did the workmen on the quay.

Percy loved it. "Oh thank you!" he said. He liked the last line best of all.

Percy's Promise

A MOB of excited children poured out of Annie and Clarabel one morning, and raced down to the beach.

"They're the Vicar's Sunday School," explained Thomas. "I'm busy this evening, but the Stationmaster says I can ask you to take them home."

"Of course I will," promised Percy.

The children had a lovely day. But at tea-time it got very hot. Dark clouds loomed overhead. Then came lightning, thunder, and rain. The children only just managed to reach shelter before the deluge began.

Annie and Clarabel stood at the platform. The children scrambled in.

"Can we go home please, Stationmaster?" asked the Vicar.

The Stationmaster called Percy. "Take the children home quickly please," he ordered.

The rain streamed down on Percy's boiler. "Ugh!" he shivered, and thought of his nice dry shed. Then he remembered.

"A promise is a promise," he told himself, "so here goes."

His Driver was anxious. The river was rising fast. It foamed and swirled fiercely, threatening to flood the country any minute.

The rain beat in Percy's face. "I wish I could see, I wish I could see," he complained.

They left a cutting, and found themselves in water. "Oooh my wheels!"

shivered Percy. "It's cold!" but he struggled on.

"Oooooooooooooshshshshshsh!" he hissed, "it's sloshing my fire."

They stopped and backed the coaches to the cutting and waited while the Guard found a telephone.

He returned looking gloomy.

"We couldn't go back if we wanted," he said, "the bridge near the junction is down."

The Fireman went to the Guard's Van carrying a hatchet.

"Hullo!" said the Guard, "you look fierce."

"I want some dry wood for Percy's fire please."

They broke up some boxes, but that did not satisfy the Fireman. "I'll have some of your floor boards," he said.

"What! My nice floor," grumbled the Guard. "I only swept it this morning," but he found a hatchet and helped.

Soon they had plenty of wood stored in Percy's bunker. His fire burnt well now. He felt warm and comfortable again.

"Buzzzzzzzzzzzzzzzzzz! Buzzzzzzzzzzzzzzzzzz! Buzzzzzzzzzzzzzzzzzz!"

"Oh dear!" thought Percy sadly, "Harold's come to laugh at me."

Bump! Something thudded on Percy's boiler. "Ow!" he exclaimed in a muffled voice, "that's really too bad! He needn't *throw* things."

His driver unwound a parachute from Percy's indignant front.

"Harold isn't throwing things at you," he laughed, "he's dropping hot drinks for us."

They all had a drink of cocoa, and felt better.

Percy had steam up now. "Peep peep! Thank you, Harold!" he whistled. "Come on, let's go."

The water lapped his wheels. "Ugh!" he shivered. It crept up and up and up. It reached his ash-pan, then it sloshed at his fire. "Oooooooooooooshshshshshshshshshshsh!"

Percy was losing steam; but he plunged bravely on. "I promised," he panted, "I promised."

They piled his fire high with wood, and managed to keep him steaming.

"I *must* do it," he gasped, "I must, I must, I must."

He made a last great effort, and stood, exhausted but triumphant, on rails which were clear of the flood.

He rested to get steam back, then brought the train home.

"Three cheers for Percy!" called the Vicar, and the children nearly raised the roof!

The Fat Controller arrived in Harold. First he thanked the men. "Harold told me you were – er – wizard, Percy. He says he can beat you at some things . . ."

Percy snorted.

" . . . but *not* at being a submarine." He chuckled. "I don't know what you've both been playing at, and I won't ask! But I do know that you're a Really Useful Engine."

"Oh Sir!" whispered Percy happily.

THE RAILWAY SERIES NO. 12

The Eight Famous Engines

THE REV. W. AWDRY

with illustrations by

JOHN T. KENNEY

DEAR FRIENDS,

The Fat Controller's engines are now quite famous. They have been on the Wireless, and had many other adventures. But he had another plan too for his engines, and this book will tell you what it was.

THE AUTHOR

Percy takes the Plunge

SOMETIMES Percy takes stone trucks to the other end of the line. There, he meets engines from the Other Railway.

One day, Henry wanted to rest in the Shed; but Percy was talking to some tank engines.

". . . It was raining hard. Water swirled under my boiler. I couldn't see where I was going; but I struggled on."

"Ooooh Percy, you *are* brave."

"Well," said Percy modestly, "it wasn't anything really. Water's nothing to an engine with determination."

"Tell us more, Percy," said the engines.

"What are you engines doing here?" hissed Henry. "This shed is for the Fat Controller's Engines. Go away."

"Silly things," Henry snorted.

"They're not silly." Percy had been enjoying himself. He was cross because Henry had sent them away.

"They are silly, and so are you. 'Water's nothing to an engine with determination.' Pah!"

"Anyway," said cheeky Percy, "I'm not afraid of water. I like it." He ran away singing,

"Once an engine attached to a train
Was afraid of a few drops of rain . . ."

Percy arrived home feeling pleased with himself. "Silly old Henry," he chuckled.

Thomas was looking at a board on the Quay. It said "DANGER".

"We mustn't go past it," he said. "That's Orders."

"Why?"

" 'DANGER' means falling down something," said Thomas. "I went past 'DANGER' once, and fell down a mine."

Percy looked beyond the board. "I can't see a mine," he said.

He didn't know that the foundations of the Quay had sunk, and that the rails now sloped downward to the sea.

"Stupid board!" said Percy. For days and days he tried to sidle past it; but his Driver stopped him every time.

"No you don't," he would say.

Then Percy made a plan.

One day at the Top Station he whispered to the trucks. "Will you give me a bump when we get to the Quay?"

The trucks were surprised. They had never been asked to bump an engine before. They giggled and chattered about it the whole way down.

"Whoah Percy! Whoah!" said his Driver, and Percy checked obediently at the "distant" signal.

"Driver doesn't know my plan," he chuckled.

"On! On! On!" laughed the trucks. Percy thought they were helping. "I'll pretend to stop at the station; but the trucks will push me past the board. Then I'll make them stop. I can do that whenever I like."

If Percy hadn't been so conceited, he would never have been so silly.

Every wise engine knows that you cannot trust trucks.

They reached the station, and Percy's brakes groaned. That was the signal for the trucks.

"Go on! Go on!" they yelled, and surged forward together.

They gave Percy a fearful bump, and knocked his Driver and Fireman off the footplate.

"Ow!" said Percy, sliding past the board.

The day was misty. The rails were slippery. His wheels wouldn't grip.

Percy was frantic. "That's enough!" he hissed.

But it was too late. Once on the slope, he tobogganed helplessly down, crashed through the buffers, and slithered into the sea.

"You are a very disobedient engine."

Percy knew that voice. He groaned.

The Foreman borrowed a small boat and rowed the Fat Controller round.

"Please, Sir, get me out Sir, I'm truly sorry Sir."

"No, Percy, we cannot do that till high tide. I hope it will teach you to obey Orders."

"Yes, Sir," Percy shivered miserably. He was cold. Fish were playing hide and seek through his wheels. The tide rose higher and higher.

He was feeling his position more and more deeply every minute.

It was nearly dark when they brought floating cranes, cleared away the trucks, and lifted Percy out.

He was too cold and stiff to move by himself, so he was sent to the Works next day on Henry's goods train.

"Well! Well! Well!" chuckled Henry, "Did you like the water?"

"No."

"I *am* surprised. You need more determination, Percy. 'Water's nothing to an engine with determination' you know. Perhaps you will like it better next time."

But Percy is quite determined that there won't be a "next time".

Gordon goes Foreign

LOTS of people travel to the Big Station at the end of the line. Engines from the Other Railway sometimes pull their trains. These engines stay the night and go home next day.

Gordon was talking one day to one of these.

"When I was young and green," he said, "I remember going to London. Do you know the place? The station's called King's Cross."

"King's Cross!" snorted the engine, "London's Euston. Everybody knows that."

"Rubbish!" said Duck, "London's Paddington. I *know*. I worked there."

They argued till they went to sleep. They argued when they woke up. They were still arguing when the other engine went away.

"Stupid thing," said Gordon crossly, "I've no patience."

"Stupid yourself," said Duck, "London's Paddington, PADDINGTON, do you hear?"

"Stop arguing," James broke in, "you make me tired. You're both agreed about something anyway."

"What's that?"

"London's not Euston," laughed James. "Now shut up!"

Gordon rolled away still grumbling. "I'm sure it's King's Cross. I'll go and prove it."

But that was easier said than done.

London lay beyond the Big Station at the other end of the Line. Gordon had to stop there. Another engine then took his train.

"If I didn't stop," he thought, "I could go to London."

One day he ran right through the station. Another time he tried to start before the Fireman could uncouple the coaches. He tried all sorts of tricks; but it was no good. His Driver checked him every time.

"Oh dear!" he thought sadly, "I'll never get there."

One day he pulled the Express to the station as usual. His Fireman uncoupled the coaches, and he ran on to his siding to wait till it was time to go home.

The coaches waited and waited at the platform; but their engine didn't come.

A porter ran across and spoke to Gordon's Driver. "The Inspector's on the platform. He wants to see you."

The Driver climbed down from the cab and walked over the station. He came back in a few minutes looking excited.

"Hullo!" said the Fireman, "what's happened?"

"The engine for the Express turned over when it was coming out of the Yard. Nothing else can come in or out. They want us to take the train to London. I said we would, if the Fat Controller agreed. They telephoned, and he said we could do it. How's that?"

"Fine," said the Fireman, "we'll show them what the Fat Controller's

engines can do."

"Come on!" said Gordon, "let's go." He rolled quickly over the crossings and backed on to the train.

It was only a few minutes before the Guard blew his whistle; but Gordon thought it was ages!

"COME ON! COME ON!" he puffed to the coaches.

"Comeoncomeoncomeon!"

"We're going to Town, we're going to Town," sang the coaches slowly at first, then faster and faster.

Gordon found that London was a long way away. "Never mind," he said, "I like a good long run to stretch my wheels."

But all the same he was glad when London came in sight.

The Fat Controller came into his office next morning. He looked at the letters on his desk. One had a London post-mark.

"I wonder how Gordon's getting on," he said.

The Stationmaster knocked and came in. He looked excited.

"Excuse me Sir, have you seen the news?"

"Not yet. Why?"

"Just look at this Sir."

The Fat Controller took the

Newspaper. "Good gracious me!" he said, "there's Gordon. Headlines too! 'FAMOUS ENGINE AT LONDON STATION. POLICE CALLED TO CONTROL CROWDS.'"

The Fat Controller read on, absorbed.

Gordon returned next day. The Fat Controller spoke to his Driver and Fireman. "I see you had a good welcome in London."

"We certainly did Sir! We signed autographs till our arms ached, and Gordon had his photograph taken from so many directions at once that he didn't know which way to look!"

"Good!" smiled the Fat Controller, "I expect he enjoyed himself. Didn't you Gordon?"

"No Sir, I didn't."

"Why ever not?"

"London's all wrong," answered Gordon sadly, "they've changed it. It isn't King's Cross any more. It's St Pancras."

Double Header

THE Fat Controller gave Gordon a rest when he came back from London. He told James to do his work.

James got very conceited about it.

"You know, little Toby," he said one day, "I'm an Important Engine now; everybody knows it. They come in crowds to see me flash by. The heaviest train makes no difference. I'm as regular as clockwork. They all set their watches by me. Never late, always on time, that's me."

"Sez you," replied Toby cheekily.

Toby was out on the Main Line. The Fat Controller had sent him to the Works. His parts were worn. They clanked as he trundled along.

He was enjoying his journey. He was a little engine, and his tanks didn't hold much water, so he often had to stop for a drink. He had small wheels, too, and he couldn't go fast.

"Never mind," he thought, "the Signalmen all know me; they'll give me plenty of time."

But a new Signalman had come to one of the stations.

Toby had wanted to take Henrietta, but the Fat Controller had said, "No! What would the passengers do without her?"

He wondered if Henrietta was lonely. Percy had promised to look after her; but Toby couldn't help worrying. "Percy doesn't understand her like I do," he said.

He felt thirsty and tired; he had come a long way.

He saw a "distant" signal. "Good," he thought, "now I can have a nice drink, and rest in a siding till James has gone by."

Toby's Driver thought so too. They stopped by the water-crane. His Fireman jumped out and put the hose in his tank.

Toby was enjoying his drink when the Signalman came up. Toby had never seen him before.

"No time for that," said the Signalman. "We must clear the road for the Express."

"Right," said the Driver. "We'll wait in the siding."

"No good," said the Signalman, "it's full of trucks. You'll have to hurry to the next station. They've got plenty of room for you there."

Poor Toby clanked sadly away. "I must hurry! I must hurry!" he panted.

But hurrying used a lot of water, and his tanks were soon empty.

They damped down his fire and struggled on, but he soon ran out of steam, and stood marooned on the Main Line far away from the next station.

The Fireman walked back. He put detonators on the line to warn James and his Driver; then he hurried along the sleepers.

"I'll tell that Signalman something," he said grimly.

James was fuming when Toby's Fireman arrived and explained what had happened.

"My fault," said the Signalman, "I didn't understand about Toby."

"Now James," said his Driver, "you'll have to push him."

"What, me?" snorted James. "ME, push Toby *and* pull my train?"

"Yes, you."

"Shan't."

The Driver, the Firemen, the passengers and the Guard all said he was a Bad Engine.

"All right, all right," grumbled James. He came up behind Toby and gave him a bump.

"Get on you!" he said crossly.

James' Driver made him push Toby all the way to the Works. "It serves you right for being cross," he said.

James had to work very hard and when he reached the Works Station he felt exhausted.

Some little boys ran along the platform. "Coo!" said one, "The Express *is* late. A double header too. Do you know what I think? I think," he went on, "that James couldn't pull the train, so Toby had to help him."

"Cor!" said James and disappeared in a cloud of steam.

The Fat Controller's Engines

ONE evening, Thomas brought his last train to the junction. He went for a drink.

"I'm going to the Big Station," he said to Percy and Toby.

"So are we," they answered.

"Do you know," Percy went on, "I think something's up." Toby looked at the sky, "Where?"

"Down here, silly," laughed Thomas.

"How," asked Toby reasonably, "can something be up when it's down?"

"Look!" said Thomas excitedly, "Look!"

Seven engines from the Other Railway were coming along the line.

"Hullo Jinty!" whistled Percy, "Hullo Pug!

"They're friends of mine," he explained. "I don't know the others."

Jinty and Pug whistled cheerfully as they puffed though the station.

"What *is* all this?" asked Thomas.

"The Fat Controller's got a plan," answered his Driver, "and he's going to tell it to us. Come on."

So they followed to the Big Station at the end of the line where all the engines had gone.

The Fat Controller was waiting for them there.

"The people of England," he said, "read about Us in the Books; but they do not think that we are real. . . ."

"Shame!" squeaked Percy. The Fat Controller glared. Percy subsided.

". . . so," he continued, "I am taking My Engines to England to show them."

"Hooray! Hooray!" the engines whistled.

The Fat Controller held his ears. "Silence!" he bellowed.

"We start the day after tomorrow at 8 a.m. Meanwhile as these engines have kindly come from the Other Railway to take your place, you will show them your work tomorrow."

Next day, as Annie and Clarabel were going to England too, Thomas and Jinty practised with some other coaches.

Thomas was excited. He began boasting about his race with Bertie. "I whooshed through the tunnel and stopped an inch from the buffers. Like this!"

——— CRASH — The buffers broke.

No one was hurt; but Thomas' front was badly bent.

They telephoned the Fat Controller. "I'll send up some men," he said, "but if they can't mend Thomas in time, we'll go to England without him."

Next morning the engines waited at the junction. Toby and Percy were each on a truck and Duck had pushed them into place behind Edward.

Henrietta stood on a siding. The Fat Controller had called her a "curiosity". "I wouldn't dream of leaving you behind," he said, "I'll fit you up

as my private coach." She felt very grand.

Gordon, James and Henry were in front. They whistled impatiently.

The Fat Controller paced the platform. He looked at his watch. "One minute more," he said, turning to the Guard.

"Peep peep peeep!" whistled Thomas and panted into the station.

Annie and Clarabel twittered anxiously. "We hope we're not late; it isn't quite Eight."

"Thomas," said the Fat Controller sternly, "I am most displeased with you. You nearly upset My Arrangements."

Thomas, abashed, arranged himself and the coaches behind Duck, without saying a word!

The Fat Controller climbed into Henrietta. The Guard blew his whistle and waved his flag.

The engines whistled, "Look out England, here we come!" and the cavalcade puffed off.

The engines stood side by side in a big airy shed. Hundreds of people came to see them, and climbed in and out of their cabs every day.

They liked it at first, but

presently felt very bored, and were glad when it was time to go.

The people along their line put the flags out, and cheered them home. "We are glad to see you," they said. "Those others did their best; but they don't know our ways. Nothing anywhere can compare with our Fat Controller's engines."

THE RAILWAY SERIES NO. 13

Duck and the Diesel Engine

THE REV. W. AWDRY

with illustrations by

JOHN T. KENNEY

DEAR FRIENDS,

We have had two visitors to Our Railway. One of these, "City of Truro", is a very famous engine. We were sorry when we had to say "goodbye" to him.

The other visitor was different. "I do not believe," writes the Fat Controller, "that all Diesels are troublesome; but this one upset our engines, and made Duck very unhappy."

THE AUTHOR

Domeless Engines

A SPECIAL train arrived one day, and the Fat Controller welcomed the passengers. They looked at everything in the Yard, and photographed the engines. Duck's Driver let some of them ride in his cab.

"They're the Railway Society," his Driver explained. "They've come to see us. Their engine's 'City of Truro'. He was the first to go 100 miles an hour. Let's get finished, then we can go and talk to him."

"Oh!" said Duck, awed. "He's too famous to notice me."

"Rubbish!" smiled his Driver. "Come on."

Duck found "City of Truro" at the coaling stage.

"May I talk to you?" he asked shyly.

"Of course," smiled the famous engine, "I see you are one of Us."

"I try to teach them Our ways," said Duck modestly.

"All ship-shape and Swindon fashion. That's right."

"Please, could you tell me how you beat the South Western?"

So "City of Truro" told Duck all about his famous run from Plymouth to Bristol more than fifty years ago. They were soon firm friends, and talked "Great Western" till late at night.

"City of Truro" left early next morning.

"Good riddance!" grumbled Gordon. "Chattering all night keeping important engines awake! Who *is* he anyway?"

"He's 'City of Truro'. He's famous."

"As famous as me? Nonsense!"

"He's famouser than you. He went 100 miles an hour before you were drawn or thought of."

"So he says; but I didn't like his looks. *He's got no dome,*" said Gordon darkly. "Never trust domeless engines, they're not respectable.

"I never boast," Gordon continued modestly; "but 100 miles an hour would be easy for me. Goodbye!"

Presently Duck took some trucks to Edward's station. He was cross, and it was lucky for those trucks that they tried no tricks.

"Hullo!" called Edward. "The famous 'City of Truro' came though this morning. He whistled to me; wasn't he kind?"

"He's the finest engine in the world," said Duck, and he told Edward about "City of Truro", and what Gordon had said.

"Don't take any notice," soothed Edward, "he's just jealous. He thinks no engine should be famous but him. Look! He's coming now."

Gordon's boiler seemed to have swollen larger than ever. He was running very fast. He swayed up and down and from side to side as his wheels pounded the rails.

"He did it! I'll do it! He did it! I'll do it!" he panted. His train rocketed past and was gone.

Edward chuckled and winked at Duck. "Gordon's trying to do a 'City of Truro'," he said.

Duck was still cross. "I should think he'll knock himself to bits," he snorted. "I heard something rattle as he went through."

Gordon's Driver eased him off. "Steady boy!" he said. "We aren't running a race."

"We are then," said Gordon; but he said it to himself.

"I've never known him ride so roughly before," remarked his Driver.

His Fireman grabbed the brake handle to steady himself. "He's giving himself a hammering, and no mistake."

Soon Gordon began to feel a little queer. "The top of my boiler seems funny," he thought; "it's just as if something was loose. I'd better go slower."

But by then it was too late!

They met the wind on the viaduct. It wasn't just a gentle wind; nor was it a hard steady wind. It was a teasing wind which blew suddenly in hard puffs, and caught you unawares.

Gordon thought it wanted to push him off the bridge. "No you don't!" he said firmly.

But the wind had other ideas. It curled round his boiler, crept under his loose dome, and lifted it off and away into the valley below. It fell on the rocks with a clang.

Gordon was most uncomfortable. He felt cold where his dome wasn't, and besides, people laughed at him as he passed.

At the Big Station, he tried to "Wheeeesh" them away; but they crowded round no matter what he did.

On the way back, he wanted his Driver to stop and find his dome, and was very cross when he wouldn't.

He hoped the Shed would be empty; but all the engines were there waiting.

"Never trust domeless engines," said a voice. "They aren't respectable."

Pop Goes the Diesel

"CITY OF TRURO'S" visit made Duck very proud of being Great Western. He talked endlessly about it. But he worked hard too and made everything go like clockwork.

The trucks behaved well, the coaches were ready on time, and the passengers even stopped grumbling!

But the engines didn't like having to bustle about. "There are two ways of doing this," Duck told them, "the Great Western way, or the wrong way. I'm Great Western and . . ."

"Don't we know it!" they groaned. They were glad when a visitor came.

The visitor purred smoothly towards them. The Fat Controller climbed down. "Here is Diesel," he said, "I have agreed to give him a trial. He needs to learn. Please teach him, Duck."

"Good morning," purred Diesel in an oily voice, "pleased to meet you, Duck. Is that James? – *and* Henry? – *and* Gordon too? I am delighted to meet such famous engines." And he purred towards them.

The silly engines were flattered. "He has very good manners," they murmured, "we are pleased to have him in our Yard."

Duck had his doubts.

"Come on!" he said shortly.

"Ah! Yes!" said Diesel, "The Yard, of course. Excuse me, engines," and he purred after Duck, talking hard. "Your worthy Fat . . ."

"Sir Topham Hatt to you," ordered Duck.

Diesel looked hurt. "Your worthy Sir Topham Hatt thinks I need to learn. He is mistaken. We Diesels don't need to learn. We know everything. We come to a yard and improve it. We are revolutionary."

"Oh!" said Duck, "If you're revo-thingummy, perhaps you would collect my trucks, while I fetch Gordon's coaches."

Diesel, delighted to show off, purred away. With much banging and clashing he collected a row of trucks. Duck left Gordon's coaches in the station and came back.

Diesel was now trying to take some trucks from a siding nearby. They were old and empty. Clearly they had not been touched for a long time.

Their brakes would not come off properly. Diesel found them hard to move.

Pull — Push — Backwards — Forwards. "Oheeeer! Oheeeer!" the trucks groaned. "We can't! We *won't!*"

Duck watched the operation with interest.

Diesel lost patience. "GrrrrrRRRRRrrrrrRRRRR!" he roared, and gave a great heave. The trucks jerked forward.

"Oher! Oher!" they screamed. "We *can't!* We *WON'T!*" Some of their brakes broke, and the gear hanging down bumped on the rails and sleepers.

"WE CAN'T! WE WON'T! Aaaaah!" Their trailing brakes caught in the points and locked themselves solid.

"GrrrrrRRRRRrrrrrRRRRRrrrrrRRRR!" roared Diesel; a rusty

coupling broke, and he shot forward suddenly by himself.

"Ho! Ho! Ho!" chuckled Duck.

Diesel recovered and tried to push the trucks back; but they wouldn't move, and he had to give up. Duck ran quietly round to where the other trucks all stood in line. "Thank you for arranging these, Diesel," he said, "I must go now."

"Don't you want this lot?"

"No thank you."

Diesel gulped. "And I've taken all this trouble," he almost shrieked. "Why didn't you tell me?"

"You never asked me. Besides," said Duck innocently, "you were having such fun being revo-whatever-it-was-you-said. Goodbye."

Diesel had to help the workmen clear the mess. He hated it. All the trucks and coaches were laughing. Presently he heard them sing. Their song grew louder and louder, and soon it echoed through the Yard.

Trucks are waiting in the Yard;
tackling them with ease'll
"Show the world what I can do,"
gaily boasts the Diesel.
In and out he creeps about,
like a big black weasel.
When he pulls the wrong trucks out —
Pop goes the Diesel!

"Grrrrr!" he growled, and scuttling away, sulked in the Shed.

Dirty Work

WHEN Duck returned, and heard the trucks singing, he was horrified. "Shut up!" he ordered, and bumped them hard. "I'm sorry our trucks were rude to you, Diesel," he said.

Diesel was still furious. "It's all your fault. You made them laugh at me," he complained.

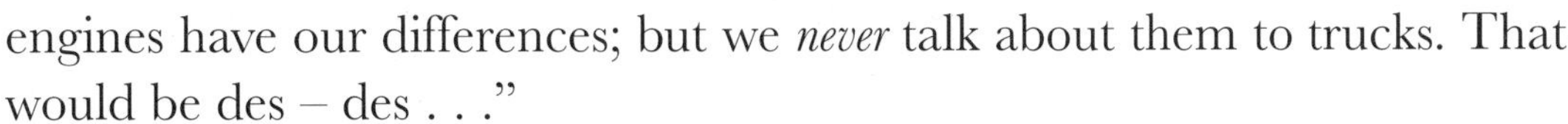

"Nonsense," said Henry, "Duck would never do that. We engines have our differences; but we *never* talk about them to trucks. That would be des – des . . ."

"Disgraceful!" said Gordon.

"Disgusting!" put in James.

"Despicable!" finished Henry.

Diesel hated Duck. He wanted him to be sent away. So he made a plan.

Next day he spoke to the trucks. "I see you like jokes," he said in his oily voice. "You made a good joke about me yesterday. I laughed and laughed. Duck told me one about Gordon. I'll whisper it. . . . Don't tell Gordon I told you," and he sniggered away.

"Haw! Haw! Haw!" guffawed the trucks. "Gordon will be cross with Duck when he knows. Let's tell him and pay Duck out for bumping us."

Diesel went to all the sidings, and in each he told different stories. He said Duck had told them to him. This was untrue; but the trucks didn't know.

They laughed rudely at the engines as they went by, and soon Gordon,

Henry and James found out why.

"Disgraceful!" said Gordon.

"Disgusting!" said James.

"Despicable!" said Henry. "We cannot allow it."

They consulted together. "Yes," they said, "he did it to us. We'll do it to him, and see how *he* likes it."

Duck was tired out. The trucks had been cheeky and troublesome. He had had hard work to make them behave. He wanted a rest in the Shed.

"Hoooooooosh! KEEP OUT!" The three engines barred his way, and Diesel lurked behind.

"Stop fooling," said Duck, "I'm tired."

"So are we," hissed the engines. "We are tired of *you*. We like Diesel. We don't like you. You tell tales about us to trucks."

"I don't."

"You do."

"I don't."

"You do."

The Fat Controller came to stop the noise.

"Duck called me a 'galloping sausage'," spluttered Gordon.

". . . rusty red scrap-iron," hissed James.

". . . I'm 'old square wheels'," fumed Henry.

"Well Duck?"

Duck considered. "I only wish Sir," he said gravely, "that I'd thought of those names myself. If the dome fits . . ."

"Ha! Ahem!" The Fat Controller coughed.

"He made trucks laugh at us," accused the engines.

The Fat Controller recovered. "Did you, Duck?"

"Certainly not Sir! No *steam* engine would be as mean as that."

"Now Diesel, you heard what Duck said."

"I can't understand it Sir. To think that Duck of all engines . . . I'm dreadfully grieved Sir; but know nothing."

"I see." Diesel squirmed and hoped he didn't.

"I am sorry, Duck," the Fat Controller went on; "but you must go to Edward's station for a while. I know he will be glad to see you."

"Beg pardon Sir, do you mean now?"

"Yes please."

"As you wish Sir." Duck trundled sadly away, while Diesel smirked with triumph in the darkness.

A Close Shave

SO Duck came to Edward's station.

"It's not fair," he complained, "Diesel has made the Fat Controller and all the engines think I'm horrid."

Edward smiled. "I know you aren't," he said, "and so does the Fat Controller. You wait and see."

Duck felt happier with Edward. He helped him with his trucks and coaches, and sometimes helped foreign engines by pushing their trains up the hill.

But Gordon, Henry and James never spoke to him at all.

One day he pushed behind a goods train and helped it to the top.

"Peep peep! Goodbye!" he called, and rolled gently over the crossing to the other line. Duck loved coasting down the hill, running easily with the wind whistling past. He hummed a little tune.

* * *

"Peeeeeep! Peeeeeep! Peeeeeep!"

"That sounds like a Guard's whistle," he thought. "But we haven't a Guard."

His Driver heard it too, and looked back. "Hurry, Duck, hurry," he called urgently. "There's been a break-away, some trucks are chasing us."

There were twenty heavily loaded trucks. "Hurrah! Hurrah! Hurrah!" they laughed, "We've broken away! We've broken away! We've broken away!"

and before the Signalman could change the points they followed Duck on to the down line.

"Chase him! Bump him! Throw him off the rails!" they yelled, and hurtled after Duck, bumping and swaying with ever-increasing speed.

The Guard saved Duck. Though the trucks had knocked him off his van, he got up and ran behind, blowing his whistle to attract the Driver's attention.

"Now what?" asked the Fireman.

"As fast as we can," said the Driver grimly, "then they'll catch us gradually."

They raced through Edward's station whistling furiously, but the trucks caught them with a shuddering jar. The Fireman climbed back, and the van brakes came on with a scream.

Braking carefully, the Driver was gaining control.

"Another clear mile and we'll do it," he said.

They swept round a bend.

"Oh glory! Look at that!"

A passenger train was just pulling out on their line, from the station ahead.

The Driver leapt to his reverser; Hard over — Full steam — Whistle.

"It's up to you now, Duck," he said.

Duck put every ounce of weight and steam against the trucks.

They felt his strength. "On! On!" they yelled; but Duck was holding them now.

"I must stop them. I *must*."

The station came nearer and nearer. The last coach cleared the platform.

"It's too late," Duck groaned, and shut his eyes.

He felt a sudden swerve, and slid, shuddering and groaning along a siding.

A barber had set up shop in a wooden shed in the Yard. He was shaving a customer.

There was a sliding groaning crash, and part of the wall caved in.

The customer jumped nervously; but the barber held him down. "It's only an engine," he said calmly, and went on lathering.

"Beg pardon Sir!" gasped Duck, "Excuse my intrusion."

"No. I won't," said the barber crossly, "you've frightened my customers and spoilt my new paint. I'll teach you." And he lathered Duck's face all over.

Poor Duck.

They were pulling the trucks away when the Fat Controller arrived. The Barber was telling the workmen what he thought.

"I do *not* like engines popping through my walls,"

he fumed. "They disturb my customers."

"I appreciate your feelings," said the Fat Controller, "and we'll gladly repair the damage; but you must know that this engine and his crew have prevented a serious accident. You and many others might have been badly hurt."

The Fat Controller paused impressively. "It was a very close shave," he said.

"Oh!" said the barber, "Oh! Excuse me." He ran into his shop, fetched a basin of water, and washed Duck's face.

"I'm sorry, Duck," he said. "I didn't know you were being a brave engine."

"That's all right, Sir," said Duck. "I didn't know that either."

"You were very brave indeed," said the Fat Controller kindly. "I'm proud of you. I shall tell 'City of Truro' about you next time he comes."

"Oh Sir!" Duck felt happier than he had been for weeks.

"And now," said the Fat Controller, "when you are mended you are coming home."

"Home Sir? Do you mean the Yard?"

"Of course."

"But Sir, they don't like me. They like Diesel."

"Not now." The Fat Controller smiled. "I never believed Diesel. After you went he told lies about Henry; so I sent him packing. The engines are sorry and want you back."

So, when a few days later he came home shining with new paint, there was a really rousing welcome for Duck the Great Western engine.

THE RAILWAY SERIES NO. 14

The Little Old Engine

THE REV. W. AWDRY

with illustrations by

JOHN T. KENNEY

DEAR FRIENDS,

You remember in *Four Little Engines* that Sir Handel Brown, The Owner, sent Skarloey away to be mended. These stories tell what happened when the "Little Old Engine" came home.

Skarloey is not real. You can only see him in these books. *But there is a real engine just like Skarloey*. He is very, very old, and has been mended. His name is Talyllyn, and he lives at Towyn in Wales.

You would all enjoy going to see him at work.

THE AUTHOR

The author gratefully acknowledges the help given by fellow members of the Talyllyn Railway Preservation Society in the preparation of this book.

Trucks!

SIR HANDEL and Peter Sam had hard work while Skarloey was away. The Owner gave them buffers, and even bought a Diesel named Rusty; but Sir Handel grumbled continually.

One day Gordon saw him shunting, and laughed.

"My Controller *makes* me shunt," Sir Handel said sheepishly, "*and* take trucks to quarries too. I'm highly sprung, and I suffer dreadfully."

"Our Controllers don't understand our feelings," sympathised Gordon. "Now, if you were ill" – he winked – "you couldn't go, could you?"

"Good idea," said Sir Handel. "I'll try it."

"I don't feel well," he groaned next morning.

There wasn't time to examine him then, so some of the trucks were coupled behind Peter Sam's coaches, and Rusty promised to follow with the rest.

"He! He! He!" sniggered Sir Handel; but no one noticed. They were all too busy.

Peter Sam didn't mind the extra work. He left his coaches at the Top Station, and trundled cheerfully through the woods. The trucks chattered behind him in an agitated way, but he paid no attention.

It might have been better if he had.

Slates come from quarries high up in the hills. They travel down in trucks on a steep railway called an Incline. Empty trucks at the bottom are hitched to a rope. Loaded ones at the top are hitched to one another. By their weight, loaded trucks run down the Incline pulling up empty ones.

There are strong brakes in the Winding House at the top to prevent loaded trucks from running down too fast. The ropes are very strong too, but in spite of this, trucks sometimes play dangerous tricks.

Peter Sam never bumped trucks unless they misbehaved. Sir Handel bumped them even if they were good; so they didn't like him, and played tricks whenever they could.

Peter Sam pushed the empty trucks to a siding where his Fireman hitched them to the rope. Then, on another siding, he pulled back some loaded trucks. With these in front of him, he stood waiting.

More loaded trucks stood at the top of the Incline, ready to come down. They couldn't see Peter Sam. They thought he was Sir Handel, and wanted to pay him out.

They began to move. "Faster! Faster!" they grumbled. They reached halfway, gathering speed.

"Scrag him! Scrag him!" they yelled.

"No! No!" wailed the empty trucks. "It's Peter Sam! It's Peter Sam!" But it was no use. The loaded trucks were straining at the rope.

They broke it with a CRACK! "Hurrah! Hurrah!" they roared, hurtling down the hill.

Peter Sam heard them. He shut his eyes. His Driver and Fireman

crouched in his cab.

The crash jerked him violently backwards.

"Ouch!" he shivered. "I didn't expect a cold bath!"

The water poured from a channel smashed by flying slates. He was soaked from funnel to cab.

"Peep! Peep!" he spluttered, and was glad when he heard Rusty's answering "Toot!"

"Bust my buffers!" exclaimed Rusty. "What a mess! Never mind, Peter Sam, we'll get you out." He soon pulled him away from the water and the trucks.

Peter Sam felt battered. His funnel was cracked and his boiler dented, but he was glad his Driver and Fireman were unhurt.

He thanked Rusty, and limped slowly home. Rusty stayed to help clear the wreckage.

"I'm sorry about your accident, Peter Sam," said Sir Handel. "I always stand well back. Trucks don't like me, you see."

"Why didn't you warn me?"

"I didn't think . . ."

"You never do," said a stern voice. "You can start now while you are doing Peter Sam's work as well as your own. That'll teach you to pretend you are ill."

Sir Handel did start thinking. He thought about Thin Controllers, and he thought about Gordon. He wanted to give Gordon a piece of his mind!

Home at Last

PETER SAM wanted to start work; but the Thin Controller wouldn't let him. "Another day's rest will do you good," he said. "Besides, I've got a surprise for you."

"For me Sir! How nice Sir! What is it Sir?"

"Wait and see," smiled the Thin Controller.

The "Surprise" was Skarloey. "Oh!" said Peter Sam, "I am glad you've come home."

They lit Skarloey's fire, and he sizzled happily. "I feel all excited," he said, "just like a young engine. I'm longing to pull my dear old coaches again. Are they running nicely?"

"Yes, they're running well," Peter Sam answered, "but we have five other coaches now."

Skarloey was interested. "Oh!" he said, "tell me about them."

"Cora is a Guard's Van. She isn't as big as Beatrice, and she hasn't a Ticket Window, but I like her best. She was my Guard's Van in the old days. Ada, Jane and Mabel are plain. They have no roofs. Sir Handel says they are trucks; but they have seats," said Peter Sam, "so *I* say they're coaches. What do you think, Skarloey?"

The old engine smiled. "If they have seats, they're coaches," he said firmly.

"Sir Handel likes Gertrude and Millicent best," Peter Sam went on. "He always tries to take them alone. They have bogies, and he says they're the only real coaches we have. They remind him of when he used to pull our Express.

Both have seats for passengers, but Millicent has a Guard as well. He sells tickets and travels in a tiny cupboard place."

"I don't like that," he remarked earnestly. "Guards are very important. They need Vans. They shouldn't be put into cupboards."

Skarloey said nothing, so Peter Sam continued.

"Did Rusty help you off your truck?"

"Yes, he says he's come to mend the line and do odd jobs. I like him," smiled Skarloey.

"So do I." Peter Sam explained how kind Rusty was when he had his accident. "It's a pity Duncan doesn't like him."

"Who is Duncan?"

"He came as a spare engine after my accident."

"Is he Useful?"

"He'll pull anything, and I'm sure he means well: but he's bouncy and rude. He used to work in a factory, and his language is often strong."

"I understand," said Skarloey gravely.

Just then the telephone rang, and Skarloey's Driver and Fireman climbed into his cab.

"Come on, Old Boy," they said, "Duncan is stuck in the tunnel, and we'll have to get him out."

Skarloey was pleased. He wanted a run, and looked forward to meeting Duncan.

They found Cora and some workmen, and hurried up the line.

"How nice and smooth the rails are!" thought Skarloey. "They've mended all the old bumps. Rusty has helped to do that. I must tell him how nice it is."

Duncan had stuck at the far end of the tunnel. His coaches were outside, and the passengers were helping the Driver and Fireman to dislodge some rocks wedged between the top of his cab and the tunnel roof.

Duncan was cross. "I'm a plain blunt engine," he kept saying, "I speak as I find. Tunnels should be tunnels, and not rabbit holes. This Railway is no good at all."

"Don't be silly," snapped his Driver. "This tunnel is quite big enough for engines who don't want to Rock 'n' Roll."

They cleared away the rocks, and Skarloey pulled Duncan and his coaches safely through. Cora was left on a siding, and the workmen stayed to make sure all was safe.

Duncan grumbled all the way home, but Skarloey paid no attention.

The Thin Controller was waiting for them.

"Listen to me, Duncan," he said, "there is nothing wrong with that tunnel. You stuck because you tried to do Rock 'n' Roll. If it happens again, I'll cut down your cab, and your funnel too."

Duncan, abashed, was neither plain nor blunt for a whole evening.

Rock 'n' Roll

WHEN Skarloey's turn came, he was glad to take out the coaches and meet old friends. He met Rusty up the line. "You know," he said, "if I couldn't see the old places, I'd think I was on a different railway."

Rusty laughed. "We hoped you would. Mr Hugh, our Foreman, said 'Rusty, Skarloey's coming home. Let's mend the track so well that he won't know where he is!' And we did, and you didn't; if you take my meaning."

Skarloey chuckled away. He liked this hard-working, friendly little engine.

"There's still one bad bit," said Rusty anxiously that evening. "It's just before the first station. We hadn't time."

"Never mind!" said Skarloey. "It's much better now than it was."

"Maybe better; but it's not good," replied Rusty. "An engine might come off there. Peter Sam and Sir Handel take care, and so do you, but I'm worried about Duncan. He *will* do Rock 'n' Roll. I shouldn't like his passengers hurt."

"What's that about me? I'm a plain engine and believe in plain speaking. Speak up, and stop whispering in corners."

Rusty told Duncan about the bad bit of line, and warned him to be careful.

"Huh!" he grunted, "I know my way about, thank you! *I* don't need

smelly Diesels to tell me what to do."

Rusty looked hurt.

"Never mind," said Skarloey, "you've done your best." He said no more, but he thought a great deal.

Next morning Rusty left Duncan to find his own coaches. Duncan snorted and banged about the Yard, then clattered crossly to the station.

James was there already. "You're late," he snapped.

"I know," said Duncan, "it's that smelly Diesel's fault. He thinks he can teach me how to stay on the rails, and then goes off and leaves me to find my own coaches."

"You poor engine," sympathised James. "I know all about Diesels. One crept into our Yard, and ordered us about. *I* soon sent him packing."

Duncan gazed at him admiringly. He didn't know that James was boastful, and sometimes didn't tell the truth.

"Send him packing! Send him packing!" snorted Duncan. He climbed the first hill furiously.

"Well done, boy! Keep it up!" encouraged his Driver.

They were soon near the first station.

Duncan was pleased. "Nothing's happened! Nothing's happened!" he chortled. "Silly old Diesel! Clever me!" and he swaggered along doing his Rock 'n' Roll.

"Steady, boy!" his Driver tried to check him, but too late.

There was a tearing, cracking, crunching sound, and Duncan stopped bumpily.

"Sleepers and ballast!" he exclaimed. "I'm off!" And he was!

"I warned him," said Rusty crossly.

" 'Duncan,' I said, 'you be careful on that bit of line'; but all he did was to call me names."

Mr Hugh kept turning Rusty's handle.

"Come on!" he urged. "Start up."

"No, Mr Hugh Sir, I'm sorry to disoblige, but I *won't* help that Duncan."

"I'm ashamed of you, Rusty," said Skarloey severely, "think of the passengers. What are they going to do?"

"Oh!" said Rusty, "I'd forgotten them. I'm sorry, Mr Hugh Sir. We must help the passengers," and his engine roared into life.

"Oh dear!" thought Duncan, "now everyone will know how silly I am."

Presently Mr Hugh and Rusty brought sleepers and old rails. Mr Hugh showed the passengers how to use them, and they soon levered Duncan back to the line.

Duncan was extra careful all day.

"Rusty," he whispered that night, "thank you for helping. I'm sorry I was rude."

"That's all right."

"I wish all Diesels were like you. Let's be friends."

"Suits me," smiled Rusty. "We'll mend that bad bit first thing tomorrow."

Little Old Twins

ONE day the Owner brought some people to see the Railway. He showed them everything. They travelled in the trains, and looked at stations, and bridges, and coaches.

"Yes," they would say thoughtfully, "we'll take this"; or "No, we won't take that."

They made notes in their books.

Peter Sam whispered to Sir Handel. "Men came and did that on our old line."

"And then," said Sir Handel, "soon afterwards, it was . . . it was . . . "

"Sold," finished Peter Sam mournfully.

Peter Sam didn't sing any more. He wanted to cry. The other engines were sad too.

"What's the matter with you all?" his Driver asked him one day. "You look like dying ducks!"

"We don't want to be sold," said Peter Sam miserably.

"Sold!" the Driver was surprised. "Who to?"

"To those people who came and talked about taking things."

"You silly little engine," laughed his Driver. "They're not going to buy us. They're going to take our pictures on Television." And he tried to explain what that meant.

"Not going to be sold! Not going to be sold!" sang Peter Sam. He could hardly wait to tell the others. He told them about the Television as well, and they were pleased and excited too – all except Sir Handel.

"I don't hold with it," he grumbled. "Vulgar, I call it. Fancy traipsing about making an exhibition of yourselves. I won't do it, I tell you. Tellysomething indeed! Just let the Thin Controller come here, I'll tell him something!"

Skarloey said nothing. He just winked at Peter Sam – like this.

But next day, when the Thin Controller did come to explain about the Television, Sir Handel kept strangely quiet!

"Now," said the Thin Controller at last, "I want every engine to take part."

"I d-d-don't feel well," quavered Sir Handel.

"You poor engine," said the Thin Controller gravely, "you can stay in the Shed . . . "

Sir Handel smiled broadly!

". . . and your Driver and Fireman shall take you to pieces. That will make a very interesting picture. Just what we need."

Sir Handel's feelings were beyond words!

"That's that," said the Thin Controller.

"Now Skarloey, will you take Agnes, Ruth, Lucy, Jemima and Beatrice?"

"Yes please Sir. I was hoping you would let me have them."

"Duncan shall have a goods train, while Rusty, with Mr Hugh and the men, can show how we mend the line."

"Please Sir! What about me Sir?" asked Peter Sam anxiously.

The Thin Controller smiled. "You, Peter Sam, shall pull the special

Television train."

"Oh Sir! Oh Sir!" bubbled Peter Sam in ecstasy.

The Television men built towers for cameras beside the line. They put cameras on Ada too, and filled Gertrude with wires and instruments. Some trucks, coupled behind, carried aerials and generators.

Everyone practised hard till they knew just what they had to do.

At last the time came, and the Announcer gave the signal. "We're on the air! We're on the air!" puffed Peter Sam, and he rolled the heavy train to the "Shops", where Sir Handel was being mended.

Sir Handel did *not* enjoy their visit!

"We're on the air! We're on the air," chanted Peter Sam. He trundled over the bridge near the Middle Station. "Peep Peep!" he whistled to Duncan, "we're coming!"

The Announcer talked to Duncan, and then they puffed over the second bridge to Quarry Siding, where Rusty, Mr Hugh and the men were waiting to explain about their work.

Soon they had to go. Peter Sam whistled, Rusty tooted in reply, and they clattered through the tunnel, rumbled over the viaduct near the waterfall, and rolled at last into the Top Station.

The Owner climbed down. "We arranged for Television," he said, "to let everyone see our Little Old Engine. We are proud of him, 95 years old and good as new! There's nothing like him anywhere. Three cheers for Skarloey."

"Peep! Peep! Peep!" whistled Peter Sam, and everybody joined in.

Skarloey smiled. "I'm very glad to be home again. Thank you Sir, and all, for your nice surprise. Now I'll surprise you. Listen! When I was mended in England, I found my Twin!"

The Owner stared. "Is there really another engine like you?"

"Yes Sir," chuckled Skarloey, "there is. Another engine came to be mended too, called Talyllyn. When the workmen saw us together, they laughed and called us their 'little old twins'.

"Talyllyn told me about his Railway. It is a lovely one, at Towyn in Wales.

"Well Sir, they mended us both and sent us home; but I often think of Talyllyn. He's 95 years old too, just like me.

"Please go to see him, all of you, and wish him 'Dry rails and good running' from Skarloey, his 'Little Old Twin'."

We are indebted to John Adams (Publicity) Ltd for help in the preparation of the picture opposite.

THE RAILWAY SERIES NO. 15

The Twin Engines

THE REV. W. AWDRY

with illustrations by

JOHN T. KENNEY

DEAR FRIENDS,

The Fat Controller has just been having a Disturbing Time! He ordered one goods engine from Scotland, and was surprised to receive two!

They had both lost their numbers, and no one knew which was which. So he didn't know which engine to keep.

THE AUTHOR

'Hullo Twins!'

MORE and more people travelled on the Fat Controller's Railway. More and more ships came to the harbours. Everyone had to work very hard indeed.

The trucks complained bitterly; but then, trucks always do, and no one takes much notice.

The coaches complained too. No sooner had they arrived with one train, than they had to go out again with fresh passengers as another.

"We don't know whether we're coming or going," they protested. "We feel *quite* distracted."

"No one can say," grumbled Henry, "that we're afraid of hard work, but . . . "

". . . we draw the line at goods trains," finished Gordon.

"Dirty trucks, dirty sidings. Ugh!" put in James.

"What are you boiler-aching about?" asked Duck. "I remember on the Great Western . . ."

"That tin-pot railway . . ."

"Tin-pot indeed! Let me tell you . . . "

"Silence!" ordered a well-known voice. "Let me tell you that an engine for goods work will arrive from Scotland tomorrow."

The news was received with acclamation.

The Fat Controller stared. "Did you say *two* engines, Inspector?"

"Yes, Sir."

"Then send the other back at once."

"Certainly Sir, but which?"

The Fat Controller stared again. "Engines have numbers, Inspector," he explained patiently. "We bought No. 57646. Send the other one back."

"Quite so Sir, but there is a difficulty."

"What *do* you mean?"

"The two engines are exactly alike Sir, and have no numbers. They say they lost them on the way."

The Fat Controller seized his hat. "We'll soon settle that nonsense," he said grimly.

The two engines greeted him cheerfully.

"I hear you've lost your numbers," he said. "How did that happen?"

"They maun hae slyly slippit aff Sirr. Ye ken hoo it is." The engines spoke in chorus.

"I know. Accidentally on purpose."

The twins looked pained. "Sirr! Ye wadnae be thinkin' we lost them on purrpose?"

"I'm not so sure," said the Fat Controller. "Now then, which of you is 57646?"

"That, Sirr, is juist what we canna mind."

The Fat Controller looked at their solemn faces. He turned away.

He seemed to have difficulty with his own.

He swung round again. "What are your names?"

"Donal an' Douggie, Sirr."

"Good!" he said. "Then your Controller can tell me which of you is which."

"Och! Ye'll no get muckle help fae him, Sirr."

"Why?"

"He disna ken oor names Sirr. Hoo cud he? We only gien oorsels names when we lost oor nummers."

"One of you," said the Fat Controller, "is playing truant. I shall find him out and send him home. Inspector," he ordered, "give these engines numbers, and set them to work."

He walked sternly away.

The Missing Coach

SOON workmen came to give the twins their numbers. Donald was 9 and Douglas 10. When the men went away, they were left alone in the Shed.

"Ye may hae noticed, Douggie, that yon penters forgot somethin'."

"What did they forget?"

"They pented braw new nummers on oor tenders, but they put nane on uz." Donald winked broadly at his twin.

"Ye mean," grinned Douglas, "that we can . . ."

"Juist that," chuckled Donald. "Haud yer wheesht. Here's the Inspector."

"Now 9 and 10," smiled the Inspector, "here's Duck. He'll show you round before you start work."

The twins enjoyed themselves, and were soon friends with Duck. They didn't mind what they did. They tackled goods trains and coaches easily; for, once the twins had shunted them, trucks knew better than to try any tricks.

"We like it fine here," said Donald.

"That's good," smiled Duck, "but take my tip, watch out for Gordon, Henry and James. They're sure to try some nonsense."

"Dinna fash yersel," chuckled Douglas. "We'll suin settle them."

Donald and Douglas had deep-toned whistles.

"They sound like buses," said Gordon.

"Or ships," sniggered Henry.

"Tug-boat Annie!" laughed Gordon. "Ha! Ha!"

Donald and Douglas cruised quietly up, one on each side. "Ye wadnae be makkin' fun o' uz wad ye noo?" asked Donald.

Gordon and Henry jumped. They glanced nervously from side to side.

"Er, no," said Gordon.

"No, no, certainly not," said Henry.

"That's fine," said Douglas. "Noo juist mind the baith o' ye, and keep it that wey."

That was the way Gordon and Henry kept it!

Every day, punctually at 3.30, Gordon steams in with the Express. It is called "The Wild Nor' Wester", and is full of people from England, Wales, and Scotland. There is also a special coach for passengers travelling to places on Thomas' Branch Line.

When the other coaches are taken away empty, engines have to remember to shunt the special coach to the bay platform. It does not wait there long. Thomas, with Annie and Clarabel, comes hurrying from the junction to fetch it. Thomas is very proud of his Special Coach.

One afternoon Douglas helped Duck in the Yard while Donald waited to take a goods train to the other end of the line. As Duck was busy arranging Donald's trucks, Douglas offered to take away Gordon's coaches.

Douglas was enjoying himself, when an awful thought struck him. "I hope

the Fat Controller disna find oot I shudna be here. I cudna abide gooin' back." He worried so much over this that he forgot about Thomas' special coach.

He pushed it with the others into the carriage siding, then ambled along to join Donald at the water column. As he went, Thomas scampered by whistling cheerfully.

Soon Thomas came fussing. "Where's my coach?"

"Cooch?" asked Donald. "What cooch?"

"My special coach, that Gordon brings for me. It's gone. I must find it." He bustled away.

"Losh sakes!" said Douglas. "I maun hae stowed the special cooch wi the ithers."

"D'ye see that?" exclaimed Donald's Driver. A mob of angry passengers erupted from the siding. "They're complainin' tae the Fat Controller. He'll be comin' here next."

"Noo listen," said Douglas' Driver. We'll chainge tenders. Then awa' wi ye, Donal, an' tak yon Guids. Dinna fash aboot uz. Quick noo! Dae as I say."

The Fat Controller and three passengers walked towards them; but Donald, with Douglas' tender (10), was out and away with the Goods before they came near. Douglas and his Driver waited with innocent expressions.

"Ah!" said the Fat Controller, "No. 9, and why have you not taken the Goods?"

"My tender is awa' Sirr." The Driver showed him the tender, still uncoupled.

"I see, some defect no doubt. Tell me, why did No. 10 leave so quickly?"

"Mebbe Sirr," put in Douglas, "he saw ye comin' an' thocht he was late."

"Hm," said the Fat Controller.

He turned to the passengers. "Here, Gentlemen, are the facts. No. 10 has been shunting the Yard. Your coach disappeared. We investigate. No. 10 – er – disappears too. You can draw your conclusions. Please accept my apologies. The matter will be investigated. Good afternoon, Gentlemen."

The Fat Controller watched them till they climbed the station ramp. His shoulders twitched; he wiped his eyes. Douglas wondered if he was crying. He was not.

He swung round suddenly. "Douglas", he rapped, "why are you masquerading with Donald's tender?"

Break Van

THE Fat Controller scolded both engines severely.

"There must be no more tricks," he said. "I shall be watching you both. I have to decide which of you is to stay." He strode away.

The twins looked glum. Neither wanted to stay without the other. They said so.

"Then what is tae dae?" wondered Douglas.

"Och!" said Donald. "Each maun be aye guid as ither. Syne he'll hae tae keep uz baith."

Their plan was good; but they had reckoned without a spiteful Brake van.

The van had taken a dislike to Douglas. Things always went wrong when he had to take it out. Then his trains were late, and he was blamed. Douglas began to worry.

"Ye're a muckle nuisance," said Donald one day. "It's tae leave ye behind I'd be wantin'."

"You can't," said the van, "I'm essential."

"Och are ye?" Donald burst out. "Ye're naethin' but a screechin' an' a noise when a's said an' done. Spite Douggie wad ye? Tak that."

"Oh! Oh! Oh!" cried the van.

"Haud yer wheesht," said Donald severely. "There's mair comin' syne ye misbehave."

The van behaved better after that. Douglas' trains were punctual, and the twins felt happier.

Then Donald had an accident. He backed into a siding. The rails were slippery. He couldn't stop in time, and crashed through the buffers into a signal box.

One moment the Signalman was standing on the stairs; the next, he was sitting on the coal in Donald's tender. He was most annoyed.

"You clumsy great engine," he stormed, "now you must stay there. You've jammed my points. It serves you right for spoiling my nice new signal box."

The Fat Controller was cross too. "I am disappointed, Donald," he said. "I did not expect such – er – such clumsiness from you. I had decided to send Douglas back and keep you."

"I'm sorry, Sirr," but Donald didn't say what he was sorry for. We know, don't we?

"I should think so too," went on the Fat Controller indignantly. "You have upset my Arrangements. It is Most Inconvenient. Now James will have to help with the goods work, while you have your tender mended. James won't like that."

The Fat Controller was right. James grumbled dreadfully.

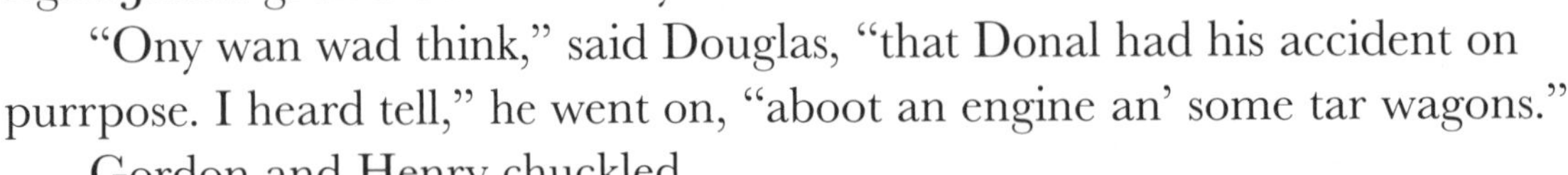

"Ony wan wad think," said Douglas, "that Donal had his accident on purrpose. I heard tell," he went on, "aboot an engine an' some tar wagons."

Gordon and Henry chuckled.

"Shut up!" said James. "It's not funny."

"Weel, weel, weel!" said Douglas innocently. "Shairly Jeames it wasna you? Ye dinna say!"

James didn't say. He was sulky next morning, and wouldn't steam properly. When at last he did start, he bumped the trucks hard.

"He's cross," sniggered the spiteful Brake van. "We'll try to make him crosser still!"

"Hold back!" whispered the van to the trucks.

"Hold back!" giggled the trucks to each other.

James did his best, but he was exhausted when they reached Edward's station. Luckily Douglas was there.

"Help me up the hill please," panted James. "These trucks are playing tricks."

"We'll show them," said Douglas grimly.

"ComeonComeonCOMEON," puffed James crossly.

"Get MOV-in' you! Get MOV-in' you!" puffed Douglas from behind.

Slowly but surely the snorting engines forced the unwilling trucks up the hill.

But James was losing steam. "I can't do it. I can't do it," he panted.

"LAE IT TAE ME! LAE IT TAE ME!" shouted Douglas. He pushed and he puffed so furiously that sparks leapt from his funnel.

"Ooer!" groaned the van. "I wish I'd never thought of this." It was squeezed between Douglas and the trucks. "Go on! Go on!" it screamed; but they took no notice.

The Guard was anxious. "Go steady!" he yelled to Douglas. "The van's breaking."

It was too late. The Guard jumped as the van collapsed. He landed safely on the side of the line.

"I might have known it would be Douglas!"

"I'm sorry Sirr. Mebbe I was clumsy, but I *wadna* be beaten by yon tricksie van."

"I see," said the Fat Controller.

Edward brought workmen to clear the mess.

"Douglas was grand Sir," he said. "James had no steam left, but Douglas worked hard enough for three. I heard him from my yard."

"Two would have been enough," said the Fat Controller drily. "I want to be fair, Douglas," he went on. "I admire your determination, but . . . I don't know, I really don't know."

He turned and walked thoughtfully away.

The Deputation

"HE'LL send uz awa' for shair, Donal."

"I'm thinkin' ye're richt there, Douggie. The luck's aye been agin uz. An engine disna ken what tae dae for the best."

Snow came early that year. It was heavier than usual. It stayed too, and choked the lines. Most engines hate snow. Donald and Douglas were used to it. They knew what to do. Their Drivers spoke to the Inspector, and they were soon coupled back to back, with a van between their tenders. Then, each with a snow plough on their fronts, they set to work.

They puffed busily backwards and forwards patrolling the line. Generally the snow slipped away easily, but sometimes they found deeper drifts.

Then they would charge them again and again, snorting, slipping, puffing, panting, till they had forced their way through.

Presently they came to a drift which was larger than most. They charged it, and were backing for another try. There was a feeble whistle, people waved and shouted.

"Losh sakes, Donal, it's Henry! Dinna fash yersel, Henry. Bide a wee. We'll hae ye oot!"

* * *

The Fat Controller was returning soon. The twins were glum. "He'll send uz back for shair," they said.

"It's a shame!" sympathised Percy.

"A lot of nonsense about a signal box," grumbled Gordon. "Too many of those, if you ask me."

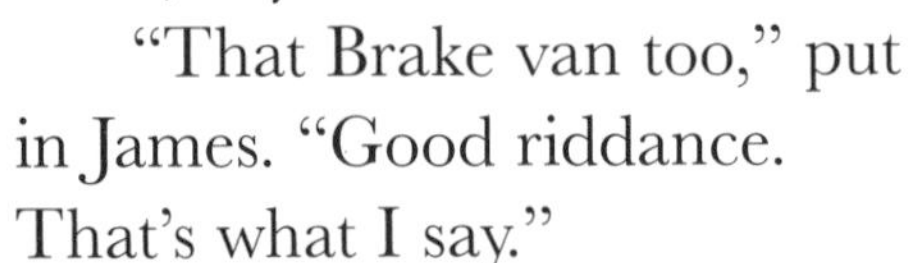

"That Brake van too," put in James. "Good riddance. That's what I say."

"They were splendid in the snow," added Henry. "It isn't fair." They all agreed that Something Must Be Done, but none knew what.

One day Percy talked to Edward about it.

"What you need," said Edward, "is a Deputation." He explained what that was.

Percy ran back quickly. "Edward says we need a Depotstation," he told the others.

"Of course," said Gordon, "the question is . . ."

" . . . what is a desperation?" asked Henry.

"It's when engines tell the Fat Controller something's wrong, and ask him to put it right."

"Did you say *tell* the Fat Controller?" asked Duck thoughtfully. There was a long silence.

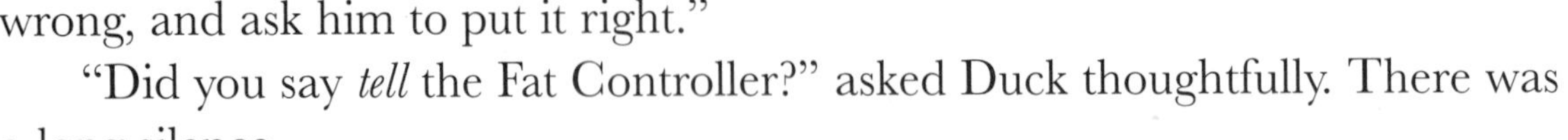

"I propose," said Gordon at last, "that Percy be our – er – hum – disputation."

"HI!" squeaked Percy. "I can't."

"Rubbish Percy," said Henry. "It's easy."

"That's settled then," said Gordon.

Poor Percy wished it wasn't!

"Hullo Percy! It's nice to be back."

Percy jumped. Some trucks went flying.

"Er y-y-yes Sir, please Sir."

"You look nervous, Percy. What's the matter?"

"Please Sir, they've made me a Desperation Sir. To Speak to You Sir. I don't like it Sir."

The Fat Controller pondered. "Do you mean a Deputation, Percy?" he asked.

"Yes Sir, please Sir. It's Donald and Douglas Sir. They say, Sir, that if you send them away, Sir, they'll be turned into Scrap, Sir. That'd be dreadful, Sir. Please Sir, don't send them away, Sir. They're nice engines, Sir."

"Thank you, Percy. That will do." He walked away.

"I had a – er – deputation yesterday," said the Fat Controller. "I understand your feelings but I do *not* approve of interference." He paused impressively. "Donald and Douglas, I hear that your work in the snow was good. What colour paint would you like?"

The twins were surprised. "Blue, Sirr, please."

"Very well. But your names will be painted on you. We'll have no more 'mistakes'."

"Thankye Sirr. Dis this mean that the baith o' uz . . . ?"

The Fat Controller smiled. "It means . . ."

But the rest of his speech was drowned in a delighted chorus of cheers and whistles.

THE RAILWAY SERIES NO. 16

Branch Line Engines

THE REV. W. AWDRY

with illustrations by

JOHN T. KENNEY

DEAR FRIENDS,

We never have a dull moment on our Branch Line. Thomas was silly and got into trouble, so a Diesel Rail-car called Daisy came. She caused trouble, but has now promised to be good, so the Fat Controller has kindly given her another chance.

Meanwhile Toby chased a bull, Percy got into a predicament and . . .

But you must read the stories for yourselves.

THE AUTHOR

Thomas Comes to Breakfast

THOMAS the Tank Engine has worked his Branch Line for many years. "You know just where to stop, Thomas!" laughed his Driver. "You could almost manage without me!"

Thomas had become conceited. He didn't realise his Driver was joking.

"Driver says I don't need him now," he told the others.

"Don't be so daft!" snorted Percy.

"I'd never go without *my* Driver," said Toby earnestly. "I'd be frightened."

"Pooh!" boasted Thomas. "I'm not scared."

"You'd never dare!"

"I would then. You'll see!"

It was dark next morning when the Firelighter came. Thomas drowsed comfortably as the warmth spread through his boiler. He woke again in daylight. Percy and Toby were still asleep. Thomas suddenly remembered. "Silly stick-in-the-muds," he chuckled. "I'll show them! Driver hasn't come yet, so here goes."

He cautiously tried first one piston, then the other. "They're moving! They're moving!" he whispered. "I'll just go out, then I'll stop and 'wheeeeesh'. That'll make them jump!"

Very, very quietly he headed for the door.

Thomas thought he was being clever; but really he was only moving because a careless cleaner had meddled with his controls. He soon found his mistake.

He tried to "wheeeeesh", but he couldn't. He tried to stop, but he couldn't. He just kept rolling along.

"The buffers will stop me," he thought hopefully, but that siding had no buffers. It just ended at the road.

Thomas' wheels left the rails and crunched the tarmac. "Horrors!" he exclaimed, and shut his eyes. He didn't dare look at what was coming next.

The Stationmaster's family were having breakfast. They were eating ham and eggs.

There was a crash – the house rocked – broken glass tinkled – plaster peppered their plates.

Thomas had collected a bush on his travels. He peered anxiously into the room through its leaves. He couldn't speak. The Stationmaster grimly strode out and shut off steam.

His wife picked up her plate. "You miserable engine," she scolded. "Just look what you've done to our breakfast! Now I shall have to cook some more." She banged the door. More plaster fell. This time, it fell on Thomas.

Thomas felt depressed. The plaster was tickly. He wanted to sneeze, but he didn't dare in case the house fell on him. Nobody came for a long time. Everyone was much too busy.

At last workmen propped up the house with strong poles. They laid rails through the garden, and Donald and Douglas, puffing hard, managed to haul Thomas back to the Yard.

His funnel was bent. Bits of fencing, the bush, and a broken window-frame festooned his front, which was badly twisted. He looked comic.

The Twins laughed and left him. He was in disgrace.

"You are a very naughty engine."

"I know, Sir. I'm sorry, Sir." Thomas' voice was muffled behind his bush.

"You must go to the Works, and have your front end mended. It will be a long job."

"Yes, Sir," faltered Thomas.

"Meanwhile," said the Fat Controller, "a Diesel Rail-car will do your work."

"A D-D-Diesel, Sir?" Thomas spluttered.

"Yes, Thomas. Diesels *always* stay in their sheds till they are wanted. Diesels *never* gallivant off to breakfast in Stationmasters' houses." The Fat Controller turned on his heel, and sternly walked away.

Daisy

THE Fat Controller stood on the platform. Percy and Toby watched him anxiously. "Here," he said, "is Daisy, the Diesel Rail-car who has come to help while Thomas is – er – indisposed."

"Please, Sir," asked Percy, "will she go, Sir, when Thomas comes back, Sir?"

"That depends," said the Fat Controller. "Meanwhile, however long she stays, I hope you will both make her welcome and comfortable."

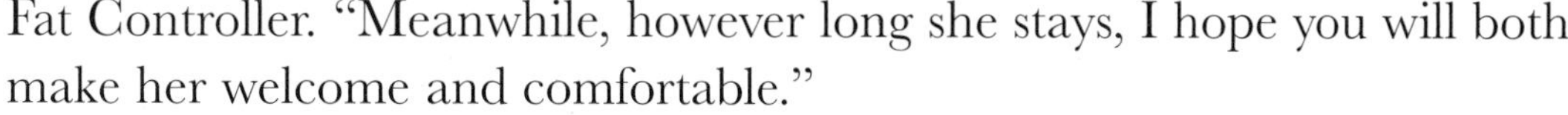

"Yes, Sir, we'll try, Sir," said the engines.

"Good. Run along now, and show her the Shed. She will want to rest after her journey."

Daisy was hard to please. She shuddered at the Engine Shed. "This is dreadfully smelly," she announced. "I'm highly sprung, and anything smelly is bad for my swerves."

They tried the Carriage Shed. "This is better," said Daisy, "but whatever is that rubbish?"

The "rubbish" turned out to be Annie, Clarabel, and Henrietta, who were most offended.

"We won't stay to be insulted," they fumed. Percy and Toby had to take them away, and spend half the night soothing their hurt feelings.

The engines woke next morning feeling exhausted.

Daisy, on the other hand, felt bright and cheerful. "Uu-ooo! Uu-ooo!" she

tooted as she came out of the Yard, and backed to the station.

"Look at me!" she purred to the waiting passengers. "I'm the latest Diesel, highly sprung and right up to date. You won't want Thomas' bumpy old Annie and Clarabel now."

The Passengers were interested. They climbed in and sat back comfortably, waiting for Daisy to start.

Every morning a van is coupled to Thomas' first train. The farmers send their milk to the station, and Thomas takes it down to the dairy.

Thomas never minds the extra load, but Daisy did. As soon as she saw that the van was to be coupled to her, she stopped purring. "Do they expect me to pull that?" she asked indignantly.

"Surely," said her Driver, "you can pull one van."

"I won't," said Daisy. "Percy can do it. He loves messing about with trucks."

She began to shudder violently.

"Nonsense," said her Driver. "Come on now, back down."

Daisy lurched backwards. She was so cross that she blew a fuse. "Told you," she said, and stopped.

The Shunter, the Guard, the Stationmaster, and her Driver all argued with her, but it was no use.

"It's Fitter's orders," she said.

"What is?"

"My Fitter's a very nice man. He is interested in my case. He comes every week, and examines me carefully. 'Daisy,' he says, 'never, never pull. You're highly sprung, and pulling is bad for your swerves.'

"So that's how it is," finished Daisy.

"Stuff and nonsense!" said the Stationmaster.

"I can't understand," said the Shunter, "whatever made the Fat Controller send us such a feeble . . ."

"F-f-f-feeble!" spluttered Daisy. "Let me . . ."

"Stop arguing," grumbled the passengers. "We're late already."

So they uncoupled the van, and Daisy purred away feeling very pleased with herself.

"That's a good story," she chuckled. "I'll do just what work I choose and no more."

But she said it to herself.

Bull's-eyes

TOBY the Tram Engine has cow-catchers and side-plates. They help to prevent animals getting hurt if they stray on to the line. Daisy thought they were silly. She said Toby was afraid of getting hurt himself.

"I'm not," said Toby indignantly.

"You are. *I've* not got stupid cow-catchers, but *I'm* not frightened. I'd just toot, and they'd all get out of the way."

"But they don't," said Toby simply.

"They would with me. Animals *always* run if you toot and look them in the eye."

"Even bulls?"

"Even bulls," said Daisy confidently.

Daisy had never met a bull, but she purred away quite unconcerned. At the level-crossing cars waited behind gates to let her pass. She tooted at a farm-crossing, and a horse and cart halted while she went by.

"Pooh!" she said. "It's easy. I just toot, and they all stand aside. Poor little Toby! I *am* sorry he's frightened."

At the next station, a policeman was waiting. "There's a bull on the line," he warned them. "Please drive it along towards the farmer."

Daisy was excited. "Now," she thought, "I'll show Toby how to manage bulls."

Champion wasn't really a fierce bull, but this morning he was cross. They had driven him away before he had finished breakfast, and tried to put him in

a cattle-float. They had pulled him and pushed him, prodded and slapped him, but he wouldn't go.

He broke away, and trotted down the road. He saw a fence, jumped it, and slithered down a slope.

Champion was surprised. This was a new kind of field. It had a brown track at the bottom, but there was plenty of grass on each side, and he was still hungry.

"Uuuu Oooo!" tooted Daisy. "Go on!"

Champion had his back to her. He was too busy to pay any attention.

"Uuuuuuu Ooooooo!" said Daisy again.

Champion went on eating.

"This is all wrong," thought Daisy. "How can I look him in the eye if he won't turn round? Uuuuuuuuuu Oooooooooo!"

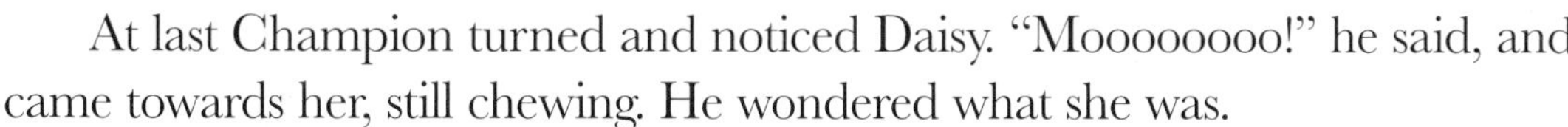

At last Champion turned and noticed Daisy. "Mooooooooo!" he said, and came towards her, still chewing. He wondered what she was.

"Uuu Ooo!" said Daisy feebly. "Why doesn't he run away?"

The Guard and the policeman tried to "shoo" Champion. But he wouldn't stay "shooed". As soon as they turned away, he came back. He was a most inquisitive animal.

"Go on, Daisy," said her Driver. "He's harmless."

"Yes," said Daisy unhappily. "*You*

know he's harmless, and *I* know he's harmless, but does *he* know? Besides, look at his horns. If I bumped into him he might hurt – er – them. The farmer wouldn't like that."

Champion came close, and sniffed at Daisy. "Oooof," she said, backing hastily.

Toby was surprised to find Daisy back once more at the station. The passengers told him about the bull. He chuckled.

"Bulls *always* run if you toot and look them in the eye. Eh Daisy?"

Daisy said nothing.

"Ah well!" Toby went on. "We live and learn. I'd better chase him for you, I suppose."

He clanked away.

But Champion took no notice of Toby's bell or whistle. He didn't move till Toby "hooshed" him with steam. Then Toby gently "shooed" him along the track to where the farmer and his men were waiting.

Daisy had an exhausting day. Toby and Percy often met her on their journeys, and though they never mentioned bulls, they gave her pitying looks. It made her so cross!

Her last journey ended at the Top Station. Some boys were on the platform. Suddenly one of them came running, holding a paper bag. "Look!" he shouted. "I've got a quarter of bull's-eyes. I think they're super, don't you?"

They shared the sweets and sucked happily.

"Grrrrrh!" said Daisy. "Keep your old bull's-eyes." She scuttled to her shed.

Percy's Predicament

TOBY brought Henrietta to the Top Station. Percy was grumpily shunting. "Hullo, Percy," he said, "I see Daisy's left the milk again."

"I'll have to make a special journey with it, I suppose," grumbled Percy. "Anyone would think I'd nothing to do."

Toby pondered the problem. "Tell you what," he said at last, "I'll take the milk; you fetch my trucks."

Their Drivers and the Stationmaster agreed, and both engines set off. They thought it would be a nice change.

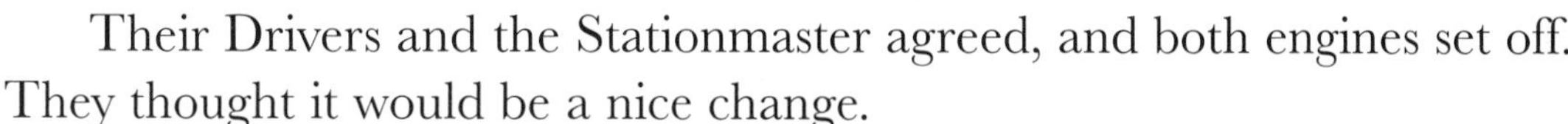

Percy trundled away to the Quarry. He had never been there before. "It's steep," he thought, "but I can manage. Trucks don't dare to play tricks on me now."

He marshalled them in a lordly way. "Hurry along there," he said, and bumped them if they dallied. The trucks were annoyed.

"This is Toby's place," they grumbled, "Percy's got no right to poke his funnel up here and push us around."

They whispered and passed the word.

"Pay Percy out!"

At last they were all arranged. "Come along," puffed Percy sharply. "No nonsense."

"We'll give him nonsense!" giggled the trucks, but they followed so quietly that Percy thought they were completely under control.

They rumbled along the twisty line till they saw ahead the notice saying ALL TRAINS STOP TO PIN DOWN BRAKES.

"Peep! Peep! Peep!" whistled Percy. "Brakes, Guard, please!" But before he could check them the trucks surged forward. "On! On!" they cried.

Percy, taken by surprise, could not stop them, and in a moment they were careering down the hill.

"Help! Help!" whistled Percy. The man on duty at the street-crossing rushed to warn traffic with his red flag, but was too late to switch Percy to the "runaway" siding.

A slow-moving cockerel lost his tail feathers as Percy thundered across, but Percy couldn't bother with him. He had other things to worry about.

Frantically trying to grip the rails, he slid past the Engine Shed into the Yard, "Peeep peeeeeeeep! Look out!" he whistled. His Driver and Fireman jumped clear. Percy shut his eyes and waited for the end.

At the end of the Yard there are sheds where workmen

shape rough stone brought from the Quarry. Then they load it into trucks, which are pulled to another siding out of the way. A train of these stood here when Percy came slithering down.

The Guard had left his van. He was talking to the Stationmaster. They heard frantic whistling and a splintering crash. They rushed from the office.

The brake van was in smithereens. Percy, still whistling fit to burst, was perched on a couple of trucks, while his own trucks were piled up behind him.

The Fat Controller arrived next day. Toby and Daisy had helped to remove most of the wreckage, but Percy still stood on his perch.

"We must now try," said the Fat Controller crossly, "to run the Branch Line with Toby and a Diesel. You have put us in an Awkward Predicament."

"I'm sorry, Sir."

"You can stay there," the Fat Controller went on, "till we are ready. Perhaps it will teach you to be careful with trucks."

Percy sighed. The trucks wobbled beneath his wheels. He quite understood about awkward predicaments.

The Fat Controller spoke severely to Daisy, too. "My engines do not tell lies," he said. "They work hard, with no shirking. I send lazy engines away."

Daisy was ashamed.

"However," he went on, "Toby says you worked hard yesterday after Percy's accident, so you shall have another chance."

"Thank you, Sir," said Daisy. "I *will* work hard, Sir. Toby says he'll help me."

"Excellent! What Toby doesn't know about Branch Line problems," the Fat Controller chuckled, "such as – er – bulls, isn't worth knowing. Our Toby's an Experienced Engine."

Thomas came back next day, and Percy was sent to be mended. Annie and Clarabel were delighted to see Thomas again, and he took them for a run at once because they hadn't been out while he was away.

Thomas, Toby, and Daisy are now all friends. Daisy often takes the milk for Thomas and when Toby is busy, she takes Henrietta.

Toby has taught Daisy a great deal. She "shooed" a cow off the line all by herself the other day!

That shows you, doesn't it?

THE RAILWAY SERIES NO. 17

Gallant Old Engine

THE REV. W. AWDRY

with illustrations by

JOHN T. KENNEY

DEAR FRIENDS,

On the second page of *Four Little Engines* Rheneas was taken away to be mended. He was away for a long time, but has now come home.

All the Little Engines are together at last. They are delighted. Rheneas is their hero. He had saved the Railway. . . .

There is a *real engine* like Rheneas. His name is Dolgoch and his home is at Towyn in Wales.

Some years ago *he* saved the Talyllyn Railway. We are proud of our gallant old engine.

THE AUTHOR

The author gratefully acknowledges the help given by fellow members of the Talyllyn Railway Preservation Society in the preparation of this book.

Special Funnel

PETER SAM'S funnel had never been quite the same since his accident with the slate trucks. Now, as he puffed up and down the line, the winter wind tugged at it, trying to blow it away.

"My funnel feels wobbly," he complained. "I wish the Thin Controller would hurry up with my new one. He says it will be 'Something Special!' "

"You and your special funnel!" said the other engines, and laughed.

They were all fond of Peter Sam; but he talked so much about his special funnel that it had become quite a joke.

The winter weather worried Mr Hugh. Wind broke branches from trees, while rain turned hillside streams into torrents which threatened to wash the line away.

Mr Hugh and the men patrolled the line every day with Rusty. They removed branches and cleared culverts so that the water could flow away. But one morning they found bad trouble.

A fresh torrent had broken out, and Mr Hugh had to stop all trains. "There's been a 'wash-out' near the tunnel," he said. "The track-bed is swept away."

The men worked hard and repaired the damage in a week. While they worked, the weather changed. It became frosty and very cold. They finished just in time for Market Day, and Peter Sam took the morning train very carefully over the mended piece of line.

The tunnel was short, but curved, so they could not see right through it. Suddenly the Driver shouted, "There's something hanging from the roof!" He braked. There was a clanging crash. When Peter Sam and his coaches stopped in the open air, he no longer had his funnel.

The Guard found the funnel and a thick icicle. "That's what hit you, Peter Sam," he said.

They started again, but the Passengers grumbled at the smoke, so when the Fireman saw an old drain-pipe, they stopped and wired it on.

The engines laughed and laughed when Peter Sam came home. Sir Handel made up a rhyme:

Peter Sam's said again and again,
His new funnel will put ours to shame,
He went into the tunnel,
And lost his old funnel,
Now his famous new funnel's a drain!

They teased Peter Sam dreadfully, but his new funnel arrived quite soon.

"Oh dear!" he said, "someone's squashed it."

The Thin Controller laughed. "It's a Giesl, the most

up-to-date funnel there is. Listen! When you puff, you draw air through your fire to make it burn brightly. With your old funnel puffing is hard work. It uses strength you need for pulling trains. Your new funnel has special pipes which help the air come easily. Puffing will be easier, so you will have more strength for your work."

"Yes, Sir," said Peter Sam doubtfully.

At first Peter Sam's special funnel was a great joke. Sir Handel and Duncan asked him why he had sat on it, and then hooted with laughter. But when Peter Sam started work it was a very different story.

Even Sir Handel was impressed. "I can't understand it," he said. "Peter Sam never seems to work hard. He just says 'Tshe, Tshe, Tshe, Tshe,' and simply strolls away with any train he's given. He makes it look so easy!"

They don't laugh at Peter Sam's funnel now. They wish they had one like it!

Steam-roller

SIR HANDEL kept slipping between the rails, so they gave him new wheels with broad tyres.

The other engines teased him. "Look at his 'steam-roller' wheels," they laughed.

"You shut up!" Sir Handel snorted. "You're jealous. My wheels are special, like Peter Sam's funnel. Now, I'll go faster than any of you."

"You'll never!" The engines were surprised. Sir Handel's trains were usually late.

Skarloey winked. "With your grand new wheels, Sir Handel," he said gravely, "you're just the engine to tackle George."

"Who's George?" Sir Handel asked.

While Sir Handel was in the Shed waiting for his new wheels, workmen had come to widen the road which ran for a mile or two beside the railway. They pulled down the wall, and nothing now protected the line.

George was their steam-roller. He chuffered to and fro, making rude remarks when the engines passed. "Railways are no good," he would say. "Pull 'em up. Turn 'em into roads."

Skarloey had often heard that talk before, and he warned the others to take no notice; but he hoped that, when the two boastful engines met, he and the others would have some fun!

"Don't worry any more," said Sir Handel importantly when they told him about George. "Leave him to me. I'll soon send him packing."

This story is adapted from an incident in *Narrow Gauge Album* by Mr P. B. Whitehouse. We gratefully acknowledge his permission to use it.

Next morning George was standing near the halt by the level crossing. "Huh!" he said. "You're Sir Handel, I suppose."

"And you, I suppose, are George. Yes, I've heard of you."

"And I've heard of you. You swank around with steam-roller wheels, pretending you're as good as me."

"Actually," said Sir Handel sweetly, "I'm better. Goodbye." He puffed away.

George chuffered, fuming.

One afternoon Sir Handel had to bring a special load down after the last train had gone. When he reached the road, he saw George trundling home.

"Peep-pip-peep!"

George took no notice. He trundled along close to the track. There was barely room to pass.

"Peeeep-pip-peeeeep!" Sir Handel slowed and crept cautiously alongside. "Get out of my way, you great clumsy road-hog," he hissed.

"I don't move for imitation steam-rollers," retorted George with spirit.

They lumbered along side by side, exchanging insults.

No one could ever explain what happened next. George's Driver says he signalled for Sir Handel to stop. Sir Handel's Driver says he signalled to George.

There was a crash. The brake van tilted sideways, and the Guard scrambled out to find George's front roller nuzzling his footboard. The two drivers were hotly arguing whose fault it was.

A policeman strolled up in time to stop the argument turning to fisticuffs, and when Sir Handel's Fireman came back with Rusty and Mr Hugh, they all set to work clearing up the mess.

Neither engine had been going fast enough to cause much damage. So Sir Handel was able to bring his train on when George had backed himself away.

Next day, the workmen put a fence between road and railway and then went away, taking George with them. This was because they had finished their work; but Sir Handel thought *he* had made George go away.

He was more conceited than ever, and talked everlastingly about steam-rollers.

"Oh dear!" whispered Skarloey one evening. "He's worse than ever. I'm sorry my plan was no good."

"Never mind," said Rusty. "We'll think of something else."

But they had no need to do that, for some boys came and asked Mr Hugh if they could look at the engines. Almost at once one called out, "Look! Here's Sir Handel. He raced a steam-roller last week. The Roller nearly beat him too. It was most exciting."

Sir Handel never mentions steam-rollers now!

Passengers and Polish

NANCY is a Guard's daughter. She was working on Skarloey with some polish and a rag.

"Wake up lazybones!" she said severely. "Your brass is filthy. Aren't you ashamed?"

"No," said Skarloey sleepily. "You're just an old fusspot. Go away!"

She tickled his nose. "Rheneas comes home tomorrow. Don't you want to look nice?"

Skarloey woke suddenly. "What! Tomorrow!"

"Yes, Daddy told me. I'm going now."

"Nancy, stop! Do I really look nice? Please polish me again. There's a good kind girl."

"Now who's an old fusspot?" laughed Nancy.

She gave him another rub, then climbed down.

"Aren't you going to polish me?" asked Duncan.

"Sorry, not today. I'm helping the Refreshment Lady this

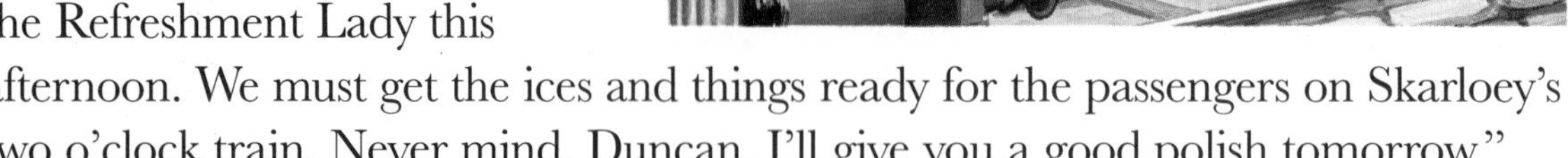

afternoon. We must get the ices and things ready for the passengers on Skarloey's two o'clock train. Never mind, Duncan, I'll give you a good polish tomorrow."

But Duncan did mind. "It isn't fair!" he complained. "Peter Sam gets a special funnel, Sir Handel gets special wheels, passengers get ices, and I'm never even polished."

This, of course, wasn't true; but Duncan liked having a grievance. He began to sulk.

That afternoon a message came from the Station by the Waterfall. "One of Skarloey's coaches has come off the rails. Please send some workmen to put it right."

Duncan was "in steam", so he had to go.

"All this extra work," he grumbled, "it wears an engine out!"

"Rubbish," said his Driver. "Come on!"

The derailed coach was in the middle of his train, so Skarloey had gone on to the Top Station with the front coaches. Duncan left the workmen, and brought the passengers in the rear coaches home. He sulked all the way.

He arrived back just in time for his own four o'clock train. "I get no rest! I get no rest!" he complained.

He was sulky and short of steam, so his Driver waited a few minutes in the hope of raising more; but Duncan wouldn't try.

"We can't keep the passengers waiting any longer," his Driver said at last.

"You always think about passengers," muttered Duncan crossly, "and never about *me*. I'm never even polished. I'm overworked, and I won't stand it."

He grumbled away, brooding over his "wrongs".

Duncan made "heavy weather" of the journey, but at last they reached the viaduct. This is long, high and narrow. No one can walk on it when a train is there.

"Come on, Duncan!" said his Driver. "One more effort, and you'll have a

rest and drink in the station."

"Keep your old station!" said Duncan rudely. "I'm staying here!"

He did too! He stopped his train right on the viaduct, and nothing his Driver or Fireman could do would make him move another yard.

Skarloey came from the Top Station to haul Duncan and his train to the platform. The passengers were very cross. They burst out of the train, and told the Drivers, the Firemen, and the Guard what a Bad Railway it was.

Skarloey had to pull the train to the Top Station, too. Duncan wouldn't even try.

The Thin Controller was waiting at the Shed for Duncan that evening. He spoke to him severely. But Duncan still stayed sulky. He muttered to himself, "No polish, no passengers," in an obstinate sort of voice.

Gallant Old Engine

"I'M ashamed of you, Duncan," said Skarloey, "You should think of your passengers."

"Passengers are just nuisances. They're always complaining."

Skarloey was shocked. "That's no way to talk," he said. "Passengers are our coal and water. No passengers means no trains. No trains means no Railway. Then we'd be on the scrap-heap, my engine, and don't you forget it. Thank goodness Rheneas is coming home. Perhaps he'll teach you sense before it's too late."

"What has Rheneas to do with it?"

"Rheneas saved our Railway," said Skarloey.

"Please tell us about it," begged Peter Sam.

"The year before you came," said the old engine, "things were very bad. We were on our last wheels. Mr Hugh was Driver and Fireman, while the Thin Controller was Guard. He did everything else too, *and* helped Mr Hugh mend us in the Shed.

" 'We expect two fresh engines next year,' they told us, 'but we *must* keep the trains going *now*; if we don't, our Railway will close.' "

"How awful!" said Peter Sam in sympathy.

"I tried hard, though I couldn't do much, but Rheneas understood. 'It's my turn now,' he said. 'You've done more than your share of hard work.' "

This story is adapted from an incident in *Railway Adventure* by Mr L. T. C. Rolt.
We gratefully acknowledge his permission to use it.

He was often short of steam, but he always tried to struggle to a station, and rest there. "That," said Skarloey earnestly, "is *most* important with passengers."

"Pshaw!" exclaimed Duncan.

"Passengers," Skarloey continued, "don't mind stopping at stations. They can get out and walk about. That's what stations are for. But they get very cross if we stop at wrong places like viaducts. Then they say we're a Bad Railway, and never come back.

"I remember Rheneas stopping in a wrong place once," said Skarloey. "He couldn't help it. But he made up for it afterwards.

"That afternoon he had damp rails and a full train. There were passengers even in Beatrice, the Guard's van. His wheels slipped dreadfully on the steep bit after the first station, but they gripped at last. 'The worst's over,' he thought. 'Now we're away.'

" 'Come along, come along,' he sang to the coaches. 'Come al —— Oooooh! I've got Cramp!' he groaned. He stopped, unable to move, on the loneliest part of the line.

"The Thin Controller and Mr Hugh examined him carefully. The passengers watched and waited. Rheneas eyed them anxiously. They looked cross.

"At last the Thin Controller stood up. 'Your valve gear on one side had jammed,' he said. 'We've unfastened the rods and tied them up. Now

Rheneas,' he went on, 'we need to reach the next station. Can you pull us there on one cylinder?'

" 'I'll try, Sir, but the next station isn't the right station. Will the passengers be cross?'

" 'Don't worry,' smiled the Thin Controller. 'They know we can't reach the Top Station today.'

"The Thin Controller sanded the rails, passengers from Beatrice pushed behind; Mr Hugh gently eased out the regulator. The train jerked and began to move.

" 'I'll . . . do . . . it! I'll . . . do . . . it!'

"Everyone cheered, but Rheneas heard nothing. 'The Thin Controller's relying on me. If I fail, the Railway will close. It mustn't! It mustn't! I'll get there or burst.'

"Everything blurred. He was too tired to move another yard; but he did! And another . . . and another . . . and another . . . till, 'I've got there at last,' he sighed with relief.

" 'It's proud of you I am indeed,' said Mr Hugh.

"All Rheneas remembered about the journey down was having to go on going on. At the Big Station the passengers thanked him. 'We expected a long walk,' they said, 'but you brought us home. We'll come again, and bring our friends.'

" 'You're a gallant little engine,' said the Thin Controller. 'When you're rested, we'll mend you ready for tomorrow.' "

"Was Rheneas always 'ready for tomorrow'?"

"Always," smiled Skarloey. "Whatever happened, Rheneas always pulled his trains."

It was Duncan who broke the silence. "Thank you for telling us about Rheneas," he said. "I was wrong. Passengers *are* important after all."

All the Little Engines were at the wharf on the day that Rheneas came home. Some of the Fat Controller's Engines were there too.

Edward pushed Rheneas' truck to the siding, and Skarloey pulled him neatly to his own rails. This was the signal for a chorus of whistles from engines large and small. You never heard such a noise in all your life!

The Owner, Rheneas, and other Important People made speeches, the Band played and everyone was very happy.

But Rheneas was happiest of all in his own place that night, next to his friend Skarloey. "This helps a little engine to feel," he said, "that, at last, he has really come home."

THE RAILWAY SERIES NO. 18

Stepney the "Bluebell" Engine

THE REV. W. AWDRY

with illustrations by

GUNVOR & PETER EDWARDS

DEAR READERS,

Percy is a kind-hearted little engine. He feels sad because many fine steam engines are cut up on the Other Railway (B.R.).

Percy's ideas, however, though natural for an engine, are a little muddled. British Railways Officials are *not* cruel. They are sad to lose faithful steam friends, and glad to help engines to go to places like the Bluebell Railway at Sheffield Park in Sussex, where they can be cared for, and useful, and safe.

THE AUTHOR

The author gratefully acknowledges the help given by fellow members of the Bluebell Railway Preservation Society, in the preparation of this book.

Bluebells of England

"The Bluebells are coming! Oho! Oho!
The Bluebells are coming! Oho! . . ."

"IF ye must sing, Percy," grumbled Douglas, "can't ye sing in tune? Anyway our song's aboot Campbells."

"And mine's about Bluebells."

"Then it's daft. Bluebells are flowers. Flowers can't come. They grow."

"My song isn't daft." Percy was indignant.

"It is then. I ken fine aboot bluebells. We've a song called 'The Bluebells of Scotland'."

"But," said Percy triumphantly, " 'The Bluebells of England' are different. They're engines, and one of them's coming with his Controller.

"Didn't you listen," he went on severely, "to the Fat Controller telling us about it?"

"I was away."

"Oh dear! I couldn't understand it all; but engines on the Other Railway aren't safe now. Their Controllers are cruel. They don't like engines any more. They put them on cold damp sidings, and then," Percy nearly sobbed, "they . . . they c-c-cut them up."

"Ye're right there," agreed Douglas. "If I hadn't escaped, I'd have been cut up too. It's all because of yon Diesels. They're all devils," he added fiercely.

"Fair play, Douglas," reminded Percy. "Some are nice. Look at Rusty and Daisy."

"Maybe so," answered Douglas, "I'd never trust one myself. But what I cannot understand is all your blether aboot bluebells."

" 'The Bluebells' are kind people who want to save engines. They've made a place in England called 'The Bluebell Railway'. Engines can escape there and be safe . . ."

"Like me winning away here?"

"Yes," Percy went on, "just like that. If they are old or ill, a Fitter makes them well. They can have their own special colours, all the coal and water they need, and pull trains too."

"That's braw hearing," said Douglas with feeling.

"The Fat Controller says Stepney was the first engine to escape there, so he's asked him to visit us and bring his Controller."

"But," objected Douglas, "how aboot yon Diesels? Mightn't they catch him on the way?"

"We thought so too," said Percy, "but the Fat Controller says there's no danger of that. Stepney's a match for any Diesel. Besides, his Controller will take care of him."

"He's a brave engine for all that," said Douglas admiringly. "Fancy fighting his way through all those Diesels just to see us."

"Look!" squeaked Percy. "The station's crowded."

"Silly! How can I look? Unless I'd be a cork-screw."

"Why've they all come? There's no train."

But Percy was wrong. The signal dropped, and from far away an engine whistled.

A gleam of yellow shone through the bridge girders. "Here he comes!" yelled Douglas.

"Poop! Poop! Peep! Peep!" the two engines whistled excitedly in welcome.

"Peeeep! Peeeeep!" replied Stepney, as with passengers and people waving and cheering, he puffed proudly through the junction on the last stage of his long journey.

Stepney's Special

" . . . SO I tried very hard, but I couldn't work properly, and they put me on a siding. I stayed there for days and days. Other engines were there too. I was afraid. . . ."

"I'd have been frightened too," said Edward.

"But then, some workmen came. They mended me and even gave me a coat of paint. I couldn't understand it till my Driver came. He was very pleased. 'Stepney, you lucky old engine,' he said, 'you've been saved! The Bluebell Railway has bought you!' "

"What a lovely surprise," smiled Edward.

"Have they saved other engines besides you?" he asked.

"Oh yes," answered Stepney. "You'd like our Bluebell and Primrose. They're twins," he chuckled, "and as like as two peas. They only had numbers at first, Bluebell is 323 and Primrose is 27. They were very pleased when our Controller gave them names. Some say he was wrong to do it. It's certainly made them cocky, but they do work hard, and I think our Controller was right. *All* engines ought to have names."

"Yes," agreed Edward, "it's *most* important."

"That's why," Stepney continued, "we've given names to our 488 and 2650. But our Controller doesn't know. It's a secret. Don't tell him, will you?"

"Of course not," smiled Edward.

"They are both very pleased about it, because now they feel part of the

family. We call 488 'Adams', after his designer, you know. He's a lovely engine, a South-Western from Devon. He can stroll away with any load he's given.

" 'Cromford', who's 2650, has been pulling trucks up high peaks in Derbyshire. He's tough is Cromford. He had to be for that job.

"Captain Baxter's tough, too,"

Stepney went on, "and rather rude. But he's worked in a quarry, and you know what *that* does to an engine's languages and manners."

"I do indeed," said Edward gravely.

"He's a good sort really," said Stepney. "I like him. We both miss our work with trucks."

He paused. "I oughtn't to say this," he went on, "after everyone's been so kind, but Our Line is very short, and I never get any good runs now. I miss them dreadfully."

"Never mind," smiled Edward. "Perhaps you'll get some while you're here."

Stepney said Goodbye to Edward and then returned to the Big Station. There he helped Duck shunt the Yard. They were soon great friends, and enjoyed their afternoon together.

Thomas arrived before they'd finished, and stayed till it was time for his last branch line train; but that train's tail lamps were hardly out of sight when the two engines heard a commotion at the station.

"Hullo!" said Duck, "I wonder what's up."

Presently the night-duty Shunter came hurrying to the Shed . . .

The bell in the cabin on the branch line rang once, then five, pause five. (That means shunt to allow following train to pass.) The Signalman was puzzled. He telephoned Control.

" . . . A Special is it? . . . I see. . . ."

Thomas and his passengers grumbled at being delayed, but there was no help for it. Soon they heard an unfamiliar puffing, "Express" headlamps swayed and twinkled, then Stepney, pulling one coach, loomed in the station lights. He slowed to exchange Tablets, whistled a greeting, then gathered speed into the night.

"Well! Bust my boiler!" said Thomas the Tank Engine.

"Shunted!" fumed Thomas next morning. "On my own Branch too! It's a disgrace!"

"I'm sorry," said Stepney. "I was a Special," he explained.

"Why?"

"An important passenger came after you'd gone. He said he *must* get home, and ordered a Special. Duck kindly let me take it. We had a splendid run. No record-breaking, of course, but . . ."

"Ah well," said Thomas modestly. "Perhaps when you know the road as I do . . ."

"Exactly," put in Stepney. "You're such an expert." Thomas, flattered, forgot he was cross, and told Stepney all about his Branch Line.

Train Stops Play

"YOU are very lucky engines," said Stepney.

"Your Branch has got everything. It's long enough to give you a good run, and you have plenty of passengers. Then you've a Quarry, a Mine and some Factories, so you need plenty of trucks. Trucks are fun," he went on wistfully, "I miss them on Our Line."

Percy looked surprised. "You can take mine and welcome, this morning," he said.

So they asked permission, and then went off to collect them. Toby and Thomas gaped in wonderment.

Stepney took his trucks to the harbour, picked up a load of empties, and started back.

On the way they were stopped by a signal near a cricket field, where a match had just started. They settled down to watch.

Presently some fielders came towards them, and waved. "Could you move, please?" they asked. "Your last few trucks are behind the bowler's arm."

"Sorry," smiled the Driver. "Will this do?" and he eased Stepney forward till he stood under the signal.

The cricketers shouted their thanks, and play started again. The batsmen hit out, and soon a "skyer" towered towards the train.

Clunk – down went the signal.

There was another clunk, too, as the ball fell on the train, but neither

Driver nor Fireman heard it. They were too busy.

"STOP!" yelled the fieldsmen; but Stepney's noisy starting drowned their shouts.

"Come along! Come along!" he puffed to the trucks, and left the frantic fieldsmen behind.

"Our one and only ball!" they said sadly.

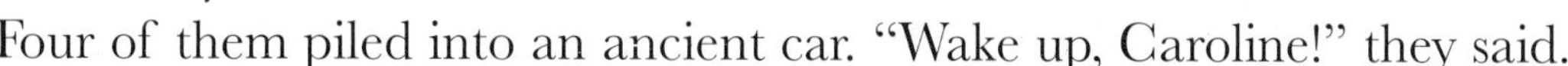

Four of them piled into an ancient car. "Wake up, Caroline!" they said.

Caroline coughed crossly, reluctantly came to life, and they rolled out on to the road.

Stepney wasn't hurrying. He had just crossed the river when Caroline came up behind.

"Tooooot! Tooooot!" she wailed.

Road and rail ran side by side. The cricketers waved and shouted, but they were too far away for the Fireman to recognize them or hear clearly what they said.

"If those jokers want a race," remarked the Driver, "they can have one." He advanced his regulator, and Stepney drew ahead.

Poor Caroline wasn't happy. She rattled along at twice her usual speed. "Master shouldn't treat me like this," she grumbled. "This pace is too hot for my system. It'll fuse all my circuits."

"Hurrah!" she exclaimed. "That silly train has run into a hole, so we can't catch it. Now Master will have to be sensible and go home."

But Master didn't go home.

Caroline nearly boiled with fury when he made her climb a steep hill and run down to the station on the other side.

Caroline arrived just as Stepney had shunted the trucks. His crew were going off duty. The cricketers explained what had happened.

The Driver and Fireman were surprised. "Did you say the third truck from the van?" they asked.

They all went and looked. The ball was there, nestling under some straw.

"We're very sorry," the Driver said.

"Never mind. You couldn't help it. Now we must get back quickly."

"That's just it," said the Driver. "You'll never be quick in Caroline. She looks worn out. . . . Wait a minute," he went on. "I've got a plan."

The Driver spoke to the Stationmaster and Signalman. Then they rolled Caroline on to a flat truck, and coupled a brake van behind. The cricketers got in, and Stepney pulled the train. They reached the field in no time.

Stepney watched from a siding while Driver, Fireman and Guard sat in the pavilion. There were no more lost balls, and the game was played to an exciting finish.

Even Caroline was pleased. She doesn't think trains silly now. "They have their uses," she says. "They can save the wear on a poor car's wheels."

Bowled Out

THE big Diesel surveyed the Shed. "Not bad," he said. "I've seen worse. At least you are all clean."

The engines gaped.

"It's not your fault," he went on, "but you're all out of date. Your Controller should scrap you, and get engines like me. A fill of oil, a touch on the starter, and I'm off, with no bother, no waiting. They have to fuss round you for hours before you're ready."

At last the engines found their voices. An Inspector had to come and stop the noise!

They held an indignation meeting early next morning round the turntable.

"Disgraceful!" rumbled Gordon.

"Disgusting!" said James.

"Despicable!" spluttered Henry.

"To say such things to us!" burst out Donald and Douglas. "It's to teach him a lesson we'd be wanting."

But no one had any good ideas, and at last they all went off to work except for Duck and Stepney. "Never mind," said Duck. "We'll be sure to think of something."

"We'll have to be quick then," warned Stepney.

But their chance came sooner than expected.

Diesel purred comfortably. He was being warmed up well before time. An Inspector watched a Fitter making adjustments. The wind tugged at the Inspector's hat.

The Fitter replaced the air-intake cover. "O.K., mate," he said.

Diesel saw his coaches waiting at the platform. He rolled proudly towards them. "Look at me, Duck and Stepney," he purred. "Now I'll show you something." He advanced a few yards, then suddenly he coughed – faltered – choked – and stopped.

The Inspector meanwhile had seen nothing of this. He was looking for his hat.

"Can we help you at all?" asked Duck and Stepney sweetly. Diesel seethed with baffled fury as they pushed him back to the Shed.

"My hat!" exclaimed the Inspector, as the cavalcade went by.

"Bother your hat!" said the Fat Controller crossly. "The train's due out in ten minutes, and you'll have to take it, Duck."

Duck looked doubtful, but when Stepney asked, "Can I help him, Sir?" he felt better. The Fat Controller was pleased too, and hurried away almost cheerfully to make the arrangements.

The engines and their crews made careful plans. "A good start's

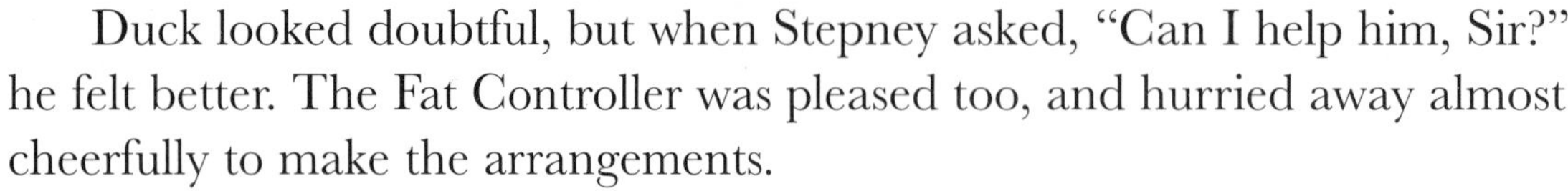

on a job like this," warned Stepney, so, as they backed down, they dropped sand on the rails, rolling it firm with their wheels.

Both Controllers were there to see them off. "Gordon will take over from half way," said the Fat Controller, "so get the train there. Never mind about being late. Good luck!"

"Don't worry, Sirs," smiled Stepney. "We'll get there, *and* be early too!"

They stood waiting, sizzling with excitement, ready and eager to be off.

At last the Guard's flag waved. The engines dug their wheels into the sand, and gave a mighty heave. "Come On! Come ON!" puffed Duck, while Stepney barked excitedly in front. Moving carefully over the points, they reached the open line.

"Now for a sprint," wuffed Stepney.

"I'm ready when you are," puffed Duck.

Faster and faster they went, till their wheels were turning at such speed that the side-rods were merely blurs. Under clear signals they whizzed through Edward's Station, and charged at Gordon's Hill beyond.

They felt the drag of their fifteen coaches here. It was hard work, but once over the top the last ten miles were plain running, and they swept into the Big Station in fine style.

"Hullo!" said Gordon. "You're early. That's one in the headlamp for old Diesel! Have you heard the latest?" he chuckled. "Diesel had sucked the Inspector's hat into his air-pipe. That's why he broke down. James says he's sick as boiler sludge, and sulking in the Shed. Out of date are we? Ho! Ho! Ho!" and still laughing, Gordon puffed away.

Everyone was sad next day when Stepney had to go. All the engines who could, came to see him off. The Fat Controller made a speech, and so did Stepney's Controller.

Donald and Douglas made everyone sing "Auld Lang Syne", and then Stepney and his Controller puffed off to a chorus of cheers and whistles.

"Goodbye, Stepney. Come again, Goodbye, Goodbye."

But what about Diesel? He'd slipped away the night before. He said Goodbye to no one, but left two things behind: the nasty smell of bad manners, and a battered bowler hat!

THE RAILWAY SERIES NO. 19

Mountain Engines

THE REV. W. AWDRY

with illustrations by

GUNVOR & PETER EDWARDS

DEAR FRIENDS,

A Rack Railway climbs the mountain called Culdee Fell. Lord Harry Barrane is Chairman of the Railway Company. Lots of people travel on it in the summer.

Mr Walter Richards, the Manager, does not have an easy time. There are seven engines, one of whom, No. 5, is still away being mended. Another, No. 6, was named Lord Harry. This was a mistake. It made him conceited and . . . But you must read the stories for yourselves.

I hope you will enjoy this book about a different kind of railway.

THE AUTHOR

The author gratefully acknowledges the help cheerfully and willingly given by members of management and staff of the Snowdon Mountain Railway Ltd, in the preparation of this book.

Mountain Engine

SIR HANDEL had had a bad day. The old coaches, Agnes, Ruth, Lucy, Jemima and Beatrice, had been "awkward". They had made him slip to a standstill twice. He was furious.

"Those cattle-trucks should be scrapped," he fumed.

Skarloey was shocked. "I won't have it," he protested. "Those old dears need kindness, not bad names."

"Exactly so," agreed Rheneas. He winked at Skarloey. "You be thankful, Sir Handel, that we're not a mountain railway."

"A mountain railway! What's that?"

"A railway which climbs mountains, of course."

"But it can't," said Sir Handel. "Its engines' wheels would slip!"

"But it can," said Rheneas firmly. "We've heard of one quite near here."

"It can't."

"It can."

A noisy argument started just as Donald shunted a flat truck to the siding nearby. On the truck was a queer-looking engine. He had six small wheels and a stove-pipe chimney. His boiler was tilted downwards, and his cylinders were "back to front".

'Wheesht!" whispered Donald hoarsely. "Dinna wake the wee engine. It's tired he is. He's away back from England after being mended. Ye ken how it is."

"We understand; but who is he?"

"He's called Culdee, after the mountain his railway climbs."

"Well! Did you ever . . . !" exclaimed the two old engines. They looked at Sir Handel and chuckled.

"I don't believe it!" said Sir Handel.

"Och, ye'd best ask him yeself. Then maybe ye'll learn it's the truth I've been telling ye."

Donald puffed away, offended.

Culdee woke to find the engines gazing at him. "Where am I?" he asked.

They told him. "That's good," he said. "I'm nearly home now."

"Do you really climb mountains?" asked Skarloey.

"I've done it for years."

"You *must* be clever. We couldn't. Our wheels would slip."

"I'm not really clever," laughed Culdee. "I was just drawn like that."

"Like what?"

"With pinion wheels on my driving axles. They have teeth, you see, which fit into a rack rail. I can't slip, however steep the line is."

"That," said Rheneas, "must help you going up; but if your line is so steep, aren't you frightened coming down?"

"Why? We have good brakes."

"Coaches," went on Rheneas, "are sometimes silly and try to push us downhill. Some . . . hrm . . . engines find it hard to stop them."

Sir Handel blushed and looked at his buffers.

"Our coaches," answered Culdee, "are never silly like that. They know such tricks are dangerous. I've never had that sort of accident. But," he went on thoughtfully, "I was frightened once – very frightened indeed."

"Please tell us," said all the engines.

"One day, long ago, before our line was opened, our drivers made all five of us engines stand ready outside our shed. 'The Inspector's coming,' they said. 'We don't know which of you he'll choose.'

"He chose me, climbed into my cab, and made me push two coaches to the Summit.

" 'So far, so good,' he said. 'Now, we'll test your brakes.'

"So he went and stood on the steepest part of the line. Down, down it fell, with a nasty curve below, edging a precipice.

" 'Brakes off, Driver. Let him roll.' "

"Oooh!" gasped the little engines in horror.

"The coaches nudged me. We gathered speed downhill. I was terrified . . .

"My Driver's hand stole to the brake. 'Hands off,' ordered the Inspector.

"Then I remembered I had automatic brakes. I could put these on myself. Perhaps the Inspector wanted to see if I could. They worked beautifully.

" 'Well done, Culdee,' said the Inspector. 'You'll do!'

"I smiled, of course, but felt *very* shaky. My Driver and Fireman mopped their faces. They'd been nervous too!

"I'm never nervous now," finished Culdee. "Why should I be? There's no need."

Bad Look-out

RHENEAS and Skarloey were talking quietly to Culdee next morning when Duncan stormed up, followed by Sir Handel.

"Hullo," chuckled Rheneas, "here we go!"

"I nearly came off," fumed Duncan. "Those coaches *pushed* me. The Thin Controller says they didn't. He says I kept a Bad Look-out.

" 'We've no money to mend you,' he said, 'and if it happens again I'll leave you at the back of the Shed.' Why does he always pick on me? It's not fair . . ."

Skarloey said nothing. He just winked at Rheneas like this.

"As you were saying, Culdee," remarked Rheneas. "You had two coaches on your trial trip. Do you ever take more?"

"No; our line is so steep that we're only allowed one. We each have our own. Mine's called Catherine. I know her well. That's most important."

"Why?" asked Sir Handel. "They're only coaches."

"Ours," said Culdee, "are something more. You pull your coaches, and you can see ahead. We *push* ours up, so we can't see. They watch the line for us. The Guard watches too, of course, but Catherine's so clever that I know at once if anything is wrong."

"That must take a load off your mind," said Skarloey.

Culdee smiled. "But not off my buffers! Climbing's hard work, and needs

a lot of steam. My Fireman and I have a tiring time. Coming down," he went on, "it's different. Catherine and I just roll. We need no steam for that."

Sir Handel sighed enviously. "I should like that," he said. "With your automatic brakes, it sounds like a Rest Cure."

"That," replied Culdee, "was just the mistake poor Godred made!"

"Who," asked the little engines, "is Godred?"

"Godred *was* our No. 1, and named after a king," Culdee replied. "Perhaps that went to his smokebox and made him conceited. He'd never keep a Good Look-out. He'd roll down the line looking anywhere but at the track.

" 'You'll have an accident,' I told him.

" 'Pooh!' he said. 'I've got automatic brakes, haven't I? And Driver's got his air brake. What more do you want?'

" 'More sense from you,' I said. 'No engine can stop at once if he isn't ready to obey his Driver's controls.' "

"The first thing a young engine learns," agreed Skarloey.

"Godred never learnt sense. His Driver and Fireman and the Manager all spoke to him. They even took him to pieces to see if anything was wrong; but he still went on in the same old way.

"One day I was going up, and waited at a station for Godred, coming down, to pass me. As I waited, so it happened. One moment he was on the

track; the next, his Driver and Fireman jumped clear as he rolled over.

"No one was hurt. His coach stayed on the rails, and the Guard braked her to a stop.

"They brought Godred home next day.

" 'We've no money to mend you,' said our Manager, 'so you'll go to the back of the Shed!'

"As time went on, poor Godred got smaller and smaller till nothing was left."

"Wha . . . what happened?" asked Duncan anxiously.

"It's not nice to talk about," said Culdee.

"But what *happened*? Why isn't it nice?"

"Our drivers used Godred's parts to mend us," answered Culdee mournfully.

Sir Handel and Duncan were unusually silent long after Culdee had gone home.

Neither Skarloey nor Rheneas ever mentioned that Culdee had made the story up.

Danger Points

DONALD brought Culdee up the valley to the exchange-siding, where he was soon off-loaded by crane.

His Driver and Fireman and the Manager were there. They all said "Goodbye" and "Thank you" to Donald. Then they lit Culdee's fire, and while waiting for the steam, they looked him over carefully.

"A very good job," they said at last.

Culdee sizzled happily. "It's lovely to be at home and in steam again," he said. "I'm longing to have a run with Catherine."

"Come on then," said his Driver, and they trundled to the Shed.

Catherine was pleased to see him, and they went for a short run. "I've had to go with Lord Harry lately," she said. "He takes risks and frightens me. When I warn him, he laughs."

"Never mind," comforted Culdee. "It'll be all right now."

Later, he met two old friends, Ernest (No. 2), and Wilfred (No. 3). After some happy gossip, Culdee asked, "Who is Lord Harry?"

"He's one of the new engines," they said, "who came while you were away. He's No. 6; Alaric and Eric are 7 and 8. They're nice quiet engines, but old Harry's a 'terror'."

Next afternoon, Lord Harry rolled by with a reluctant coach, on his way to the platform.

"Stupid things," he grumbled. "They're all scared of coming with me."

"You're too reckless," said Culdee. "That's why."

"Rubbish! I'm up-to-date, that's all. I can go twice your speed in perfect safety."

"All the same, we don't take such risks on mountain railways."

"There's no risk. Why, with my superheat . . ."

"Oh!" interrupted Culdee, "it's superheat, is it? I'd have said it was conceit, myself."

Lord Harry snorted furiously away.

"Ooooh!" screamed the coach as her wheels ground on the curves. "Be careful!"

"Pooh!" snorted Lord Harry. "I like things to be exciting."

Every wise mountain engine knows that you do not take risks, and that points *must* be taken slowly; for there, the rack rail can have no guards.

"Steady boy! Steady!" warned his Driver; but Lord Harry paid no attention. He was thinking what he'd say to Culdee next time they met. "There's no danger," he boasted, storming up the final slope. "That patched-up old ruin was talking nonsense."

The telephone rang in the Shed, and Culdee's crew were joined by the Manager. "Lord Harry's 'off' at the Summit," he said. "We shall have to go and put things right."

So they collected some workmen and the tool-van, and set out at once.

It was getting dark when they arrived. Lord Harry's shape loomed against the sky. He had come off at the points and blocked both roads of the station. Wilfred was there with his coach, unable to start his journey down. The passengers buzzed round Lord Harry like angry bees. He was feeling harassed!

The Manager pacified the passengers, while Culdee buffered up behind to take the strain when the men levered the engine's front wheels on to the rails.

"Wilfred," he called, "who is this wreck?"

"It's Lord Harry; didn't you know?"

"It looks like Old Harry; it's fat as Old Harry, but of course it can't be Old Harry."

"Why ever not?"

"You see, Old Harry's an up-to-date engine. He can go twice our speed in perfect safety."

"Tee hee hee!" tittered the coaches.

Lord Harry seethed in silence.

They pushed Lord Harry out of the way, and took the passengers home. Then Culdee helped him back to the Shed.

"It was that coach, Sir," blustered Lord Harry. "She never . . ."

"No tales," said the Manager sharply. "It was your fault, and you know it. You upset our passengers and damaged yourself by taking risks. We cannot have that on our Mountain Railway."

"But, Sir . . ."

"That's enough. You will stay in the Shed till we have decided what to do with you."

He turned, and walked sternly away.

"Devil's Back"

AS a punishment, they took Lord Harry's name away, and put him at the back of the Shed. He soon heard Culdee's story about Godred.

"Pooh!" he said. "That couldn't happen to me." But he was anxious all the same.

"Please, Sir, I'm sorry. I'll try to be different."

"The passengers don't trust you," said the Manager. "You will take the 'Truck' instead."

So No. 6 took supplies to Summit Hotel, and he took gangers to work in the morning and brought them home in the evening. He found it dull, and grumbled.

"It's important work," protested Wilfred, "and tough, too."

"Tough! That little lot?"

"Yes, tough," said Culdee. "Have you ever been across Devil's Back in a gale?"

"No," said No. 6 thoughtfully, "but I see what you mean."

A mile below Summit, the line runs along a rocky ridge. Always there is wind. Sometimes it is gentle; at others it is fierce and very dangerous. Then all passenger trains stop at Devil's Back Station, but whatever the weather, stores trains and rescue trains *must* get through.

A few days later, No. 6 reached Devil's Back at 5.15. He was on his way, with the Truck, to fetch railway staff from Summit.

"All clear now," said the Stationmaster, as the last "down" train left the loop. "Don't waste time. The wind's rising. We'll have a gale in half an hour."

He went inside to set the points, but the telephone rang and he came out looking worried. "There's trouble," he told the crew. "Come in and discuss it out of the wind."

They filled the Truck's big tank with water, and sandbags ballasted the van. The wind whistled round them as they worked.

"What is all this?" asked No. 6.

"There's been a climbing accident," explained his Driver. "Culdee and Catherine are bringing up a Doctor and a Rescue Team, but Catherine's too light to stand this gale, so we'll go up ourselves. The water and the sandbags will steady us if you can keep going, we have a good chance of getting through. Can you do it?"

"I'll have a jolly good try," said No. 6.

When Culdee arrived, the Doctor and the Rescue Team changed trains. The Manager was there too. "Splendid!" he said, when he saw the preparations. "Now, No. 6, it's up to you."

The Guard signalled the Driver, and they were off.

"A real job at last," crowed No. 6 exultantly. "Now I'll show them! Now I'll show them . . ." Leaving the shelter of the station, the full force of the gale struck him like a blow.

Culdee and Catherine saw him waver. "Go it! Go it!" they yelled.

No. 6 heard them for a moment; the next, he was battling on alone.

He didn't feel so brave now. All he wanted was to get out of the vicious, stinging, icy wind which seemed to come at him from all directions.

The Truck lurched and swayed as the wind tore at it. It whimpered and groaned as though in pain.

"She wants to go back," thought No. 6. "And so do I; but we can't. The Manager's relying on me to save those climbers. We must go through – we must! We must!"

Slowly, doggedly he struggled on, till in shelter, again on the other side, they climbed the final steep ascent, and rolled triumphant into Summit Station.

They brought the climbers safely down, and an ambulance whisked them to hospital. Next morning, their leader came to say "Thank you".

"My friend Patrick," he said, "hurt himself helping me, but he's mending now, thanks to you and your brave engine. We'd all be proud if you'd call him Patrick, too."

The Manager smiled. "Well, No. 6, would you like that?" he asked?

"Oh, Sir! Yes, please."

Patrick and the others are all good friends. He is still brave, still ready to take risks when needed, but he knows now that it is stupid to take them just for the sake of showing off!

THE RAILWAY SERIES NO. 20

Very Old Engines

THE REV. W. AWDRY

with illustrations by

GUNVOR & PETER EDWARDS

DEAR FRIENDS,

One hundred years ago, when Skarloey and Rheneas first arrived on their railway, they were young and silly. Skarloey was sulky and bouncy. He and Rheneas quarrelled. . . . But they learned sense, and the Owner has just given them a lovely 100th birthday.

Talyllyn and Dolgoch, at Towyn, are 100 too.

How about going to wish them "Many Happy Returns"?

THE AUTHOR

The author gratefully acknowledges the help given by fellow members of the Talyllyn Railway Preservation Society in the preparation of this book.

Crosspatch

SKARLOEY made a face. "Not again, Nancy, *please*."

"Just a teeny polish," she coaxed. "You must look nice for your 100th birthday."

"I *am* nice. You're just a fusspot."

"And you're a horrid old crosspatch." Nancy polished him vigorously.

Skarloey smiled. "Nancy," he said, "I really was a crosspatch once. Shall I tell you?"

"Yes, please."

"Well, come down. I can't tell it properly while you're fussing up there."

"Just five minutes then; no longer." Nancy sat down on a box, and the old engine began.

"Talyllyn, Dolgoch, Rheneas and I, were built together in England."

"Who," asked Nancy, "are Talyllyn and Dolgoch?"

"Talyllyn is my twin; Dolgoch is Rheneas'. Their Railway is at Towyn in Wales, and they're 100 too. They were green, and we were red. Talyllyn and I had four wheels then, and no cab. We thought we were wonderful, and talked about how splendid we'd look pulling coaches."

"What about trucks?" asked Nancy.

Skarloey chuckled. "We had no use for *them*," he said.

"I was finished first, and sent away on a ship. I didn't like that. It wobbled dreadfully. At the port the Big Railway kept me waiting. They had no cranes to lift me out. It wasn't the Fat Controller's Railway then. He would have managed much better."

"What did they do?" asked Nancy.

"They used the ship's derricks. They nearly turned me upside down," said Skarloey indignantly, "and left me hanging while they arranged the truck."

"You must have looked funny," gurgled Nancy.

"Yes, and I felt it too! I got crosser and crosser.

"They fastened me to the truck at last, and an engine took me away. His name was Neil – he was ugly but kind, and we were soon friends.

" 'So ye're bound for the Wee Railway,' he said. 'Ye must put some order into those trucks. The havers they make, ye'd hairdly believe.'

"I didn't like the sound of that. But I was too tired to say anything.

"Plenty of people were waiting when we got there, but they weren't used to engines, and it was dark before I was on my rails.

"Then they left me, lonely and unhappy, and wishing Rheneas would come.

"Trucks were everywhere next morning. Suddenly, with a rattle and a roar, a train of loaded ones came in. I was surprised. 'There's no engine!' I said.

"A workman laughed. 'They've come down by gravity,' he said. 'The empty ones need pulling up, though. That's why *you've* come.'

" 'But can't they go up by gra-whatever-it-was-you-said?'

" 'Gravity only brings things down. We need horses, or engines like you to pull them up.'

" 'What! Have *I* to pull *trucks*?'

" 'Of course.'

" 'I won't! I want coaches.'

"He just laughed and walked away.

"Soon, Mr Mack, the Manager, arrived with some men. He showed them my parts from a book. 'We're going to steam you, Skarloey,' he said.

" 'Can I pull coaches, Sir?'

" 'No, certainly not!'

"I gave him such a look!

"They didn't understand engines, so it was easy! My fire wouldn't burn, and I made no steam. I just blew smoke at them! They called me bad names, but I didn't care.

"Next day they tried again, and the next, and the next. I just gave them my Look, and wouldn't do a thing!

"At last the Manager said, 'Very well, *be* a crosspatch; but we're not going to look at your sulky face all day. We'll cover you up and leave you till you're a better engine.'

"They did, too," chuckled Skarloey. "They fetched a big tarpaulin, and covered me right up. I didn't like that at all!"

"I think it served you right," said Nancy severely.

"Never mind her, Skarloey. Please tell us what happened next."

Nancy turned in surprise. A group of people had quietly come up to listen while Skarloey was telling her his story.

Bucking Bronco

"I WAS lonely and miserable," Skarloey continued, "till at last the Manager came.

" 'I hope, now, that you're a better engine . . .'

" 'Yes, Sir, please, Sir.'

" '. . . Because I've asked Mr Bobbie to come and look after you.'

"Mr Bobbie had helped to build me in England. I liked him, so we soon had steam up.

" 'Come on, Skarloey!' he said. 'We must help the workmen finish the line before the Inspector comes.'

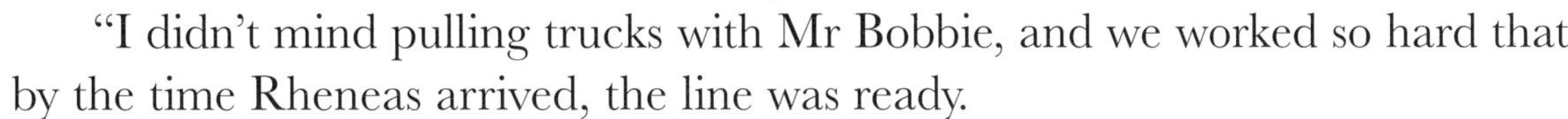

"I didn't mind pulling trucks with Mr Bobbie, and we worked so hard that by the time Rheneas arrived, the line was ready.

"Rheneas never got so excited and bouncy as I did. He worked without hurry or fuss. Trucks often played tricks on me to make me cross, but they soon found that teasing Rheneas was a mistake!

"He was shunting one day when I came alongside. I was excited. 'I'm pulling the Directors' train,' I said, 'and taking the Inspector tomorrow. Think of that!'

"Rheneas pondered. 'You mind your bucks and bounces, then, Skarloey,' he said at last. 'The Directors won't like them.'

" 'Pooh!' I snorted, and bounced away to fetch the coaches.

" 'Peep peep!' I whistled. 'Hullo, girls!'

" 'Who is it?' Agnes' deep voice echoed from the back of the Shed.

" 'It's an engine,' whispered Beatrice, the Guard's Van. 'He's come to take us out.'

" 'Beware of Strange Engines!' warned Agnes. 'We must be On Our Guard.'

" 'Our Guard has just come,' giggled Beatrice. Jemima and Ruth, the other coaches, sighed with relief.

"I pulled them all happily to the station. Agnes, still suspicious, kept muttering, 'Be On Your Guard. Be On Your Guard.' But I was too excited to listen. It might have been better if I had.

"I was sizzling with excitement as I ran round and backed down on Agnes. 'It's fun! It's fun!' I chortled.

" 'You may *look* harmless,' she whispered, 'but we'll watch you! We'll watch you!'

"She took me quite aback.

"But even Agnes couldn't complain about our upward journey. We stopped at every station, and the Directors got out to admire the arrangements. Everything went well, I forgot about Agnes; and the Manager, smiling, joined us on the footplate for the journey home.

" 'It looks so easy, Mr Bobbie,' he said, as we rolled gently down. 'Can I drive him, please?'

"We were running nicely. 'First rate! First rate!' I hissed happily, gaining speed, and, all unknowing, I began to bounce.

"The Manager, alarmed, closed my regulator – too quickly, and too much.

"Agnes' buffers clashed. 'He's — playing — tricks! Bump — him — girls, bump — him!'

"They surged against me, urging me on. I bounced and lurched. I couldn't help it.

"The Manager lost his footing, grabbed wildly for a handhold, and disappeared.

" 'Peep! peep! peeeeep! Brakes, Guard, please!' Mr Bobbie seized my controls, stopped the train and looked back.

"Two legs waved wildly from a bush.

"The Manager was unhurt, but very cross. 'I'll not ride *that* bucking bronco again,' he said. He sat in Beatrice for the rest of the journey.

"The Directors complained they'd been badly shaken. They said it was my fault. 'Rheneas will take the Inspector tomorrow,' they ordered. 'You will stay out of sight in the Shed.'

"But, late that evening, the Manager came.

" 'I'm sorry, Sir, I did *try* to be good.'

" 'It wasn't your fault, Skarloey. I'm sorry I was cross. We must do what the Directors say now, but I'll make it up to you later.'

"The Inspector was pleased with Rheneas. 'You've done very well,' he said kindly, 'for a new engine.'

"He told the Directors about some improvements which were needed. 'But,' he went on, 'on the whole, your arrangements are good.'

"He came to see me, and the Directors told him what they thought had happened.

" 'I think, gentlemen,' he said, 'that you are mistaken. Skarloey should

prove to be a Useful Engine, but he needs another pair of wheels. Take my advice, and have them fitted. Then, you'll see the difference. Good day.' "

Stick-in-the-Mud

"THE Manager was as good as his word,' Skarloey continued. "I came home from the Works with six wheels and a cab.

" 'A cab is the latest thing for engines,' he told me. 'I hope it will cheer you up after your disappointment.' "

Rheneas chuckled. "It cheered him too much! And those silly coaches made him worse. 'Such a handsome engine!' they tittered. 'Six wheels and a *cab – so* distinguished, my dears! It's a pleasure to see him.' He soon got too big for his wheels."

Skarloey smiled ruefully. "I did, too," he said. "Go on, Rheneas."

"He boasted about his cab till I was tired," said Rheneas.

" 'You should get one like me, and be up-to-date,' he would say.

" 'No thank you! You look like a snail with that house on your back. You don't go much faster, either.'

" 'Slow, am I? Let me tell you . . .'

" 'Who was late three times last week?'

" 'Oh, it's no use talking. You're just an old stick-in-the-mud.'

"He called me more names, and we quarrelled. We ended up back to back – not speaking. It went on for days and days.

"One dark Monday morning, Skarloey had to take the workmen's train to the Quarry. It had rained for three days. 'You always pick on me for wet

days,' he complained.

" 'You,' said Mr Bobbie, 'have got a cab to keep us dry. Come on!'

"Skarloey slipped and snorted on the damp rails. He began to wonder if cabs were worth it.

"An hour later, I was warming up when Skarloey's Guard came coasting down in an empty truck. He stopped by our shed.

" 'There's a landslide beyond the tunnel,' he said. 'Skarloey's run into it. He's stuck.'

" 'Show a wheel, Rheneas – look lively!'

" 'I'm sorry Mr Peter, Sir, but that Skarloey's too swanky. He says I'm a stick-in-the-mud. He can jolly well stick in the mud himself. It serves him right.'

" 'But,' went on my Driver, 'there's poor Mr Bobbie, and the quarrymen. Does it serve them right too? The Guard says the mud's like treacle . . .'

" 'Oh dear!' I said. 'That will never do. We must save them before they get sucked in.'

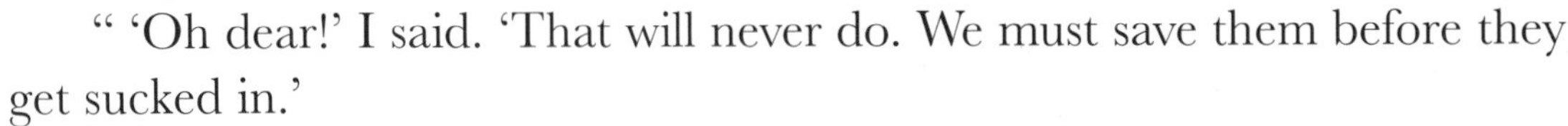

"And off we puffed with two trucks and some workmen.

"Things weren't too bad after all. The men had partly cleared the line, and had levered Skarloey back. He was hissing and grumbling dreadfully, but we didn't listen to him.

"We cleared the rest of the line, and I pushed Skarloey out of the way before taking the quarrymen to work.

"Mr Bobbie cleaned and oiled his wheels and motion so that when I

returned with the coaches I could help him back to the Shed.

" 'I'm sorry I was swanky,' he said, at last. 'Thank you for helping me.'

" 'Not at all,' I said, but I was still cross.

"Then Skarloey began to laugh. 'I'm the stick-in-the-mud after all,' he gurgled helplessly, 'not you!' I laughed too, I couldn't help it, he looked so funny. We were laughing when the cleaners came; we were still laughing when they left. 'Poor engines!' they said, tapping their foreheads; but we weren't mad. We'd learned sense, and we've been firm friends ever since."

It was nearly dark. The listeners stirred and stretched. "Thank you, Skarloey and Rheneas," they said. "Now you've told us about the 'old days', we can give you both a splendid birthday next week."

Duck and Dukes

". . . BUT I keep telling you," said Duck. "There *are* no Dukes. They were fine and stately, but they've all been scrapped."

Peter Sam goggled in horror. "This is dreadful," he wailed. "The Thin Controller said the Owner said the Duke said he was coming to our Centenary to open our extension round the lake, and now he's scrapped and Skarloey's and Rheneas' birthday will be spoilt. Oh dear! Oh dear!"

He bustled away with his empty coaches to tell his bad news.

"I think," said Skarloey, "that Duck was pulling your wheels."

"No, Skarloey, he was quite serious."

"He always jokes like that," chuckled Skarloey, but no one agreed, and they argued so loudly that the Thin Controller came to stop their noise. They told him about Duck, but he paid no attention. "I've no time for his nonsense now," he snapped. "There's a change in tomorrow's work. Skarloey, you will meet the Duke at 11.0 instead of 10.30." And he hurried away.

"If there *is* a Duke," said Duncan, but they were all too tired to argue any more.

They spent a gloomy night, but cheered up next morning when the cleaners greeted the birthday engines with an "All-metal Band". Drivers and Firemen joined in, and even the Thin Controller banged a metal plate as loudly as anyone. The engines punctuated the "music" with their whistles.

The Owner laughed and held his ears. Presently he looked at his watch. "That's enough," he ordered, so Rusty, Sir Handel and Duncan went at once to find their coaches.

Visitors crowded the Big Station. They wanted to go to places along the line to watch the celebrations.

Peter Sam and Rheneas had carefully practised their parts. Passengers in Agnes, Ruth, Lucy, Jemima and Beatrice all wore clothes of 1865. Rheneas had to pull them behind Peter Sam's Television train, not too close and not too far away, so that the cameramen could take their pictures.

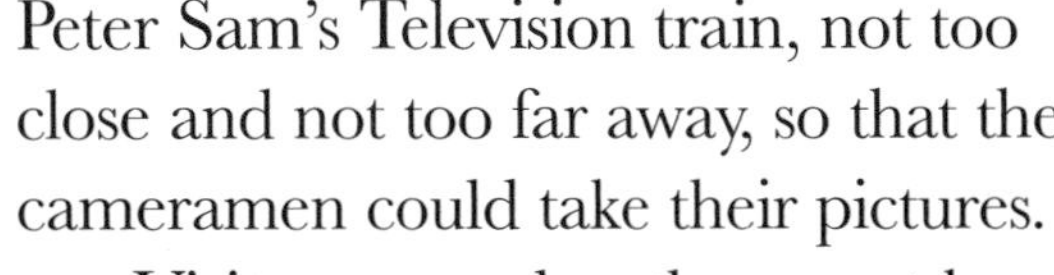

Visitors waved as they went by, and at last they reached the special sidings near the extension, where they settled down to wait. "Listen!" said Peter Sam at last. "Here's Skarloey; they're cheering him."

"Good!" answered Rheneas. "Perhaps that will make up for his disappointment over the Duke."

Skarloey wasn't disappointed at all. "I've brought the Duke! I've brought the Duke! I've brought the Duke! I've brought the Duke!" he puffed, and triumphantly came to a stand between the two trains.

A distinguished-looking man stepped out, climbed to Skarloey's footplate, and drove him on the new line round the lake and back again.

Then, standing on Skarloey's front bufferbeam, he said, "Ladies, Gentlemen, and Engines, I have pleasure in declaring your lovely lakeside loopline now open . . ."

Peter Sam could bear it no longer. "Excuse me, Sir Duke," he burst out. "Are you real?"

There was shocked silence.

The Duke smiled. "Skarloey said you'd been listening to Duck," he answered. "Duck thinks Dukes were Great Western engines, but Dukes are really people. I am happy to assure you, Peter Sam, that I am a real live Duke."

"I'll give Duck 'Dukes'!" muttered Peter Sam, but he was sternly hushed!

The Duke turned to the Owner. "I congratulate you, Sir, on your remarkable Railway. It must be a record indeed to have two locomotives in regular service, and both a hundred years old. Long life, then, and good running to Skarloey and Rheneas, your famous old engines."

The cheering and clapping died away. "Speech!" shouted someone, and the cry was taken up. "Go on, Rheneas," whispered the Owner, so rather nervously the old engine began.

"Thank you, your Grace, and everyone, for your kind wishes. You've given us both a lovely 100th birthday; but, your Grace, Skarloey and I aren't the only 'record' engines. We've got twin brothers. Talyllyn and Dolgoch were built at the same time as us, so they are 100 too, *and* they're still at work. Their Railway's at Towyn, in Wales. Please go and see them, your Grace, and everybody, and wish them Many Happy Returns from Skarloey and Rheneas, their 'Little Old Twins'."

THE RAILWAY SERIES NO. 21

Main Line Engines

THE REV. W. AWDRY

with illustrations by

PETER AND GUNVOR EDWARDS

DEAR FRIENDS,

Bill and Ben are a shameless pair. I meant to write about Main Line Engines, and give the twins a treat by letting them into the first story. But I couldn't keep them in order! Before I knew it they had crept into the others. They even wanted me to change the book and make it about them!

But I have been very firm. I am *still* calling it Main Line Engines. That will serve Bill and Ben right for ragging poor Gordon so disgracefully.

He hasn't got over it yet!

THE AUTHOR

The Diseasel

BILL and Ben are Tank Engines who live at a port on Edward's line. Each has four wheels, a tiny chimney and dome, and a small squat cab.

They are kept busy pulling trucks for ships in the harbour and engines on the Main Line.

The trucks are filled with China Clay dug from the nearby hills. China Clay is important. It is needed for pottery, paper, paint, plastics, and many other things.

One morning they arranged some trucks and went away for more. They returned to find them all gone.

They were most surprised.

Their Drivers examined a patch of oil. "That's a diesel," they said, wiping the rails clean.

"It's a what'll?" asked Bill.

"A diseasel, I think," replied Ben. "There's a notice about them in our shed."

"I remember, 'Coughs and sneezles spread diseasels.' "

"Who had a cough in his smokebox yesterday?"

"Fireman cleaned it, didn't he?"

"Yes, but the dust made him sneezle: so there you are. It's *your* fault the diseasel came."

"It isn't!"

"It is!"

"Stop arguing, you two," laughed their Drivers.

"Come on! Let's go and rescue our trucks."

Bill and Ben were aghast. "But he'll magic us away like the trucks."

Their Drivers laughed. "He won't magic us; we'll more likely magic him! Listen. He doesn't know you're twins; so we'll take your names and numbers off and then this is what we'll do . . ."

Bill and Ben chuckled with delight. "Come on! Let's go!" they said eagerly.

Creeping into Edward's Yard they found the diesel on a siding with the missing trucks. Ben hid behind, but Bill went boldly alongside and stood facing the diesel on the points leading out to the Main Line.

The diesel looked up. "Do you mind?" he asked.

"Yes," said Bill, "I do. I want my trucks please."

"These are mine," said the diesel. "Go away."

Bill pretended to be frightened. "You're a big bully," he whimpered. "You'll be sorry."

He moved over the points, ran back, and hid behind the trucks on the other side.

Ben now came forward. The diesel had to stop suddenly.

"Truck stealer," hissed Ben. He ran away too, and Bill took his place.

This went on and on till the diesel's eyes nearly popped out.

"Stop!" he begged. "You're making me giddy!"

The two engines gazed at him side by side. He shut his eyes. "Are there

two of you?" he whispered?

"Yes, we're twins."

"I might have known it," he groaned.

Just then, Edward bustled up. "Bill and Ben, why are you playing here?"

"We're *not* playing," protested Bill.

"We're rescuing trucks," squeaked Ben.

"What do you mean?"

"Even *you* don't come in our yard without asking."

"And you only take the trucks we give you."

"But," they both squeaked indignantly, "this diseasel didn't even ask. He just took the lot!"

"There is no cause to be rude," said Edward severely. "This engine is a 'Metropolitan-Vickers, diesel-electric, Type 2.' "

The twins were abashed. "We're sorry Mr – er . . ."

"Never mind," he smiled, "call me BoCo. I'm sorry I didn't understand about the trucks."

"That's all right then," said Edward. "Off you go, Bill and Ben. Fetch BoCo's trucks, then you can take these."

The twins scampered away. Edward smiled.

"There's no real harm in them," he said, "but they're maddening at times."

BoCo chuckled. "Maddening," he said, "is the word."

Buzz Buzz

BoCo reached the Big Station and arranged his trucks. Then he went to the Shed, and asked politely if he could come in.

Duck was not pleased to see a diesel but, presently, when he found that BoCo knew Edward, he became more friendly. And by the time BoCo had told him about Bill and Ben they were laughing together like old friends.

"Have they ever played tricks on *you*?" asked BoCo.

"Goodness me! Yes!" chuckled Duck. "Edward is the only one who can keep them in order."

"You know," went on Duck, "I sometimes call them 'The Bees'."

"A good name," chuckled BoCo. "They're terrors when they start buzzing round."

Just then James bustled in. "What's that, Duck? Are you terrified of bees? They're only insects after all: so don't let that buzz-box diesel tell you different."

"His name is BoCo, and he didn't. We . . . "

"I wouldn't care," interrupted James, "if hundreds were swarming round. I'd just blow smoke and make them buzz off."

"Buzz Buzz Buzz," retorted Duck.

James retired into a huff.

James was to pull the Express next morning, and when Duck brought his coaches the platform was crowded.

"Mind your backs! MIND YOUR BACKS!" Two porters were taking a loaded trolley to the front van. Fred drove, while Bert walked behind.

"Careful, Fred! Careful!" warned Bert, but Fred was in a hurry and didn't listen.

Suddenly an old lady appeared in front.

Fred stopped dead, but the luggage slid forward and burst the lid of a large white wooden box.

Some bees flew out, and, just as James came backing down, they began to explore the station.

Someone shouted a warning. The platform cleared like magic.

The bees were too sleepy to be cross. They found the empty station cold. James' Fireman was trying to couple the train. They buzzed round him hopefully. They wanted him to mend their hive. Then they could go back and be warm again.

But the Fireman didn't understand. He thought they would sting him.

He gave a yell, ran back to the cab and crouched with his jacket over his head.

The Driver didn't understand either. He swatted at the bees with the shovel.

The bees, disappointed, turned their attention to James.

James' boiler was nice and warm. The bees swarmed round it happily.

"Buzz off! Buzz off!" he hissed. He made smoke, but the wind blew it away, and the bees stayed.

At last one settled on his hot smokebox. It burnt its feet. The bee thought James had stung it on purpose. It stung James back – right on the nose!

"Eeeeeeeeeeeeee!" whistled James. He had had enough: so had his Driver and Fireman. They started without waiting for the Guard's whistle.

They didn't notice till too late, that they'd left their train behind.

In the end it was BoCo who pulled the Express. He was worried at first about leaving his trucks, but Duck promised to look after them and so it was arranged. He managed to gain back some of the lost time, and the Fat Controller was pleased with him.

No one seemed to notice when James came back to the Shed. They were talking about a new kind of beehive on wheels. It was red, they said. Then they all said "Buzz, buzz, buzz," and laughed a lot.

James thought that for big Main Line Engines they were being very silly.

Wrong Road

THOMAS' Branch Line is important, and so is Edward's. They both bring in valuable traffic, but their track and bridges are not so strong as those on the Main.

That is why the Fat Controller does not allow the heavier Main Line Engines such as Gordon and Henry to run on them.

If, however, you had heard Gordon talking to Edward a short while ago, you would have thought that the Fat Controller had forbidden him to run on Branch Lines for quite another reason.

"It's not fair," grumbled Gordon.

"What isn't fair?" asked Edward.

"Letting Branch Line diesels pull Main Line trains."

"Never mind, Gordon. I'm sure BoCo will let you pull his trucks sometimes. That would make it quite fair."

Gordon spluttered furiously. "I *won't* pull BoCo's dirty trucks. I *won't* run on Branch Lines."

"Why not? It would be a nice change."

"The Fat Controller would never approve," said Gordon loftily. "Branch Lines are vulgar."

He puffed away in a dignified manner. Edward chuckled and followed him to the station . . .

Gordon, his Driver and his Fireman all say it was the lady's fault. She wore a green floppy hat, and was saying "Goodbye" to a friend sitting in the coach nearest the Guard's Van.

It was almost time to start. The Fireman looked back. He was new to the job. He couldn't see the Guard but he did see something green waving. He thought it was the flag.

"Right away, Mate," he called.

But the Guard had not waved his flag. When Gordon started he left some luggage, several indignant passengers and the Guard all standing on the platform.

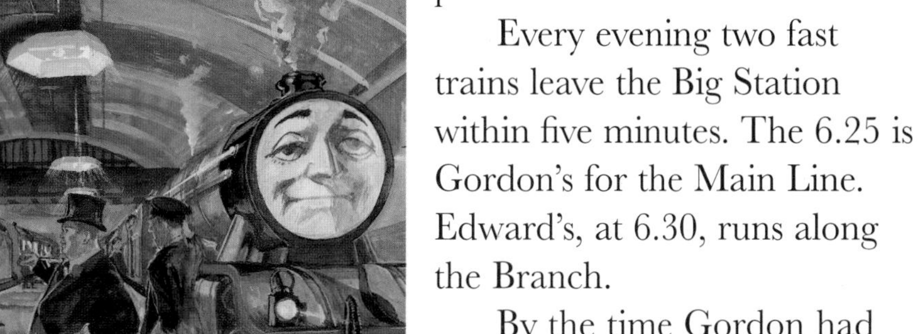

Every evening two fast trains leave the Big Station within five minutes. The 6.25 is Gordon's for the Main Line. Edward's, at 6.30, runs along the Branch.

By the time Gordon had been brought back, Edward's train was overdue.

"You've missed your 'path', Gordon," said the Fat Controller, crossly. "Now we must clear Edward's train before you can start."

This should have put everything right with the least possible trouble; but Control at the Big Station made things worse. They forgot to warn the Signalman at Edward's Junction about the change of plan.

It was dark by the time the trains reached the junction, and you can guess what happened – Edward went through on the Main, while Gordon was switched to the Branch . . .

It took the Fat Controller several hours to sort out the tangle and pacify the passengers.

In the end Gordon was left, with his fire drawn, cold and cross on one of Edward's sidings.

Bill and Ben peeped into the Yard next morning. They wondered if BoCo had brought them some trucks. There were no trucks, but they didn't mind that.

Teasing Gordon, they thought, would be much better fun!

"What's that?" asked Bill loudly.

"Ssh!" whispered Ben. "It's Gordon."

"It *looks* like Gordon, but it can't be. Gordon *never* comes on Branch Lines. He thinks them vulgar."

Gordon pretended he hadn't heard.

"If it isn't Gordon," said Ben, "it's just a pile of old iron . . . "

". . . which we'd better take to the scrapyard."

"No, Bill, this lot's useless for scrap. We'll take it to the harbour and dump it in the sea."

Gordon was alarmed. "I *am* Gordon. Stop! Stop!"

The twins paid no attention. Gordon shut his eyes and prepared for the worst.

The twins argued loudly and long. Bill favoured the scrapyard, while Ben said that the cutting up in such places was something cruel.

It would be kinder, he urged, to give these remains a quick end in the sea.

Besides, he went on, they would make a lovely splash.

Gordon could not view either prospect with any enthusiasm.

Up to that time he had disapproved of diesels.

They were, he considered, ugly, smelly, and noisy; but when he opened his eyes and saw BoCo coming into the Yard, he thought him the most beautiful sight he had ever seen.

"BoCo my dear engine!" he gasped. "Save me!"

BoCo quickly sized up the situation, and sent Bill and Ben about their business.

They were cheeky at first, but BoCo threatened to take away the trucks of coal he had brought for them. That made them behave at once.

Gordon thought he was wonderful. "Those little demons!" he said. "How do you do it?"

"Ah well," said BoCo. "It's just a knack."

Gordon thinks to this day that BoCo saved his life; but we know that the twins were only teasing – don't we?

Edward's Exploit

EDWARD scolded the twins severely, but told Gordon it served him right. Gordon was furious.

A few days later, some Enthusiasts came. On their last afternoon they went to the China Clay Works.

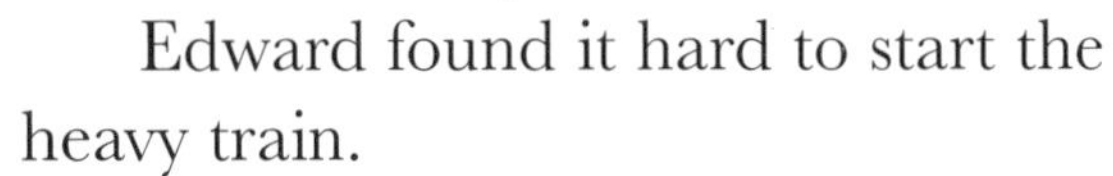

Edward found it hard to start the heavy train.

"Did you see him straining?" asked Henry.

"Positively painful," remarked James.

"Just pathetic," grunted Gordon. "He should give up and be Preserved before it's too late."

"Shut up!" burst out Duck. "You're all jealous. Edward's better than any of you."

"You're right, Duck," said BoCo. "Edward's old, but he'll surprise us all."

Bill and Ben were delighted with their visitors. They loved being photographed and took the party to the Workings in a "Brake Van Special".

On the way home, however, the weather changed. Wind and rain buffeted Edward. His sanding gear failed, his wheels slipped, and his Fireman rode in front dropping sand on the rails by hand.

"ComeOn-ComeOn-ComeOn," panted Edward breathlessly. "This is dreadful!"

But there was worse to come. Before his Driver could check them, his wheels slipped fiercely again and again.

With a shrieking crack, something broke and battered his frame and splashers up and out of shape.

The passengers gathered round while the crew inspected the damage. Repairs took some time.

"One of your crank-pins broke, Edward," said his Driver at last. "We've taken your side-rods off. Now you're a 'single' like an old fashioned engine. Can you get these people home? They must start back tonight."

"I'll try, Sir," promised Edward.

They backed down to where the line was more nearly level. Edward puffed and pulled his hardest, but his wheels kept slipping and he just could not start the heavy train.

The passengers were getting anxious.

Driver, Fireman and Guard went along the train making adjustments between the coaches.

"We've loosened the couplings, Edward," they said. "Now you can pick your coaches up one by one, just as you do with trucks."

"That will be much easier," said Edward gratefully.

So, with the Fireman sanding carefully in front, the Driver gently opened the regulator.

Come . . . on! puffed Edward. He moved cautiously forward, ready to take the strain as his tender coupling tightened against the weight of the first coach.

The first coach moving, helped to start the second, the second helped the third, and so on down the train.

"I've done it! I've done it!" puffed Edward, his wheels spinning with excitement.

"Steady, Boy!" warned his Driver, skilfully checking the wheel-slip. "Well done, Boy!"

"You've got them! You've *got* them!" And he listened happily to Edward's steady beat as he forged slowly but surely up the hill.

The passengers were thrilled. Most had their heads out of windows. They waved and shouted, cheering Edward on.

The Fat Controller paced the platform. Henry with the Special train waited anxiously too.

They heard a "Peep peep!" Then, battered, weary, but unbeaten, Edward steamed in.

The Fat Controller stepped angrily forward. He pointed to the clock, but excited passengers swept him aside. They cheered Edward, his Driver and Fireman to the echo, before rushing off to get in Henry's train.

Henry steamed away to another storm of cheers, but not before everyone knew Edward's story.

Edward went thankfully to the Shed, while Duck and BoCo saw to it that he was left in peace. Gordon and James remained respectfully silent.

The Fat Controller asked BoCo to look after Edward's line while he was being mended. BoCo was pleased. He worked well, and now they run it together. Bill and Ben still tease him, but BoCo doesn't mind.

He lives at Edward's station, but is welcome anywhere, for he is now one of the "family".

Donald and Douglas were the last to accept him, but he often helps with their goods trains, and the other day they were heard to remark, "For a diesel, yon BoCo's nae sich a bad sort of engine."

That, from the Caledonian Twins, is high praise indeed!

THE RAILWAY SERIES NO. 22

Small Railway Engines

THE REV. W. AWDRY

with illustrations by

PETER AND GUNVOR EDWARDS

DEAR FRIENDS,

Some leadmines up in the hills have long been closed, but their waste-heaps still spoil a lovely valley.

The Fat Controller has now found that the waste is good weed-killing railway ballast. He talked to the Owner and the Thin Controller of the Skarloey Railway, and other important people. They "went shares" and built a Small Railway to fetch it away.

The Small Engines are managed by a Controller. They call him the Small Controller; but that is only in fun. He is bigger than either of the others!

THE AUTHOR

The author gratefully acknowledges the help given by fellow members of the Ravenglass and Eskdale Railway Preservation Society in the preparation of this book.

Ballast

THE Fat Controller's Railway has a new look. From end to end they are clearing old ballast from the track and packing the sleepers with fresh stones. The gangers are pleased. "Weeds don't grow in it," they say; and even James has stopped grumbling about dirty sidings!

Douglas and Donald disappeared regularly behind the Big Station, along a line on which none of the others had ever gone. They returned with loaded ballast trains, and were most mysterious about it.

"Verra wee engines bring the ballast doun fra the hills," was all they would say.

Soon the engines could talk of nothing else. James and Henry thought the "Verra wee engines" must be some kind of magic.

"I don't believe it," said Gordon. "Donald and Douglas have pulled our wheels before."

But Duck wanted to see for himself, so he asked permission to take some trucks. When he arrived, he was told to push them under the "chute". This was like a tunnel made of steel girders. On top of it stood some queer-looking trucks.

"What d'you think of our 'chute'?" said a voice. "Good, isn't it?"

Duck blinked. Standing beside him was a small green engine.

"Where did you spring from?" asked Duck.

"I've been here all the time," smiled the small engine. "I'm Rex, and you,

I'm sure, are Duck."

"How *did* you know?"

"That's easy; there's only one Great Western engine in these parts."

There was a sudden rattling and roaring. Duck's whole train shuddered.

"Wh-what was that?" he asked, startled.

"That was our 'chute'. The bottoms of those wagons slide out, and the stones fall through the chute into your trucks. We may be small, but we're quite efficient."

Duck puffed away much impressed.

Next time, there were three Small Engines. Rex introduced Duck to Bert and Mike. "As you can see," he went on, "the Small Controller's given us different coats."

"Silly nonsense," grumbled Mike.

"I *like* being blue," protested Bert.

"It's all right for *you*," fumed Mike, "but not for me. Passengers'll say I look like a pillarbox!"

"Shocking!" said Rex, and winked at Duck. "Consider *my* feelings. When we were both green, passengers kept calling me Mike!"

"You . . . you . . ." spluttered Mike.

"Stow it you two," said Bert. "Duck," he went on, "have you seen our coaches?"

"Where are they?" asked Duck.

"Over there," said Bert.

"But they're tru . . . I mean they're not like ours," he finished lamely.

Rex smiled. "I agree. They are like trucks, but they behave surprisingly well."

"Sez you," put in Mike rudely.

"They're all right," said Bert, "if you treat 'em right. Besides, passengers like 'em. They won't use 'covereds' on a fine day. It's this scenery – you know, trees, mountains and such – can't understand it myself; but then, passengers are queer."

"You're right there," said Mike. "Give me goods trains every time."

"Do you *like* trucks?" Duck was surprised.

"Not all of them," smiled Mike, "but our big ballast hoppers are different. They run on bogies as sweetly as any coach. We take them to the old mines, fill them up, and run them down here to the chute. The men pull some levers, and the whole lot's unloaded before you can say 'Small Controller'. No trouble at all."

"How about hot axleboxes?" put in Rex.

"We soon cured *that* nonsense."

"You mean the Small Controller did!"

"Same thing," grinned Mike.

Duck chuckled delightedly. Rex and Mike loved teasing each other.

"I can't understand," said Duck, "why I've never heard about you before."

The Small Engines all answered at once.

"We've only just come . . ."

" . . . from our Railway in England which closed."

" . . . Your Fat Controller asked us to come and fetch ballast for him . . ."

" . . . and he said he'd bring us plenty of passengers too."

"Haven't you had passengers before?" asked Duck.

"Only in England. It's our first season here."

"Oh!" promised Duck. "Then I'll bring you lots. Goodbye! Goodbye!" and he puffed excitedly away to see about it.

Tit for Tat

THE engines were being cleaned and polished for the day. Bert, who was going out first, had a tall chimney in his funnel to draw up his fire.

"We've got Visitors today," said his Driver.

Rex yawned. "We have 'em every day," grunted Mike.

"But these are Special," said the Driver. "One takes 'moving pictures', and the other writes books. So mind you all behave."

"I don't want to be a moving picture in a book," protested Bert. "I want to stay as I am."

They all tried to explain, but Bert was still muddled when he went to take his train.

The visitors were clergymen, one fat, the other thin. They arrived in a little car. Both had cameras.

They shook hands with Bert's Driver. "The Small Controller," he told them, "says you can ride with me in Bert's tender, if you like."

"Thank you," they said. "May we come later please? Just now, the sun is shining so nicely that we want to take photographs."

Then they asked Bert his name and told him how smart he looked.

"These visitors," he thought, "do at least know how to speak to engines."

He puffed away feeling happier.

Wherever the line came near the road – level crossings, bridges, stations – there the two clergymen were, squinting into their cameras.

Bert found this rather upsetting. "They might wave at an engine," he complained.

"They can't wave *and* get good pictures," said his Driver; but Bert didn't understand. He thought they were being unfriendly.

"Poop! Poop!" The little car shot past them once more, but Bert made no reply.

"They'll be at the Lane next."

The Lane is a side-road. It runs for a short distance alongside the railway. There is no fence.

It had rained hard in the night. There were puddles in the Lane. The Thin Clergyman sat in the car. The Fat One waited with his camera. He took his pictures, jumped in, and off they went, racing the train to the Lane's end.

Unluckily, just as they passed Bert, they went through a puddle.

"Schloooooosh" – muddy water splashed over Bert's boiler.

"Ouch!" said Bert.

But the clergymen didn't know. They were ahead and out of the car. Smiling they waited for Bert to catch up.

Bert wasn't smiling. "They did it on purpose," he snorted crossly.

"They splashed me! They SPLASHED me!" Bert hissed, rolling into the last station.

"Pictures indeed!" he grumbled, running round his train.

"I'm a nice picture; covered in mud!"

He sizzled crossly when the Fat Clergyman sat in his tender for the journey back. "Driver oughtn't to allow him after what he's done!"

Suddenly he stopped sizzling, and let off steam "Whoooooooooosh!"

"I know," he thought, "how to pay the Fat One out. It's a *lovely* plan. I only wish the Thin One was there too," he said. But he said it to himself.

Bert ran nicely till they reached the woods.

The line climbs steeply here. Bert usually "rushes" the hill. This time, he deliberately dawdled.

"Come on!" said his Driver giving him full steam.

This was just what Bert wanted.

"Tit for Tat! TIT for TAT!" he shouted, storming up the slope.

Rain-soaked branches met close overhead. Bert's blast, shooting straight up, shook them wildly. Showers of water fell on Clergyman and Driver. Their soaking did not stop till they had topped the rise, and steam could be reduced for the downward run.

The Small Controller soon found out what had happened. He sent Bert back to the Shed. "You're a Very Naughty Engine," he said sternly. "I won't have rudeness to visitors."

"They *splashed* me," faltered Bert. "I only . . ."

"That's no excuse. I'm ashamed of you."

Bert went sadly away.

But he was happy again when Rex and Mike came in.

"Those Visitors are Nice," he told them. "They came and said 'sorry', and I said 'sorry' too. Then they cleaned me like Driver does. They know lots about engines," he went on. "The Thin One's writing about me in a book. He promised he'd write about you too. Think of that!"

Mike's Whistle

ONE morning when he arrived, Duck's whistle was out of order. They had worked late the night before and his Driver and Fireman had used it to boil eggs for their supper.

But something had gone wrong, and next morning, when he wanted to whistle, Duck found he could only make burpling noises. He was upset about it.

"Never mind," said his Driver, "it must be a bit of that egg which broke. We'll clean it out presently when we've got time. Meanwhile, no one will mind."

But Mike made rude remarks about it.

"Shplee! Shplee!" mimicked Mike. "It's shocking! If engines can't whistle properly, they shouldn't try."

"Then why do you?" asked Bert.

"Why do I what?"

"Try to whistle, of course."

"Shut up! You're jealous." Mike was proud of his shrill whistle. "Mine's better than yours, anyway."

"Listen, Mike," said Rex. "If I had a whistle like yours, d'you know what I'd do?" He paused impressively. "I'd lose it."

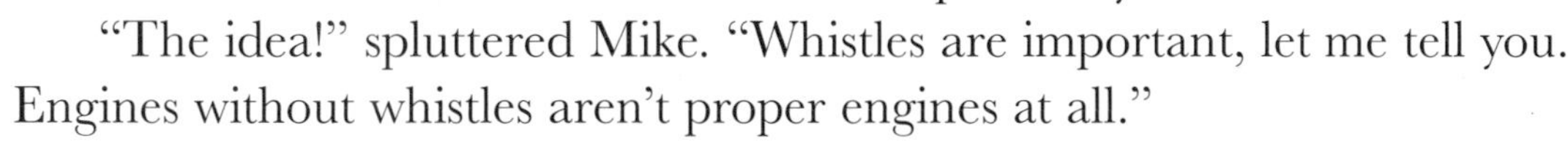

"The idea!" spluttered Mike. "Whistles are important, let me tell you. Engines without whistles aren't proper engines at all."

Mike went redder than ever with fury. His steam pressure went up suddenly, and his safety-valves blew off, "Whoooooosh!"

"Hullo!" said his Driver. "As you're ready first, you'd better take the 'passenger'."

"What! and leave my 'goods'?"

"Yes, Bert can do that. We can't have you blowing off in here. Come on!"

Mike backed down on the coaches "whoooooshing" angrily. When all was ready, he started with a rude jerk. "Come on! Come on! COME ON!" he puffed.

"What's bitten him?" wondered his Driver. "He doesn't like coaches, but he's never been as bad as this."

Mike whistled loudly at the least excuse. "They're jealous, they're jealous," he muttered as he bucketted along. "I'll show 'em! I'll show 'em!"

"He's in a flaming temper about something," remarked his Driver. He was relieved when they reached the End Station safely. He looked Mike all over, but saw nothing wrong. He tried to soothe him, but Mike still sizzled crossly. "It beats me," he said at last.

Then, soon after they had started back, he heard a thin persistent tinkle. "That's something loose on his boiler," he thought. "I'll tighten it at the next station."

But he never got the chance.

It was the cow's fault. She stood on the track busily cropping grass. She took no notice of the train.

Mike stopped. He wasn't frightened. He had met her before. She only made him cross.

He came slowly forward whooshing steam from his cylinders.

"Shooooh! Shooooh! Shooooh!"

The cow just flicked her tail and went on eating. Mike felt exasperated.

He tried whistling. He wanted to say "Get out of my way you stupid animal!" but he didn't get far. His second "peep" turned into a tremendous "Whoooooosh!" as his whistle-cap shot up like a rocket, and landed in a field.

Driver and Guard started to look for it, but some passengers objected. "We can't waste time with whistles," they said. "We must catch our train."

Mike was dismayed. "There are boards saying 'WHISTLE'," he protested. "I mustn't pass those without whistling. That's 'Orders'. Please find it."

"Sorry," said the passengers. "We can't wait. We'll have to whistle for you; that's all." And so it was arranged.

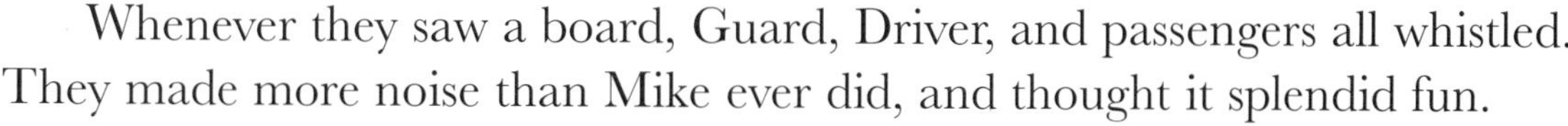

Whenever they saw a board, Guard, Driver, and passengers all whistled. They made more noise than Mike ever did, and thought it splendid fun.

Mike mourned for his lost whistle.

Mike hoped his Driver would give him a new whistle when they got home. He was disappointed.

"I've no spare whistles," said the Small Controller sternly. "So you'll have to wait. It serves you right for being such a crosspatch."

Mike worked in the quarries for the rest of the day. It was nearly dark when he reached the Shed.

"What's that?" asked Bert, as Mike came in.

"Shsh!" whispered Rex. "Take no notice. It's an Improper Engine."

"Why Improper? He looks all right to me."

"It's got no whistle."

"Oh dear!" said Bert. "How shocking! We don't approve of his sort, do we?"

Useful Railway

MIKE had had trouble with some sheep. He grumbled about them dreadfully.

"They're silly," said Rex, "but they're useful."

"What!"

"Farmers," went on Rex, "sell their wool."

"What's that?"

"People make clothes from wool. You know – things they wear instead of paint."

"Quite right, Rex." The engines were startled. The Small Controller stood in the doorway. "The farmers," he went on, "want us to take their wool to market. If we do it well, they'll know we're Really Useful. So you must all do your best."

"But I don't understand, Sir," Bert protested. "We can't drive sheep down the line. They wouldn't go straight."

"Silly!" said Rex. "We don't drive sheep, we take their wool, in bales on trucks. It'll be easy."

The Small Controller laughed. "Very well, Rex," he said. "You seem to know all about it, so you shall take the first train."

They started loading at the Lane. Then Rex came gently down the line stopping at all the farms and level crossings on the way.

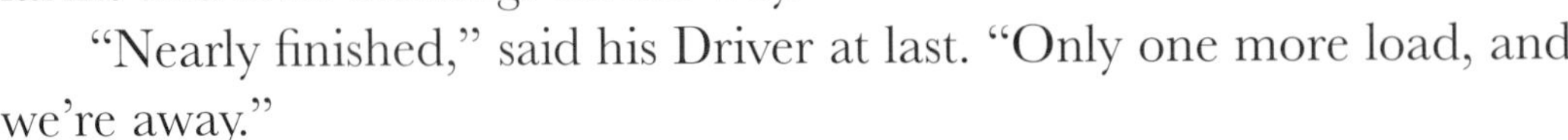

"Nearly finished," said his Driver at last. "Only one more load, and we're away."

But he'd reckoned without Willie.

Willie was late. He'd been dawdling. Rex's whistle roused him, and he set off at top speed.

"Your load's slipping," someone shouted.

"Oh dear!" thought Willie. "I can't stop now. I hope it'll hold."

It did, but not quite long enough. Willie dashed into the Yard, and swept round to bring his trailer alongside the line. The trailer tilted, the strain loosened the ropes, and the topmost wool-bales slid sideways to the track.

"Crumbs!" burst out Willie. "That's torn it! I must warn Rex."

He jumped down and ran along the line.

Rex's trucks were running nicely. "I *said* it was easy! I *said* it was easy!" he chuntered happily to himself.

Then everything happened at once. Willie waved and shouted, and behind Willie, through the bridge, Rex glimpsed the bales lying on the track.

"Stop! Stop! Stop!" he whistled.

"On! On! On!" urged the stupid trucks.

But Rex's brakes checked them. "Oooooer!" he groaned, and shut his eyes. His front hit something soft. He tilted sideways, and found himself off the line leaning against the cutting side, while his Driver felt him all over to find if he was hurt.

When the Small Controller came, Willie said he was very sorry, and, with his master's permission, he stayed and worked very hard clearing the mess.

They put the trucks to rights, and Bert lost no time in taking them away. But Rex had to stay where he was. He didn't like that a bit.

Trains kept passing, and passengers would point at him and say "Oooh! Look! There's been an accident!"

Mike and Bert would laugh and remark how easy it was to pull wool trains.

Poor Rex.

They lifted Rex to the rails at last and Bert and Mike helped him home.

"That accident served me right for being swanky."

"No," said Bert. "It wasn't your fault at all."

"Sorry we laughed." This came from Mike.

The Small Controller was waiting. "I'm proud of you all," he said. "Thanks to Rex, the accident did little harm. Bert and Mike worked like heroes, and our customers all admire the way we managed. They thought we were a 'toy railway', but now they say we're Really Useful. They've promised us plenty more work when the wool traffic is done."

If you have enjoyed these stories, you will also enjoy a visit to the Ravenglass and Eskdale Railway in Cumberland.

THE RAILWAY SERIES NO. 23

Enterprising Engines

THE REV. W. AWDRY

with illustrations by

GUNVOR & PETER EDWARDS

DEAR RICHARD,

Do you remember the photographs you took of what happened to your train on the way to Waterloo in April 1967?

Your Mother, very kindly, gave me a set, and they helped our artist to draw at least two of the pictures for "Super Rescue".

Anyway, "Super Rescue" is the story which your pictures told me. I hope you will enjoy it, and the other three stories as well.

THE AUTHOR

The author gratefully acknowledges the ready help given by Flying Scotsman's owner, Mr A. F. Pegler, and his assistant, Mr E. Hoyle, in the preparation of this book.

Tenders for Henry

"I'M not happy," complained Gordon.

"Your fire box is out of order," said James. "No wonder, after all that coal you had yesterday."

"Hard work brings good appetite," snapped Gordon. "*You* wouldn't understand."

"I know," put in Duck, brightly. "It's boiler-ache. I warned you about that standpipe on the Other Railway; but you drank gallons."

"It's *not* boiler-ache," protested Gordon. "It's . . . "

"Of course it is," said Henry. "That water's bad. It furs up your tubes. Your boiler must be full of sludge. Have a good wash-out. Then, you'll feel a different engine."

"Don't be vulgar," said Gordon huffily.

Gordon backed down on his train, hissing mournfully.

"Cheer up, Gordon!" said the Fat Controller.

"I can't, Sir. The others say I've got boiler-ache, but I haven't, Sir. I keep thinking about the Dreadful State of the World, Sir. Is it true, Sir, what the diesels say?"

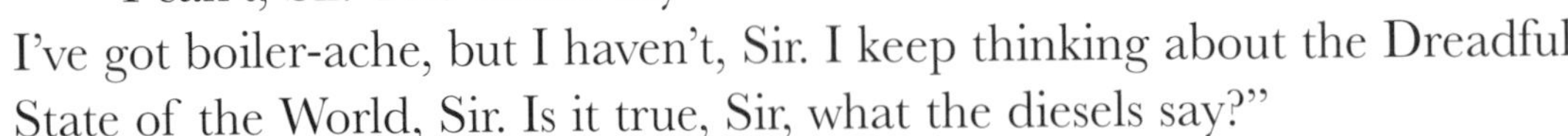

"What do they say?"

"They boast that they've *abolished Steam*, Sir."

"Yes, Gordon. It is true."

"What, Sir! All my Doncaster brothers, drawn the same time as me?"

"All gone, except one."

The Guard's whistle blew, and Gordon puffed sadly away.

"Poor old Gordon!" said the Fat Controller. "Hmm . . . If only we could! . . . Yes, I'll ask his Owner at once." He hurried away.

Arrangements took time, but one evening, Gordon's Driver ran back, excited. "Wake up, Gordon! The Fat Controller's given you a surprise. Look!"

Gordon could hardly believe it. Backing towards him were two massive green tenders, and their engine's shape was very like his own. "It's Flying Scotsman!" he gasped. "The Fat Controller's brought him to see me. Oh thank you, Sir!"

Gordon's toot of joy was drowned by Flying Scotsman's as he drew happily alongside.

Next day the two engines were photographed side by side.

"You've changed a lot," smiled Flying Scotsman.

"I had a 'rebuild' at Crewe. They didn't do a proper Doncaster job, of course, but it serves."

"I had a 'rebuild' too, and looked hideous. But my Owner said I was an Extra Special Engine, and made them give me back my proper shape."

"Is that why you have two tenders, being Special?"

"No. You'd hardly believe it, Gordon, but Over There, they've hardly *any coal and water.*"

"But surely, every *proper* railway . . ."

"Exactly. You are lucky, Gordon, to have a Controller who knows how to run railways."

Everyone got on well with Flying Scotsman except Henry. Henry was jealous.

"Tenders are marks of distinction," he complained. "Everybody knows that. Why's he got two?"

"He's famous," explained Duck and Donald. "He was the second to go 100 miles an hour; besides, the Other Railway has no coal and water."

"Pooh!" sniffed Henry. "I can't believe *that*! I never boast," he continued, "but I always work hard enough for two. I deserve another tender for that."

Duck whispered something to Donald.

"Henry," asked Duck innocently, "would you like *my* tenders?"

"Yours!" exclaimed Henry. "What have *you* got to do with tenders?"

"All right," said Duck. "The deal's off. Would you like them Donald?"

"I wudna deprive ye of the honour."

"It *is* a great honour," said Duck, thoughtfully, "but I'm only a tank engine, so I don't really understand tenders. Perhaps James might . . ."

"I'm sorry I was rude," said Henry hastily. "How many tenders have you, and when could I have them?"

"Six, and you can have them this evening."

"Six lovely tenders," chortled Henry. "What a splendid sight I'll be! That'll show the others the sort of engine I am!"

Henry was excited. "D'you think it'll be all right?" he asked for the umpteenth time.

"Of course," said Duck. "Just go where I told you, and they'll all be ready."

Meanwhile, word had gone round, and the others waited where they could get a good view. Henry was cheered to the echo when he came, but he wasn't a splendid sight. He had six tenders, true, but they were very old and very dirty. All were filled with boiler sludge!

"Had a good wash-out, Henry?" called a voice. "That's right. You feel a different engine now." Henry was not sure, but he thought the voice was Gordon's.

Super Rescue

THE two diesels surveyed the Shed. "It's time, 7101," said one, "that we took this railway over."

"Shsh, 199! It's *their* railway, after all."

"Not for long," persisted 199. "Our Controller says, 'Steam engines spoil our Image'."

"Of course we do," snapped Duck. "We show what frauds you are. Call yourselves engines? If anything happens, *you* care nothing for your train. *You* just moan for a Fitter. *We* bring it home, if only on one cylinder."

"Nothing," boasted 199, "*ever* happens to us. *We* are reliable."

Vulgar noises greeted this.

"How rude!" said 199.

"You asked for it," growled 7101. "Now shut up!"

Next day, Henry was rolling home, tenderfirst. "I'm a 'failed engine'," he moaned. "Lost my regulator – Driver says it's jammed wide open, and he can't mend it till I'm cool."

"However," he went on, "I've got steam, and Driver can use my reverser; but it *would* happen after Duck fooled me with those tenders. Now they'll laugh at me again."

He reached a signal box and stopped, whistling for a "road".

Opposite the box, on the "up" line, stood diesel 199 with a train of oil-tankers.

"Worse and worse," thought Henry. "Now 'Old Reliable' will laugh at me, too."

The Signalman came out. "For pity's sake take this Spamcan away. It's failed. The 'Limited' is behind, and all he does is wail for his Fitter."

"Spamcan!" fumed 199. "I'm . . ."

"Stow it!" snapped the Signalman, "or I'll take my tin-opener to you. Now then!"

199 subsided at this dreadful threat, and Henry pulled the train out of the way. The diesel didn't help. He just sulked.

The "Limited" rushed by with a growl and a roar. Henry gave a chuckle. "Look, Spamcan," he said. "There's your little pal."

The diesel said nothing. He hoped 7101 hadn't noticed.

7101 hadn't noticed. He had troubles of his own. He was cross with his coaches. They seemed to be getting heavier. He roared at them, but it did no good.

Engines have a pump called an ejector which draws air out of the train's brake pipes to keep the brakes "off". If it fails, air leaks in and the brakes come "on", gently at first, then harder and harder.

7101's ejector had failed. The brakes were already "leaking on" while he passed Henry. He struggled on for half a mile before being brought to a stand, growling furiously, unable to move a wheel.

"Well! Well! Well! Did you hear what Signalman said?"

"I thought they'd be laughing at me!" chuckled Henry. "Now, the joke's on them!"

"Moving two 'dead' diesels and their trains?" said his Driver thoughtfully. "That's no joke for a 'failed' engine. D'you think you can do it?"

"I'll have a good try," said Henry with spirit. "Anyway, 7101's better than old Spamcan. He did try and shut him up last night."

"Come on, then," said his Driver. "We mustn't keep the passengers waiting."

"GET MOV – ING YOU!" Henry puffed the sulky diesel into motion, and started to the rescue.

Henry gently buffered up to the Express. While the two Drivers talked, his Fireman joined his front brake-pipe to the coaches.

"It's better than we thought, Henry," said his Driver. "The diesel can pull if we keep the brakes 'off'. So the only weight we'll have is Spamcan's goods."

"Whoosh!" said Henry. "That's a mercy." He was, by now, feeling rather puffed.

"Poop poop poopoop! Are you ready?" tooted 7101.

"Peep peep peeeep! Yes I am!" whistled Henry.

So, with 7101 growling in front, and Henry gamely puffing in the middle, the long cavalcade set out for the next Big Station.

Donald and Flying Scotsman were waiting. They cheered as Henry puffed past.

He braked the coaches thankfully; Spamcan and the tankers trailed far behind.

The passengers buzzed out like angry bees; but the Fat Controller told them about Henry, so they forgot to be cross and thanked Henry instead. They called him an Enterprising Engine, and took his photograph.

They were thrilled too, when Flying Scotsman backed down on their train. If the Guard hadn't tactfully "shooed" them to their coaches the train would have started later than ever.

Donald took the "goods". "Return 199 to the Other Railway," ordered the Fat Controller. "I will write my views later."

Henry and 7101 went away together.

"I'm sorry about last night," ventured the diesel.

"That's all right. You did shut 'Old Reliable' up."

"And," said the diesel ruefully, "made a fool of myself today too."

"Rubbish! A failed ejector might happen to anyone. I'd lost my regulator."

"You! Failed?" exclaimed the diesel. "And yet . . ." His voice trailed away in admiration.

"Well!" said Henry. "Emergency, you know. Trains *must* get through."

7101 said no more. He had a lot to think about.

Escape

DOUGLAS had taken the "Midnight Goods" to a station on the Other Railway. He was shunting ready for his return journey, when he heard a faint "Hisssssssssssss".

"That sounds like an engine," he thought.

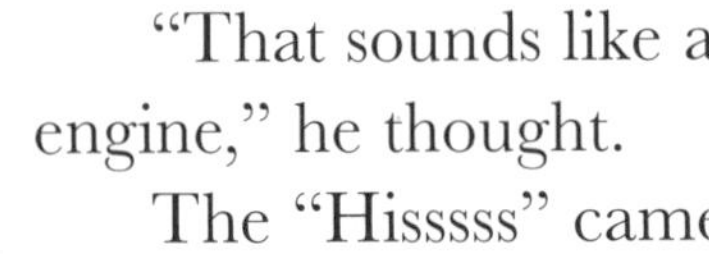

The "Hisssss" came again. This time, it sounded almost despairing. "Who's there?" he asked.

A whisper came. "Are you a Fat Controller's engine?"

"Aye, and proud of it."

"Thank goodness! I'm Oliver. We're escaping to your railway, but we've run out of coal, and I've no more steam."

"Is it from scrap ye're escaping?"

"Yes."

"Then it's glad I'll be to help ye; but we maun wurrk fast."

Both crews joined in. They took off Oliver's side-rods, wrote out transit labels, and chalked SCRAP everywhere they could. Douglas marshalled Oliver in front of his train. "No time to turrn round," he panted. "I maun run tender furrst."

"Yoohoo! Yoohoo!" yelled a passing diesel. "A steamer's escaping! Yoohoo!"

Douglas puffed firmly on. "Take no notice," he counselled; but they were stopped before they could clear the station throat.

The Foreman's lamp shone on Oliver. "Aha!" he exclaimed. "A 'Western' engine!" His light flickered further back. "A 'Western' auto-coach, and goods-brake too! You can't take these."

"Can we no!" said Douglas' Driver. "They're all fer uz. See fer yeself."

Douglas' Guard showed him the labels and papers. Oliver's crew, hiding in the coach, hardly dared to breathe.

"Seems in order," said the Foreman grudgingly, "but it's queer."

"Sure, and it is," began the Guard, "but I could tell you queerer . . ."

"So could I!" interrupted the Foreman. "Right away, Guard."

"A near thing," puffed Douglas with relief.

"We've had worse," smiled Oliver. "We ran at night. Friendly Signalmen would pass us from box to box when no trains were about. We got on well till 'Control' heard about a 'mystery train'. Then, they tried to hunt us down."

"What did you do?"

"A Signalman let us hide on an old quarry branch. Driver, Fireman and Guard blocked the cutting with rubbish, and levered one of the approach rails away. We stayed there for days, with diesels baying and growling like hounds outside. I was very frightened then."

"Small blame to you," said Douglas feelingly.

Presently they rumbled over the bridge and on to the Fat Controller's Railway.

"We're home! They can't catch ye noo."

"Tell Isabel and Toad please."

Douglas called out the news, and heard a joyful "Tingalingaling! Tingalingaling!" He was surprised.

Oliver chuckled. "That's Isabel," he said. "There is a bell on her you see. She's clever. When we go out together, I pull one way, and push the other. When I pull, I can see ahead. When I push, I can't; so Isabel keeps a good look-out, and rings her bell to talk to me."

"Ye dinna say!" Douglas was impressed.

"Aboot this Toad," he continued. "Is he . . ."

"Haud yer wheesht," said his Driver. "Yon's the Wurrks. We maun slip in unbeknownst, and find a place for Oliver."

Douglas tried hard to be quiet, but the Night Foreman heard them, and had to be told their secret. "I know just the place," he said, and showed them an empty siding nicely hidden away.

Oliver said "Goodbye" and "Thank you", and Douglas puffed away. "Yon's an enterprising engine," he thought. "I won away here with Donald; but I'd've been feared to do it on my own."

Little Western

DOUGLAS arrived back in time to see Flying Scotsman take his Enthusiasts home.

The Fat Controller said they had all been honoured, and thanked Flying Scotsman and his Owner for their help. "Please tell everyone," he went on, "that whatever happens elsewhere, Steam will still be at work here. We shall be glad to welcome all who want to see, and travel behind, *real* engines."

This announcement was greeted with cheers, and Flying Scotsman departed to the strains of "Will ye no come back again?" led, as one might expect, by Donald and Douglas.

At last Douglas could tell his news. They were all excited about it, and agreed that something must be done for Oliver.

"I'm feared," said Donald, "some murdering diesel may creep in, and him there alone, lacking steam even to whistle for help."

"You're right," said James. "He won't be safe till the Fat Controller knows."

"Douglas should tell him at once," said Gordon firmly.

"Is it me speak to the Fat Controller? It's forward he'd think me, and maybe interfering."

"Well, here he is!" said a cheerful voice. "Now, what's this all about?"

Duck broke the awkward silence. "Beg pardon, Sir, but we do need another engine."

"I agree, Duck. That is why I am giving 7101 another chance." Their faces showed such dismay that the Fat Controller had difficulty with his own!

"Sir," ventured Gordon at last. "We had hoped for a *real* engine."

"They," said the Fat Controller gravely, "are rare, and unless one escapes, there's little hope . . ."

"But, Sirr," burst out Donald, "one *has* . . ."

" . . . and, thanks to Douglas, is now at our Works," announced the Fat Controller.

"Sirr," gasped Douglas, "Is there anything ye don't know?"

"More than you think," he laughed. "Oliver's crew told me all you did, Douglas . . ."

"Och, Sirr! Ye couldna' see a braw wee engine, and him in trouble, and no do a wheel's turn . . ."

"More than 'a wheel's turn', I fancy. Douglas, I'm pleased with you. Oliver, Isabel, and Toad will soon be ours. Oliver and Isabel are just what we need for Duck's Branch Line . . ."

Loud cheers greeted this announcement.

" . . . and Toad wants to be your brake van, Douglas."

"Thank you, Sirr. I'd hoped for that. He and I'll do brawly together."

That, of course, made everything right. Henry spoke a good word for 7101, and the others gave him a welcome.

He had good manners for a start, so Henry didn't find it hard to teach him our ways. 7101 finds them different from those of the Other Railway, but much more interesting. He is now quite a useful engine.

They teased him at first because of his growls. They said he was like a bear. He still growls, not because he is cross, but because he can't help it. His name, "Bear", has stuck. He likes it.

"It's nicer than just a number," he says. "Having a name means that you really belong."

The Fat Controller soon had Oliver, Isabel, and Toad mended and painted in full Great Western colours. Then, he rescued three more

"Western" auto-coaches. Two, Alice and Mirabel, he gave to Duck. The third, Dulcie, joined Oliver and Isabel.

Duck and Oliver are happy on their Branch Line. It runs along the coast to the Small Railway. "We *re-open* Branches," they boast.

They are very proud of this indeed.

The others laughed at first, and called their Branch "The Little Western". Duck and Oliver were delighted, and now, no one ever thinks of calling it anything else.

THE RAILWAY SERIES NO. 24

Oliver the Western Engine

THE REV. W. AWDRY

with illustrations by

GUNVOR & PETER EDWARDS

DEAR M.,

We both wanted to call this book Little Western Engines; but Publishers are stern men. They did not approve.

They, of course, don't know the trouble we've had with Oliver. We hope he has learnt sense, but goodness knows what will happen when he finds he has a book all to himself. . . .

I know! If Oliver gets uppish, we'll set Messrs. Kaye & Ward on to him. That'll teach him!

W.

Readers may like to know that "Olivers" and "Ducks" still work on the Dart Valley Railway in Devonshire; and "Small Railway Engines" are at Ravenglass in Cumberland.

Donald's Duck

THE Fat Controller has re-opened a Branch Line. It runs along the coast by sandy beaches and seaside towns till it meets the Small Railway at a port to which big ships come.

As Duck had made friends with the Small Railway Engines, the Fat Controller asked him to take charge. "Your work in the Yard has been good," he said kindly. "Would you like to have this Branch Line for your own?"

"Yes, please, Sir," said Duck.

"Very well," said the Fat Controller. "I hope you will work hard, and be a credit to me."

Duck is very proud of his Branch Line, and he works very hard. His two coaches, Alice and Mirabel, are painted in Great Western colours. They take passengers to the Small Railway.

Duck also has some trucks in which he hauls away the ballast that the Small Engines bring down from their valley. The Fat Controller uses this ballast for his railway.

Duck cannot do all the work himself, so Donald and Douglas take turns to help him. The Fat Controller has built them a shed at the station by the Small Railway.

Duck felt his responsibility deeply. He talked endlessly about it.

"You don't understand, Donald, how much the Fat Controller relies on me."

"Och aye," muttered Donald sleepily.

"I'm Great Western and . . ."

"Quack, quack, quack."

"What?"

"Ye heard. Quack, quack ye go, syne ye'd an egg laid. Now wheesht, and let an engine sleep."

"Quack yourself," said Duck indignantly. He stayed awake wondering how to pay Donald out. At last he said to himself sleepily, "I'll ask Driver in the morning."

"He says I quack as if I'd laid an egg. Let's pay him out."

"Quack, do you?" His Fireman pondered. "I know," he said, and whispered.

Duck giggled, and his Driver slapped his leg in delight. "Just right," he said. He dearly loved a joke.

That night, when Donald was asleep, they popped something into his water tank. "We've done it!" they whispered to Duck.

"They won't hurt her, will they?" asked Duck anxiously.

"Bless you, no. They're both kind men. She'll come to no harm.

A duckling popped out of Donald's tank at the first water-stop. Both Driver and Fireman goggled with surprise, but Donald laughed.

"Na doot at a' who's behind this," he said, and told them what had happened in the Shed.

The duckling was tame. She shared the Driver's and Fireman's sandwiches, and rode in the tender, quacking at intervals. The other engines enjoyed teasing Donald about her.

Presently, however, she hopped off at a station, and, as they couldn't wait to catch her – there she stayed.

But before they reached home, Donald, and his Driver and Fireman, consulted together, and made a plan.

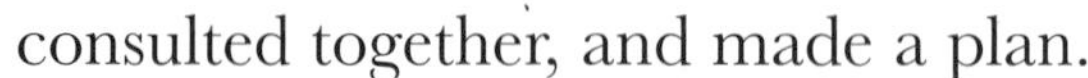

That night, Donald's Driver and Fireman got busy.

When Duck's crew arrived to look him over in the morning, they found something which made them laugh till they cried.

"Look, Duck!" they said. "Look what was under your bunker – a nest-box with an egg in it!"

Duck peered at it unbelievingly.

Donald opened a sleepy eye. "Ye dinna say!" he exclaimed. "D'ye mind what I said, Duck? Ye must ha' laid it this night, all unbeknownst!"

Then Duck laughed too. "You win, Donald," he said. "It'd take a clever engine to get the better of you!"

The duckling settled at the station, and became a pet with passengers and staff.

She carefully inspects all parcels and luggage, and sees that the porters stow them properly in the vans.

When she wants a swim, she flies to a nearby pond, but always returns to welcome the trains. She stands by the cab, quacking imperiously, till Driver or Fireman gives her something to eat.

Donald is her favourite, and she sometimes allows him to give her rides, but always gets off at her own station.

The Stationmaster calls her Dilly, but to everyone else, she is always Donald's Duck.

Resource and Sagacity

OLIVER is a Great Western tank engine. The Other Railway wanted to scrap him, so he ran away. Isabel, his faithful coach, came too, and so did Toad, a brake van.

At the last moment they were nearly caught, but Douglas saved them. The Fat Controller was pleased, and said that when Oliver was mended he could help Duck with his Branch Line.

"We'll give you Great Western colours, like Duck," he said kindly. That will help you to forget your troubles."

"Oh, thank you, Sir," said Oliver happily.

Duck's Branch starts from the Big Station. When Oliver started work, he often met other engines there. They all wanted to know about his adventures.

"Amazing!" Henry would remark.

"Oliver," said James, "has resource . . ."

" . . . and sagacity," put in Gordon. "He is an example to us all."

"You're *too* kind," giggled Oliver modestly. But he was only a tank engine after all. No big engine had ever said admiring things to him before. I'm sorry to say that it made him puffed up in the smokebox.

The Fat Controller rescued another coach, called Dulcie. She trundled along with Isabel.

Oliver sang "Oh, Isabel's a funny coach and so is Dulcie too. If I didn't look after them, they'd not know what to do!"

"Just listen to him. Just *listen* to him," twittered Dulcie.

"He's proud, he's conceited; he's heading for trouble," Isabel sadly replied. "I feel it in my *frames*," she shrieked as they rounded a curve.

Oliver just laughed. "Henry says I'm amazing. He's right. What do I care for trouble. I just push it aside."

All trucks are badly behaved, but ballast trucks are worst of all. Donald, Douglas, and Duck warned Oliver about this.

"You think I can't manage," he said huffily. "Gordon knows better. *He* says I'm sagacious."

"You may be 'goodgracious', but . . ."

"Say no more, Duck. It's mebbe a peety, but the wee engine'll juist ha ta learrn."

Today, Oliver took the trucks by himself for the first time.

He pulled the loaded ones to a siding and pushed "empties" to the Chute. Then he came back full of confidence to take the loaded wagons away.

The loaded trucks were comfortable, and didn't want to move. They had just realised, too, that they had a different engine. "Duck, we know," they grumbled, "and Donald, and Douglas. What right has Oliver to poke his funnel in here?"

"Look sharp!" puffed Oliver. "Smartly there!"

"That's not the way to speak! Pay him out!" The trucks moved off easily, and Oliver thought he had them in control.

"Trucks," he told himself proudly, "daren't play tricks on ME! I'll arrange them on the middle road, and start away as soon as Duck arrives. I can't understand why he says they're so troublesome."

They reached the station throat. Oliver's brakes came on with a groan. But brakes were useless against loaded surging trucks. They pushed forward yelling, "ON! ON! ON!"

Oliver fought hard, but still they forced him on, and on, and on.

Their effort slackened at last. "I'm winning," he gasped. "If only . . ."

But it was too late. One moment his rear wheels were on the rails; the next, they had none, and he was bunker down in the turntable well, with a deluge of ballast all round him.

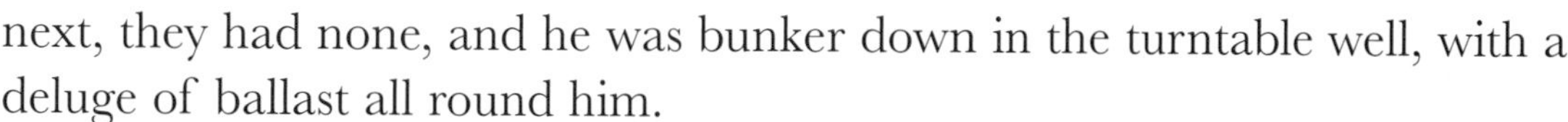

When Duck arrived, he was stopped outside the station, and flagged to the platform.

He surveyed the wreckage. "Hullo Oliver!" he remarked. "Are you being a 'goodgracious' engine? Beg pardon, of course, but we don't *really* like that sort of surprise. Donald and Douglas will miss their turntable."

Later that day, Donald and Douglas spoke pungently in Scots, and the Fat Controller spoke pointedly in English. All three left Oliver in no doubt at all, that so far from being sagacious, he was a very silly engine.

Toad Stands by

WHEN Oliver came home again, the trucks sang rude songs. They were led by Scruffey, a "Private Owner" wagon.

"Oliver's no use at all; thinks he's very clever.

Says that he can manage us; that's the best joke ever!

When he orders us about, with the greatest folly,

We just push him down the well. Pop – goes old Ollie!"

The engines bumped them. "Shut up!" they ordered. But they couldn't be everywhere; and everywhere they weren't, the trucks began again.

At last they gave it up. "We're sorry, Oliver," they said.

"It's really my fault," he answered sadly.

"I'm worried, Mr Douglas," said Toad next morning. "This nasty spirit of disrespect for engines. Where's it going to end?"

"Dear knaws," said Douglas gloomily.

"It must be stopped before it gets worse. I believe Mr Oliver can do it."

"Mebbe so, but how?"

"I've a plan, Mr Douglas. May I stay here today and help him? We are both Great Western and must stand together. Would you ask him, before you go, to favour me with a word?"

"I'll take ye to him; but he's ower sma' for the wurrk ye ha in mind."

" . . . No, Duck, Toad's right. This trouble's my fault, and I must put it right."

"I meant no disrespect, you understand."

"Of course not, Toad. Anyway, Driver says the same, and he's arranged it with Stationmaster."

"Very well, Oliver; but I must hurry. My passengers'll be waiting. Don't forget Stepney's tip about sand. Lay it on the rails as you back down, and roll it firm with your wheels. You get a splendid grip that way. Good luck! We three'll be there to cheer you on while you give those trucks a lesson."

"So long!" smiled Oliver bravely; but he felt dreadfully nervous inside.

"I expect, Mr Oliver, you'll want me on the middle road as a stop-block, like."

"Er – Yes, please."

Oliver marshalled the worst trucks two by two in front of Toad.

"This way, Mr Oliver, takes longer, but they can't give trouble, and if you leave that Scruffey till last, you'll have him behind you. Then you can bump him if he starts his nonsense."

Duck arrived to find them ready and waiting.

"Three cheers for Oliver and Toad!" he called. Alice and Mirabel responded with a will, and so, wonderingly, did the passengers.

"Hold back!" whispered Scruffey. The trucks giggled as they passed the word.

Oliver dug his wheels into the sand, and gave a mighty heave.

"Ooer!" groaned Scruffey. His couplings tightened. He was stretched between Oliver and the trucks. "I don't like this!"

"Go it!" yelled Duck. "Well done, Boy, WELL DONE!"

"OW! OW!" wailed Scruffey, but no-one bothered about him. "OW! OOOOOW! I'm coming apaaaaaart!"

There came a rending, splitting crash.

Oliver shot forward suddenly. Scruffey's front end bumped behind his bunker, while Scruffey's load spread itself over the track.

"Well, Oliver, so you don't know your own strength! Is that it?"

"N-n-no, Sir," said Oliver nervously.

The Fat Controller inspected the remains.

"As I thought," he remarked. "Rotten wood, rusty frames – unserviceable before it came." He winked at Oliver, and whispered, "Don't tell the trucks that – bad for discipline!"

He strode away, chuckling.

Nowadays, Oliver only takes trucks when the other engines are busy; but they always behave well. "Take care with Mr Oliver," they warn each other. "He's strong he is. You play tricks on him, and he'll likely pull you in half."

Bulgy

IT was Bank Holiday morning. The Small Railway Engines were working hard. Their station was crowded. No sooner had one train started than another was filled with people waiting to go.

Duck, Oliver, Donald and Douglas were busy too; but they had not brought everybody. The Yard was full of parked cars and coaches.

Duck was waiting for his next turn. Alice and Mirabel complained of the heat, so he backed them into the Goods Shed while he basked outside in the sun.

Near him stood a huge red bus. He had never seen it before.

The bus watched the passengers happily "milling" round the Small Railway.

"Stupid nonsense!" he grumbled. "Wouldn't have brought 'em if I'd known. I'd have had a breakdown or something."

"I'm glad you didn't," smiled Duck. "You'd have spoilt their fun. Look how they're enjoying themselves!"

"Pah!" snorted the bus. "Enjoyment's all you engines live for, taking the petrol from the tanks of us workers. Come the Revolution," he went on fiercely, "railways'll be ripped up. Cars 'nd coaches 'll trample their remains."

"Free the roads," he growled. "Free the roads from Railway Tyranny!"

At the passing station Duck told Oliver about the bus. “I call him ‘Bulgy’,” he chuckled. “He’s painted bright red and shouts ‘Down with railways’.”

But next time they met, Oliver didn’t laugh.

“Bulgy’s friend has come,” he said. “He’s red and rude too. He’s taking Bulgy’s passengers home, so’s to leave him free to steal ours.”

“But he can’t,” objected Duck. “Ours want to go to the Big Station.”

“Bulgy bets he can get there before us.”

“Rubbish! It’s much further by road.”

Oliver looked anxious. “Yes, but Bulgy says he knows a short cut.”

That evening Donald, Oliver and Duck were preparing for the homeward rush. Duck’s train was to be first out, but he had few passengers. He was soon to know why!

“Look!” shrilled Oliver. “Look at Bulgy! He’s a mean Scarlet Deceiver!”

Bulgy had turned to leave. They could now see his other side. It had on it RAILWAY BUS.

“STOP!” yelled Staff and engines, but too late.

“Yah! Booh! Snubs!” jeered Bulgy. He roared away. The unsuspecting passengers waved happily.

“Come on!” puffed Duck. He, Alice and Mirabel trundled unhappily away.

Alice and Mirabel chattered crossly. “The nasty old thief, he’s stolen our people!”

Duck wondered how to pay Bulgy out.

Then, far ahead, a man clambered up the embankment waving a red scarf. "Danger!" he shouted.

The line here crosses a narrow road. Duck came as close as he could. "So *this* was Bulgy's short cut!" He chuckled.

Bulgy was wedged under the bridge. Drivers of cars trapped in front and behind were telling him what they thought. Angry passengers, cornering the Conductor, demanded their money back.

From time to time loosened bricks fell making Bulgy yelp.

Bulgy's passengers swarmed round Duck.

"He tricked us," they complained. "He said he was a railway bus, but wouldn't accept our return tickets. He wanted us to think railways are no good. Please help us."

Duck's crew examined the bridge. It's risky," they said, "but we must help the passengers."

"Passengers are 'Urgent'," agreed Duck. "Besides," he chuckled, "it'll pay Bulgy out!"

They laughed, and told the passengers to wait on the other side of the bridge.

"STOP!" wailed Bulgy. "It might *fall* on me!"

"That," said Duck severely, "would serve you right for telling 'whoppers'."

Bulgy howled as he felt the bridge quiver, but it didn't collapse. Duck made good time to the Big Station, and all passengers caught their trains.

The Fat Controller arranged a "shuttle service" on the Branch. Passengers changed trains at Bulgy's Bridge.

Bulgy had to stay till it was mended, but he never learnt sense. He told "whoppers" till no-one could believe his destination boards, and no passengers would travel in him.

He is a henhouse now, in a field beside the railway. If he still tells "whoppers" they can do no harm. The hens never listen to them anyway!

THE RAILWAY SERIES NO. 25

Duke the Lost Engine

THE REV. W. AWDRY

with illustrations by

GUNVOR & PETER EDWARDS

DEAR FRIENDS,

An engine lost in the South American jungle was found after 30 years. A tree had grown through its chimney and hornets nested in its firebox. When mended it gave good service for 30 more years.

"The Duke" was lost too; not in the jungle but in his own shed which a landslide had buried. Not long ago he was dug out and mended. His own railway had been pulled up, so he is now at the Thin Controller's.

THE AUTHOR

"Duke" looks like a real engine called PRINCE. You can see PRINCE running on his own railway at Portmadoc in Wales.
"Small Railway Engines" can be seen at Ravenglass in Cumberland.

Granpuff

ONCE upon a time three little engines lived in their own little shed on their own little railway. Duke was brown, Falcon blue, and Stuart green.

Duke was the oldest. He had been the first engine on the line, and named after the Duke of Sodor. He was proud of this and wanted everything "just so". Whenever the others did anything they shouldn't, he would say, "That would never suit His Grace."

Other engines came and went, but Duke outlasted them all. Stuart and Falcon used to call him Granpuff.

Duke was fond of them, and tried to keep them in order. They were fond of him, too, as he was so wise and kind, but they did get tired of hearing about His Grace. Sometimes they would wink at each other and chant solemnly:

"Engines come and engines go,
Granpuff 'goes on' for ever!"

"You impertinent scallywags," Duke would say indignantly. "Whatever are young engines coming to nowadays?"

"Never mind, Granpuff. We're only young once."

"Well, you'd better mind; unless you want to end up like No. 2"

"Ooooh! Granpuff. Whatever happened?"

"No. 2," said Duke, "was American, and very cocky. He rode roughly and often came off the rails. I warned him to be careful.

" 'Listen, Bud,' he drawled. 'In the States we don't care a dime for a few spills.'

" 'We do here,' I said, "but he just laughed."

"But he didn't laugh when the Manager took away his wheels, and said he was going to make him useful at last."

"Why? W–W–What did he do?"

"He turned him into a pumping engine. That's what. He's still there, behind our shed."

Stuart and Falcon were unusually good for several days!

Stuart and Falcon became Useful Engines and all three were happy together for many years.

But hard times came, the mines closed one by one, and the engines had little to do.

At last, their line was closed and people came to buy the engines.

"We'll take Stuart and Falcon," they said; but no one wanted Duke. They thought him too old.

"Cheer up, Granpuff!" called Stuart, as they went away. "We'll find a nice railway, and then you can come and keep us in order!"

They all laughed bravely, but not one of them thought it would ever come true.

Duke's Driver and Fireman oiled and greased him. They sheeted him snugly, and said goodbye. They had to go away and find work.

Duke was alone, locked up in the Shed.

"Where's His Grace?" he wondered. "It's not like him to forget me."

But His Grace had been killed in the War, and the new Duke, a boy, hadn't heard of his Little Engine.

"Oh, well," said Duke to himself. "I'll go to sleep. It'll help to pass the time."

Years passed. Winter torrents washed soil from the hills over the Shed. Trees and bushes grew around. You wouldn't have known a shed was there, let alone a little engine asleep inside it.

Have you guessed about Stuart and Falcon? Yes, you're quite right. They came to the Thin Controller's Railway. He gave them new coats and new names. Stuart became Peter Sam, and Falcon Sir Handel. They prefer their new names.

That was a long time ago, but they never forgot Granpuff, and often talked about him when alone.

They were excited to hear that the Duke was coming to Skarloey's and Rheneas' 100th birthday; but most disappointed with the Duke who actually came. For he was only a man. . . .

But we must say no more, or we'll spoil the next story.

Bulldog

EVER since Skarloey and Rheneas had their 100th birthday, Peter Sam had been worried. He kept on saying that the real Duke never came.

"Rubbish!" said Duncan. "Of course he was real!"

"All the same," Peter Sam persisted, "he wasn't *our* Duke."

"Our Duke," said Sir Handel, "is an engine."

"You're as bad as he is. *All* 'engine Dukes' were scrapped. Ask Duck."

"Duck doesn't know everything," Skarloey put in quietly. "Tell us about him, you two."

Here is one of the stories that Peter Sam and Sir Handel told about Granpuff.

It happened when Sir Handel was new to the line. Now, have you remembered that in those days he was called Falcon, and painted blue?

You have? Now we can begin.

The Manager came to see him one day and said he was pleased with his work, so far. "Now, Falcon," he went on, "you must learn the 'Mountain Road' . . ."

"Yes please, Sir," said Falcon, excited.

". . . So, tomorrow you shall go 'double-heading' on it with Duke. He'll explain everything."

Falcon didn't like this. He thought Duke was a fuss-pot, and a regular old fuddy-duddy.

Duke's train was one for holiday-makers. He called it "The Picnic".

Falcon was ready when Duke arrived. Duke drew forward beside him. "Listen," he said. "The 'Mountain Road' is difficult. You take the train and I'll couple in front."

"No," said Falcon, "I'll lead. How can I learn the road with you lumbering ahead, blocking the view?"

"Suit yourself," said Duke shortly, "but never mind the view. Attend to the track."

"LOOK AT THE TRACK," he puffed again, on starting, "Never mind the view."

"Fuss-pot, Fuss-pot," puffed Falcon, on starting. "Fud-dy dud-dy, Fud-dy dud-dy, Fud-dy dud-dy!"

They rattled through the first tunnel, looped round, recrossed the river and entered the second, climbing all the time. Their speed grew slower and slower.

"Don't dawdle! Don't dawdle!" urged Falcon.

"No hurry, no hurry," puffed Duke stolidly.

The tunnel was curved and pitch dark. Falcon felt stifled. He wanted to get out.

Presently the light grew. Two ribbons of track appeared ahead in the gloom.

"Watch the track! Watch the track!" warned Duke.

"Fuss-pot! Fuss-pot!" scoffed Falcon.

The tunnel mouth grew larger and larger till at last they burst into the sunshine.

The line here swung sharply right. It was laid on a ledge cut in the hillside. Below lay the valley up which they had come. Track and buildings looked tiny, like toys.

No one quite knows what happened next.

Duke said there must have been something on the track and Falcon hadn't kept a good look-out.

Falcon said he was dazzled, so how could he keep a good look-out?

Anyway, their coaches had barely cleared the tunnel when Falcon lurched. His front wheels, derailed, crunched over sleepers and ballast. He came to rest with one wheel uncomfortably near the edge.

Duke had saved Falcon. Now he held on grimly with locked wheels and taut couplings.

"Young idiot!" he hissed. "Stop it! I can't hold you if you shake."

Falcon tried hard to stop shuddering.

Quickly, Duke's Driver and Fireman chocked his wheels, and strengthened the coupling between the two engines.

"Thank you!" said Duke. "Now I'll manage."

With Duke secure, the two crews, helped by a Platelayer, propped up Falcon's front end. They were looking forward to a rest when Duke began "wheeshing" in an alarming way.

His Fireman ran to his cab.

"Water!" he cried. "We want water, quickly."

The Platelayer's cottage stood nearby. He explained to his wife, and the passengers borrowed jugs, buckets, kettles, saucepans – anything in fact which would hold water.

They formed a chain from the well to the engine, and passed them from hand to hand.

The Fireman, meanwhile, reduced his fire, and anxiously watched the gauge.

It was hot and tiring work, for Duke needed many gallons; but at last the Fireman shouted cheerfully, "We're winning! Don't weaken!" And they all set to work again with a will.

They cheered again when the Breakdown Gang arrived. They showed other passengers how to help them lever Falcon back to the rails.

The Manager was at the Top Station. He said he was sorry about the accident, and thanked the passengers for their help.

"Not at all," they said. "We admired the way you put things right, and enjoyed the adventure."

"They thanked Duke and his crew for preventing a nasty accident."

"Your Duke," they said, "is a hero. He stood firm like a bulldog, and just *wouldn't* let go."

Falcon said, "Thank you" too. "I don't know why you bothered after I'd been so rude."

"Oh, well!" replied Duke. "You'd just had a new coat of paint. It would have been a pity if you'd rolled down the mountain and spoilt it. That would never have suited His Grace."

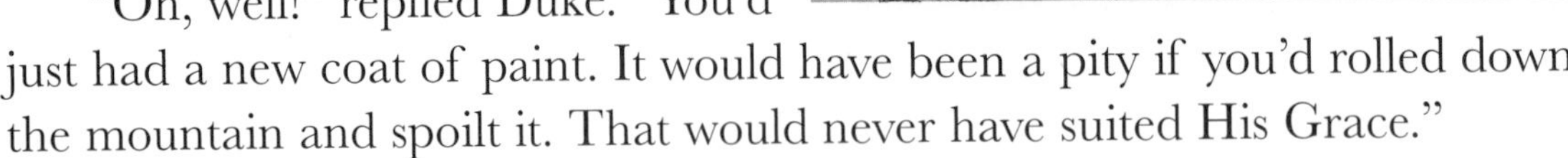

You Can't Win!

DUKE'S "Picnic" was a train for summer visitors. It was his special train. Many people came year after year, just to see him.

He always pulled it even if he felt poorly. "I mustn't disappoint my friends," he would say. "That would never suit His Grace."

The morning run gave no trouble. He took his passengers up the line, and stopped anywhere they wanted. He and his Driver knew all the best places for picnics.

"Peep, pip, peep!" he whistled as they waved goodbye. "Please don't be late when I come back. We might miss the boat, and that would never do."

One day Duke felt poorly at the end of his first "Picnic" journey. He had been short of steam, and was glad of a rest before starting back. His Driver and Fireman had just finished cleaning his tubes, when Stuart bustled in.

"Hullo, Granpuff! Are you short of puff?"

"Nothing of the sort. Routine maintenance."

"Tell you what, Granpuff. You're getting old. You need to take care. We'll have to keep you in order, or one day you'll break down."

"Humph," said Duke. "That'll be the day! You keep me in order! Impudence!"

He puffed away, hooshing crossly from his draincocks.

Duke couldn't stay cross for long. It was a lovely evening. All the picnic parties were ready. The coaches ran well, and they lost no time anywhere. "Couldn't be better! Couldn't be better!" he chuntered happily.

They began to climb. The work was harder, but Duke didn't mind.

"I've plenty of steam," he panted. "We'll be up in a couple of puffs."

He needed more than that, though. His puffs changed to wheezes. "It's not so easy! It's not so easy! My old valves *would* start 'blowing' now; but I'll manage. I'll manage!"

But the leaks became worse, and soon he was "Hoooochroooochshing" hoarsely with escaping steam.

Duke's Driver examined him carefully at the next station while the Guard went to telephone. Anxious passengers gathered round.

"Two engines are coming," the Guard reported. "With luck we'll be away in 15 minutes. You'll easily catch your boat."

Falcon buffered up in front. "Poor old Granpuff," he hooshed importantly. "What a shame you've broken down!"

"Peep, peep, pip, peep! This is the Day!" whistled Stuart cheekily. He was coupled on behind.

"Peep, pip, peep? Are you ready?" whistled Falcon.

"Peep, peep, peep! Yes I am!" replied Stuart, and away they went.

Falcon had left his train at the Middle Station. Arrived there, the calvacade split up. Falcon went down to the port with Duke's "Picnic", while Stuart headed Falcon's train with Duke coupled behind.

Stuart was excited. "Fancy me rescuing Granpuff! This is the Day! This is the Day! This is the Day! This is the Day!" he chortled gleefully.

"Poor Granpuff," he thought. "He's much too old. We'll have to keep him in order now. Kindly but firmly; that's it. We'll allow him to have runs sometimes, but Falcon and I'll do the real work. Granpuff'll be cross, but we can't help that."

"Poor old engine! Poor old engine!" he puffed kindly.

Duke was by no means crippled. His valves sounded worse than they were. He could have kept his train, but his Driver said, "No. Our passengers will only be worried."

Duke agreed. He didn't want to spoil their day. He listened to Stuart chortling, and smiled. He and his Driver had their own joke ready.

At first, they used just enough steam to keep moving; but the last half-mile was uphill.

"Now!" said his Driver. He advanced the regulator, and Duke responded with a will. He puffed and roared as though the whole train's weight was on his buffers. People heard the noise from far away. They ran to see what was happening.

At the Works Station Duke uncoupled and went along the loop to the water-tank.

A boy on the platform asked, "Why were there two engines on this train, Daddy? It's most unusual."

"It is," said his father, "but today was different. Stuart broke down, you see, and they had to call Duke out to help him. Duke had a hard job, too, by the sound of it."

"Well, for crying out loud!" exclaimed Stuart. He vanished in a cloud of steam.

Duke wheezed alongside. "Poor old engine!" he chuckled. "It's no good, Stuart; you can't win!"

Sleeping Beauty

DUKE'S story soon spread. The engines told Mr Hugh; Mr Hugh told the Thin Controller; the Thin Controller told the Owner; the Owner told His Grace; His Grace told the Small Controller; the Small Controller told the Thin Clergyman, and the Thin Clergyman told the Fat one.

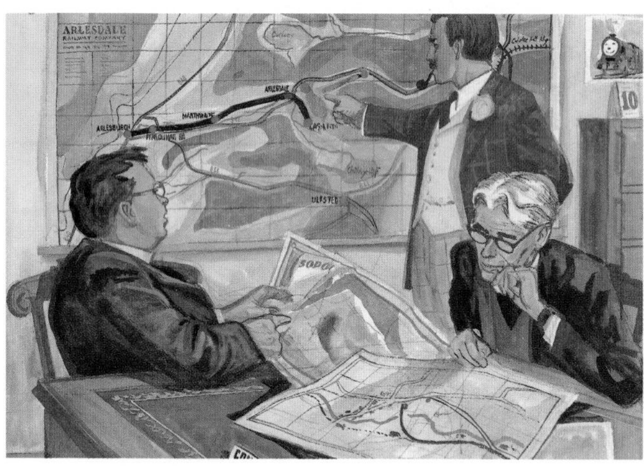

That is why, one morning, the two clergymen and the Small Controller were looking at maps.

"Our railway," said the Small Controller, "is laid on the bed of the old one, but swings round to end at the road south of that village. The old line kept straight on. It went north of the village and then to the mountains. The maps show the 'Works' at the Old Station. If Duke is anywhere, he's there."

"Are you writing another book, Sir?"

"Yes," said the Thin Clergyman, "but not about you!" He smiled at their downcast faces. "Cheer up!" he went on. "It's about a nice old engine who is lost; but, if you're good, the artist might put you in the pictures."

"Oooooh! Thank you, Sir."

So the clergyman told them about Duke, and Falcon, and Stuart. "So, you see," he continued, "poor Duke was left alone . . ."

Three Small Engines sighed sympathetically.

". . . and we want to find him, and mend him, and make him happy again. Your Controller wants to help, but he can't if you're naughty."

Three Small Engines promised to be as good as gold!

The three men spent days and days at the Old Station.

They came up every morning on Bert's train. He always whistled "Good luck!" as they walked up the track, but they had nothing in the evening except scratches and torn clothes. They wouldn't give up, though. "Duke's there, somewhere," they said.

The Fat Clergyman found him in the end. Scrambling over a hillock, he trod on something which wasn't there, crashed through a hole and landed, legs astride, on Duke's saddletank.

"Our Sleeping Beauty himself!" he shouted.

The Thin Clergyman and the Small Controller peeped through the hole above.

"Excuse me," enquired Duke. "Are you a Vandal? Driver told me Vandals break in and smash things."

The Fat Clergyman ruefully felt his bruises. "Bless you, no!" he laughed. "I'm quite respectable. I dropped in because I couldn't find your door," and he told Duke about Falcon and Stuart.

"So they *did* remember," said Duke softly; then, "Does His Grace approve?"

"Yes, he's coming."

"To see me? How kind! And I'm all dirty! That will never do. Please clean me."

So they set to work, and by the time the Small Controller had fetched His Grace, Duke was the cleanest of anyone in the Shed.

Early next morning Mike brought workmen and tools. They enlarged the Fat Clergyman's hole, lifted Duke out, and put him on a "lowloader" to take

him away by road.

"I'd be ashamed," Duke protested, "to travel by road. It's – it's – it's undignified."

"I'm sorry, Duke," said His Grace, "but the Small Railway has no suitable trucks."

Duke gave in then, but so many people came out and greeted him that he felt better. "So they still remember me," he thought happily.

Donald was waiting with a flat truck. Everyone cheered when Duke was lifted onto it, and still more when he started along the Big Railway on the last stage of his journey to his new home.

Peter Sam and Sir Handel were on "early turn". They peeped out of the Shed. "He's there!" they whispered, "Shsh! Shsh! Shsh!"

Duke opened his eyes. "You woke me," he grumbled. "In my young days engines were . . ."

". . . seen and not heard, Granpuff. Remember?"

"I remember," said Duke, "two idle good-for-nothings called Falcon and Stuart . . . "

"Good for you, Granpuff! We're glad you've come. We can keep you in order now."

"Keep *me* in order! Impertinence! Be off!"

The pair chuffed away, well content.

"Impudent scallywags," murmured Duke; but his old eyes twinkled, and for the first time in years he smiled as he dozed in the sun.

THE RAILWAY SERIES NO. 26

Tramway Engines

THE REV. W. AWDRY

with illustrations by

GUNVOR AND PETER EDWARDS

DEAR FRIENDS,

Thomas has been pestering me to write about his Branch Line. "After all," he said, "we are the importantest part of the whole railway."

"What can I write about?" I asked.

"Oh, lots of things – Percy's Woolly Bear, Toby's Tightrope and . . . "

". . . your Ghost," I added.

"Don't put that silly story in," said Thomas crossly.

I will, all the same. Thomas has been much too cocky lately. It will serve him right!

THE AUTHOR

Ghost Train

". . . AND every year on the date of the accident it runs again, plunging into the gap, shrieking like a lost soul."

"Percy, what *are* you talking about?"

"The Ghost Train. Driver saw it last night."

"Where?" asked Thomas and Toby together.

"He didn't say, but it must have been on our line. He says ghost trains run as a warning to others. "Oooh!" he went on, "it makes my wheels wobble to think of it!"

"Pooh!" said Thomas. "You're just a silly little engine, Percy. I'm not scared."

"Thomas didn't believe in your ghost," said Percy, next morning.

His Driver laughed. "Neither do I. It was a 'pretend' ghost on television."

Percy was disappointed, but he was too busy all day with his stone trucks to think about ghosts. That evening he came back "light engine" from the harbour. He liked running at night. He coasted along without effort, the rails humming cheerfully under his wheels, and signal lights changing to green at his approach.

He always knew just where he was, even in the dark. "Crowe's Farm Crossing," he chuntered happily. "We shan't be long now."

Sam had forgotten that Mr Crowe wanted a load of lime taken to Forty-acre field. When he remembered, it was nearly dark. He drove in a hurry, bumped over the crossing, and sank his cart's front wheels in mud at the field gate.

The horse tried hard, but couldn't move it. The cart's tail still fouled the railway.

Sam gave it up. He unharnessed the horse, and rode back to the farm for help. "There's still time," he told himself. "The next train isn't due for an hour."

But he'd reckoned without Percy.

Percy broke the cart to smithereens, and lime flew everywhere. They found no one at the crossing, so went on to the nearest signal box.

"Hullo!" said the Signalman. "What have you done to Percy? He's white all over!"

Percy's Driver explained. "I'll see to it," said the Signalman, "but you'd better clean Percy, or people will think he's a ghost!"

Percy chuckled. "Do let's pretend I'm a ghost, and scare Thomas. That'll teach him to say I'm a silly little engine!"

On their way they met Toby, who promised to help.

Thomas was being "oiled up" for his evening train, when Toby hurried in saying, "Percy's had an accident."

"Poor engine!" said Thomas. "Botheration! That means I'll be late."

"They've cleared the line for you," Toby went on, "but there's something worse – "

"Out with it, Toby," Thomas interrupted. "I can't wait all evening."

" – I've just seen something," said Toby in a shaky voice. "It *looked* like Percy's ghost. It s-said it w-was c-coming here t-to w – warn us."

"Pooh! Who cares? Don't be frightened, Toby. I'll take care of you."

Percy approached the Shed quietly and glided through it. "Peeeeep! peeeeeeeeeeeep! pip! pip! pip! Peeeeeeeeeeeeeeeeeeeep!" he shrieked.

As had been arranged, Toby's Driver and Fireman quickly shut the doors.

"Let me in! Let me in!" said Percy in a spooky voice.

"No, no!" answered Toby. "Not by the smoke of my chimney, chim chim!"

"I'll chuff and I'll puff, and I'll break your door in!"

"Oh dear!" exclaimed Thomas. "It's getting late . . . I'd no idea . . . I must find Annie and Clarabel . . ."

He hurried out the other way.

Percy was none the worse for his adventure. He was soon cleaned; but Thomas never returned. Next morning Toby asked him where he'd been.

"Ah well," said Thomas. "I knew you'd be sad about Percy, and – er – I didn't like to – er – intrude. I slept in the Goods Shed, and . . . Oh!" he went on hurriedly, "sorry . . . can't stop . . . got to see a coach about a train," and he shot off like a jack rabbit.

Percy rolled up alongside. "Well! Well! Well!" he exclaimed. "What d'you know about that?"

"Anyone would think," chuckled Toby, "that our Thomas had just seen a ghost!"

Woolly Bear

GANGERS had been cutting the line-side grass and "cocking" it.

The Fat Controller sells the hay to hill-farmers who want winter feed for their stock.

At this time of year, when Percy comes back from the harbour, he stops where they have been cutting. The men load up his empty wagons, and he pulls them to Ffarquhar. Toby then takes them to the hills. The farmers collect the hay from Toby's top station.

When in the wagons, the hay is covered to prevent it blowing about, but on the line-side it is stacked in the open air to dry.

"Wheeeeeeeeeeesh!" Percy gave his ghostly whistle. "Don't be frightened, Thomas," he laughed, "it's only me!"

"Your ugly fizz is enough to frighten anyone," said Thomas crossly. "You're like – "

"Ugly indeed! I'm – "

" – a green caterpillar with red stripes," continued Thomas firmly. "You crawl like one too."

"I don't."

"Who's been late every afternoon this week?"

"It's the hay."

"I can't help that," said Thomas. "Time's time, and the Fat Controller relies on me to keep it. I can't if you crawl in the hay till all hours."

"Green caterpillar indeed!" fumed Percy. "Everyone says I'm handsome –

or at least *nearly* everyone. Anyway, my curves are better than Thomas's corners."

He took his trucks to the harbour, and spent the morning shunting. "Thomas says I'm always late," he grumbled. "I'm never late – or at least only a few minutes. What's that to Thomas? He can always catch up time further on."

All the same, he and his Driver decided to start home early. It was most unfortunate that, just before they did, a crate of treacle was upset over him. They wiped the worst off, but he was still sticky when he puffed away.

The wind rose as they puffed along. Soon it was blowing a gale.

"Look at that!" exclaimed his Driver.

The wind caught the piled hay, tossing it up and over the track. The gangers tried to clear it, but more always came.

The line climbed here. "Take a run at it Percy," his Driver advised; so, whistling warningly, Percy gathered speed. But the hay made the rails slippery, and his wheels wouldn't grip. Time after time he stalled with spinning wheels and had to wait till the line ahead was cleared before he could start again.

The Signalman climbed a telegraph pole, the Stationmaster paced the platform, passengers fussed, and Thomas seethed impatiently.

"Ten minutes late! I warned him. Passengers'll complain, and the Fat Controller . . ."

The Signalman shouted, the Stationmaster stood amazed, the passengers

exclaimed and laughed as Percy approached.

"Sorry – I'm – late!" Percy panted.

"So I should hope," scolded Thomas; but he spoilt the effect as Percy drew alongside. "Look what's crawled out of the hay!" he chortled.

"What's wrong?" asked Percy.

"Talk about hairy caterpillars!" puffed Thomas as he started away. "It's worth being late to have seen you!"

When Percy got home his Driver showed him what he looked like in a mirror.

"Bust my buffers!" exclaimed Percy. "No wonder they all laughed. I'm just like a woolly bear! Please clean me before Toby comes."

But it was no good. Thomas told Toby all about it, and instead of talking about sensible things like playing ghosts, Thomas and Toby made jokes about "woolly bear" caterpillars and other creatures which crawl about in hay.

They laughed a lot, but Percy thought they were really being very silly indeed.

Mavis

MAVIS is a diesel engine belonging to the Ffarquhar Quarry Company. They bought her to shunt trucks in their sidings.

She is black, and has six wheels. These, like Toby's, are hidden by sideplates.

Mavis is young, and full of her own ideas. She is sure they are better than anybody else's.

She loves re-arranging things, and put Toby's trucks in different places every day. This made Toby cross.

"Trucks," he grumbled, "should be where you want them, when you want them."

"Fudge!" said Mavis, and flounced away.

At last Toby lost patience. "I can't waste time playing 'Hunt the Trucks' with you," he snapped. "Take 'em yourself."

Mavis was delighted. Taking trucks made her feel important.

At Ffarquhar she met Daisy. "Toby's an old fusspot," she complained.

Daisy liked Toby, but was glad of a diesel to talk to. "Steam engines," she said, "have their uses, but they don't understand . . ."

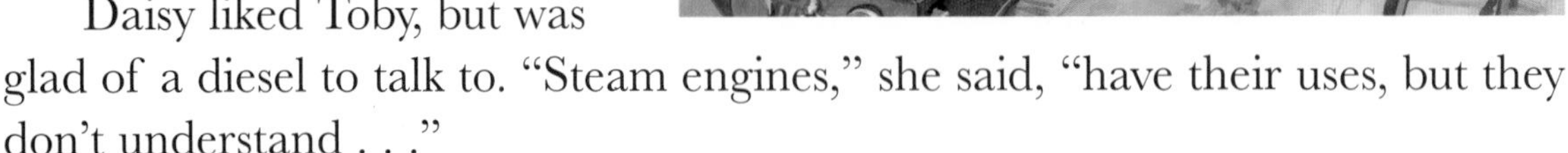

"Toby says only steam engines can manage trucks properly . . ."

"What rubbish!" put in Daisy, who knew nothing about trucks. "Depend upon it, my dear, anything steam engines do, we diesels can do better."

Toby's line crosses the main road behind Ffarquhar Station, and, for a short way, follows a farm lane. The rails here are buried in earth and ashes almost to their tops. In wet weather, animals, carts, and tractors make the lane muddy and slippery. Frost makes the mud rock-hard. It swells it too, preventing engine wheels from gripping the rails properly.

Toby found this place troublesome; so, when frost came, he warned Mavis and told her just what to do.

"I can manage, thank you," she said cheekily. "I'm not an old fusspot like you."

The trucks were tired of being pushed around by Mavis. "It's slippery," they whispered. "Let's push *her* around instead."

"On! On! On!" they yelled, as Mavis reached the "Stop" board; but Mavis had heard about Percy, and took no chances. She brought them carefully down to the lane, and stopped at the Level Crossing. There, her Second Man halted the traffic while the Guard unpinned the wagon brakes.

"One in the headlamp for fusspot Toby!" she chortled. She looked forward to having a good giggle about it with Daisy.

But she never got her giggle. She was so sure she was right, that she'd stopped in the wrong place.

In frosty weather Toby stops *before* reaching the lane, and while some of

his trucks are still on the slope. This ensures that they can't hold him back, and their weight helps him forward till his wheels can grip again.

But Mavis had given the trucks the chance they wanted. "Hold back! Hold back!" they giggled.

"Grrrrrrr Up!" ordered Mavis. The trucks just laughed, and her wheels spun helplessly. She tried backing, but the same thing happened.

They sanded the rails, and tried to dig away the frozen mud, but only broke the spade.

Cars and lorries tooted impatiently.

"Grrrrr agh!" wailed Mavis in helpless fury.

"I warned her," fumed Toby. "I told her just where to stop. 'I can manage,' she said, and called me an old fusspot."

"She's young yet," soothed his Driver, "and . . ."

"She can manage her trucks herself."

"They're *your* trucks really," his Driver pointed out. "Mavis isn't supposed to come down here. If the Fat Controller . . ."

"You wouldn't tell, would you?"

"Of course not."

"Well then . . ."

"But," his Driver went on, "if we don't help clear the line, he'll soon know all about it, and so shall we!"

"Hm! Yes!" said Toby thoughtfully.

An angry farmer was telling Mavis just what she could do with her train!

Toby buffered up. "Having trouble, Mavis? I *am* surprised!"

"Grrrrrroosh!" said Mavis.

With much puffing and wheel-slip, Toby pushed the trucks back. Mavis hardly helped at all.

The hard work made Toby's fire burn fiercely. He then reversed, stopping at intervals while his Fireman spread hot cinders to melt the frozen mud. "Goodbye," he called as he reached the crossing. "You'll manage now, I expect."

Mavis didn't answer. She took the trucks to the sheds, and scuttled home as quickly as she could.

Toby's Tightrope

THE Manager spoke to Mavis severely. "You are a very naughty engine. You have no business to go jauntering down Toby's line instead of doing your work up here."

"It's that Toby," protested Mavis. "He's a fusspot. He . . ."

"Toby has forgotten more about trucks than you will ever know. You will put the trucks where he wants them and nowhere else."

"But . . ."

"There are no 'buts'," said the Manager sternly. "You will do as you are told – or else . . ."

Mavis stayed good for several days!

Mavis soon got tired of being good.

"Why shouldn't I go on Toby's line?" she grumbled. She started making plans.

At the Top Station, the siding arrangements were awkward. To put trucks where Toby wanted them Mavis had to go backwards and forwards taking a few at a time.

"If," she suggested to her Driver, "we used the teeniest bit of Toby's line, we could save all this bother."

Her Driver, unsuspicious, spoke to the Manager, who allowed them to go as far as the first Level Crossing.

Mavis chuckled; but she kept it to herself!

Frost hindered work in the Quarry, but a thaw made them busy again.

More trucks than ever were needed. Some trains were so long that Mavis had to go beyond the Level Crossing.

This gave her ideas, and a chance to go further down the line without it seeming her fault.

"Can you keep a secret?" she asked the trucks.

"Yes! yes! yes!" they chattered.

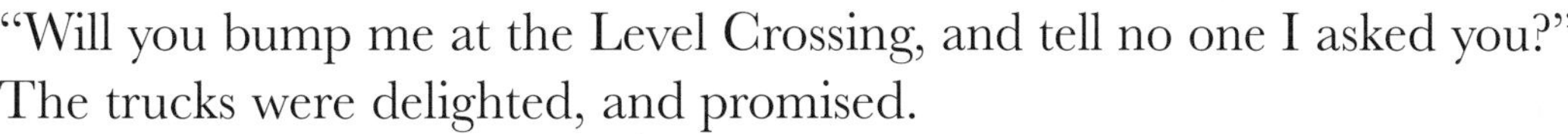

"Will you bump me at the Level Crossing, and tell no one I asked you?"

The trucks were delighted, and promised.

It was unfortunate that Toby should have arrived while Mavis was elsewhere, and decided to shunt them himself.

They reached the Level Crossing, and Toby's brakes came on. This was the signal for the trucks.

"On! On! On!" they yelled, giving him a fearful bump. His Driver and Fireman, taken unawares, were knocked over in the cab, and before they could pick themselves up, Toby was away, with the trucks screaming and yelling behind him.

What none of them realised was that with the warmer weather melted snow from the mountains had turned a quiet stream into a raging torrent, and that the supports of the bridge they were approaching had already been undermined.

Toby and his crew saw it together. The bridge vanished before their eyes, leaving rails like tightropes stretched across the gap.

"Peep Peep Peeeeep!" whistled Toby.

His Driver, still dazed, fought for control. Shut regulator – reverser hard over – full steam against the trucks.

"Hold them, boy, hold them. It's up to you."

Nearer and nearer they came. Toby whistled despairingly.

Though their speed was reduced, braking was still risky, but it was all or nothing now. The Driver braked hard. Toby went into a squealing slide, groaned fearfully, and stopped, still on the rails, but with his wheels treading the tightrope over the abyss.

Mavis was horrified. She brought some men who anchored Toby with ropes while she pulled the trucks away. Then she ran to the rescue.

"Hold on, Toby!" she tooted. "I'm coming."

Ropes were fastened between the two engines. Toby still had steam and was able to help, so he was soon safe on firm track, and saying "Thank you" to Mavis.

"I'm sorry about the trucks," said Mavis, "I can't think how you managed to stop them in time."

"Oh, well!" said Toby. "My Driver's told me about circus people who walk tightropes, but I just didn't fancy doing it myself!"

The Fat Controller thanked the Manager and his men for rescuing Toby from his "tightrope".

"A very smart piece of work," he said. "Mavis did well too, I hear."

Mavis looked ashamed. "It was my fault about those trucks, Sir," she faltered. "I didn't know . . . But if I could . . ."

"Could what?" smiled the Fat Controller.

"Come down the line sometimes, Sir. Toby says he'll show me how to go on."

"Certainly, if your Manager agrees."

And so it was arranged. Mavis is now a welcome visitor at Ffarquhar Shed. She is still young and still makes mistakes; but she is never too proud to ask Toby, and Toby always helps her to put things right.

Afterword

BY BRIAN SIBLEY

The Thomas the Tank Engine Man: The Reverend W. Awdry

Wilbert Awdry with an engine from the Dean Forest Railway.

THE man who was to create Thomas the Tank Engine and the other characters in the famous Railway Series was born on 15 June 1911, the son of the Reverend Vere Awdry, vicar of Ampfield, near Romsey in Hampshire. He was christened Wilbert Vere Awdry (his first name combining those of his father's favourite brothers, William and Herbert) and inherited a passion for steam engines which had led his father to build a model railway layout in the vicarage garden. Wilbert's father used to take him on walks around the parish during which they often met and talked with local railwaymen; and, long before he could read, Wilbert would sit poring over the pictures in his father's bound copies of *The Railway Magazine*.

A brother, George, was born when Wilbert was five and, soon afterwards, the Awdry family moved to Box in Wiltshire, near the Great Western Railway's main line from Paddington to Bristol. It was here that the seeds of the Railway Series were sown.

> *Lying in bed as a child I would hear a heavy goods train coming in and stopping at Box station, then the three whistles, crowing for a banker, a tank-engine, which would come out of his little shed to help the goods train up the gradient. There was no doubt in my mind that steam engines all had definite personalities. I would hear them snorting up the grade and little imagination was needed to hear in the puffings and pantings of the two engines the conversation they were having with one another: 'I can't do it! I can't do it! I can't do it!' 'Yes, you can! Yes, you can! Yes, you can!'*

Wilbert was educated at Dauntsey School in West Lavington, Wiltshire, before going to St Peter's Hall, Oxford, where he gained his BA and MA. Deciding to go into the ministry of the Church of England, Wilbert studied theology at Wycliffe Hall and, before being ordained, worked as a teacher at St George's School in Jerusalem. It was there that he met and became engaged to Margaret Emily Wale, a teacher at the English High School in Haifa.

Returning to England, Wilbert was ordained deacon at Winchester Cathedral in December 1936 and became a curate at Odiham in Hampshire. Marrying Margaret when she returned from the Holy Land in 1938, Wilbert moved to West Lavington in Wiltshire, as curate to the clergyman who had once been his school chaplain. Problems arose in 1939, when – as war in Europe became an inevitability – Wilbert declared himself a pacifist. He was asked to leave the parish and was on the point of giving up his work as a priest when the pacifist Bishop of Birmingham appointed him to a curacy at the parish of King's Norton.

It was in Birmingham, in 1940, that Wilbert and Margaret's first child, Christopher, was born, followed by two daughters, Veronica in 1943 and Hilary in 1946. When Christopher was two years old he was confined to bed with measles. Wilbert entertained his son with a story about a little old engine who was sad.

'Why is he sad, Daddy?'
'Because he's old and hasn't been out for a long time.'
'What's his name, Daddy?'
'Edward!'

It was the first name that came into Wilbert's head. By question and answer, he invented the Cinderella-type story of 'Edward's Day Out': how the little engine was eventually given the chance to take out a train of his own.

The story was told over and over again and was eventually written down and illustrated with simple line drawings. The adventures of Edward – along with two other engines, Gordon and Henry – might easily have been forgotten had not Margaret Awdry encouraged her husband to offer them to a publisher.

In 1945, after being turned down by several publishers, the book was accepted by Edmund Ward and published as *The Three Railway Engines*.

The master storyteller and a young admirer at a model railway exhibition.

The most famous of all Wilbert Awdry's engine characters appeared the following year in *Thomas the Tank Engine.*

In 1946, Wilbert was given his first parish at Elsworth and Knapwell, near Cambridge, where he stayed for seven years before moving to Emneth, near Wisbech. During these years, Wilbert continued writing books for children and from *James the Red Engine* in 1948, published a new Railway Series title each year until his last book, *Tramway Engines*, in 1972. The stories featured the already established engines, Thomas, Edward, Gordon and Henry, as well as introducing new characters in such volumes as *Toby the Tram Engine*, *Percy the Small Engine* and *Duck and the Diesel Engine* which featured the type of disagreeable non-steam engine that were increasingly taking over from traditional locomotives to the disgust of Wilbert Awdry and many other steam enthusiasts.

With his brother, George, Wilbert invented a fictional setting for his stories situated between the British mainland and the Isle of Man and called the Island of Sodor. The Awdry brothers made maps and wrote a long, detailed history of the island, its people and railway engines which helped shape many of the events described in the later volumes of the series.

Wilbert also pursued other railway interests: building ambitious model railway layouts in each of his vicarages, taking railway excursions at home and abroad with his brother or his friend the Reverend 'Teddy' Boston, and becoming involved with the work of various railway preservation societies, such as the Talyllyn Railway in Wales, which was to inspire the Skarloey Railway on the Island of Sodor, featured in such books as *Four Little Engines* and *The Little Old Engine.*

Another preserved railway was to honour the author of the Railway Series when, in 1987, the Dean Forest Railway named one of its engines 'Wilbert'. By this time, however, Wilbert Awdry had long ceased to be a full-time clergyman. In 1965, he had retired, or as he puts it, gone 'into private practice', and moved with his wife to Stroud in Gloucestershire. Sadly, Margaret Awdry died in 1989, the year after she and Wilbert celebrated their Golden Wedding Anniversary.

In addition to the Railway Series, Wilbert Awdry wrote two children's novels about the adventures of a little red three-wheeled car, *Belinda the Beetle* and *Belinda Beats the Band*, and co-edited and contributed to several adult books about railways.

In 1983, eleven years after Wilbert Awdry wrote his last Railway Series title, his son, Christopher, published *Really Useful Engines*, the first of, to date, fourteen books about the engines of Sodor. The book, like its successors, was illustrated by Clive Spong who – like Reginald Dalby and John Kenney before him – studied at Leicester College of Art. The following year, 1984, saw the premiere of Britt Allcroft's popular TV series, *Thomas the Tank Engine and Friends*, narrated by Ringo Starr.

The fiftieth anniversary of the first publication of *The Three Railway Engines* was celebrated in 1995 with an exhibition at the National Railway Museum in York. An InterCity 225, running on the East Coast line between London and Glasgow, was named the 'Reverend W. Awdry' and the same day saw the publication of a biography, *The Thomas the Tank Engine Man.* In recognition of his services to children's literarture, Wilbert Awdry was awarded an O.B.E. in the 1996 New Years Honours List.

In his later years, Mr Awdry suffered from osteoporosis, but despite becoming increasingly bed-ridden, he managed, nevertheless, to reply to the voluminous correspondence he received from Thomas fans all over the world.

After a prolonged illness, Wilbert Awdry died peacefully, aged 85, on 21 March 1997, at his home in Stroud.

The Man Who Set The Style: C. Reginald Dalby

C. Reginald Dalby, set the style for the series.

PUBLISHED in 1948, *James the Red Engine,* was the first of nine volumes of the Railway Series to be illustrated by C. Reginald Dalby, who also re-illustrated *The Three Railway Engines* and made a few improvements to the pictures in *Thomas the Tank Engine.*

Although Dalby's illustrations didn't entirely satisfy the author, and errors in detail caused all kinds of problems, his pictures – with their bold lines, lively energy and bright, gem-like colours – quickly caught the imagination of young readers, and he undoubtedly set the style for the series.

Born in Leicester in 1904, C. Reginald Dalby (the 'C.' was for Clarence, a name he disliked and never used) won a scholarship in 1917 to Leicester College of Art, after which he worked for five years as a commercial designer for the firm of Victor Ward, producing a variety of packaging designs – the first of which was a label for a beer bottle! He also had the distinction of painting the very first Glacier Mints Polar Bear on the side of a delivery van for Fox's, a company then based in Leicester.

With the outbreak of the Second World War, Reginald Dalby joined the Royal Air Force and served as an Intelligence Officer with the little-known MI9, where he was responsible for devising methods of 'Escape and Evasion' to be used by air-crews who baled-out behind enemy lines.

At the end of the war, Dalby was offered an intelligence post with Earl Mountbatten in India, which he turned down because he wanted to get back to the drawing-board. But with few or no openings in commercial art, he eventually had to accept a job with the Blood Transfusion Service in Sheffield. However, within six months he was back in Leicester, once more looking for work as a freelance artist.

The publisher Edmund Ward knew Dalby's work, and when an illustrator was needed for the third book in the Railway Series, he was a natural choice.

The two men met in Leicester's Royal Hotel where Ward showed Dalby the author's 'matchstick sketches' and asked him to turn them into finished illustrations.

The collaboration between author and illustrator was not an easy one and Reginald Dalby once described the creator of the Railway Series as 'a pedantic, remote man with whom co-operation was difficult'. It is true Dalby did not share the author's passion for railway engines: 'To Dalby,' Wilbert Awdry once remarked, 'one engine was very like another. Living in Leicester, he could have gone to Leicester Midland or Central any day and seen real engines, but he preferred to sit in his studio and draw what he thought was a good picture.'

Self-portraits: Dalby is the man with the case, his daughter has the dog!

Dalby certainly drew some good pictures, although his complacency about railway engineering resulted in a deluge of letters from puzzled readers. Problems came to a head in 1956 with *Percy the Small Engine.* Although the book contained some of Dalby's finest illustrations, Wilbert Awdry objected to the way in which the artist drew Percy who looked, as he put it, 'like a green caterpillar with red stripes!' In response, the artist decided to end his association with the series.

The railway illustrations were only a small part of Dalby's work, occupying him for around six weeks each year. He continued with his commercial work as well doing his own drawings and paintings and, in 1955, wrote and illustrated a children's book of his own. Inspired by the ferries that worked at Poole Harbour in Dorset, it featured a character called Tubby the Tugboat and was called *Tales of Flitterwick Harbour.*

A great traveller with an inquiring mind and a love of people and places, Reginald Dalby drove to the Costa Blanca on a six-week trip that turned into a three year sojourn! He later discovered and fell in love with Greece, making many drawings and painting of that country as well as of France and Spain.

Reginald Dalby died at the age of 79, after a short illness, in 1983.

A Lightness of Touch: John T. Kenney

John Kenney at work on an equine portrait.

EDMUND Ward's book catalogue for 1957 announced the future publication of a new title in the Railway Series, *The Fat Controller's Engines*. When it eventually appeared, the title had been changed to *The Eight Famous Engines*; and instead of Reginald Dalby's familiar illustrations, the pictures were by John T. Kenney.

The choice of John Kenney as successor to Dalby was a happy one: another Leicestershire man, he brought a freshness and a new liveliness to the twelfth title in the series with pictures that combine a lightness of touch with a more realistic look.

'We got on splendidly,' Wilbert Awdry has recalled. 'John Kenney was as different from Dalby as chalk from cheese. He was interested in the work and used to go down to his station and draw railway engines from life.' The engines which Kenney drew are longer, larger and less like the 'toy trains' of Dalby's pictures. As for his human characters, they are *real* people: pushing barrows, leaning on shovels, running along station platforms; and the scenery recalls those airy, luminous country scenes that featured on 1950s railway posters.

John T. Kenney – his full name was John Theodore Eardley Kenney – was born in 1911. Like his predecessor, he trained at Leicester College of Art before working for J. E. Slater, a local firm of commercial artists.

During the Second World War, John Kenney served with the 121st Light AA Regiment. Although not employed as a war artist, he made dozens of on-the-spot drawings recording the D-Day landings of 1944 and the triumphant sweep across Europe which followed. When the war ended, Kenney returned to Leicester and his former employers, J. E. Slater, where he met his future wife, Peggy.

In addition to being a commercial artist, Kenney began establishing himself as an illustrator of books, including two children's stories of his own –

The Grey Pony in 1954 and, the following year, *The Shetland Pony* – which were published by Edmund Ward. When, in 1957, ill-health drove Kenney to relinquish his work in commercial art and become a freelance artist, it was Ward who commissioned him to illustrate the series of adventure stories about 'Hunter Hawk, Skyway Detective' (which included such exciting titles as *Smugglers of the Skies*, *Commandos of the Clouds* and *Outlaws of the Air*) as well as the twelfth title in the Railway Series, *The Eight Famous Engines*.

John Kenney – added personality to the people as well as the engines.

Apart from the illustrations to the Awdry stories, the art of John Kenney – if not his name – has been known to millions of children through his work for another Leicestershire publisher, Ladybird books. Kenney undertook a vast amount of research to gather the authentic historical detail which he incorporated in some twenty-seven titles, including *The Story of Nelson* (with which he had endless problems over flags!), *William the Conqueror*, *Charles Dickens*, *Florence Nightingale*, *The First Queen Elizabeth* and *King Alfred the Great*. Since each book contained twenty-four full-page colour illustrations, the work was very demanding.

Although Kenney only illustrated six titles in the Railway Series, he made a significant contribution by creating naturalistic – less story-bookish – settings and giving personality to the human characters in the stories. He was also the first artist to draw a number of new engine characters, including Donald and Douglas (the Scottish Twins), Daisy, Diesel and Duncan.

The Railway Series demanded precise draughtsmanship and when John Kenney began having problems with his eyesight, he decided to give up the work, illustrating his last title, *Gallant Old Engine*, in 1962. Nevertheless, he continued drawing and painting – especially horses, for which he had a great passion.

In 1972 an exhibition of his paintings was on show in Chicago when John Kenney died, aged 61 years.

A New Look:
Peter and Gunvor Edwards

The impressionists – Peter and Gunvor Edwards.

WHEN John Kenney decided to give up illustrating the Railway Series, the books' editor, Eric Marriott, approached Swedish-born illustrator, Gunvor Edwards to see whether she would try her hand at some illustrations for the latest title, *Stepney the "Bluebell" Engine.* Gunvor accepted the commission and decided to start well into the book with a difficult picture showing the big diesel standing alongside four of the engines in their shed.

The painting had to be quite small, about ten by six inches, and Gunvor soon realised that duplicating the sort of pictures used for the series was not going to be easy. Unhappy with the project, Gunvor turned for help to her British artist husband, Peter Edwards, who was, as he puts it, 'trying to be a "serious" artist'. Although no more able to imitate the style of the earlier books than his wife, Peter Edwards managed to produce a set of illustrations that satisfied the author and publisher.

Although Edwards' style was more impressionistic than his predecessors, Wilbert liked his work because he drew from life and 'obviously had an affection for the characters'. Published in 1963, *Stepney the "Bluebell" Engine* carried the joint credit: 'with illustrations by Gunvor & Peter Edwards', but it was almost entirely Peter's work.

Peter Edwards was born in London in 1934 and, during the Second World War, was evacuated to Devon and North Wales. He was educated at Quintin School and, in 1950, began studying illustration at Regent Street Polytechnic. It was there that he met and fell in love with the Swedish artist Gunvor Ovden, who had come to Britain after a year of working on set designs for the Royal Opera in Stockholm.

At the end of their studies, Gunvor returned to Sweden and Peter entered National Service. In 1956, Peter joined Gunvor in her homeland where, the following year, they were married and received their first commissions as illustrators. Returning to London in 1958, they began prolific careers in art and design. One of Peter's earliest books was Wilkie Collins' *The Moonstone*, one of Gunvor's was Mary Hayley Bell's *Whistle Down the Wind*.

Gunvor went on to illustrate Barbara Sleigh's *Ninety-Nine Dragons*, Barbara Softly's *Magic People* and *More Magic People*, Margaret Stuart Barrie's 'Maggie Gumption' books and David Thompson's 'Danny Fox' stories, as well as her own books *Cat Samson* and *Grandmother's Donkey*.

Of the Railway Series titles illustrated by Peter Edwards, several featured interesting new landscapes such as the wind-swept peaks in *Mountain Railways* drawn from sketches made on Snowdon Mountain Railway. Such pictures came as a welcome change after those endless lines running through fields of cows or beside the sea. He also illustrated the first appearance of several new engine characters, among them Oliver, Duke and the Small Railway Engines, as well as portraying the author as the Thin Clergyman who, with the Fat Clergyman (inspired by Wilbert Awdry's friend the Reverend 'Teddy' Boston), makes an appearance in some of the stories.

*Some extraordinary new landscapes (*Mountain Engines *1964).*

Like Reginald Dalby, Edwards illustrated nine titles in the series, concluding in 1972 with *Tramway Engines*, the twenty-sixth and last book to be written by the Reverend W. Awdry.

Peter Edwards has illustrated a diversity of other children's books, including *The Great Escape* by Monica Dickens, *The Dining Room Battle* by Compton Mackenzie and John Wyndham's *The Chrysalids* and *The Trouble with Lichen*. He has also worked as a painter of murals, portraits and landscapes and as a set-designer for such projects as the Astrid Lindgren Museum in Stockholm (where he designed the train ride) and the London Dungeon.

Acknowledgements:
Brian Sibley for permission to use material previously published in *The Thomas the Tank Engine Man* (Heinemann 1995) in the Afterword section of this book; Brighton Evening Argus (jacket-flap photograph); The Gloucester Citizen (photograph, page 406); Swindon Evening Advertiser (photograph, page 408).

040-716

THE ISLAND OF
SODOR
Reference
Rivers
Main Roads
Secondary Roads
Tracks & Boundaries
Railway N.W.R.
Railway Narrow Gauge
Built-up Areas
1. Here the engines live in their shed.
2. Edward's station. He shunts here.
3. Gordon stuck on this hill.
4. Henry was shut up in this tunnel.
5. Thomas used to arrange coaches here.
6. The trucks pushed James down this hill.
7. James had his accident here.
8. This is Thomas' Junction.
9. Here James had hiccoughs!
10. James made the troublesome trucks come here.
11. Thomas left his Guard behind here.
12. Here Thomas went fishing.
13. Here Thomas stuck in the snow.
14. Thomas raced Bertie the 'bus along this valley.
15. Henry met an elephant in this tunnel.
16. James spun round on the turntable here.
17. Percy ran away from this station.
18. The 'Flying Kipper' had an accident here.
19. The quarry line, where Thomas met the policeman.
20. James bumped the tar-wagons here.
21. Mrs Kyndley's cottage.
22. Here Gordon fell in a ditch.
23. Here James slipped on the leaves.
24. Here Thomas fell down a mine.
25. Here the engines met H.M. The Queen.
26. Here Henry and Gordon met a cow.
27. Bertie the 'bus chased Edward from here.
28. Here is Trevor the Traction-engine's scrapyard.
29. James ran away from here, and Edward chased him.
30. Duck took charge of the Yard here.
31. Harold Helicopter lives at this airfield.
32. Percy brought the children through floods here.
33. Here Percy fell into the sea.
34. From here, Gordon went to London.
35. Toby ran out of water near here.
36. Here the Fat Controller spoke to the Engines before taking them to England.
37. Here Edward talked to Skarloey.
38. Here Sir Handel slipped through the rails.
39. Here is the Skarloey Railway.
40. On this viaduct, Gordon lost his dome.
41. Here Duck ran into the barber's shop.
42. Thomas' Branch-line runs from KNAPFORD to FFARQUHAR.
43. Edward's Branch-line runs from WELLSWORTH to BRENDAM.
44. Engines are made and repaired at CROVAN'S GATE.
RAMSEY
ISLE OF MAN
DOUGLAS
ARLSBURGH
CASTLETOWN
TIDMOUTH
ELSBRIDGE
KNAPFORD
CRUSBY
IRISH SEA